BOOKS BY AARON LATHAM

The Cowboy with the Tiffany Gun

Code of the West

The Ballad of Gussie and Clyde

The Frozen Leopard: Hunting My Dark Heart in Africa

Perfect Pieces

Urban Cowboy

Orchids for Mother

Crazy Sunday: F. Scott Fitzgerald in Hollywood

RIDING WITH

John Wayne

AARON LATHAM

Simon & Schuster

NEW YORK   LONDON   TORONTO   SYDNEY

SIMON & SCHUSTER
Rockefeller Center
1230 Avenue of the Americas
New York, NY 10020

SIMON & SCHUSTER and colophon are registered trademarks
of Simon & Schuster, Inc.

For information about special discounts for bulk purchases,
please contact Simon & Schuster Special Sales at
1-800-456-6798 or business@simonandschuster.com

Manufactured in the United States of America

1   3   5   7   9   10   8   6   4   2

Library of Congress Cataloging-in-Publication Data

Latham, Aaron.
Riding with John Wayne: a novel / Aaron Latham.
p. cm.
1. Screenwriters–Fiction. 2. Motion pictures–Production and direction–
Fiction. I. Title.
PS3562.A7536R53 2006
813'.54–dc22   2005055884

ISBN-13: 978-0-7432-6979-7
ISBN-10:   0-7432-6979-9

To my father, Clyde
(1910–2003)
Larger than life and death

RIDING WITH
John Wayne

Preface

"I've got some bad news for you," said director Jamie Stone.

She was holding my screenplay in what seemed contemptuous hands.

"Uh, what?" I asked.

"Most screenplays are not written in the past tense," she said severely.

"Oh," I say. "Who knew?"

BOOK ONE

1

WE WALK ACROSS A PARKING LOT FILLED WITH A LARGE
herd of fancy cars. A mammoth Mercedes SUV is parked beside a
miniature Mercedes convertible with the top down. They look like a
car cow and car calf.

"This is where the western set used to be," says JAMIE STONE,
whose ancestors were named Stein. "They tore it down and turned it
into a parking lot when they stopped making westerns."

"Maybe it's time they rebuilt it," I say, "now that they're making
westerns again."

"Chick, forget the plural," she says. "They're making western. And
we're lucky they're doing even one. I can't believe you talked them
into it. Or wrote them into it. Or roped them into it."

"Lucky for me I didn't know enough not to write one. God loves
a dumb country boy, you know."

"Dumb like a coyote."

"You know, I miss that old western set."

"You never even saw it."

"I miss it anyhow."

I miss lots of things I've never seen. I miss my great-great-great-
ever-so-great-grandfather Jimmy Goodnight, who will be the hero of
our movie. And I miss my great-great-great-ever-so-great-grandmother Revelie Goodnight, who will be our heroine. Jimmy grew up
on the Texas frontier, but Revelie was Boston-bred. According to the
script and history, Jimmy Goodnight invented ranching in West
Texas, and so you could say he invented the cowboy as well. He even
promulgated what he called the "Code of the West." After his death,

Revelie cured Texas tick fever and raised their son, my great-great-great-grandfather Percy Young "Pyg" Goodnight, who carried a silver gun made by Tiffany. I miss Jimmy Goodnight's great Home Ranch, which has long since been broken up and sold off. I miss Jimmy and Revelie and Pyg and the Home Ranch and the real Old West and the unreal Old West sets in Hollywood. I miss the values. So I am going to try to bring all that back to life as a movie.

I'm glad I'm making my first movie with Jamie Stone, who is about five seven, blond, green-eyed, and—as many have told her—too pretty to be a director. It isn't just that I like most of the movies she has directed. It is more that I feel totally relaxed with her. When I am with her, the constant tremor in my hands doesn't stop, but at least it slows down. I wonder why I feel so comfortable with Jamie. And I feel comfortable with no one—man, woman, or child.

It has been that way ever since I met Jamie that first time, at the Polo Lounge in the Beverly Hills Hotel, for breakfast. Even before the eggs arrived, I knew she was going to direct my movie. Of course, she said she was going to direct a movie based on a recent bestseller, but I somehow knew she wouldn't. I didn't try to sell myself or my movie. I knew I didn't have to. I even praised the bestseller and asked lots of questions about how she was going to translate it to the screen. But I already knew for sure that that movie had better start looking for another director. How had I known? I wish I knew.

After our breakfast together, Jamie went home, finished reading my book, and—that very afternoon—formally committed to directing my movie. The book, a biography of my family's founding father, Old Goodnight, was something I managed to write while holding down a job as a reporter for *The Washington Post*. I worked on it on my days off and whenever the city editor wasn't looking. I was surprised when Hollywood started calling. What piqued the moviemakers' interest—it turned out—were the parallels between Jimmy Goodnight's story and the legend of King Arthur. Something that had always fascinated me, too. When Paramount bought the book, I quit my job at the *Post* in order to try to write the screenplay, which was a lot harder than I expected. When I showed the results of my efforts to Jamie, she probably had second thoughts about agreeing to be my director. Anyway, that was the day she informed me that most screenplays are not written in the past tense. We decided to start all over and write the script together.

We still haven't finished the screenplay, but I am already on my way to meet the Paramount casting director. I can't believe it and yet I'm not surprised at all. I wonder what casting will be like. Will the pretty actresses want to sleep with me in order to get a job? No, of course not. Hollywood has outgrown that cliché. The studio is so big that it takes us almost ten minutes to walk from our office on the west side of the lot all the way to the administration building on the east side.

"That's it," says Jamie.

The boss building looks like the set of a movie about Henry VIII. It is faux Tudor, with white stucco walls crisscrossed by dark wooden half-timbers. My sense of well-being, of relaxation, of comfort, begins to evaporate. Now I am going to have to meet and talk to other people. Entering the casting office, a suite of two rooms, one large and the other small, another cow and calf, I can feel my mouth going as dry as West Texas.

"Chick, meet Marion Douglas," says Jamie. "She's a legend."

"You're tall," says MARION DOUGLAS, who is short and plain. "Nobody told me you were going to be tall."

I am just under six six with curly red hair.

"Oh," I say nervously.

Reaching out with a damp, trembling hand, I clasp her dry, firm hand. Of course hers is firm because, as a casting director, she has met thousands of other people, thousands of strangers. If she really is a legend, she might have met millions. She has gotten used to strangers. Having grown up in the small town of Spur, Texas, where I knew everybody, I am afraid I never will. Why don't other people notice how frightening strangers are? It isn't just that they might be dangerous; it is more that they make me feel so insignificant. I have never heard of them, and they have never heard of me. I am an amoeba in an ocean of strangers.

"Otherwise, I've heard great things about you," says Marion.

"Me too," I mumble uneasily.

Okay, I know I am lying, but I suspect she's lying, too. So we're even, aren't we? But I realize she is a better liar than I am.

"Everybody on the lot is very excited about your movie," Marion says.

All right, she is a much better liar than I am.

"That's good news," I fumble.

"Let's all sit down," Marion says.

In an unfamiliar room, I never know where to sit. Uncertain, I watch as Marion lowers herself into a well-padded chair and Jamie drops onto a couch and crosses her pretty legs. I wonder: Should I sit by Jamie or take the other chair? It seems an important decision. Fortunately, Jamie pats the cushion beside her. Grateful, I rush to join her on the couch, and exhale.

"I've got two stacks of pictures for you," Marion says. Bending forward, she picks them up from the coffee table, one in each hand. One stack is much thicker than the other. "These are the girls who can act," she says, shaking the smaller stack. "And these"—she shakes the bigger stack—"are the girls for your esteemed producer."

"What?" I ask.

"Don't ask," says Marion. "We'll start seeing people tomorrow, okay?"

As we walk back across the parking lot—the great car corral—I am still shaking my head.

"Is she serious about the girls for Buddy?" I ask.

"I'm afraid so," Jamie says. "I hope you're not too shocked."

"But I thought that was just a Hollywood myth. Or only happened in the old days. Or, I dunno, was some outmoded cliché."

"There's a lot of truth in clichés. Not that I recommend them to a writer. I guess Buddy's something of a throwback. I'm sure plenty of people think I had to sleep with him to get this job. Nothing I can do about that."

I am surprised to find myself getting prudishly angry. "You mean the casting department is pimping for Buddy Dale?"

"I guess that's one way to look at it," Jamie says. "Of course, unfortunately for them, those girls are going to make the ultimate sacrifice in vain. Like the poor Johnny Rebs at Gettysburg. He's just gonna mow them down."

"We should warn them."

"I know what, we'll hire a plane to skywrite up and down the beach."

"This isn't funny."

"See, Chick, I know from your book that you expect people to have codes. Not everybody does."

2

I GO HOME TO MY COUSIN, THE DAUGHTER OF MY father's baby brother, Uncle Johnny. She lives in an apartment that resembles a television set. It is a single-room box with one glass wall facing the lights of Los Angeles. This box is perched on the side of a hill in Laurel Canyon: It has a multimillion-dollar view for Wal-Mart rent. The glass wall has no curtains. The people down below could watch us like a television show if they cared to.

"Hi," says SHARON.

I'm not surprised to find Sharon at home. She is usually at home. She is an out-of-work actress. Where does she have to go? But I *am* surprised to find her in bed with a good-looking cowboy. I call him a cowboy because he still has his cowboy hat on.

"Oh, I'm sorry," I say, retreating back out the sliding glass door.

Closing the door, I race back up the stone steps to my car. Driving up and down the Sunset Strip, I tell myself over and over not to think judgmental thoughts about Sharon or the cowboy either. She's grown. She's entitled. He's entitled, too. She's a woman, he's a man, enough said. But I am still strangely shaken. What did I think: She was a virgin? Forget it. None of my business.

An hour later and low on gas, I return to the cul-de-sac, park once again, and slowly walk down the stone steps making lots of noise. I'm sure he's left by now, but just in case . . .

I am surprised once again: The cowboy is still there, but at least he is no longer naked. He wears a cowboy shirt, Wrangler jeans, and scuffed boots. He still has his hat on. He is good-looking with a strong straight nose, light brown hair, Skoal tobacco in his mouth, and a satisfied look on his face.

My cousin Sharon sits beside him on the couch. Sharon has long, walnut hair that falls in an inverted V from the part in the middle of her forehead. She was the prettiest girl in Spur, Texas, and is now one of the prettiest in Los Angeles. She reminds me of Audrey Hepburn with breasts. She has the long graceful neck, the fine features, and cheekbones that stand up high like the mesas back home. Her eyes would make cornflowers and blue jays jealous. When she heard I was coming to Los Angeles to make a movie, she invited me to share her space and her rent.

"Chick," Sharon says, unembarrassed, "get used to Chris Crosby." It's an expression from the Old West that she wouldn't have used on just anybody. "Chris, this is my cousin that I told you about. Mr. Beginner's Luck."

CHRIS CROSBY gets up and shakes my hand in a way that lets me know he is stronger than I am. It almost hurts but not quite.

"Glad to know you," Chris says. Not a cowboy to beat about the bush, he adds: "Maybe you could put in a good word for me. I'm a stuntman. I'd love to work on a movie about Sharon's great-great-great-ever-so-fucking-great-granddad. That would be very special."

"Please," Sharon says. "Please, please."

"Okay," I say, not meaning it.

"That's your way of saying 'no.' I'm serious," she presses. "Promise me you'll help out. You've explained to me why you can't help me, nepotism and all that bullshit, but you can at least help Chris. He is fortunate enough not to be related."

I sag under the implied accusation. "I'm so sorry, but I really couldn't . . ."

"So you owe me, put in a good word for Chris."

"Uh, well, all right, but a writer's recommendation doesn't mean much."

"But you'll do it?"

I hesitate and delay and shift feet several times. "Okay, but don't expect too much. I'm just the writer. That's all."

"But you promise to do what you can?"

"Yeah."

"I know you believe in some kinda code. Do you promise by that code that you're not just blowing smoke up my ass?"

"Yeah."

"Swear it."

"Okay, I swear."

"Thank you, thank you," says Sharon. "Now all I have to do is get cast."

"But . . ." I say.

I don't finish the sentence because Sharon and Chris are kissing in such a way that I feel I should flee the apartment once again. And do.

———

After another half hour driving around the neighborhood, I return to the apartment to find Sharon thankfully alone.

"Hi," I say, trying to pretend I'm coming "home" for the first time. "I'm working for a son of a bitch."

"You mean a bitch of a bitch, don't you?" asks Sharon.

"No, not Jamie," I say with a CHUCKLE. "I mean Buddy Dale."

"What did he do to you?"

"Nothing to me. But he's got the Paramount casting department pimping for him."

"I'm not surprised."

"You aren't?"

"I've heard rumors."

Sharon, who is six years younger than I am, has been in Hollywood almost a year longer than I have. She has done a half dozen student films, mostly USC Film School minimovies. One was a UCLA would-be feature, but the film student ran out of money halfway through. Plus she has done a thousand auditions.

"Did you ever audition for him?" I ask.

"I wish," Sharon says.

"No, you don't."

"Yes, I do. Then maybe I could work on the movie with you and Chris. Wouldn't that be perfect?"

"You're dreaming."

"That's my specialty: dreams."

We order a pizza from Domino's and watch television inside the TV in which we live. She doesn't mention getting Chris a job on my movie more than a hundred times.

I can't sleep. Stretched out on a Salvation Army couch, I keep opening my eyes and staring out at the lights of the city. I expect those lights to go out one by one until the town is dark, but as far as I can tell none of them ever fades to black. Doesn't anybody in Los Angeles sleep? It occurs to me that some of those lights probably belong to screenwriters who are busy writing while I am trying to sleep. They are getting ahead of me. Maybe I should get up and get busy, just to keep up, but then I would disturb my cousin, who is snoring softly in her bed. It is really just a mattress laid flat on the floor. I close my eyes, but they are soon open again. And all those screenwriting lights are still on and winking at me. Plus I am bored. I should get up and write, but what would my fingers say if I did get up? What if they didn't say anything? What if my fingers were dumb and just sat there staring at me?

Feeling my trembling becoming worse, I get up slowly and quietly off the couch. I am still chastely dressed in my blue jeans and a badly wrinkled shirt. I prefer to sleep in my underwear but not in my cousin's one-room apartment. Tiptoeing, I creep to my suitcase, where I have hidden my secret vice. I take them out and look at them, enjoying their familiar feel, and then I start twirling them.

These are the batons my parents gave me for Christmas long ago. Cheerleaders' batons. Lead-the-marching-band batons. They look like giant Q-tips. When I unwrapped them that Christmas morning, I was too young to know that boys didn't twirl batons. By the time I found out—or had it forcefully pointed out to me by the other boys—I liked twirling too much to give it up. From then on I twirled in secret as I am doing now. I find twirling calms me down. Standing here, spinning in the dark, I can already feel the tension flowing out of my fingers into the batons. My hands stop shaking, and my mind starts working again.

I find myself thinking: Why not take another run at the all-important ax scene? It has been giving Jamie and me so much trouble that we have skipped it, promising ourselves we'll solve it later. Maybe now is later. Here nobody is watching, not even my lightly snoring cousin, so nobody will know if it doesn't work. What do I have to lose?

Putting my batons away—hiding them once again—I feel around in the dark until I find my backpack. Unzipping it, I pull out my Toshiba laptop, the big one with the fifteen-inch screen. Trying to move quietly, I carry it to the small table where the pizza box still yawns open with a single slice remaining inside. I put the computer on the table, open it, and push a silver button. Running on battery power, the screen illuminates and brightens the small room. It isn't as bright as day, but it is twice as light as before. Sharon turns over on her mattress.

I put my hands on the keys. The trembling does not return. I open the file that contains our script in progress and stare at the big screen. Now is the moment. Either my fingers will talk to me, or they won't.

They don't.

So I open another file, this one just entitled "think," and start typing:

```
Try to think about the big scene when he locks arms
with destiny . . . I hate words like "destiny" . . .
think about the ax . . . what does he think? . . . no,
idiot, you can't do thoughts in a movie . . . what to
write? . . . Cut to the interior of Goodnight's
brain? Ha . . . Should it be a close-up? Ha ha! . . .
```

I think for a moment and then type:

```
Why not?
```

Switching from the "think" file back to the "script" file, I start typing faster:

```
EXT. COUNTY FAIR — AFTERNOON

JIMMY GOODNIGHT pushes his way through a boisterous
crowd of big farm boys. At the center of the mob, he
SEES (POV) an ax that is stuck in an anvil. It is
surrounded by the debris of failure: broken ax
```

handles left behind by all the strongmen who have
tried to pull it out and had no luck. Jimmy
approaches a CARNY MAN.

> JIMMY GOODNIGHT
> Excuse me, mister, I'd like to give it
> a try.

The Carny Man LAUGHS. His laughter is contagious.
Soon all the big men and strapping boys are
LAUGHING, too. The merriment grows and grows as the
news spreads outward from the center of the crowd.

> JIMMY GOODNIGHT
> Here's my nickel. Git outta the way.

> CARNY MAN
> Okay, kid, try not to hurt yourself,
> okay?

HEARING LAUGHTER and JEERS, Jimmy steps up to the
anvil, drops to his knees out of respect, and then
addresses the mass of iron.

> JIMMY GOODNIGHT
> Excuse me, O Great Anvil. I have great
> respect for your strength. Uh, I hope
> you also have respect for my weakness.
> I couldn't possibly take your ax away
> from you, so I won't try, but I hope
> you will give it to me willingly. You
> see, I need it a lot worse than you do.
> I need your ax so people will stop
> laughing at me.

The crowd continues to LAUGH and mock.

BIG FARM BOY #1

Look, he's prayin' to it!

BIG FARM BOY #2

It looks like he wants to hump it!

BIG FARM BOY #3

He's makin' love to it!

JIMMY GOODNIGHT

I need your ax so they will respect me.

Jimmy gets up off his knees, rises to his feet,
places his hands on the wooden handle, and pulls
gently as if helping up a girl who has fallen down.

JIMMY GOODNIGHT (CONT)

Ax, you will never leave my side. You
will be my constant companion. If you
help me, I will help you. You will no
longer be a spectacle. You will no
longer be pawed by strangers. My home
will be your home. What do you say?

The anvil begins to loosen its iron grip. Jimmy gives
the slightest tug and draws the ax from the anvil.

The crowd swallows its mean laughter and seems to
choke on it. Jimmy smiles and raises the ax high
over his head. The crowd falls utterly quiet and
everybody starts backing up to give more room.
Somebody at the back of the crowd CHEERS. Then other
voices take up the HURRAH. The cheering becomes a
mighty YELL.

"What?" gargles Sharon. "Who's there?"

I resent her interrupting me at such a crucial moment, but at the same time I am secretly relieved. Now I have an excuse to put off facing—well, not the moment of truth exactly, but something like it.

"It's me," I say. "Your cousin. Remember? I live here now."

"Oh." She lifts her head and yawns. "You mean you didn't break in to assault me."

"Sorry."

"Me too. Don't forget about Chris."

"Maybe I should get my own place."

"No. Well, maybe. No, don't do that."

"Go back to sleep."

"I'll try, but I doubt it. Not with that click-clicking going on."

"I said I'm sorry. And I won't forget about Chris. I'm almost done. Anyway I hope so."

"Good."

Sharon puts her head back down and turns her back on me. Oh, great, now I have to hurry my way to the end of a difficult and important scene. I don't need the pressure. Who asked her to wake up anyway? Well, I suppose I did with my clicking.

I have to refocus. Maybe a bite of pizza will help. I have a theory that any sensory input helps the imagination. The bite tastes good. Okay, here goes. Now it is time to do the impossible. Now I will attempt to cut to the interior of my great-great-great-ever-so-great-grandfather's mind, his brain, his unphotographable inner self:

```
Blinking, Jimmy stares up at the ax in his hand, at
the sky, at the sun.

                    JIMMY GOODNIGHT
                     (VOICE OVER)
           Horses whinny. Roosters crow. Bulls
           snort and kick up red dirt. A donkey
           brays. A red-tailed hawk screams high
```

overhead. Mice squeak, grasshoppers
leap high in the air, spiders stop their
weaving and look around. Prairie dogs
come up out of their burrows to see what
has disturbed the universe. A turtle
hurries. A baby cries in its mother's
arms. An old diamondback rattles its
tail. A single drop of rain falls out of
the pale blue sky and hits me right
between my good eye and my bad one.

We HEAR the donkey, the hawk, the mice, the rattler,
the baby CRYING. Then Jimmy lets out a SCREAM that
begins as a war cry but ends in LAUGHTER. He shakes
his new weapon at the heavens, and bees BUZZ loud
about his head.

I close the computer and go back to bed or rather to couch. The
other screenwriters' lights are still on, but I close my eyes and dissolve
in sleep.

3

I PARK MY RENTAL IN THE BIG PARKING LOT WHERE
the western town used to be. My assigned spot is at the far north edge
of the lot, about as far from the main entrance as you can get. I
glance up at a huge painting—literally half a block wide and almost as
high—of a beautiful blue sky. As if Los Angeles needed more blue
sky. Looked down on by two skies, I begin the long walk to our

office. I take a shortcut down a narrow alley, pass under the old Desilu water tower, and eventually arrive at a courtyard where our office is located. It is one of a dozen or more built around what the Italians would call a piazza. A small white shingle hangs outside with GOODNIGHT neatly lettered on it. I walk in.

"She's not here yet," says Becky, Jamie's assistant.

Her full name is REBECCA BAKER and she is short, well shaped, and a California brown.

"Oh," I say, a man of few words.

Passing through the small outer office, I move into the large inner office that I share with my director. Sinking into our puffy gray couch, I wait, more nervous than I usually am when I await Jamie. I am anxious to show her the new pages, but also apprehensive. I don't think they are a masterpiece, but I like them. And of course I want her to like them, too, and like me as an extension of the pages. If she doesn't like them, will she dislike me as well? Will she wish she had chosen the bestseller instead? Relax, just relax. My fingers play six-teenth notes on an invisible keyboard. Then thirty-second notes. I find myself staring at my single contribution to the decor of the office: a longhorn's long horns nailed to the wall.

"Hi," Jamie says. "Am I late?"

"No, I'm early," I say.

"Did you get a good rest?"

"Actually I couldn't sleep, so I did some writing."

"Good. Let's see."

"I didn't have a chance to print them out. Not yet. Maybe you could read them on my computer."

"Sure."

Balanced on my knees, my computer takes an agonizingly long time to boot up and get ready for the workday. When it finally reports for duty, I call up the new scene. Then I pass the laptop to Jamie, who carries it to our shared desk. She sits down and starts read-ing. I sit opposite her.

I WATCH (POV) as she LAUGHS and then LAUGHS again. Usually laughter is a good sign, but not in this case because this scene isn't supposed to be funny. I cringe. Had I misspelled something? Had I inadvertently slipped into the past tense? Had I violated some other thou-shalt-not commandment of screenwriting? Or is she simply laughing because it is so bad? I shrivel.

"What's so funny?" I ask, my fingers playing sixty-fourth notes.

Jamie's face sobers. Opening her black canvas bag, which serves as her briefcase, makeup kit, pocketbook, and extra closet, she fishes around until she finds what she is looking for: a handful of crumpled pages. She hands them to me.

"Read this," she says.

I start reading and I start LAUGHING. Unlike me, she had cut directly to the chase:

```
Jimmy studies the ax in his hand.

                JIMMY GOODNIGHT
                 (VOICE OVER)
         Horses whinny. Cocks crow. Mice squeal.
         A donkey hee-haws. A hawk screeches. A
         baby squalls. A diamondback hisses and
         rattles. Out of a blue sky, a drop of
         rain hits me in the face.
```

I LAUGH and LAUGH and stare at Jamie. I mouth "Oh, my God." I mouth "Fuck."

"Yeah, fuck all," she says out loud. "What's going on here? You didn't peek in my window last night, did you?"

"No," I say defensively, a little too quickly, a little too loudly. "I don't even know where you live."

"Relax, I was kidding."

"Of course, I knew that."

"Sure. Did anything like this ever happen to you before? Maybe you're psychic."

"No, never. What about you? Maybe you're the psychic one."

"Nope." She shrugs. "Funny thing, huh?"

I CHUCKLE. "Yeah."

"Before I read your scene, I wasn't sure I was going to show you mine," she says. "Because theoretically I'm sort of against voice-overs." She pauses and then explains: "I learned screenwriting from the late and much lamented Jim Bridges. You know, he wrote and directed *The Paper Chase* and *The China Syndrome*. And before that, he worked for Alfred Hitchcock."

"Oh," I say, impressed.

"Hitchcock had a rule: Always try to write it without a voice-over. That's cleaner. But if you're having serious trouble, sometimes a voice-over will solve your problems."

"Well, we tried, didn't we?" I say.

"We did indeed. It would seem that somebody up there—or something out there, or something in here—wants us to use a voice-over. Sorry, Hitch. And not just any voice-over, but this voice-over. It feels like magic, doesn't it? In a creepy but nice creepy sort of way?"

"Yeah, like the ax itself."

"But that's made up."

"Not according to my family." Then I remember, speaking of family, my promise to Sharon. "By the way, my cousin is completely besotted by a stuntman. She wants me to put in a good word for him. Maybe he could work on the show. I know this is totally inappropriate, but I promised her."

"What's his name?"

"Chris Crosby."

"I've heard he's good."

We face each other like gunfighters on Main Street. But closer. She sits on the west side of the big desk. I sit on the east side. Her weapon is a big Dell desktop with all the trimmings. My weapon is of course my laptop. I feel outgunned.

"Why don't you insert your scene into the script?" Jamie says.

"Sure," I say with a smile. "But there are a few differences between yours and mine. Maybe I should—?"

"No, yours is fine. Besides, there are damn few differences. I'm beginning to think you're 'pixilated.'"

"Pixilated?" I scratch my memory. "That's *Harvey*, isn't it?"

"No, it's *Mr. Deeds Goes to Town*."

Of course, I should have known. I hate getting things wrong in front of her. I feel like an idiot. Looking down at my screen, I start to type. She types faster. I try to type still faster, but I am already typing faster than I can think. I slow down, wishing I could find something that I can do better than she does. I wonder if she is any good at basketball. Since I am almost a foot taller than she is, roundball might be my best chance.

At ten to four in the afternoon, Jamie says: "We'd better head on over to the casting office. There'll be a whole bunch of girls who'll be very disappointed if they don't get to meet you."

"Yeah, right. What about the boys who want to meet you?"

"The boys want to meet you, too."

We head over.

4

"DID YOU GIVE THE ACTORS THE SIDES?" ASKS JAMIE.

"We're handing them out as soon as they sign in," says Marion Douglas.

I want to ask: What the hell are you two talking about? But I don't want to appear dumb, so I decide to bide my time and try to figure it out as I go along.

Marion hands us both xeroxed lists of the actors we will be meeting this afternoon. I glance at it but don't recognize any of the names. We want young actors and there are surprisingly few famous ones. Even in Hollywood, it evidently takes a while to make a name for yourself.

"I thought we might bring them in two by two," Marion says.

"Like the Ark," says Jamie.

"That's right. A boy and a girl. So they can play the scene together."

"Good."

I want to ask: What scene? But I decide to play smart, as if I know, as if I have no questions.

Marion leads in the first brace of frightened actors: a young woman named MARCIE DANIELS, who has big tits, and a young man named DANNY WORTH, who has big pimples. They both bring eight-by-ten glossies with their résumés stapled to the back, but they don't look much like their heavily retouched photographs. Glancing at their professional histories—plays and television shows and bit parts in movies—I don't know what is important and what isn't. We all shake hands. Then the actors sit on the couch while the rest of us find chairs.

"Thanks for coming in," Jamie says. "Before we get down to the reading, my partner, Chick, has a few questions to ask you. He's a trained journalist and good at interviewing people."

I am?

Everybody looks at me and my hands tremble faster than ever, as if somebody has just floored the gas pedal on a rough road. I am embarrassed because I hate to be the center of attention and because I had no warning. I fall back on my standard routine: I ask a question that contains the word *first*. Almost everybody remembers the first time they did something important. Who doesn't remember the first time he or she made love? Who remembers the tenth time?

"When did you first start thinking about acting?" I ask.

"When I was a kid, maybe nine years old," says Marcie. "My friends and I would go out in the wheat fields and stamp out a square room that we used as a stage. While we were in that room, we weren't supposed to be ourselves. We were all supposed to play roles."

"Really?" I prompt.

"They all broke the rules but me," she goes on. "I would get so mad at them. Then I found out there was a profession where nobody broke the rules. I knew I wanted to be an actress."

I like her.

"I got interested in college," says Danny. "It was the only thing I was good at."

Which is what Paul Newman once told me in an interview. I don't like Danny as much as Marcie, but I don't dislike him.

"Where are you from?" asks Jamie.

"Chicago," says Danny.

"Topeka," says Marcie.

"Good," says Jamie. "I have a theory that the best actors don't come from Los Angeles. Not that there's anything wrong with L.A. It's my favorite city in the whole world. Really. But it's so easy for somebody who grew up in L.A. to want to be an actor. Too easy. I prefer actors who have come from a little farther away. Who had to make an effort. Who had to leave home to look for what they want."

"Good," says Marcie.

"Of course, that rule doesn't always work. Some great actors have grown up right here. Debra Winger was a Valley girl. Are you ready to read?"

"Sure."

"Uh-huh."

Marcie takes two folded xeroxed pages from her purse. Danny removes identical pages from the inside pocket of his sport coat.

"Chick, why don't you set the scene?" Jamie says. "You know, catch them up on where we are in the story."

I look and feel ambushed. "Uh, where are we?" I ask. "I haven't seen the pages."

"Oh, I'm sorry," Jamie says. "It's the 'tender grass' scene. That's what I gave them."

"Okay, well, uh," I begin uncertainly. Then I launch into a speech I have made many times before, every time anybody ever asked me what my book was about: "Okay, well, uh," I begin uncertainly. "See, Jimmy Goodnight and Revelie happen to meet when he finds her hanging by her thumbs in a one-horse Texas cow town." I expect the actors to ask why she was so hanging, but they are too frightened. So I continue: "Goodnight rescues her, then falls in love with her, but she runs home to Boston. He follows her with letters and then in person. Okay, cut to the horse race: They get married and he brings his Boston Brahman bride home to the barbarian wilds of West Texas. Goodnight really loves Revelie and wants her to love his strange new land. But will she? He has visions of the West as it can be. She has memories of the comfortable, civilized East as it already is. Does this marriage have any chance in hell?" I pause. "That's where we are. The newlyweds have just arrived at Goodnight's Home Ranch, Revelie's new home."

"Any questions?" asks Jamie.

The still-frightened actors have none.

"Okay," she says. "When you're ready."

The two actors look at her and then glance at each other. They adjust themselves on the casting office sofa, trying to get comfortable.

"This grass'll git tough later on," says Danny, playing the young, newlywed Jimmy Goodnight, "but right now it's nice an' tender."

"Oh yes," says Marcie, playing Revelie, not particularly interested.

I remember writing this scene with Jamie—talking it out line by line—just a couple of days ago. Now I'm excited because I have never seen anything I've written—all right, cowritten—acted out before. I'm also anxious: How will the scene play?

"The thing is, a person could lie down on it now," Danny says, not getting the accent quite right, "while it's tender like this."

He gets up from the couch and lies down on the carpet. He stretches out and smiles. He rolls over and smiles again.

"How is it?" Marcie asks.

"Good," Danny says. "Wanna try it?"

Marcie moves tentatively from the sofa to the "young grass." Danny rolls closer to her, places his face over hers, and kisses her. His right hand reaches for her left breast.

"Wait," Marcie protests. "What do you think you're doing?"

He pulls his hand away. He is surprised, confused, and a little angry.

"What's the matter?" Danny asks in a choked voice.

"This isn't a bedroom," she says.

"It's a great bedroom. The best bedroom in the whole damn world."

"What if somebody comes along? One of the cowboys?"

"They won't. I sent 'em all to work t'other end a the canyon."

"You did?" Marcie grins. "You really did?"

"Unh-hunh."

Danny reaches for Marcie's breast once again.

"Wait," she says. "No, it still doesn't seem right. I don't know. Out here, God can see us."

"God won't mind."

"You don't know. How do you know?"

"Because he made Adam and Eve."

"And you're telling me this is Eden?"

"Purdy near."

"So you really think it would be all right?"

"Unh-hunh."

When Danny reaches for Marcie's breast this time, she doesn't stop him. I feel like a voyeur spying on an intimate scene. Peeping.

We thank the actors and they leave.

"What do you think?" Marion asks Jamie.

"I think they were acting their asses off," my director says and then turns to me: "Chick, what's your take on them?"

"They looked good to me," I say, "but what do I know? I liked her better than I liked him, but that may be because I liked her story about the wheat fields."

"I liked her better, too," Jamie says. "How did you think the scene played?"

"It was good enough to make me feel kind of embarrassed."

"Then we're on the right track." She turns. "Marion, who's next?"

We finish about five-thirty—with none of our casting questions answered—and head on back to our office. When we arrive, we discover we have a visitor.

"Jamie, Kelly Hightower is here to see you," Becky says. "He's inside."

"Oh, my God," Jamie says. "I forgot all about him. How long has he been here?"

"About half an hour."

"Fuck me, I feel terrible." Jamie turns to me and explains: "I asked

Kelly to come in because he's an old friend and I thought he might be good to play Loving. I used him in my first movie, *Baby Factory.* He played a sperm donor who made hundreds of kids."

"Of course, I remember him," I say proudly.

"Anyway this isn't an audition, just a meeting. I mean, I already know he can act. The question is: Is he right for the part?"

Jamie and I enter our private office, where I am introduced to KELLY HIGHTOWER, father of hundreds. He is as good-looking off screen as on, but off he looks harder. His eyes are blue-green. His face is brown and weathered as if he were a ski instructor or a motorcycle cop or a real cowboy. I not only like him immediately, but I like him for the part of Loving. While Jamie and Kelly are chatting about old times, I am leaning more and more toward offering him the part right here and now.

"Kelly, see that hat hanging from that horn?" Jamie asks.

"Sure," says the would-be Loving.

The hat is the color of a badly soiled dove. It is a special hat, at least to me, because it once belonged to our hero, Jimmy Goodnight. The brim isn't quite as wide as those cowboys and pretend cowboys wear today.

"Would you mind trying it on?"

"Sure."

Kelly Hightower stands up, crosses the room, and plucks the cowboy hat off the bull's horn. He lowers it onto his head. It fits, but . . .

After he leaves, Jamie asks: "What did you think?"

I say: "He looked like Howdy Doody."

"He did, didn't he? Guess we have to keep looking for Loving."

5

WHEN I ARRIVE FOR WORK THE NEXT MORNING—
another day in the dream salt mine—I am surprised to find Jamie
already hard at work. It turns out that entertaining people is harder
work than I ever imagined.

"Am I late?" I ask.

"No, I'm early," Jamie says. "Shelley Bingham summoned me for
a breakfast meeting. The commissary breakfast is surprisingly not disgusting. She came bearing news. It seems Tom Bondini has been in
touch with her and he wants to do our movie."

"Oh no," I say before I can stop myself.

"Well, Shelley thinks it's an interesting idea and she's the boss."

I just sit there and shake my head. There goes the movie. Tom
Bondini is about as cowboy as spaghetti. As the New Jersey Turnpike.
As mob hits and "fergittaboutit." He could play a young Godfather,
but I couldn't see him as the young King Arthur of the West.

"Speak," says Jamie.

"He'll ruin the movie," I respond. "You aren't seriously considering him, are you?"

"I'm not sure," she says.

"That means you are."

"Well, as Shelley pointed out to me, he's made a lot of money for
this studio. Saved the studio actually. Makes it kind of hard to spit in
his face." She thinks for a moment, studying my scowl. "If the
biggest movie star in the world wants to make your movie, what can
you do?"

"Shoot him, a mob hit."

"I'm afraid we'll at least have to talk to him. He'll be here this afternoon at two."

"Oh." My hands start shaking double time. "Do you know him?"

"Seen him a couple of times. The last time was when I was doing *Plan B*. He dropped by to meet Cameron Diaz. There was some script they were both considering. That movie never happened, but as soon as they saw each other, her ovaries started jangling, and his prick turned into a compass, and she was the North Pole."

I can feel my face warming.

"Oh, I made you blush. I'm sorry. Whatever must you think of Hollywood?"

"What about your ovaries?"

She blushes.

A little after two in the afternoon—pretty much on time—TOM BONDINI walks into our office. I like a superstar who is punctual. He stands almost six feet tall, is incredibly thin, and his jeans are incredibly tight. His hair is blond and his feet are puce, thanks to his bright puce running shoes. I wonder if they glow in the dark. His eyes look like Godiva chocolate truffles. I keep studying his nose, trying to decide if it was ever broken, since it takes a tiny detour halfway down his face. I can't quite tell. I suppose that is part of the fascination. I hope he doesn't notice the tremor in my hands.

"If I have to audition," Tom Bondini says with a LAUGH, "I won't do the movie."

Jamie and I LAUGH, too. We all know that the biggest star in the world doesn't audition. Everybody in Hollywood knows it. Probably everybody in the whole damn world. So it's funny. As they say, you had to be there.

"Have you seen Cameron Diaz lately?" asks Jamie.

"No, the last time was the *Plan B* thing," Tom says. "The costarring gig didn't happen, but our meeting was fun."

"Of course it was fun," Jamie says. "As I remember, you spent about half an hour kissing her hand."

"That's right. I'd just come back from Paris, the hand-kissing capital of the world. So I told Cameron: In France, there are lots of ways to kiss hands. Some men kiss hands this way . . ."

Tom Bondini demonstrates how he kissed Cameron Diaz's hand by kissing his own hand: planting a wet one on the back of his paw. He is the perfect couple. Surely it is true love, and yet he doesn't seem too narcissistic.

"Others," he continues, "kiss them this way . . ."

The world's biggest movie star kisses his own knuckles.

"Still others do it this way . . ."

This time he kisses his own fingers.

"And then there is always . . ."

He kisses his own palm and then presses it to his cheek.

Maybe he won't audition, but he is playing a great love scene in our office. Which makes me begin to like him better. He is somehow charming as he courts himself. My hands calm down somewhat.

I notice that Tom is sitting beneath the long horns that are mounted on the wall. Our historic cowboy hat still hangs from the tip on one of those horns. Hovering above the head of the big star, it looks like a sweat-stained Texas halo.

"I wonder how you'd look in Jimmy Goodnight's hat," I say, surprised to hear my voice. "It's a family heirloom. That's it hanging over your head."

"Goodnight's, huh?" Tom says. "I'd be honored."

He half stands, reaches up, and plucks the dirty dove off its perch. Sitting back down, he slowly lowers it onto his head. It is a little too big but not by much.

"You look great," says Jamie, relieved.

"Yeah," I say, ever a man of few words.

He does look good. Am I turning into a star fucker?

"I want to see how it looks," Tom says. "Do you guys have a mirror?"

"In the john," Jamie says.

"Where's that?"

"I'll show you," I volunteer.

I lead Jamie and Tom down a truncated hall and into our bathroom. Or rather our shower room. (We have an office shower but not an office bathtub.) Tom stares at himself in the shower room mirror for a long, long time. I stop breathing because now I want him to like the hat. I want him to like how he looks in the hat.

At last, he says: "I want to play a cowboy."

We troop back to the office. Tom hangs the hat on the bull horn. We all sit down.

"I want to play a cowboy," the biggest star in the world repeats, "but I'd like to read a script."

"We don't have one," Jamie tells him. "Not yet. We're working on it."

"I can't decide until I see a script."

Somehow he has turned the tables. Before I hadn't wanted him, but now he wants to read our script. Of course, I want him to like it. I want everybody to like it. Now he is passing judgment on us instead of us passing on him.

"As soon as we've got a first draft," Jamie says.

"Maybe I could just look at what you've written so far," Tom suggests. "I hate reading whole scripts anyway."

"Maybe."

6

TWO DAYS LATER, TOM BONDINI, HAVING READ JUST
twenty pages, agrees to play Jimmy Goodnight in return for $25 mil-
lion. Plus we have to agree to give bit parts to his sister and brother and
a host of friends and hangers-on. So one piece of the puzzle is in place.

Hoping to fit the next piece to the first piece, Jamie and I keep
making our trips to the casting office every day at four. We see lots of
beautiful girls. Some of the beauties are simply too beautiful to play
Revelie, who—in my mind's old tintypes—was beautiful but not that
beautiful. These poor actresses are cursed with over-the-top beauty.
They look unreal, unbelievable. Their extreme beauty is as much a
handicap as a harelip. Eventually I begin to think that I never want to
see another beautiful blonde. Enough is enough. Too much.

Then a brunette walks in who isn't all that pretty. She is wearing
cowboy boots, a western shirt, and a cowboy belt with a big buckle.

"I'm Sarah Marks," she says, "and you're Jamie Stone, but who
the hell are you?"

"Chick Goodnight," I say.

"Any relation to our hero?" asks SARAH MARKS.

"Afraid so."

"Pleased to know you." Her handshake is firm.

"Sarah, where are you from?" asks Jamie.

"Well, I was born in Boston, but I was an Army brat. I've lived all
over: Arizona, Nevada, Texas."

"Where in Texas?" I ask, interested.

"You've never heard of it. A little bitty town called Idalou."

"Idalou? Idalou! I'm from Spur."

"Spur, no kidding? That's just down the road. The Spur Bulldogs, right?"

"Right!"

"I hate to interrupt this family reunion," interrupts Jamie with an edge to her voice, "but we've got an audition scheduled here. Sarah, would you be willing to read a scene for us?"

"Sure," Sarah says, pulling her folded sides out of her hip pocket.

"Good."

Jamie does not ask me to catch Sarah up on the story so far. By now, my director has heard my summary so many times that she is sick of it.

"Who's going to play Jimmy Goodnight?" asks Sarah.

"Chick is," says Jamie.

Taken by surprise, I feel my cheeks blushing. My face is so hot it hurts. I know I can't act. In high school, I had tried playing Marc Antony in *Julius Caesar*. Some people actually laughed at my attempts to speak iambic. Then I mounted a platform to make my funeral speech and it collapsed. My acting career has been all downhill from there.

"No," I decline.

"Come on, handsome," Sarah says, "you're good-looking enough to be a leading man."

"You must want this part awfully bad," I tell Sarah. Then I turn to my director: "Jamie, you do it."

"But I've got to watch. Come on, please."

My hands are shaking like an eight-point earthquake and I am sweating. I am always afraid of being the center of attention, which is why I fear acting, and I'm scared of this actress. She has impressed me, and I don't want to embarrass myself in front of her. At the same time, I don't want to hurt her chance to get the part. She has to act the scene with somebody.

"Go on, 'handsome,'" Jamie says, making quotes with her fingers. "Hurry up. We're wasting time."

I fear acting irrationally, the way some people fear flying, or heights, or enclosed spaces. But I'm also afraid of playing the coward in front of Jamie and Sarah. Feeling as if I am going over the top in combat, I get up stiffly from my chair and slouch toward Sarah's couch. I slump down without looking at her. I don't want her to see the terror in my eyes.

"Okay, when you're ready," Jamie says.

I look at "Revelie" shyly, timidly, which is how I feel, but which is also how "Jimmy" is supposed to feel, so it fits the scene. She looks more confident, which befits her status as a more experienced actor, but which fits her part as well.

"Chick," Jamie prompts me, "talk."

"This grass'll git tough later on," I say haltingly, playing my own great-great-great-ever-so-great-grandfather, reading every word, the pages shaking in my quivering hands, "but right now it's nice an' tender."

"Oh yes," Sarah says casually, playing my great-great-great-ever-so-great-grandmother.

"The thing is, a person could lie down on it now," I say, indicating the grass, getting the accent right but not anything else. "While it's tender like this."

Now comes a moment I have been dreading. I can't believe I'm really going to lie down on the floor. I do it anyway. Trying to lie down gracefully, I lose my balance and fall flat. It reminds me of the platform collapsing under me in *Julius Caesar.*

"How is it?" Sarah asks.

"Good," I say unconvincingly, frowning, scowling. "Wanna try it?"

Sarah moves gracefully to the floor. Now comes the second moment I have been dreading and longing for at the same time. My hand reaches for her breast.

"Wait," Sarah reprimands me, and I flinch. "What do you think you're doing?"

I do a hot-stove reaction and actually feel burned.

"What's wrong?" I ask, getting my own line wrong.

"This isn't a bedroom," she says.

"It's a great bedroom. The best bedroom in the whole damn world."

I stumble through the rest of the scene until we get to the ultimate moment, feared, longed for, impossible, possible . . .

"So you think it would be all right?" asks Sarah.

"Unh-hunh," I stammer.

When I reach for Sarah's breast this time, she not only doesn't stop me but grasps my hand and presses it harder into her softness. That isn't in the pages.

"Cut," Jamie says.

7

I FOLLOW JAMIE TO A SMALL DOOR CUT INTO THE SIDE of a huge Hollywood soundstage—Stage 7—which looks like an airplane hangar. Entering, I pass from bright sunlight into darkness, from the known world into the unknown, from reality into dream. I feel myself leaving the open plain and entering the dark forest. Down Alice's rabbit hole, through the looking glass, into the belly of the whale. It is dark in here. It is huge in here. It is quiet in here.

As my eyes begin to adjust to the dark, I can barely make out the shadow of Jamie moving ahead of me, my guide in this underworld. I trip and almost fall because I don't see a cable the size of a boa constrictor that snakes its way across the black floor. In the dark distance up ahead, I SEE (POV) a dim light. Is it a will-o'-the-wisp? Or a campfire? The light attracts us and we move toward it. The glow resolves into a cluster of lights on stands.

"I love this," Jamie says softly, "but it scares me."

"Really?" I ask, surprised.

"Sure, I see all the machinery and the crew and my stomach starts to hurt. I feel like I've swallowed a baby."

"A baby?" I ask, dreaming of cannibals.

"Oh, that's one of those big lights over there. It's a baby the way Little John was little. Anyway I feel it right in the pit of my stomach. Very hot and very heavy."

"I thought you'd be used to it by now."

"Never."

From our hundreds and hundreds of office readings, we have selected a half dozen actresses for screen tests. Jamie says sow's ears in the office can be silk purses on screen. Buddy Dale puts it differently: Some assholes turn out to be real pussies through the camera lens.

Drawing nearer our destination, we can make out the outlines of our set. It is the living room borrowed from a prime-time soap opera. It is so bland it could readily be turned into anybody else's room if the soap is canceled tomorrow.

"As Ethel Barrymore once said of a set where she was supposed to live, 'I don't have very good taste, do I?'" Jamie says.

"Right," I LAUGH.

Our scene is supposed to take place in a log cabin with windows covered by curtains made from flour sacks. The floor should be packed earth partially obscured by a rug woven from rags.

"It'll do for a screen test," Jamie says as we advance a little closer. "But that won't do." All the humor is gone from her voice. "Look at that camera. I might've known."

I study the camera, which is staring directly at a couch at a perpendicular angle. What's the matter with it? It looks all right to me. But then what do I know about cameras?

"You might have known what?" I ask.

"It's in the wrong place," she says.

"Oh."

"It's set up for a two shot. But we already know Tom can act. Anyway, he'd better be able to at these prices. So we don't need to see him. We need to see the girls. So why not put the camera on them. Shoot over his shoulder. Get our girls full face."

While I hang back, Jamie plunges into the light and starts giving orders. A couple of huge men, who look as if they play on the offensive line of the Dallas Cowboys, unlock the camera wheels and start rolling it. Then another team of workers, who are almost as big, start shifting the clusters of lights.

"It's always like this," Jamie says. "Everybody works so hard and then you have to come in and change everything. Too bad."

Tom Bondini comes strolling out of the dark, practicing his cowboy walk. In no hurry. He wears jeans, a floppy flannel shirt, and a leather vest. He lowers himself slowly onto the soap opera couch.

Then Buddy Dale escorts an actress named MAGGIE FAITH into our light, looking deer-startled. As usual, he is dressed all in black, and his nose is running. She is wearing a translucent tank top, and her nose is running, too. The big eyes in her head look frightened, but the big eyes on her chest seem confident. She is simultaneously timid and bold. What a piece of work is woman.

"Tom," Buddy addresses the biggest star in the world, "could you come here a minute?"

Giving Jamie a funny look, Tom Bondini gets up off the couch and ambles toward the producer and his protégée.

"What can I do for you?" Tom asks.

"Maggie's a little upset," explains Buddy. "She needs to talk to you before she does the scene. Why don't you go for a walk outside?"

Tom looks over at Jamie and shrugs. She shrugs back.

"Okay," Tom says.

The star and the would-be actress walk off together, disappearing into the soundstage's artificial night.

"If we cast her," Jamie whispers to me, "it'll take two years to shoot this movie."

We all just stand around, wasting time is money, waiting for our actors to return. I shift my weight from one foot to another, from one hundred-dollar bill to another, like a tethered horse. I try to think ahead about our story, but it is no use.

"When I was about to direct my first movie," Jamie says, "I asked a wise old director to give me some advice. Know what he said?"

"'Do storyboards,'" I guess.

"No," she says. "He said, 'Get comfortable shoes.'"

My feet, pinched in cowboy boots, start to hurt.

When our actors return after about fifteen minutes, Tom looks sadder, but Maggie seems happier.

"Maggie, come over here," Jamie says. "Please."

Maggie walks over and faces the director. She stops looking quite so happy. Buddy Dale scowls.

"Maggie, you're wearing too much makeup," Jamie says. "Go wash your face, please. And wipe your nose."

Maggie looks appealingly at Buddy: Do I have to do this? You're in charge here, aren't you?

Buddy just shrugs. Sorry about that. Got to humor these directors.

With a petulant frown, Maggie stalks off and disappears into the gloom.

After what seems a long time, Maggie returns to the light and looks younger. Hesitantly, Maggie gives Jamie a big smile.

"Go wash your face again," Jamie orders.

Looking miserable, Maggie retreats into the darkness once again.

"What're you doing to her?" demands Buddy, materializing out of the gloom. "I don't get you."

"Look, these young actresses make a mistake," Jamie says. "They put on too much makeup to look older and more sophisticated. But their greatest asset is their youth and innocence." She fixes Buddy with a stare. "But I guess maybe they're not all that innocent after they meet you, are they?"

"Remember who you're speaking to," Buddy stammers. "I'm—"

"I know who you are. That's the problem."

Jamie turns her back and walks away. I catch up with her in the shadows.

"Fuck him," she spits out. "These girls have the rest of their lives to look older. I just don't understand why they don't want to look young, the one and only time in their lives when they are young. They're hiding their gift."

Maggie materializes out of the shadows and stands at Jamie's elbow.

"Oh, hello," says Jamie. "Let me see you in the light."

She leads her into a bright field and studies her. Maggie cringes. Jamie frowns.

"I'm sorry," she says. "You're going to have to wash again."

Maggie seems close to tears as she disappears into the gloom once more.

Buddy approaches. "Stop picking on her."

"I hate having to do that," Jamie says, "but there's no point in doing a screen test if we can't see her face."

"Yeah, sure."

When Maggie finally returns, she looks terrified. Jamie once again escorts her into the light and examines her.

"That's much better," Jamie says. "You're lovely." She looks around. "Where's Tom? Somebody find Tom and tell him we're ready."

When Tom Bondini appears a few minutes later, the two actors take seats on the soap couch. Next to flannel-and-denim Tom, Maggie in her translucent top looks almost naked. It occurs to me that she should have put more cover on her body and less on her face. Maybe she has been auditioning for too many Buddys and not enough Jamies.

"Ready?" asks the director.

"Sure," Tom says.

Maggie just nods.

Jamie takes up a position behind and slightly to the right of the camera. I move over and stand behind and slightly to the right of her. A young man stretches a carpenter's tape measure from the lens of the camera to the tip of Maggie's nose.

"That's called 'pulling focus,'" Jamie whispers to me.

"Picture is next," says a young man with a beard. The soundstage gets quieter and tenser. "Stand by." The set gets quieter still. "We're rolling."

"We *are* rolling," confirms the camera operator.

"Speed," says the sound man.

A seedy-looking young man with a wispy mustache steps in front of the camera and holds up a slate.

"*Goodnight* screen test," he says in a loud, clear voice. "Maggie Faith. Take one. Mark." The arm of the slate comes down, *whack*.

"And action," Jamie says in what seems an artificial voice. Then she whispers to me: "It always embarrasses me to say that."

"What's the matter?" Tom (as Goodnight) asks Maggie (as Revelie).

"Well, I was just thinking," Maggie/Revelie says, "maybe it's time."

"Time for what?" he asks.

"Time to write out your code," she says.

"What?"

"Don't you remember?" she says, sounding both overanxious and sleepy at the same time. "Back when you were courting me by mail, you wrote you were planning to write down some rules for life in this country. And you implied that you could use my help. Well, was that just something you said to get me to fall in love with you? Or were you serious about a code?"

"Uh, well, both to tell you the truth," he says, not trying too hard, weaving Texas rhythms into his speech. "See, I wanted you to love me and I wanted help to write this stuff down. Wha'd you call it?"

"A code," she says. "I think it's a good idea." Then the well-scrubbed actress begins to stumble: "I've . . . I've . . . Let's see, I've . . ."

"'I've been waiting for you to bring it up,'" Jamie prompts.

"I've," Maggie stammers. "I've . . ." Then she bursts into tears. She is crying out her pretty, well-washed eyes. Very impressive tears—a measure to some of acting ability—are flowing down her soap-and-water cheeks. Unfortunately, it isn't that kind of scene.

"Give her a minute," interrupts Buddy Dale.

"With pleasure," Jamie says under her breath.

I follow my director back into the dark reaches of the soundstage, stumbling over a couple of electrical boa constrictors as I go. Deep in purgatory, Jamie finally stops.

"It seems," Jamie says in a conspiratorial voice, "that Buddy flew Maggie in from New York yesterday. She's some kind of model. She spent last night at his house, and he gave her certain chemicals that he assured her would make her a better actress. And she didn't get any sleep and she's a mess with a runny nose."

Ten minutes later, Buddy Dale waves everybody to come back. We reassemble around the electronic campfire.

"I'm sorry," Maggie says from behind cry-red eyes.

"Okay," Jamie says. "Are you ready to continue?"

"Yes," Maggie sniffs.

So we go through the same routine again . . . "Picture is next" . . . "Stand by" . . . "We're rolling" . . . *Whack!*

Everybody on set takes a deep hopeful breath and prays: Let her get through this.

"Can we take it from the top?" asks Maggie with film threading through the camera.

"No, we'll take it from where we left off," Jamie says.

"Please," asks Maggie, her tears on the verge of beginning again. "Sorry."

"Give the kid a break," interrupts Buddy Dale.

"Cut!" Jamie orders, then turns on her producer: "That wouldn't be fair to the others. We pick up where we left off. I'm sorry, but I'm falling way behind schedule. Let's go, ready or not."

Maggie wipes her tears. She plays the martyr. Unfortunately, martyrdom isn't the part. At least not in this scene.

"I underestimated her," Jamie whispers to me. "It would take five years to make this movie."

Tearfully Maggie tries again: "I've been waiting for you to bring it up, but . . . but . . . but . . ."

". . . but you never did," says Sarah Marks/Revelie, who is no crybaby, "so I thought I might mention it. You still want to, don't you?"

"Sure," Tom/Goodnight says, purposely nervous.

"Good, so do I," she says, her Boston accent believable, to me, at least.

Sarah picks up paper and a historically inappropriate ballpoint pen from the soap opera coffee table. "Let's begin. Perhaps when we finish, we might persuade all of our cowboys to sign it."

"Sounds good to me," Tom says. "We'll puzzle it out together, okay?"

"Of course. How do you want to start?"

"I dunno. Mebbe we oughta start with number one."

"That sounds good to me," Sarah CHUCKLES, writing a "1."

"Less see," Goodnight says, "put down how you gotta be trustworthy. That's number one. Now you do number two."

"All right," says Revelie, "shall we make two bravery? How shall we put it? 'I promise always to strive to be brave.' How's that?"

"Real purdy. Now it's my turn. I reckon three oughta be self-reliant. Is that okay?"

"That's fine. Now four." She writes the numeral. "Maybe four could be fair, always striving to be fair. Fair and impartial."

"Yeah, fair and like you said because ever'body's worth the same amount."

"Equal?"

"That's it."

Her pen scratches across the paper.

"Read it to me," Goodnight says. "Read me what you wrote."

"All right," Revelie says. "'In all my dealings, I promise to be fair and impartial and to treat all people as equals.'"

"You ever think a writin' poetry?"

"As a matter of fact I did—when I was a girl. Thank you for the implied compliment. But go on about your conception of equality."

"You know, a white man ain't worth more'n an Injun ain't worth more'n a Meskin ain't worth more'n a black man. A cow ain't worth more'n a buffalo. A dawg ain't worth more'n a wolf ain't worth more'n a coyote. A rose ain't worth more'n a horehound flower and t'other way 'round. A man ain't worth more'n a woman.'"

"Mr. Goodnight, did you ever think of writing poetry?"

"Not hardly. Don't make funna me. I'm real sensitive in this here area."

"Believe me, I'm not making fun. And I'm more than willing to prove it."

Sarah attacks Tom.

At the end of all the screen tests, I feel tired and a little light-headed. Casting is harder work than I would have imagined. It is like interviewing in that it requires prolonged concentration. As the gaffers and grips and gripes pack up their equipment, the rest of us mill about. We are packing up our impressions.

"Who'd you like best?" Buddy Dale asks me.

I jump because I didn't see him coming. His black clothing and dark hair make him almost invisible in this light. Only his face and hands are visible. And of course his omnipresent dandruff—looking like stars—on his black sweater.

"Uh, Sarah Marks," I gasp.

"Really? Why?"

"I like her freckles."

I don't know why I say it. The words just jump out. I do like her freckles, but I like a lot more besides. I like her intensity. I like her being from Idalou. I like it seeming like fate that a girl from Idalou might play my great-great-great-ever-so-great-grandmother who had lived the best years of her life only a few miles away from that dusty dying cotton town.

"Freckles?" Buddy Dale asks. "Maggie's got freckles. Really. Go look at her."

"I believe you," I say, a little embarrassed that I hadn't noticed whether she had freckles or not.

"Come on," Buddy insists.

He takes me by the elbow and marches me away. Looking back over my shoulder, I SEE (POV) Jamie smiling at me. I trip again over the boa constrictors. When we emerge into the daylight, it takes a moment for my eyes to adjust. Then I SEE (POV) Maggie sniffling in front of me. She looks up at me with eyes bright with tears.

"Look at her nose," Buddy orders, pointing. "See, freckles."

8

AT 3 P.M. THE NEXT DAY, WE ALL GATHER IN PARA-mount's full-sized Gary Cooper Theater to look at the screen tests.

Here is the biggest screen on the lot. Studio president Shelley Bingham is missing, but the chairman of the board is there—which is rare—as well as the head of production and various vice presidents. Buddy Dale, who was once the studio head, is late. We wait for him. When he finally arrives, wearing black, we roll.

Up on the huge screen, the first test scene looks surprisingly like real life, at least to me. This is my first preview of what the movie will look like, and I like what I see. I'm excited. I believe Tom Bondini is Jimmy Goodnight. I believe at least one of the actresses could be Mrs. Goodnight, Revelie. It takes half an hour to see all the tests.

The lights go up.

"I think Maggie was head and shoulders above the others," says Buddy Dale.

"Head and tits above," says RICK LIVINGSTON, head of production, and the only Alaska native ever to make it big at a Hollywood studio.

Buddy Dale blows his runny nose on a Kleenex and drops it on the floor of the theater.

"I like Sarah Marks," I say, surprising myself at being so bold. I don't say: I thought she was even better on the screen than in real life.

"I like her, too," says Jamie, "now that I've seen her on the screen."

I take a deep breath, relieved, no longer the center of attention, no longer alone. But my hands are still vibrating as if I were riding a fast motorcycle through the badlands. Of course, that could never happen because my mother made me swear a blood oath at a young age that I would never ride anything with a motor and less than four wheels.

"I'd never fuck Sarah Marks," Buddy Dale says disdainfully. "I wouldn't fuck her with a ten-foot pole."

"Yeah, I had the same reaction," says Rick Livingston, Alaska's contribution to the age's most popular art form. "I kept wondering: Is she fuckable enough? I don't think she is."

"Not fuckable?" says MICKEY BERNSTEIN, Paramount's chairman of the board. "I don't know what you guys are talking about. I guess that's because I'm married. Let me tell you, they all look fuckable to me."

Nervous LAUGHTER.

"*I* still wouldn't fuck her with a ten-foot pole," Buddy says. "I'd like to see more girls."

"I'll bet you would," says the chairman.

9

BACK IN OUR OFFICE A FEW MINUTES LATER, JAMIE says: "Come with me."

We make our way to the great parking lot, turn left, and tread narrow alleys until we reach a huge warehouse labeled CONSTRUCTION DEPARTMENT. When we enter this glass palace, none of the workers pay any attention to us. The interior looks like God's own hardware store. We pass down aisles stocked with boulders, aisles crowded with trees, aisles stacked with columns (Ionic, Doric, Corinthian).

Jamie stops in front of the columns, so I do, too. She studies these giant sticks very carefully, studies them the way she studied the actors during auditions. At last, she makes up her mind.

"Help me," Jamie says. "We'll take this one."

I can't believe she wants us to pick up and carry a marble pillar. Who does she think we are? Some of the columns are standing or leaning, but this one is lying on the floor. When Jamie bends down to grasp one end, I reach for the other. Giving it my all, I lift and almost fall over backward. The marble pillar is as light as an angel food cake. I should have known. Where do I think I am, anyway? I hope Jamie hasn't noticed me straining to lift this toothpick. My face reddens but not from exertion.

"Too heavy for you?" Jamie asks.

"Never," I huff unconvincingly.

As we carry the column—which happens to be Corinthian, my favorite, so we are still in sync—out of the Construction Department, nobody pays any attention to us. The workers seem to expect people to come along and carry away parts of their temple.

Toting our burden, we thread our way through Paramount's parking lot. The longer we carry the pillar, the more it feels like stone instead of papier-mâché. I'm determined not to let down my end.

"How're you doing?" asks Jamie.

"Fine," I lie breathlessly.

"You know," she says, not out of breath at all, "Sarah's much better on screen than she was in the room. When we were shooting the test, I didn't think she had much of anything. But on film she's almost another person. And a much better actress. Some actors are like that."

"I thought she was pretty good in the room," I huff.

"Yeah, but what room was that?" Jamie winks. "Besides, she let you feel her up, right? That day on the casting-office floor?"

"She made me. She grabbed my hand—"

"Poor baby."

When we reach Buddy Dale's bungalow—with his name in huge script letters on the front door—Jamie puts her head inside. "Would somebody mind giving us a hand?" she asks. "Please hold the door. We've got a delivery here."

A pretty, peroxided secretary comes to our aid and holds the door open while we file inside toting our Corinthian column. She seems to be impressed by our pillar. At last, somebody is paying attention.

"What's that?" asks the blonde.

"A Corinthian column," Jamie explains.

"Yes, but . . ."

"We need to see Buddy right now."

"Just a moment."

Not waiting, Jamie opens the door to Buddy Dale's inner office. This time no secretary helps us, but we get through the door anyway. I SEE (POV) office walls covered with posters of movies that Buddy Dale has produced over the years. Jamie and I march right up to the producer's desk, which is as big as a barge. As we approach, he retreats, pushing his padded leather chair backward.

"Here, Buddy," Jamie says. "Catch."

We toss the column across the desk. While it is in the air, Buddy Dale's face changes into a terrible mask from some gruesome horror movie.

"No!" he SHOUTS.

The Corinthian column lands in Buddy's lap. He looks as if he thinks he has been crushed by a ton of marble. As if he has been cut in half. As if his sex life has been smashed to pudding. In his terror, he, too, has forgotten where he is.

"There's your ten-foot pole," Jamie says, "which is what you seem to need for intercourse. But I don't want you using it on our new leading lady because you said you never would. You know, Buddy, I'm beginning to think you're just a little bit perverted."

"You're crazy!" sputters Buddy Dale.

"And proud of it," I say, surprising myself.

"Don't mind him," Jamie says, grinning at me. "Sarah let him touch her breast and he hasn't been the same since."

10

AFTER WORK, I DRIVE MY HUMBLE RENTED FORD TO my cousin's box home. Sharon greets me wearing her bathrobe and moving unnaturally, like an old lady who needs a cane.

"What happened to you?"

"I got hit. Places it wouldn't show."

"Who?"

"You know who—Chris. I told him my girlfriend found out he was fucking somebody else. And I said I didn't want to see him anymore. And that I'd tell you. And then you wouldn't help him anymore. Forget about working on your movie. And then he started punching me in the stomach and just kept on hitting me."

"I'm calling the cops."

"No, don't. Please, don't. If you care for me at all, don't do that. I'll be all right in the morning. He just kept apologizing. I feel sorry for him."

"Why?"

"Really, I'm okay. Forget it. Men do this."

"No, they don't. I don't. I don't know any man who does."

"Well, then you just don't know many men. But let's change the subject. Please. Pretty please. You're just making it worse. How was your day? Better than mine, I hope."

"Tell me what he did. I'm sure it's a crime."

"Not unless I say so, and I say it wasn't. Now cheer me up. What's going on with your movie?"

I am reluctant to change the subject, but I finally acquiesce. "Okay, well, we had a showdown with Buddy the asshole. We cast

Sarah as Revelie over his objections. Over his obscenities. Over and out, I hope." I stare for a long time at my cousin. "I want you to promise me that you won't ever audition for that predator. He's like a Chris with real power. And Chris is bad enough."

"Still—"

"Don't say that. I'm not kidding. He convinces girls to"—I pause because it has always been hard for me to say the word *fuck*—"well, you know, which is bad enough. But even worse, it doesn't do them any good. They're rejected because they slept with him." I decide to overcome my *fucking* scruples to make a point: "Fucking Buddy means no fucking talent. Everybody who counts knows that. Those poor girls."

"I still say I should be so—"

"Shut up!" I almost yell. "Don't say that, don't think that, don't ever do that. Not that—"

"Not that he would ever consider me," Sharon says.

"No, not that you ever would—really would—consider such a thing."

"Oh, you never know. If I hadn't broken up with Chris, he was going to recommend me. Unlike you."

I am about to give my cousin another lecture when the phone RINGS. Sharon answers it.

"Hello." Listens. "It's for you."

"Hello," I say, taking the phone.

"Hi," says Jamie.

"What's up?" I ask.

"I'm sorry to disturb you so late, but I thought you should know."

"What?"

"Buddy Dale just called. He ordered me to fire you. Your last day as a screenwriter was today."

11

I COME IN EARLY THE NEXT MORNING TO CLEAN OUT my desk, but I'm too early. Jamie's assistant, Becky, has not yet arrived and the office is still locked. I don't have a key. I wonder if that is some sort of Hollywood rule: No keys for the writers. I sit down and lean back against the locked door. The stoop starts to get hard, but I don't move, anyway not much, until Becky arrives at nine-thirty.

"Good morning," I greet her, struggling stiffly to stand up.

"I didn't mean to keep you waiting," she apologizes.

"That's all right."

"Did you lose your key?"

"No, I never got one."

"Oh, I'm sorry. I'll get you a key today."

So it isn't a rule after all.

"No need," I say. "This is my last day. Actually yesterday was."

"What?" she says. "You just started . . ."

"I know."

"That's too bad. I'm sorry."

She unlocks the door and we go inside. I start packing up my things, which doesn't take long because—Becky is right—I've just started. Then I sit down on the office couch and wait for the telephone to ring. Wait for the summons. Wait for my screenwriting career to end. Wait to get fired.

At a quarter to eleven, Jamie arrives, finally. She explains she is late because her dog is sick. She had to take Betcher to a veterinarian. She sits down beside me on the couch.

"Why?" I ask simply.

"Because you defied him," Jamie says. "Didn't like his girl. And I didn't make things any better with that column stunt. I'm sorry. I guess I went a little crazy and you're having to pay for it."

I like Jamie more than ever.

"Let's go," she says.

"Where?"

"To see Buddy Dale."

"What?"

"Come on," she says. "Don't sit around here all day while you're not getting paid."

When we enter Buddy Dale's office, it seems to me that my own life is turning into a movie. Real drama, reel drama. And I see this drama as if in the third person. Outside myself. Through the lens of a camera rather than through my own eyes. I even wonder how I would write it . . .

INT. BUDDY DALE'S OUTER OFFICE — MORNING

Jamie and Chick enter and look around. They SEE (POV) a RECEPTIONIST. They also SEE (POV) a PRETTY REDHEADED MODEL who is new to them. They approach the receptionist.

                    JAMIE
        Is Buddy free?

                    RECEPTIONIST
        What are you going to throw at him
        today?

                    JAMIE
        Darn it, I knew we forgot something.

> RECEPTIONIST
>
> Let me see if he is brave enough to
> receive you.

The receptionist picks up her phone and punches
several numbers.

> RECEPTIONIST
> (into phone)
>
> Jamie and—uh—

> CHICK
>
> Chick Goodnight.

> RECEPTIONIST
> (into phone)
>
> —and Chick Goodnight are here to see
> you.

The receptionist hangs up the phone.

> RECEPTIONIST (CONT)
>
> Okay, but don't hurt him too badly.

INT. BUDDY DALE'S INNER OFFICE — MORNING

Jamie and Chick enter. BUDDY DALE looks up from a
script he is pretending to read and smiles.

> BUDDY DALE
>
> Hello. It was good of you to drop in,
> Jamie. But I'm a little surprised to
> see you, Chick. I thought—

> JAMIE
>
> Let's cut to the chase, as they say in
> the so-called movie business. Chick and

                    JAMIE (CONT)
I just dropped by to tender our
resignations.

                    BUDDY DALE
No, Jamie, not you. The studio loves
you. I love you.

                    JAMIE
Chick and I are kinda tied together, like
a two-man chain gang. Where one of us
goes, the other one is bound to follow.

CLOSE ON BUDDY DALE
He stares at Jamie, his expression puzzled, then
irritated, then angry, then puzzled again.

                    BUDDY DALE
Okay, Jamie, you win this one.

                    JAMIE
Chick, let's get back to work.

Jamie and Chick turn and leave the office.

12

WHEN I ARRIVE BACK AT THE SMALL BOX DUG INTO THE
big hill, my cousin Sharon rushes to meet me at the sliding glass
door. The lights of Los Angeles are already sparkling below our glass

wall, and there are lights in Sharon's eyes as well. She is excited. She is happy. She has news. I'm happy for her. Her smile is as big and bright as the HOLLYWOOD sign on the side of another hill nearby. I smile back.

"Buddy Dale called," Sharon almost shouts her news. "Well, not him personally, but his office. He wants me to audition for a part in your movie."

I stop smiling.

"Isn't that great?" she asks, her smile becoming more tentative.

"No, it's not," I say. "You know how I feel about Buddy. Don't do it. Come up with some excuse, but don't do it."

"Why? What's the matter with you? Why can't you be happy for me? I've been waiting to get noticed. Not that I'll get the part. But if I do, just think, both of us working on the same movie. Your movie. Don't bring me down."

Fog or smog is blowing in, dimming the lights below.

"I'm sorry, but I know Buddy Dale," I say. "I don't mean to spoil your fun, but he's a very bad man. He only holds auditions for one reason and that isn't to hand out roles. The casting department keeps any actresses who can act away from him—"

"Well, thank you very much!"

"I didn't mean that the way it sounded. I know you can act. But that isn't why Buddy wants to see you. He wants to get on top of you—I'm sorry to be so blunt—because you're my cousin."

"So everything is about you! Is that right? I know you were a bigger deal back home in Spur than I ever was. But we're not in Spur anymore in case you haven't noticed. This is just as much my town as it is your town. More, I got here first. You still ask me directions. How do you know this isn't about me?"

I feel terrible. Am I just being an arrogant bastard?

"I told you he wanted to fire me," I say. "I told you about the column in his lap. He hates me, and I hate him. He's trying to get back at me through you."

Sharon is crying. She was so happy and now she is in tears. Why did I have to open my big mouth? Why couldn't I just celebrate with her? But she is my cousin, and I'm older, so I still feel the need to protect her. I step forward to take her in my arms, but she pushes me away.

"Did it ever occur to you that the world doesn't always revolve around you?" she scolds tearfully. "Anyway not planet Hollywood. When I was little, my parents used to hold you up to me as an example. Be like fucking Chick. Study, grind your nose off, get a scholarship. What I got was sick of it."

"But Buddy's a real menace. I don't want him to use you. I don't want him anywhere near you."

"I'm a big girl. Besides, he probably doesn't even know I'm your cousin."

I hadn't thought of that possibility. Her professional name isn't Goodnight. It's Loving. Unfortunately, when she entered the acting fraternity, the name Sharon Goodnight was already taken. So she settled on Sharon Loving, since Loving was her great-great-great-ever-so-great-grandfather's best friend, his Lancelot, in every way.

"He knows," I say at last. "I'm sure he knows."

"No you aren't," Sharon says. "You just can't let me have my chance. What are you afraid of? That I might get the job? That I might invade *your* movie?"

"Wait, I'm not the enemy," I say, wondering if I'm right. "Please tell me you aren't going to do this. Please."

"Now it's my turn to be sorry," she says. "I'm sorry I'm not sorry. I'm declining your advice. If you don't like it, you can find a new place to live. I'm seeing him tomorrow."

13

A PICNIC LUNCH IS SPREAD IN TOM BONDINI'S DRESS-
ing room. A small crowd stands around munching sandwiches and
lemon cake and plums while the biggest star in the world takes off his
pants. He is trying on different outfits that may or may not be used in
his hit television series. Tom stands there in his jockey shorts until the
wardrobe mistress hands him a pair of charcoal slacks to try on. He
looks in the mirror. Then he takes off his pants again and waits in his
jockeys until he is handed a pair of blue jeans. I would have imagined
that achieving stardom meant you didn't have to get undressed in
front of people anymore, but there he is stripping unself-consciously.
It is as if he knows he belongs to the people.

All the while I keep thinking about my cousin meeting with
Buddy Dale. Like Tom, would she be undressing soon? Right here at
the studio? Or would it be later at his home?

Sarah Marks enters the dressing room and smiles at Tom in his
skivvies. "Lucky me," she says. "I married horse hung."

Tom bows in his underwear.

"Isn't it unlucky for a bride to see her groom in his underpants?"
Sarah asks. She walks up and extends her hand: "Hello, Mr. Goodnight, I'm Mrs. Goodnight."

"Loved your screen test," Tom says. "Hello, Revelie, I'm Jimmy."

"Pleased to meet you, husband."

"Pleased to know you, wife."

"Do you mean biblically?"

They kiss, which surprises me but nobody else. It is a long kiss.
Her cheeks crater. He in his underwear, she in her jeans. I hate to

admit it, but I look to see if there is any stirring in his skivvies. I don't see any movement, but what do I know?

"Chick and I still have some work to do," Jamie says. "So I hope we'll see you both tonight for a celebration dinner."

We celebrate Sarah's casting at Jamie's favorite restaurant: Dr. Hogly Wogly's Tyler Texas Bar B Que, way way out on Sepulveda Boulevard in the Valley. The world-famous actor, the sort of famous director, the brand-new actress, and the obscure writer are seated—after a fifteen-minute wait—in a booth with a scratched Formica table and paper place mats. Nobody pays any attention to the celebrities, not the customers, not even our waitress.

"This is the best barbecue in the world," says Jamie.

"A four-star dive," says Sarah.

"What do you mean by 'dive'?" asks the director.

"I'm sorry. Does your family own a piece of this little sliver of hog heaven?"

When our waitress finally gets around to visiting our booth, Jamie insists that we all order combination plates with lots of side dishes. Ribs. Pulled pork. Sliced beef. Barbecued links. Potato salad. Coleslaw. Red beans. Extra biscuits.

"You know about the Greek column, right?" Jamie asks.

"Yeah, I heard," Sarah says.

"I'll never forgive Buddy for what he said."

"I wasn't surprised."

"You weren't?"

"No, not after I wouldn't fuck him."

"What?"

"You don't know?"

"No."

"Oh, yeah, when I first heard about this project, I knew I wanted to play Revelie. I told my agent and he arranged a meeting with

Buddy. I met him in his office, where he seemed to like me. Then I went for a second meeting at his home, where he didn't like me so much. It was dumb of me to go."

"What happened?" asks Tom.

"He welcomed me at the door wearing a robe and slippers. Then he handed me a robe and told me to change into it."

(Of course, I imagine my cousin Sharon enduring the same trial by desire.)

"Sarah, what did you do?" asks Jamie.

"I said I preferred the wardrobe I'd come in. That's when he gave me the stardom lecture. He said the definition of a star is somebody you want to fuck. So I was supposed to fuck him to prove he wanted to fuck me, to prove I was star fuck material. I wasn't swept off my boots."

(I find myself hoping my cousin is equally uncooperative, but unfortunately I have my doubts. She was so excited about meeting him. Too excited. I imagine her accepting the robe and all it implies.)

"That sounds like Buddy," I say.

"So I told him that I'd fuck anybody. Anybody at all. Except somebody who could give me a job. That's my code."

I like Sarah more than ever because she has a code.

(I only wish my poor cousin had one. I imagine her even now flaring her nose for coke or spreading her legs for Buddy. And here I sit helpless. Some cousin's keeper.)

The waitress comes bearing a heavy tray of heavy foods. Ribs and links that seem sexual only because Buddy Dale hovers over our celebration dinner. Sliced beef and barbecued chicken also take their bows. Followed immediately by a chorus of potato salad and beans and coleslaw.

"Anybody want bibs?" asks the waitress.

We all shake our heads. We're all too tough to care about a few stains. Did cowboys at the chuck wagon ask for bibs? Shaking her head, the waitress departs.

"A toast to Sarah," says Jamie, lifting her bottle of Bud. Lots of CLINKS. "Welcome to the Goodnight family."

"Thank you," says Sarah.

I pick up a rib, bite into it, and feel sauce spread across my face. I'm embarrassed. Barbecue is not something I feel comfortable eating in front of people I want to impress. And I want to impress our leading lady, who let me touch her breast. But even more, I don't want to disappoint Jamie. And there is the biggest star in the world staring at the runny red barbecue clogging my pores.

"I know what, Tom," Sarah says, "you feed me and I'll feed you. Go on, feed me a link. That'll be sexy."

(I cannot help imagining something similar in Buddy's bedroom.)

"What?" asks a surprised Tom.

"What's wrong?" she asks.

"Nothing," he says.

"I'm waiting and I'm really hungry," she says, opening her mouth.

There is a silence that seems as endless as *Moby-Dick*. Our hero and heroine stare at each other.

"Sarah," Tom says at last, "you're not one of those actresses who believe you have to live the part, are you?"

They continue to stare at each other. *Moby-Dick the Sequel.*

"The ribs are good," says Jamie. "Try the ribs."

"They're great," I echo.

"Listen to your director," Jamie says, "and eat up."

Our two stars stop staring at each other and turn their attention to their plates. Tom picks up a rib and bites into it without getting sauce all over his face. I try to study how he does it. Then Sarah picks up a sausage link with her fingers, pushes three-quarters of it into her mouth, and bites down fiercely. She isn't nearly as neat as Tom. She gets sauce on her face and a large glop on her T-shirt which is silver and black, and says: RAIDERS.

"I guess I'm messy," Sarah says.

"At least it wasn't a good shirt," Tom says.

"You don't like my shirt," she flares.

"No, I just meant it's only a T-shirt," he defends himself.

"Well, if you don't like it, then I'd better do something about it." Sarah puts two fingers in her mouth and whistles loudly. "Waitress!"

The young woman in uniform hurries—for the first time this evening—to our table, looking worried.

"Waitress, I've changed my mind," says our leading lady. "Would you please bring me a bib and a steak knife?"

"Of course, miss, right away."

Now the rest of the restaurant is studying our booth. Dozens of baseball-cap bills point in our direction. Several recognize Tom but don't make a fuss. They just whisper to each other. The waitress soon returns with a bib and a steak knife and hands them to our new leading lady.

"Thank you very much," Sarah says primly.

Then she ties the white plastic bib—with DR. HOGLY WOGLY'S TYLER TEXAS BAR B QUE printed in red—around her graceful neck. When she picks up the steak knife, I expect her to slice into the meat on her plate, but instead she attacks the shirt on her back. Reaching under the bib, she slices her T-shirt vertically from top to bottom as if opening a body at an autopsy. The rending fabric sounds loud even in the noisy restaurant. Then she puts down the knife and slips completely out of the dangling remnants of the T-shirt. She drops this rag on the floor.

"Okay, Tom, you don't like it," Sarah says. "I'll never wear it again." She picks up a rib and eats hungrily. "Mmmm, good barbecue."

I am so riveted, I no longer think of my cousin and what she may be going through. Or whether she may need my help.

14

I HURRY DOWN THE UNEVEN STONE STEPS THAT LEAD from the road to my cousin's box on the side of the hill. I'm anxious to be reassured she isn't spending the night with Buddy Dale, and I can't wait to tell her the story of the bib. I'm disturbed to see no lights on. Maybe she is with Buddy. Or out with friends. I tell myself it isn't really late, only a few minutes past eleven o'clock. I enter the unlocked door. Ever trusting, ever faithful to her West Texas roots, Sharon never locks up. She says her box is hard to find and there's nothing worth stealing. Lock up anyway. No. Well, it's her place. She's too trusting to live in Lubbock, much less Los Angeles. She's too trusting for planet Earth. And obviously too trusting to be left alone with Buddy Dale.

Inside, I turn on the lights and television. The local news appears. I pay particular attention to make sure there hasn't been an accident or a murder in which my missing cousin might figure. There is plenty of local-news crime, but none that seems to threaten Sharon. I relax ever so slightly and wait.

Jay Leno doesn't amuse me tonight. Neither does Conan O'Brien. I'm not in the mood. I switch to CNN. Even less amusing. Death and destruction. Just what I want to escape thinking about.

Channel surfing, I find *The Searchers,* directed by John Ford. I don't know much about movies, but I know a lot about westerns. This one happens to be one of the best ever made. Maybe the best. John Wayne sets out in search of his niece, who has been carried off by Indians. He believes Indians are evil and anyone who has had intimate contact with them is better off dead. The touch of the Indian—

I'm thinking Buddy Dale—is or should be fatal. If she won't kill herself, then John Wayne will do it for her. But when John Wayne finds his niece, he changes. She is still his niece. He clasps her to him.

I tell myself that I must forgive my cousin, but, of course, who asked me? Who made me Mr. God or Mrs. God—no matter what she has done with Buddy? Oh hell, let's be honest: I'm pissed off. I warned her. Whatever happens to her is her own prewarned fault. Why doesn't she come home so we can at least argue about whether or not she is an actress/slut? Oh no, did I think that? I'm sorry.

Reverting to my secret vice, I get out my batons and start twirling, but this time they don't help. I give up and lie down on the couch. Will I ever get to sleep . . . ?

KNOCKING awakens me. Only half awake, I pull myself off my couch and slouch toward the door. Glancing at my watch, I see it is just after six in the morning. Checking Sharon's bed, I see nobody.

"Who is it?" I ask, sleep-hoarse.

"Police," a voice says.

"Show me," I say, opening the door a crack.

They show me. I read the badges. They seem real to me. What do I know?

"Excuse me, but could you tell me if this is the home of one Sharon Goodnight?" says a uniformed officer.

"Yes," I say, beginning to feel uneasy.

"Are you her husband?"

"No, her cousin."

"Oh, I'm very sorry, but I'm afraid we have some bad news for you."

He pauses as if waiting for me to articulate the bad news for him. I silently refuse.

"Your cousin . . ." he begins.

"Was she raped?" I ask.

"No, it was hit-and-run."

"How badly . . . ?"

"I'm sorry. Would you mind coming with us to officially identify the body?"

I go numb. It is worse than the worst writer's block. I can't feel. I can't function. My severed head is rolling helplessly inside a revolving cement mixer. I feel I've let my cousin down. A Goodnight should protect a Goodnight, not get her killed. Smog-thick guilt clouds my vision. I feel as if I am going to faint—and I want to, want to dissolve into oblivion—but I get to the very edge and then revive. No.

"Are you all right?" asks a policeman.

"I'm afraid so," I say.

"What?"

"Where, uh, where did it happen?" I finally stammer.

"Her body was found in a ditch beside the Pacific Coast Highway a few miles this side of Malibu."

"What was she doing there?"

"Walking along the highway. Anyway that's what it looks like."

"Why?" I mean it in every sense of the word. Rhyme *why* with *I* and I'm back to blaming myself.

15

I FLY HOME TO SPUR FOR SHARON'S FUNERAL, OR RATHER I fly to Lubbock and then drive seventy miles to reach Spur. When I see the black mailbox with the red reflectors, I turn into my parents' small ranch. The rented car rumbles over the cattle guard that keeps forty head of cattle from escaping. They are all white-face Herefords except for a lone brindle longhorn munching grass in the front yard. Watching him, I think—not for the first time—of Larry McMurtry's *Horseman, Pass By* in which the death of a lonely longhorn represents the passing of the Old West. I wonder how Mom and Dad's longhorn is feeling. Pulling up in front of my parents' double-wide, I get out stiffly and walk back into the world of my childhood. This trailer is new and bigger than the ones I grew up in, but it feels the same as the others.

I hug my emotional mother, ANNIE, who taught school in and around Spur for almost fifty years, starting out at the age of seventeen in a one-room schoolhouse, ending at age sixty-five in a mud-colored brick building that looked like a big trailer house without wheels. She has permed gray hair and high cheekbones. Standing about five feet seven inches, she is still remarkably pretty in spite of her sixty-six years. I'm not sure, but I think I feel her tears soak through my shirt.

I shake hands with my seventy-one-year-old father, CLYDE, who started out as a cowboy and ended up a high school football coach. He coached teams in and around Spur a little less than half a century, winning bi-district twice and having countless high school yearbooks dedicated to him. He was always the most important man in town, and the handsomest. At six and a half feet tall, he still weighs just over two hundred pounds, and is about one-eighth Cherokee, with the nose and bearing of a proud chief. I have always been, let's face it, jealous of his ease, good looks, and charm.

"I figure you're probably purdy tuckered," says my dad, "and maybe you wanna rest. But we was about to go on over to see John and Jean. They ain't doin' too good. We'd be proud to have you come along with us if'n you're up to it."

Even though I can hear the siren song of a nap calling to me, I reluctantly say: "Sure."

So the three of us crowd into my dad's beat-up red pickup. He drives, my mom is in the middle, and I'm riding shotgun. We rumble over the cattle guard and then turn left on Highway 70. We rattle the two miles into Spur and pull up in front of a small, pale green stucco house with a huge backyard full of pecan trees. Growing up, I fell out of those trees many times. I am relieved to see no other cars parked out front. I hate crowd scenes.

Entering through the kitchen door without knocking—a local custom—we walk in on what looks like a sad potluck supper. I realize food has been arriving all day. Starve a fever, feed unbearable grief. Pecan pies. Lemon meringues. Bean casseroles. Better, tamale casseroles. Tortilla casseroles. And good intentions. Good wishes. Bad feelings. Bitter tears and bittersweet memories. More bitter than sweet at the moment. Such moments are why God or Einstein or Whoever made small towns. According to Lyndon Johnson, small towns are where people know when you're sick and care when you die. Like the people of Spur.

Sitting at the groaning kitchen table are Sharon's parents, UNCLE JOHNNY and AUNT JEAN GOODNIGHT. She was once a Powers model in New York and still looks it. He was once a writer of paperback westerns and still churns one out every now and then. He was the one who gave me the idea of trying to write. I owe him whatever I might or might not become. Well, him and my mom. Well, him, my mom, and my dad.

"What happened?" Uncle Johnny asks me.

"I don't really know," I say with a shiver, "but I'll try to find out."

"Good," my mother sniffles.

"You really don't have any idea?" asks Aunt Jean. "We were kinda countin' on you. Please, cain't you tell us anything?"

"Well, the police say it was hit-and—"

"We know all that," interrupts Uncle Johnny, "but what do you say? Please. Because what the police say doesn't make any sense. She wouldn't have been walking along a big highway in the middle of the night. She hated walking. If she had to cross the street, she'd drive. I'm just not buying it."

"We're counting on you," says Aunt Jean.

I shiver.

On the morning before the funeral, I go for a walk in Spur's small cemetery. I SEE (POV) the open grave waiting to receive my cousin. And just past it I come across the final resting place of a black former slave who, according to the dates on his tombstone, was 120 years old when he died. My cousin's stone will show that she was only twenty-one. The world has never heard of either one of them. All the while, as I pace the graves, I keep thinking of what my uncle said: Sharon wasn't the type to go for a hike.

At the burial, I want to cry—I need that release—but for some reason, I can't.

Afterward, I drive and drive. I drive four-lane Highway 82. I drive two-lane Highway 70. I drive one-lane dirt roads. I drive the back country. I drive the breaks. I drive until I get stuck and have to dig myself out. I drive to be alone. I get lost and feel utterly lost. Once I was lost, but now am found. Why don't I feel anything as amazing as grace?

The landscape is drought brown, seemingly lifeless, fitting my mood. The wind always blows in West Texas, but now every windmill I pass is still. I can hardly believe it. It is as if even the wind is in mourning. The sky is bright blue and cloudless, which means it is not only beautiful but killing. It is a killing sky. Out here cloudless means rainless, which means death by thirst. Cotton dies, the economy dies, the boll weevils die, hope dies. I am in a hope-dying frame of mind. No rain in the soul.

I slam on the brakes. The car skids sideways and stops, shuddering on the brink of a gully that cuts the dirt road. Proof it once rained here but not recently. The floor of the gully is dry powder.

Stopped here, with brain-numbing radio pounding, I promise myself: I really will try to find out who killed Sharon. Sure. Of course. Fat chance. But if it wasn't an accident, who could have done it? Buddy of course. Surely it was Buddy. But what about Chris? What about the stuntman with the bruising fists? He had already hurt her once that I knew about. What if he had come back to finish the job? I had always supposed that I would like stuntmen, but I don't like him.

Back at the double-wide, my mother hugs me tightly and liquidly once again. My father shakes my hand firmly again.

When my parents go to bed, I call Jamie, but then I don't know what to say. She doesn't know what to say either. We are supposed to be good at dialogue, but we are no good at all.

There is thunder at midnight but no rain.

16

I DRIVE MY RENTED CAR TO THE HOTEL THAT TOM Wolfe once recommended to me, saying: "When you're in Los Angeles, always stay at the hotel that sounds like a bottle of wine." I turn into a minuscule parking garage and give my rent-a-pig to the attendant. After Sharon's death, I couldn't bear staying at her apartment. I tried it for half of one night and then checked into the Chateau Marmont.

I make my way to a bungalow that stands next door to the one where John Belushi overdosed. Then I sit down, utterly at a loss. What should I do about this murder? How should I go about investigating it? Am I up to it? Where do I begin?

Eventually, I take out my computer, set it up on a small table, and do what I do when I don't know what comes next in a story: I start typing up possibilities.

> What should be the first thing I do? ... call
> her girlfriends, call her agent ... that is
> probably what I should do ... spy on Buddy ...
> maybe ... call out the Texas Rangers ... call
> the cavalry ...

Deciding to call Sharon's agent, I keep staring at the hotel telephone. At last, moving slowly, as if lifting a heavy load, I pick up the receiver and dial information. Armed with the agent's phone number, I put down the receiver and stare some more. It is hard to talk about my cousin's death—it is hard to talk about her at all—so I wait. I wait a long time, but eventually I feel I am letting Sharon down. I tell myself that if I call, I won't get through anyway. You never get through—anyway I never get through—to an agent on the first call, even my own. Especially my own. So I'll just put my name on a callback list.

"Rosalie Cort's office," says a cheerful voice.

"Hello, this is Chick Goodnight," I say. Then I ask pro forma: "Is Rosalie available?"

"Of course. I'll put you right through."

Oh no!

"Hello, Chick, I'm so sorry," says ROSALIE CORT in a voice used to commiserating. How many times has she had to tell clients: No, you didn't get the part. No, they don't like the script. "I've been thinking about you a lot."

Oh no!

"Chick, are you there?"

"Uh, yes." I pause too long. "I was just hoping you could tell me a little about what—" I break off because I can't say her name.

"What?"

"What my cousin"—that is easier than naming her—"did that day."

"Just a moment. I'll look it up."

"She saw Buddy, didn't she?"

"I think so. I'm not sure. Just a minute. I'm checking." A computer BEEPS. "Okay, here it is. Are you still there?"

It takes me a moment to catch my breath. "Yes."

"Let's see, yes, that's right. Buddy Dale at five o'clock."

"How long?"

"I don't know. It says here that she called after the meeting, but I was unavailable. I was sorry then and I'm sorrier now. I called her back the next morning, but, you know . . ."

"So you don't know if she met Buddy later that night?"

"So that's what you're interested in?"

"You don't know, right?"

"I don't, but I wouldn't be surprised. If he's interested in a girl, he often asks her to meet him later on."

My tremor goes from eighth notes to sixteenths. The phone shakes in my hands. "Interested how? Interested in her as an actress, or interested in 'fucking' her?"

Unused to swearing, I say the dirty word as if it has quotes around it. But used to daydreaming, I imagine Buddy's last moments on this earth: me "fucking" him up the ass with a hot branding iron.

"You're not very good at swearing, are you?" says the agent.

"No," I admit.

"Anyway, Buddy is pretty much what you think he is. I've had lots of complaints. But I don't know if Sharon was with him that night or not. I'm sorry."

"Me too." I'm about to say good-bye and hang up when another question occurs to me. "Did my cousin ever mention a stuntman named Chris Crosby?"

"No, *she* didn't, but *I* can tell you this much: He's a meanness machine. A Ted Bundy wannabe. He just loves hurting women."

17

JAMIE AND I HAVE DINNER AT THE GALLEY ON MAIN
Street in Santa Monica, a tiny restaurant with nets, buoys, a pool
table, and six booths. Also great T-bone steaks in addition to seafood.
They must have accidentally caught some cows in their nets.

"I'm sorry I was no good at work today," I say.

"That's okay," she says. "Maybe you should consider going back
to Texas for a while. Take some time off."

"No."

"I'm worried about you."

And she reaches across the booth and grips my trembling hand.
With her touch, I stop shaking. The healing touch. Arise and walk
and all that.

"I'm sure he did it," I say.

"Really sure?" she asks.

"Almost really sure."

"Why almost?"

"Because she had a boyfriend who used to beat her up. So I guess
it could've been him. But probably not. It was Buddy. Maybe, almost
certainly, almost probably. I don't really know, okay?"

"Well, I'm on your side," she says, "whoever turns out to be on
the other side."

Jamie gives my hand a squeeze to add a physical exclamation
point to her declaration. Then she starts to pull away, but I hang on.

"Thank you very much," I say. "But if I go after Buddy, what's it
going to mean for your movie?"

"Our movie," she says sharply.

"Okay, ours," I say. "What's it going to mean for our movie? My suspicions versus everybody on the payroll?"

"It's just a movie."

"Everybody says that, but nobody believes it, do they?"

"I suppose not. But it's worth remembering that a movie can't save your life or love you back."

The waitress comes and we order a cowboy dinner: two steaks. I almost say "burn mine," the way John Wayne did in *The Man Who Shot Liberty Valance*. But I resist.

"Medium-rare," I say.

"If you go after him," Jamie says, "do it quietly, okay?"

Jamie and I walk side by side to the public parking lot behind the Galley. We are so close to the ocean, I can smell it. My rented Chevy is parked a couple of slots over from her baby-blue vintage Mercedes ragtop. Her ride is about fifty years old, dating from a time when Hollywood made more westerns than anything else.

"See you tomorrow," I say.

"If you think you're up to it," she says.

"I'll be better tomorrow."

"You sound like Scarlett O'Hara."

"Yeah, and frankly I don't give a damn."

I walk Jamie to her vintage Mercedes and notice a small rip in its rag hat. While I am distracted by this imperfection, Jamie reaches up and kisses me lightly on the lips. She so surprises me, I pull back. Then I surprise myself and her by leaning down and kissing her back. The kiss keeps lasting. I reach around her, still kissing, and lift her up with one arm. I feel her feet kicking in the air like a hanged man's.

Driving back to the hotel that sounds like a bottle of wine, I feel like the dangling man. Had I gone too far? Did I misinterpret her quick kiss? What would our working relationship be like now? Don't fish off the company dock. Don't shit where you eat, and all that. Would she lose respect for me now? No, that's some kind of joke.

I pull into the handkerchief parking garage at the Chateau Marmont. The parking attendant, bubbly as a bottle of champagne, seems very glad to see me. I walk past the swimming pool, where two nude lovers are trying to get it on underwater without obvious success. Underwater sex has its drawbacks.

Reaching my stucco bungalow, I use an oversized key to open a front door lock that could be picked by a paper clip. I undress and go right to bed. I want not the semiunconsciousness of late-night television, but the complete erasure of sleep. But I can't fall into welcome oblivion in spite of my glasses of wine at dinner. That kiss keeps on kicking. I know from recently acquired Hollywood lore that screenwriters are supposed to fall in love with their leading ladies and be bitterly disappointed. Screenwriters never fall in love with their directors. But I'm not in love. I just kissed her. That's all. Maybe I should call her and tell her. Tell her what? Tell her I'm not in love with her? Just what every woman waits by the phone to hear. Not that she is waiting by the phone. Not that she even remembers. Not that she would care. Maybe I'm an idiot.

I am an idiot. Jamie and I go together like a rental wreck and a Mercedes. I roll over and over until the hotel sheets are a straitjacket. I actually experience a moment of panic as if I am trapped underwater. Rolling, bucking, I finally free myself. And then the old conundrum: What do you do when you can't sleep in the middle of the night?

I get up and twirl my batons. I even go out on my front porch and toss them high in the air. I always catch them. My only audience is a ten-foot-high cowboy on a nearby billboard. He doesn't seem to think I'm a sissy.

When my hands stop shaking, I exchange my batons for my computer. I plug in and fire it up. Sitting at my tacky hotel kitchen table, I type out my usual brainstorming beginning:

What happens now? What should I work on? I don't
know. Come on. Maybe I should take another run at
the "starry night" scene. Once again, they are
outside, like the couple in the pool. Try to make
it memorable. Good luck. Well, what the hell? Try.

So I try to write the scene. It doesn't come as Keats's leaves to a
tree, more like thorns to a cactus, but it does eventually come, for
better or worse. I type:

EXT. RED RIVER — STARRY NIGHT

Revelie and Goodnight are making love by the Red
River in God's own bedroom.

> GOODNIGHT
> (VOICE OVER)
>
> And then ... almost ... almost ...
> almost ... A rooster crows in the
> night. Coyotes take up the howl. A
> screech owl screams. Beneath the earth,
> moles and earthworms stop burrowing,
> wondering what has happened up there in
> the vast spinning world. Nighthawks
> dive and moths clap their wings. And I
> realize my heart is losing its
> virginity, too.

As I'm typing, it crosses my mind that Jamie may be typing, too. I
dismiss the thought. That sort of thing could never happen twice.

Closing the lid of my laptop, I put myself to bed once again.
Soon I am asleep, dreaming of roosters, screech owls and nighthawks,
earthworms and moles, howling coyotes, and the sound of moths
clapping.

18

AS SHE READS MY PAGES, JAMIE STARTS *LAUGHING*.
What a great audience she is! The only problem is, once again, the
scene isn't supposed to be funny. We are sitting side by side on the
gray office couch. I feel her shaking next to me. When she finishes,
she takes a moment to catch her breath.

"Over the top?" I ask, hands trembling.

"No, I love it," Jamie says. "By the way, I couldn't sleep either.
Don't know why. So I made some notes. They're just notes, remember. Not really a scene like yours."

She fishes out her pages and hands them to me.

```
Goodnight and Revelie make love under the stars.
Goodnight does another VOICE OVER like the one
when he pulled out the ax. Now he is putting
something in and it feels even better. He talks
about coyotes and owls and moles, et al. Need some
sentimental coda, something like: His heart just
popped its cherry. I'll get Chick to pretty it up.
```

"Jesus!" I say.

"Watch it," Jamie says. "I'm Jewish. Don't go all Jesus on me. I
thought we were really in sync and then you pull this." She smiles as
if she is joking, but there is an edge to her voice that says she isn't
entirely.

"Holy shit!" I say.

"Much better," she says, and this time she means her smile.

"What does this mean?" I ask.

"I don't know," she says, "but I don't mind it."

"I don't either."

"Except I'm not the kind of person who believes in this kind of shit."

"Me either."

"That's the spirit."

I stare at Jamie to see if that kiss in the parking lot left any sort of mark on her. Any tenderness. Any irritation. Anything at all. Her face says it never happened. Is that good or bad? If only emotions left footprints. Or maybe I'm just a bad tracker.

"If you're sure you're okay, let's go to work," Jamie says. "Insert your scene in the script. I'll try my hand at the next scene. Try my fingers really." She wiggles them, calisthenics for the imagination. "My fingers are usually smarter than I am."

I get to work cutting and pasting on my computer. She gets busy typing not only faster than I can type, but even faster than I can think.

"Last night, after I finished writing," I tell her, "I had a dream. I don't suppose you had a dream, too. Maybe the same dream."

"Sorry," she says. "I mean, well, maybe, but I usually don't remember my dreams. What did you dream?"

"Oh, nothing."

"That good, huh?"

"Yeah. Sorry you missed it. Or don't remember it. It was actually one of the great ones."

"Give me a hint."

"No, ma'am."

"Then go to work and stop wasting my time."

She goes back to writing faster than the speed limit. Not wanting to do nothing while she is working so hard, I begin typing, too.

"Read me what you've written," she says. "I want to see if we're writing the same thing again."

"We aren't," I say.

"How do you know?"

"I know."

"Please, read it. I can't write another word until I know what you've written. Miss Dollar waiting on Mr. Dime. That's you."

"Okay, you asked for it."

"I did."

I clear my throat and wish I could simply choke to death right here, right now. "Okay, here goes nothing." I have a coughing fit.

"Come on, it can't be that bad. Stop stalling."

"All right, okay, I was typing: 'Now is the time for all good men to come to the aid of the quick red fox.'"

I cringe. I can't look at her. I'm a fraud.

"Oh, very nice. Thank you."

She goes back to work. I love her. Well, not love, but I something her. And the moths are clapping.

19

AFTER WORK, I DRIVE TO MY COUSIN'S SMALL APART-ment for the last time. I've been putting off packing up her few belongings and moving out, but I can't procrastinate any longer. Sharon's rent is only paid up through tonight, and the landlord is anxious to install another tenant. I know this job is going to be heavy work. Parking my rental car at the end of my cousin's dead-end street, I fetch cardboard boxes and garbage bags out of the trunk. Carrying them, I walk down the steep stone steps to Sharon's place. I try to open the sliding glass front door, but it doesn't budge. Now at last it is locked after my heart's horses have already been stolen. I fish around and come up with a key. I walk in. Emotional exhaustion bleeds into physical exhaustion. I collapse on the mattress on the floor. Soon I'm asleep.

When I rouse an hour and a half later, I'm unhappy to be awake again. Forcing myself to stand up, I walk in small circles in the small room, wondering where to start. The lights of the city are beginning to blink on. She loved those lights. I finally stop in front of the battered bureau set against the uphill wall opposite all the glass.

Opening the top drawer, I am faced with my cousin's underwear. I don't want to see Sharon's underthings. I don't want to touch them. I don't want to paw through them. What should I do with them? Give them to Goodwill? Throw them away? I decide against passing on used underpants and bras. Feeling like a pervert, I am soon grabbing fistfuls of my cousin's most intimate garments and stuffing them into a black garbage bag that reminds me of a body bag. I hate seeing how worn and stained her panties are. I feel as if I am spying on her. I find myself wondering what she wore when she went to meet Buddy.

When I finally empty the top drawer, I am relieved to move down to the second, where I find T-shirts and tank tops and frilly blouses. Deciding these can go to Goodwill, I pack them in a cardboard box. The next drawer down is crowded with blue jeans and pedal pushers and slacks. These go in the box on top of the tops.

The bottom drawer is the best and worst of all. It brims with photographs. Sharon as a baby. A tiny Sharon riding a huge horse. Even some of Sharon and me growing up in the same small town. Sharon happy at Hollywood parties. Sharon so alive. Sharon so hopeful. Sharon on her way. I want to cry—again I want the release of tears—but I can't. Evidently I don't deserve rain but only drought. One by painful one, I transfer the pictures from the bottom drawer to their own cardboard box. I feel as if I am burying Sharon again.

Standing up too quickly, I rock back and forth on my feet. What should I do now? I walk more circles, finally stopping at the telephone. This black antique phone rests on the table where we often used to eat. I lower myself into one of the two hard-backed chairs. Beside the phone lies my cousin's gray Palm Pilot. Picking it up, I punch up her electronic telephone book and scroll through it. There are studio numbers and agent numbers and pizza-delivery numbers. But there are also many names of friends and acquaintances and random contacts that I don't recognize.

I wonder: Would any of these numbers know anything about my cousin's plans for the evening that got her killed? I know there is only one way to find out. I need to call a lot of these people, but I hate talking on the phone. I especially hate talking on the phone to strangers. I tell myself: I can't do this. I tell myself : I have to do this. With trembling hands, I reach for the receiver.

I start with the *A*'s. With quivering fingers, I punch the number of somebody named Stephanie Ambrose. The phone RINGS and RINGS. I'm relieved nobody is home. When a voice comes on asking me to leave a message, I hang up. I feel as if I have dodged something unpleasant.

Should I try making another phone call, or should I go back to packing? What a choice. Damn. I decide to try the *B*'s. Scrolling down the list, I stop at Ann Benson. She lives out in the Valley with an 818 number. I dial it and listen to the RINGS. One, two, three, four. I am about to hang up—dodged another one—when someone answers.

"Hello," says ANN BENSON.

Oh no! "Uh, hello, I'm looking for Ann."

"Who's calling?"

"My name's Chick Goodnight. I'm Sharon Goodnight's cousin." I wait for a response that doesn't come, so I add: "Maybe you knew her as Sharon Loving."

"Oh, hello. I'm so sorry . . ."

"I found your name and number in my cousin's Palm Pilot. I wondered if I could ask you a couple of questions about her."

"I really didn't know her that well."

"Then you may not be able to help, but I'd like to ask anyway. I'm particularly interested in what she was doing"—my voice begins to thicken—"on the day she died."

"I'm sorry. I haven't seen or talked to Sharon in over a month. I wish I could help you, but . . ."

"Well, thank you anyway."

I'm disappointed she couldn't help, but I'm relieved the conversation is over. Now I just want to get off the phone. "Take care."

"I didn't know her that well, but I really liked her," Ann says.

"Thank you again." I can feel impatience bleeding into my voice. "Take care."

"Everybody liked her."

"That's good to hear. Take care."

"I really didn't know her that well."

"Right." This is where I came in. Time to go now.

"But I can tell you who you should call. Her best friend. But you've probably already talked to her, right?"

Hold the phone. Why was I in such a hurry to end this conversation?

"I don't think so," I say. I am suddenly feeling better, but at the same time I can't believe I don't know the name of my cousin's best friend. I didn't even know she had a best friend. "What's her name?"

"Eve Johnston. They were very tight. Call Eve. Do you have her number?"

"Let me check." I scroll Sharon's phone book until I come to the J's. There it is. "I've got it. Really, thank you very much."

"Take care," she says.

After I hang up, I know I should call Eve immediately, but I am really shy. Face-to-face shy. Phone shy. Just totally shy. I make a bargain with myself: I can wait five minutes between calls. Remembering that a watched pot never boils, I stare at the face of my watch to slow down time. But it doesn't work. The hands on the watched watch seem to race ahead. I pick up the phone and dial. It RINGS and RINGS and RINGS and RINGS.

"That's right, you got the machine," a voice that must be Eve's tells me curtly. "On your mark, get set, leave a message."

20

"DID YOU WRITE ANYTHING LAST NIGHT?" ASKS JAMIE.

"No, I'm sorry, I didn't," I confess.

"Good, I didn't either," she says. "I just wanted to make sure we are still in sync."

"I cleaned out my cousin's apartment last night."

"That's what I thought. I considered coming over to help out, but it seemed too weird. I wouldn't know what to say. You wouldn't either. It would be a very awkward silent movie. Anyway, it's too bad you had to do that alone."

"Yeah. It was . . . it was . . . I don't know what it was. I love words, but sometimes they just aren't up to the job, you know? Or maybe I'm not up to it. I'm some wordsmith, huh, some wordwright?"

"That's not a word."

"Well, I told you I wasn't a very good one."

"That's why I love movies," Jamie says. "The words are important. It all begins with words on a page. But in the end you aren't limited by language. If a picture is worth a thousand words, then a moving picture is worth a million. I hope you don't mind my pointing that out. You aren't going to pout, are you?"

The phone on our shared desk RINGS. Jamie lifts the receiver and listens.

"It's for you," she says. "Somebody named Eve."

Perhaps I simply imagine that she is curious about who Eve is, perhaps even a little jealous. I hope so. She hands me the phone and winks. Good. I take it and turn away.

"Hello."

"I got your message," EVE says.

"Good. It's good to hear from you."

"Sure, I'd do anything to help Sharon." She pauses and makes flustered sounds. "I mean, I know I can't help her, but maybe I can help you. I guess that's what I mean. I loved her. I really did."

"Me too."

I wonder what my side of the conversation sounds like to Jamie. What does she think "me too" means? Does she care? Why am I thinking this way?

"Could we get together?" I ask. What will Jamie think of that? Am I deliberately trying to tease her? No, of course not. "Maybe later on today?"

"I wish I could say I'm too busy, but I'm not. Sure. When and where?"

"How about the Chateau Marmont Hotel? You know where that is?"

"Sure."

"Say seven-thirty."

"Okay, see you there."

After I hang up, I turn and SEE (POV) Jamie staring at me.

"You work fast," she says. "Be careful. Remember what her name-sake did to Adam."

"She's a friend of my cousin's. I'm trying to piece together what Sharon was doing that last day. Thought she might help."

"Oh, sorry. Didn't mean to kid you about something like that."

"That's okay," I say, secretly pleased.

Jamie and I have lunch in the Paramount commissary, which resembles the fanciest Hollywood eateries. While we are waiting for the third member of our party, we order two Diet Cokes.

"Tom Bondini bought this place for the studio," Jamie says.

"What?" I ask. Then, assimilating what she just said, I add: "Generous of him."

"I mean, his movies saved the studio and there was enough left over to pay for this place. Before, the Paramount commissary was on the same level as Denny's."

"No wonder Paramount loves him and wants him in all their movies, including ours."

"Well, they love him and they hate him. They can't forgive him for needing him as much as they did—and do."

The Diet Cokes and Tom arrive at the same time. Even in the Paramount commissary—perhaps especially here—his entrance creates buzz and restaurant rubbernecking.

"I was just telling Chick," Jamie says, "they should call this beanery Tom's Place."

"How about Chez Tom?" says the biggest star in the world.

"Spoken like a real cowboy," she says.

"I guess I don't believe in living the roles," he says. "I hope you don't mind."

"You kidding? I'm relieved. Method actors can drive you crazy. You don't know who they really are and they don't either. And they usually want to rewrite all the dialogue and even the plot." She pauses uncertainly. "Not that that's out of the question."

I give Jamie a look. I realize she is trying to "woo" Tom, but such loose talk makes me nervous.

"What about Sarah?" Tom asks. "Is she . . ."

"I don't really know," Jamie answers.

"I heard she was method," he says, making the acting technique sound like a venereal disease. "She isn't going to want to fuck me, is she? That's what all those method maniacs want to do. Not that I don't appreciate a little friendly fucking. But if you fuck your costar, she owns you. I mean, suddenly scenes that should be yours turn out to be hers. She leads you around by your prick."

21

I SIT WAITING FOR MY COUSIN'S FRIEND EVE IN THE impressive lobby of the hotel that sounds like a bottle of wine. It reminds me of a dollhouse version of the gigantic living room in the Hearst Castle at San Simeon. Sitting on a long couch, I cross and uncross my legs. I also keep looking at my watch. Eve walks in thirty-five minutes late. Long-legged, slim but still heavy-chested, also blond, she looks like the pretty daughter on a sitcom. I recognize her because she is looking for a stranger. I know the look.

"Sorry I'm late," she says. "An audition ran a lot longer than it was supposed to. I should've just left. I knew I was wrong for the part, but I told myself: Hold on, don't get mad and walk out. If you blow them off now, they'll never consider you for anything else ever. So I stayed."

"What's the part?" I ask.

After sitting through so many auditions, I now empathize with people trying out for parts. I had never suspected it could be so demeaning, so desperate, and so arbitrary.

"It's a sitcom," Eve says. "There're two daughters, of course. I'm up for the pretty one. No chance. Miscasting. Just a waste of time. They'll never call me back. Anyway that's why I'm late."

I like her better for not knowing she is the pretty-daughter type.

"You might be surprised," I say. "I mean I wouldn't be surprised if they called you back."

"But you just fell off the turnip truck, right? Or was it a hay wagon? Your cousin told me. No offense, but what do you know? Oh, I'm sorry. You were trying to cheer me up, weren't you?"

"No, I meant it."

"Then I'm glad you aren't casting your movie all by yourself. You aren't, are you?"

"No, I've had some help. Believe me. Not all of it welcome."

"You mean Buddy. Sharon told me about your thing with Buddy."

"That's right. Why don't we have a drink on the patio."

"The patio would be nice."

We decamp to an outdoor table on a small patio squeezed between two huge billboards for movies. Billboard bookends. I can't help wondering if my film will ever grace one of those advertising acres. When the waiter appears, I order a Diet Coke and Eve asks for a banana daiquiri.

"How can I help you?" asks Eve.

"Well," I say, remembering that such an expression is called a "handle" among writers out here. "Well," I repeat, double handling, "I'm trying to piece together my cousin's last day. Last night. I thought you might know something about her plans."

"You want to play detective?" she asks. "I didn't mean 'play.'"

"No," I lie. "Well, yes and no."

"Sort of?"

"Yes, that's it. Did you talk to her that day?"

"Several times. We always did."

"Did she say anything about Buddy Dale?"

Our waiter appears—why now?—with my Diet Coke and Eve's daiquiri.

"Buddy Dale?" I prompt.

"She was very excited about meeting him, yes."

"When was that supposed to happen?"

"Afternoon, sometime in the afternoon."

"Did you talk to her after she met with him?"

"No. Oh, we tried to call each other, but we just kept playing phone keep-away. The first messages just said to call her. The last one said she couldn't meet me for dinner. Like we'd planned."

"Did she say why she couldn't make dinner?"

"No, she didn't." She pauses and is thoughtful. "But she sounded excited. Do you think he had something to do with—"

"I don't know," I interrupt. "That's what I'm trying to figure out. Did she ever mention somebody called Chris Crosby?"

"Mention him? Lately, he was mostly all she talked about. She loved him. She hated him. He was a cowboy prince. He was a fake cowboy devil. Then she heard he was cheating on her. You know he hit her?"

"Yeah, I know, and I didn't do anything about it."

"What could you? Anyway, hey, maybe she was seeing him that night. Gonna fuck and make up. Could be that was why she was so excited. Yeah, could be. You should talk to him. But if you do, bring a big old gun."

I LAUGH nervously.

22

I'M ASLEEP WHEN I *HEAR* THE 3 A.M. *KNOCK* THAT always means trouble. Good can wait, bad is in a hurry. Getting out of bed in my underwear, socks, and a Princeton T-shirt, I stumble in the general direction of my bungalow's front door. I try to press my bleary, unfocused eye to the peephole, but this door turns out not to have one. All I manage to do is butt my head against wood and peeling paint. Just then the KNOCKING starts again, pounding my ears. I open the door a suspicious crack.

"Hi, handsome," says Sarah.

My voice chokes in my throat. My hands start quivering like an outboard motor. "Huh," I say.

"If I promish not to rob you," she asks, "can I come in?"

"Huh," I say, opening the door all the way.

Sarah takes three steps into the room and falls headfirst. She doesn't even put up her hands to soften the blow. She uses her face to break the fall. Her nose squirts blood. I jump back to keep from getting the red on my socks.

I hear a voice inside my head saying: You have no earthly idea what to do. You didn't know what Hollywood was going to be like. What can I read to tell me what to do now?

Sarah doesn't move. I wonder if her nose is broken. Will we have to find a new leading lady or make do with one who looks like she is a mafioso? No longer worrying about my socks, I kneel in her blood.

"Sarah, are you all right?"

She makes a sound, but I can't make out what she is trying to say.

"What? Sarah, I didn't understand you. What did you say? Are you all right?"

She makes the sound again. It is as if she is speaking a foreign language. Her nose continues to spurt blood. Has anybody ever died of an unchecked nosebleed?

"Sarah, are you all right?" I don't know why I keep asking: She clearly isn't. "Sarah, talk to me."

She does, once again in Martian. Or is it Uranusian?

"Sarah." I nudge her shoulder.

More Martian. No, it's not Martian. I realize I know this language. I know it fairly well. Sarah is snoring.

"Sarah!"

She keeps on snoring.

I turn her over and pick her up. Blood drips from her face and hair. Her lifeblood makes a Hansel-and-Gretel trail to my still-warm bed. I lay her down, wrestle the covers out from under her, and spread them over her.

Then I retreat to my bottle-of-wine bungalow's living room. Lying down on the couch, I feel with a pang that I am back at my cousin's.

But this couch is shorter than Sharon's. It's really only a love seat. I turn over and over again, feeling like I am trying to sleep on an airplane. In coach, in the middle.

The physical twisting comes with mental contortions. Who asked her to come here anyway when I need my sleep? What's wrong with her? Did we pick the wrong standard bearer for our movie? I was the loudest voice—loudest metaphorically—in her favor. Had I made a mistake? But what do I know? Maybe this is standard actress behavior. Or perhaps she just appreciates my being on her side and came over to thank me for her getting the part. Or maybe she just likes me. Unlikely, but . . .

I can't stand this couch any longer. Getting up stiffly, I return to the bedroom. It seems that I should ask her permission before crawling into the sack with her, but she is unreachable in her present condition. Besides, it's my mattress. Carefully I lower myself onto the bed beside my leading lady. Cozy.

"What the hell do you think you're doing?" Sarah asks, her voice strong and clear and undrunk. Amazing recuperative reserves. She doesn't even sound sleepy.

Startled, I say: "It's my bed."

"Good point," she admits.

"By the way, what are you doing here?"

"I guess I freaked out."

"Why? What happened to you?"

"I was at Buddy Dale's."

"No."

"Yeah, I was. What an idiot I am. Anyway he said he wanted to make up after our 'unfortunate' beginning. And he offered me drugs, as a kind of bribe. I wish I could say I turned him down, but I didn't. It was powder and I thought it was coke, but I've never had a reaction like this one. I got confused and paranoid and really jumpy."

"I don't think it's paranoia if you're with Buddy," I say.

"We were sitting on this couch in front of the fire, and he put his hand on my leg. I said—I'm kinda proud of this—I said, 'I thought you wouldn't touch me with a ten-foot pole.'"

"Good for you," I say.

"He said that was a lie, he never said that, and what's more he was willing to prove it to me. That's why he had invited me over, to prove it to me. Then he grabbed my breast, which lots of people have done. Well, you know that, you're one of them. Normally I don't mind, but when Buddy did it, I didn't like it."

"When I did it, it was in a professional context," I say.

"Whatever. Anyway I told him I was willing to touch him, too, and to prove it I balled up my fist and lowered the boom on his balls. Just came straight down like John Henry banging his hammer."

I let out some kind of celebratory whoop.

"He crumpled and screamed at me. That's when it happened. I just got completely and absolutely terrified. Probably the drugs talking, but I was afraid in every cell of my body."

"He's a scary guy," I say. "I don't blame you."

"I actually thought he was going to kill me. Because of his balls. Because he didn't want me in the movie. Because he just hated me. So I ran out of his place and thought I was trapped inside the walls. I jumped in my car and gunned it toward the big double gates. I was going to smash right through it, but suddenly the gates just started opening on their own."

"Electric eye," I say. "The bad guys can't get in, but your guests can get out."

"You know, I'd kinda figured that out. Anyway I barreled outta there and, guess what, I didn't know where to go. I could go home, but I didn't want to be alone. I thought he might come looking for me. Or the drugs thought that. I'm not sure which one of us was doing the thinking at that point. I told myself I could go knock on my director's door, but she'd think I'm a flake and a drug addict and fire me. Anyway it would be icky. I thought about dropping in on the biggest star in the world, but I figured I'd rather freak him out later on instead of at the beginning. That's when I thought about you. Again it was probably the drugs doing the thinking. I don't get it myself."

"I'm third string?"

"Lucky to be that."

"Thank you very much."

"Thanks for taking in this Little Drunk Match Girl."

Sarah passes out once again. Maybe from Buddy's drugs. Maybe from alcohol. Maybe she is just acting. She is a mess but perhaps a telling mess. I keep picturing Sharon running out of Buddy's place the way Sarah did, only my cousin didn't have a car. Confronted with the fence, what could she have done? Where would she have found help?

Toward dawn, Sarah begins to rustle once again. I move across the mattress carefully so as not to touch her.

"Buddy, Buddy," Sarah moans, "do it to me again."

I shake her.

"Gotcha," she says. "By the way, I've never slept with a writer before."

"But we didn't—"

"I know, but we slept together. That's big news in this town. Call *Variety.* I can see the headline now: LEADING LADY SLEEPS WITH WRITER. What's the date today? This is history."

Unamused, I keep thinking about how I am going to explain this night to Jamie. Not that I owe her an explanation. And yet I feel that I do. It feels good.

"I hear Jamie's a lesbian," Sarah says, as if she knows who I'm thinking about.

"I never heard that," I say.

"Well, like my mama says, don't say they are unless you've seen them do it."

"And you haven't?"

"Of course not. Not that I'd mind. What do you think?"

"About what?"

"Is Jamie a lesbian?"

"I have no idea."

"Funny, I thought you might know. Guess I was wrong, huh?"

"Looks like it."

"Mind if I use your shower?"

"Of course not."

Sarah gets up, stands in the middle of the bedroom, and takes off all her clothes. Then she heads for the bathroom swinging her hips like a slow church bell ringing.

23

WHEN JAMIE WALKS INTO THE OFFICE THE NEXT MORN-ing, I scan her carefully for lesbianism. Which is just what Sarah wanted. Jamie's walk doesn't seem too girlish, or too boyish, or too anything. I like her walk. She walks her walk to the far side of the big desk and lowers herself into her seat. I wonder if she can tell that I am studying her in a new way.

"Did you write anything last night?" Jamie asks.

"Afraid not," I say.

"Good, me too. Or me neither. Hell, anyway, we're still synced up. Still got our sync going. What did you do instead? Anything good?"

"I didn't do much." I consider telling her about Sarah's unexpected visit, but I don't. Is it because of what our leading lady said about lesbianism? "I was pretty tired."

"Me too."

The phone on the desk RINGS.

"Hello," Jamie says. "Okay, put him on." She mouths to me

"Buddy Dale." "Of course. Right away." She hangs up the phone. "Buddy wants to see us right away."

"That's too bad," I say.

"Maybe. Maybe not. We better go find out."

Walking across the great parking lot—like the Great Plains that divide America—I wonder if Buddy knows Sarah came to my hotel last night. If he does, is that what this meeting is all about? If he knows, is it a blow to his pride he can't accept? Is he going to fire me again?

I stare at Buddy across his desk as if I'm not—what? apprehensive? scared? chicken shit?—anyway that is my intention. I hate him, and yet I still want to make this movie. Which means I don't want him to fire me. I feel like a sellout. Talk about not having a code. What is mine? The movie justifies the means?

"Bad news," Buddy says. Then he pauses to blow his nose and toss the tissue in a wastebasket.

"What?" asks Jamie.

"Paramount's big summer movie just fell through. Artistic differences, what the hell. They all hate each other. The studio just pulled the plug."

"You mean no *Summer Solstice*?" Jamie asks.

"Yeah, too bad," says Buddy. "Really a shame. But that brings me to the good news. We're going to Texas immediately. Next week. Sooner if we can do it. Because we're the new big summer movie. Remains to be seen how big, but I have faith."

"But the script's not finished," I say in a quiet voice.

"Don't ruin my good mood with details," Buddy says. "If we don't start shooting in two weeks, we'll never be ready to open next June."

"Jesus," I say.

"We can certainly use His help," Buddy says. "So try not to piss Him off, okay? Because next week I'm putting a sign on my office door that says GONE TO TEXAS."

Back in our office, our home, Jamie says: "Becky, see if Kelly can come in again. Today if possible. Anyway as soon as he can make it."

"But I thought—" I begin.

"I've got an idea."

Shortly after six, Becky ushers Kelly Hightower into our inner office.

"I thought I didn't make the cut," Kelly says.

"I thought so, too," Jamie says. "But would you mind taking a walk with us?"

"Why not?"

Having no clue where we are going, I follow Jamie and Kelly across the lot. I realize that I am slightly jealous that she is walking side by side with him, leaving me to follow. We stop in front of a great barn with a big sign that says WARDROBE. Inside, Jamie nods to a clerk and then leads us down an alley. We turn, another alley, another turn, and we are there. We are facing a thousand or more cowboy hats in great stacks.

"Okay, Kelly, pick a hat," Jamie says.

"Any hat?" he asks.

"Any hat."

Kelly takes his time, turning this one and that one in his hands, but not trying on any of them. Twisting, examining, considering.

"This one might work," he says at last, holding up a black Stetson with a wide brim.

Kelly lowers the hat onto his head. The big brim make his ears look smaller. He is no longer Howdy Doody. He is Loving. Jamie nods at me. I nod in return and smile. She smiles, too.

"We didn't have the wrong cowboy," Jamie says. "We had the wrong cowboy hat."

BOOK TWO

24

THE WEST TEXAS WIND IS BLOWING. THE WIND IS always blowing. This wind never gets tired, never takes a breath, never takes a day off, never sleeps. No wonder there are windmills everywhere. I stare out the window at the wind blowing the cotton plants low.

"Windy," Jamie says.

"It's always windy," I tell her.

"He ain't lyin'," confirms a teamster nicknamed MACK TRUCKS, who is driving our rented van.

He is fat and has a wad of Skoal between his lip and gum. In the old days, only old ladies used snuff. Now all the cowboys do. And teamsters all think they have inherited the cowboy mantle.

"The wind starts up at the North Pole," I continue, "and there's nothing to stop it till it gets to West Texas. No mountains to stop it. No trees to slow it down. It's Great Plains all the way from there to here."

"Really," she says. "I hope that won't be a problem."

"My granddaddy used to say," I tell her, "that one day the wind did stop blowin' and all the chickens fell over."

She thinks about it, LAUGHS a little, thinks about it some more. "I hope the grips, gaffers, and best boys don't start falling over."

Having flown into Lubbock, the nearest commercial airport, we still have a trip in front of us: It is ninety miles to the 6666 Ranch, the Four Sixes, named for the poker hand that won this spread over a hundred years ago. The land outside the window is griddle flat, pool-table flat, flatter than a supermodel's stomach. Flat as that line that tells you that you're dead. Or your cousin is dead.

Jamie and I have flown in ahead of the rest of the company to scout locations and generally prepare the ground for Hollywood's invasion.

"Buddy was dreaming when he said we had to roll in two weeks," Jamie says, not for the first time.

"Dreaming or on drugs," I say, not for the first time.

"The pictures of that ranch house look okay, but pictures often lie. What if I don't like it? What if I can't imagine Goodnight and Revelie living there?"

"I can imagine it. I love it."

"I hope we're still in sync."

We can't use Jimmy Goodnight's original stone ranch house because it has been gone for half a century or more. A rare earthquake cracked its walls and the roof fell in. Then over the years it was looted and burned. But strangely, the original dugout where my ancestor started out is still there and in good shape. There must be some sort of lesson in there somewhere. Ozymandias, King of Kings . . .

"This doesn't look like cattle country," Jamie complains. "Excuse my whining."

"Right," I say. "It's cotton country."

"Unfortunately, we're making a movie about cows."

"The cows are coming."

"Promise?"

"Promise. Look, this is Idalou coming up."

"Whoopee."

"Where Sarah lived as a kid."

"Or so she says."

What is going on here? Sarah accuses Jamie of being a lesbian? Jamie suggests Sarah might be a liar?

"Yeah," I say.

We pass through Idalou and soon, up ahead, Lorenzo rises out of the plains, the water tower appearing first, then the tops of the grain elevators. Next comes Ralls and its elevators. Then Crosbyton. These small, godforsaken towns are all a uniform ten miles apart because they started out as stations where the stagecoaches changed horses. Then our van plunges down into the White River Valley.

"This is better," Jamie says.

"Yeah, we just came down off the Cap Rock," I explain.

"Out here, am I going to need subtitles to understand what you're talking about?"

"Do you know anything about geology?"

"No, and I don't want to."

"Think of the Cap Rock as the big plywood board under your mattress."

"I don't have a board under my mattress."

"Okay, not you, but somebody with back trouble. The Cap Rock is this huge limestone layer that stretches from here to the top of Canada. The plywood board under the geological mattress. The Cap Rock is why the Great Plains are plains. That's why they're flat. Get it?"

"Yeah, I get it," she says. "The Cap Rock is why the chickens fall over."

"Exactly."

"Turn here," I say.

"I know," says Mack Trucks.

We turn left off State Highway 82 onto a gravel road leading north. I more or less hold my breath because I want Jamie to like it so much.

"This is it," I announce, "the set I've always had in mind. You know, the cowboy castle, sort of a combination of cow lot and Camelot."

Jamie LAUGHS merrily. I love her laugh. Mack Trucks SNORTS.

I know I shouldn't ask—it's too soon—but I can't resist: "What do you think?"

She takes forever to answer: "So far, so good. Only where's the house?"

"I'm getting ahead of myself, right?"

"I hope you aren't like this in bed."

25

WHEN THE VAN STOPS IN FRONT OF THE GREAT ROCK pile, we all get out, which is harder than it should be. Especially if you are almost six six. I feel like a lower-case chick trying to fight its way out of its eggshell. Slightly bruised, I stand in front of the house, studying it. When I was growing up in the small town of Spur (pop. 1,000)—about thirty miles from here—I always thought of this place as the Castle. It is three stories tall and shaped like an *E*. The arms of the *E* are wings containing bedrooms and torture chambers and who knows what. The spine of the *E* is the magnificent front of the house. The great front door opens and a small, gray-haired woman emerges.

"Hello, Chick," she says, "welcome to the Four Sixes."

"Hello, Miss Clark," I say, having known her for years. "Thank you very much. Miss Clark, I'd like you to meet Jamie Stone. She's directing our movie."

"You have a lovely place," Jamie says.

"Well, it's not really mine," says MISS CLARK. "I'm just the care-taker. The owners are away. Italy this month. Won't you come inside and look around?"

Of course, we knew the owners were away. Fortunately away.

Because their absence allowed us to rent the Castle to house the most important members of our band of filmmakers. The rest will have to make do with tents. Well, really good tents. Luxury tents. But only if Jamie approves my Castle as our castle.

Following Miss Clark into the manse, I am once again surprised at the size of the fireplace. It seems to me that it is as big as my cousin's whole hillside apartment. All the furniture is covered with brown-and-white cowhide. The chandelier is a herd of deer antlers. I realize I am thrilled at being here in the Castle of my dreams, on the verge of bringing a dream to life, with a woman who might just be the girl of my dreams. My pulse rate is as high as the vaulted two-story ceiling. I keep staring at Jamie but at the same time trying to hide it: What does she think? But I don't want to ask again.

"Feels right," Jamie says at last. She points to the left: "We could put the fighting deer heads over there."

Jimmy Goodnight, my forefather, had a pair of fighting deer heads in his living room. Their horns were fatally locked together when a hunter happened to come along and kill them both. And their heads were mounted with horns still eternally intertwined.

"Yeah," I say instead of *Yippeeee!*

We tour the eighteen bedrooms and three bathrooms—one per floor.

"That could be a problem," says Jamie.

"Three's a lot for the nineteenth century," I say. "Of course, we could also build an outhouse. Also very nineteenth."

"Very funny. I suppose we could park three honey wagons out back. But really I don't think our clientele would find that acceptable. Just imagine the biggest star in the world waiting in line to piss or whatever. Or Buddy. Oh, my God."

"Honey wagon . . . ?" I ask, baffled.

"Piss wagons. You know, shit trucks. What've you gotten me into? We've gotta look for another place. Maybe we can still shoot here, but we can't stay here. We can't live here. Really."

My stomach feels like Houdini trying to escape from handcuffs and chains underwater.

"I love this place," I say louder than I usually talk, shaking more than I usually shake. "I really do. I don't mean to be a problem, but it means a lot to me. From my childhood. From . . . from . . . I don't know, but it does. It seems right to me."

Jamie looks to all points of the compass, then up, down, all around.

"Okay, on second thought, maybe this'll do," she says with a semifrown, "but it's your fault. Remember that. Okay?"

"'Maybe this'll do'?" I say, suddenly defensive instead of grateful. "What're you talking about? This place is perfect." Then I can't believe I've said what I just said.

"As a director," Jamie says, "you can never admit perfection. If you do, everybody will let you down."

"Good to know," I say. Then I add: "Maybe if you're not busy this afternoon, you'd come meet my parents."

"I'd love to," she says, "but a director's always busy. We haven't even started and I'm already way behind. But you go."

"Okay. I really should."

"Invite them to visit the set while we're shooting. If we ever get that far."

I don't call ahead. I just show up—Mack Trucks drives me over—at my parents' double-wide. The longhorn is munching my mother's small front lawn and dropping cow pies on the mowed grass.

"I'll call later and ask you to pick me up," I tell Trucks, "if that's okay."

"You got yourself a deal," he says.

I'm shuffling up the walk to the back door of the double-wide when that door flies open. My mother is crying by the time she reaches the second step. She is running by the time she reaches the sundial. Then she is hugging me and wetting my western shirt and its mother of pearl buttons.

"You're really here," my mother says. "Really an' truly."

My father emerges from the double-wide, smiles, and says: "I thought I heard somebody kicking up a racket out here."

He waits for me to come to him. We shake hands.

In the double-wide's kitchen, my mom passes out drinks: a cold Diet Coke for me, a room-temperature Diet Coke for my dad, and iced tea for herself.

"How're they treating you at the Four Sixes?" my father asks.

"So far, so good," I say. "We just got there."

"Myself, I prefer the Pitchfork," says my mother, who taught generations of Pitchfork cowboys.

"I wanted a stone house," I say. "I want it to look like a castle."

"But the Pitchfor—"

"Mama, don't you tell him how to make his movie and he won't tell you how to make yours."

The kitchen falls silent except for the faint humming of the refrigerator. My father finally breaks the quiet.

"Ever'body wants to know what happened to Sharon," he says.

"I've been trying to find out," I say. "I think maybe my producer, Buddy Dale, had something to do with it, but I'm not sure. Because she also had a bad-tempered boyfriend who liked to use her as a tackling dummy." That was for my father, the ex–football coach. "Or it could be just what it looks like: a random hit-and-run."

"Oh, really?" says my mother. "Oh well."

"Yeah, not much, huh?" I admit.

"No, too bad, do you have a girlfriend?" My mother changes gears quickly. If you aren't used to it, you could wind up damaging your mental gear box. "All our friends have grandchildren."

26

JAMIE AND I COMPRESS TWO MONTHS OF PREPRO-
duction work into two weeks. Of course, we have help. We have our
driver, Mack Trucks. We have an art director named LOGAN WHIT-
MAN. We have two location scouts named JACK STURM and JILL
DRANG of all things. And we have an energetic and eager cinematographer named VICTOR HAMMER, who is just five feet tall.

Potbellied Trucks drives us all over the country, from here to eter-
nity, to hell and most of the way back. I've often been told that location scouting is the most boring part of moviemaking, but I love it.
Now I have a chance to show off my country, the country that made
me, the country I adore even though I know it isn't easy to like. This
is the locus of my chauvinism: godforsaken West Texas. The windmill
is to me what the Eiffel Tower is to a Frenchman.

We spend most of our time in Palo Duro Canyon, often called the
Grand Canyon of Texas. I show Jamie and all the others the dugout
where Jimmy Goodnight first started housekeeping. I take them to
the ruins of the original cowboy castle, the great red-stone house my
forefather built well over a century ago. We stop regularly to watch
deer grazing and wild turkeys pecking. Prairie dogs keep popping up
and vultures circle lazily overhead.

I can feel Jamie slowly beginning to accept the landscape. The definition of beauty here is harsher than she is used to, but she adjusts,
she redefines, she reeducates her eyes. She starts to appreciate dangerous beauty. Thorns. Cactus. Parched earth. Horned toads. Rattlers.
The bleached bones of cattle and horses and deer and maybe
humans. We are rarely sure about the humans because we almost

never find a skull, but I know many have died on this ground. Overhead death's handmaidens, great black turkey buzzards, are always gracefully gliding.

Now we are more or less ready for the "locusts"—Jamie's term for the rest of the company—to descend upon us.

Mack Trucks drives Jamie and me to the 6666 airstrip. No self-respecting ranch these days would be without a few planes and at least one helicopter. The runway is red dirt pocked with prairie-dog holes. And the winds here are strong and treacherous to strangers.

"How could the studio let him do this?" Jamie says. "Flying his own plane? Does our insurance company know what he's up to?"

Since these aren't really questions—just venting—I don't answer. But I'm worried, too. At the moment, it seems that my entire future is riding on the safe arrival of a plane piloted by an actor. He might be the biggest star in the world, but is he the best pilot in the world? And he has our leading lady with him. Our entire story could be wiped out with one twist of the wrong knob. And they are late. Half an hour late and counting. I picture a smoking pile of machinery somewhere in the wilds of New Mexico where no human has set foot since Coronado. I pace as eternal vultures ride the eternal wind.

"Is that a plane or just another buzzard?" Jamie asks.

"Buzzard," I say.

"No, I think it's a plane. I hope it's a plane. Yes, it's a plane unless buzzards have wheels."

"The newer models do."

"Hush."

Soon I, too, SEE (POV) the buzzard begin to metamorphose into a plane. The grasping, corpse-stripping claws turn into wheels. The sleek feathers change to aluminum skin.

"Good, I can breathe again," says Jamie.

While we watch, Tom's plane suddenly veers to the right, as if it plans to make a hockey-stop landing. Turning sideways might work on ice, but will it work for an airplane bearing all our hopes and fears?

"My God," Jamie almost yells. "Did you see that?" She grabs me, hugs me, closes her eyes. "Don't tell me if it's bad," she says.

I want to close my own eyes, too, but I can't bring myself to do so. I watch, eyes wide, as the plane struggles to straighten out. I hug Jamie harder than I have ever hugged anybody—am I breaking bones?—as the aircraft hits the runway at what looks like a forty-five-degree angle. It kicks up a huge cloud of red dust that swallows the plane.

"What's happening!" Jamie demands, eyes still closed.

"I don't know," I say. "I can't see anything."

"Why not? What's wrong?"

As the dust begins to settle, the outline of an airplane starts to take shape. It is standing upright.

"Open your eyes," I say.

"Thank God," Jamie says.

Sarah emerges from the plane with an expression I never expected to see on her face: fear. Tom follows her down the stairs.

"Well, like I always say," says the biggest star in the world, "any landing is a good landing."

"Fuck you," Sarah says.

27

OVERNIGHT WE ARE OVERRUN. I WAKE UP TO FIND A tent town set up in a mowed hayfield near the cowboy castle. I SEE (POV) hundreds of strange middle-aged men with potbellies wearing shorts hurrying this way and that as if they know what they are supposed to be doing. Dozens of younger men and women are scurrying about with earphones and walkie-talkies. Security guards in khaki uniforms are walking their beats. There are huge eighteen-wheel trucks parked all over the place. Cooks are cooking, teamsters are driving, wardrobe mistresses are fitting, and I just sit there on the big front porch thinking: Who invited them?

In the beginning, it was just me and my dream: I sat down to write a book about a man who invented the cowboy. Back then, nobody bothered me. Nobody cared—to paraphrase Raymond Chandler—whether I ever finished the book or moved to El Paso. Unfortunately, I sometimes got a little lonely. When I finally finished the book, it had a modest sale in bookstores and a big sale to Hollywood. Soon I was paired with Jamie. Then two of us shared the dream, which seemed just the right number. I was no longer lonely, but I still had elbow room. Perfect.

Then I wake up this morning to find that an army has invaded my dream. They are trampling on it in their work boots. I feel overwhelmed, pushed to the side, marginalized. I wish they would all pack up and go home.

"Quite a sight," Jamie says.

"What?" I say, spinning around, wondering how long she has been standing there.

"It's kind of intimidating, isn't it?" she says.

"Yeah," I say. We are still in sync.

"You know, driving around Los Angeles," she muses, "I often pass movie trucks parked by the side of the road. My stomach always contorts and I think: 'Those poor sons of bitches are having to make a movie.' Well, now we're those poor sons of bitches. We've got to make this movie, so suck it up and let's go."

She starts down the porch steps. I am still paralyzed.

"Come on," she says. "It's high time you made the acquaintance of a Hollywood institution: the breakfast burrito. It makes everything better."

I follow my leader into the uninvited enemy camp. Parallel rows of tents. Fort Four Sixes. And a catering wagon with lots of customers. My hands are trembling. A few minutes later, they can hardly hold a delicious burrito filled with eggs and bacon and sausage and peppers and beans and the kitchen sink.

"Good," I whimper with pleasure.

"See, moviemaking ain't all bad," Jamie says. "Hey, look, there's Chris."

"Chris?" I ask, startled. "Chris who?"

"Chris Crosby," she says. "He's right over there in the breakfast line. Look." She points.

I see him placing his order at the window.

"What's he doing here?" I demand

"He's our stunt coordinator," she says.

"Why him?"

"Because you asked me to hire him. Remember? I thought I was doing you a favor. Relax. What's the matter with you?"

"Chris used to beat Sharon up," I say, suddenly short of breath. "He's a really bad man."

"Well, somehow you failed to mention that when you were begging me to give him a break."

"I only found out later."

"Sometimes I seem to be able to read your mind, but not always. If you changed your mind about Chris, it would've been a good idea to let me know. That's what I get for trying to do a good deed. As Mark Twain said, 'No good deed goes unpunished,' right?"

"Actually it was Clare Boothe Luce."

"I should've known it'd take a chick to say something that smart."

"Anyway, now you know about Chris and his two-fisted ways. So fire the bastard."

"I can't. Not without cause. He'd sue us. The stuntmen's union would come down on our necks like a hundred wrecked police cars. We don't need problems like that before we even start shooting."

"But he beat up my cousin. He likes to hurt women. He might even have had something to do with her death."

"Really?"

"I'm not sure. But they had a big fight, a violent fight, just before . . ."

"Really?"

"Yes, really. Doesn't that give you grounds to fire his ass? Isn't that 'cause'?"

"If we could prove anything, sure. But it doesn't sound like we can."

"Not yet."

"Then I can't fire him yet. I'm sorry."

Trying to control my breathing, I want to blame somebody. How could Jamie do this to me? But then how could she have known? I'm the one who did this to me. It never occurred to me that she would hire this girl-beater just because I asked her to do it. I'm only a writer.

"Chick!" a familiar voice calls out. "Hello. Thanks. I hear I owe you big time, man."

I can't decide whether to shit, go blind, or move to El Paso. Coming to us, Chris sticks out his hand. Like an idiot, I shake it. Then I regret it. I want to wipe the shake off my hand.

"No, you don't owe me a thing," I say, trying to make my voice cold.

"Anyhow, thanks."

Then the day gets even worse as Buddy Dale appears, clutching his own burrito and blowing his nose.

"Hi," he says, with his mouth full, so it sounds more like a movie Indian saying "How."

Our new stunt coordinator steps forward and puts out his hand. "Mr. Dale, my name's Chris Crosby. I'm stunts. It's great to meet you. I can't believe I'm working on a Buddy Dale movie. If there is anything I can ever do for you, just let me know."

"Yeah, sure, welcome aboard," says Buddy. Then turning to Jamie, he says: "I'd like to get the first shot before noon. It always makes the studio happy when they see proof that a whole morning hasn't been wasted."

"Buddy, what are you talking about?" Jamie asks. "We can't possibly start shooting for another week. We're rushing it as it is."

"I promised the studio that we'd start shooting today."

"You had no right."

"I had every right. I don't care what it is. It could just be an establishing shot of the castle. But I want to shoot something before noon."

Buddy Dale turns and walks away. Chris Crosby falls in beside him. At first, they seem to be talking jerkily, but soon they are thick as outlaws. Chris is definitely an operator.

"What are we going to do?" Jamie says. "What are we going to shoot?"

"Well, instead of the castle," I say, "why don't we just shoot Buddy? And Chris, too?"

"That's cool with me," Jamie says, "but don't you do it. Outsource it."

I LAUGH.

"Seriously," she says. "I need you around, and I don't want to waste time visiting you in jail."

"I'm kind of an old-fashioned director," Jamie says at about half past eleven as we are waiting, waiting, waiting on the big front porch.

"That's okay," I say. "Ours is kind of an old-fashioned subject." I hesitate and then add: "But what do you mean exactly?"

"I don't use all the bells and whistles that most modern directors swear by. Watching the takes on a TV monitor instead of in real life. That kind of thing, you know."

"I'm afraid I don't know," I admit. "You lost me. What TV monitor?"

"Well, thanks to the miracles of technology, you can hook up a monitor to the camera and see exactly what it sees. I mean you are looking right through the camera lens. It's kind of amazing, but it's too small for me. It feels to me like I'm watching television instead of making a movie. The scale's all wrong. I prefer to stand beside the camera and watch the living, breathing actors as they live and breathe."

"Of course," I say, but I would secretly love to see how one of those TV monitors works.

At 11:51 A.M., Jamie quietly and self-consciously says: "Action."

Tom and Sarah—wearing dusty western attire—climb the steps of their cowboy castle. He has a patch over his left eye because my great-great-great-ever-so-great-grandfather wore one thanks to a knife fight with a Comanche. Tom opens the front door for Sarah. She proceeds him inside.

"Good one," Jamie proclaims. "Print. That's a camera wrap for today. Not that any of you get the rest of the day off. I know you've all got a lot to do. So get busy."

Everybody LAUGHS. Then they all scatter.

"You look puzzled," Jamie says.

"Yeah, I missed the joke," I say. "You must've been saying something in secret movie talk that I didn't understand."

"The only secret is: When you become a director, everybody laughs at everything you say."

I LAUGH.

"That's it," she says. "Just like that. It made me nervous at first. I thought I'd never get used to it, but I finally did, more or less."

I CHUCKLE.

As Jamie walks away, Sarah approaches me. I like her paying attention to me—after all, she is my leading lady—but I worry about what she is going to want.

"You have to have a talk with Tom," Sarah says.

"Sure," I say foolishly. "Why?"

"Tell him he should wear that eye patch all the time, twenty-four hours a day. So he can get used to it. Did you see the way he stumbled on the porch steps?"

"No." I feel as if I have failed some sort of test.

"Well, open your eyes. He did. And that's because he isn't accustomed to the patch. You have to talk to him."

"Why don't you tell him since you feel so strongly about it? You know nobody ever listens to the writer."

"Yeah, but the problem is: I already did talk to him, and he just blew me off saying he isn't a method actor. Promise me you'll talk to him."

"You should really talk to Jamie."

"That dyke. She hates me. No, you have to do it." She waits. I say nothing. "Well?" she prompts.

"Okay."

"But don't tell him it was my idea."

Sitting on the side of my bed in my third-floor bedroom, alone at last, I use my cell phone to call Tom Bondini on his cell phone. He answers with a touch of irritation in his voice.

"Well, today went very well," I say. Then I rush at my subject: "But I noticed that you stumbled on the steps."

"I didn't stumble," he says, his voice irritation escalating.

"Anyway I think it might be a good idea if you practiced wearing the eye patch—"

"Sarah put you up to this, didn't she? You're on her side, aren't you?"

"There aren't sides."

"Sure there are, and you aren't on mine."

"Yes, I am."

"No, you aren't. She's fucking you, isn't she?"

"No!"

The very accusation makes me feel that I've been unfaithful to Jamie, whom I'm not fucking either.

"If she isn't," Tom says, "then you're the only one. You should at least get paid for taking her side."

"But I'm not—"

"She's crazy. Wearing the patch all the time isn't a bad idea, but I'm not gonna do it. Why? Because she told me to. Okay?"

28

WE WILL START SHOOTING FOR REAL A WEEK LATER. Jamie wants to begin with a scene that doesn't require any carpenters to build anything. I suggest starting at Jimmy Goodnight's original dugout since it is still in relatively good condition. She buys the idea.

The night before the big day, I am fast asleep on the third floor of the castle when my cell phone BURPS. Rousing, I look at my Timex, which is cheap but lights up in the dark. It is almost one o'clock in the morning. I check my phone to see who is calling and find Jamie's name on the display. I answer.

"I know it's late, but can you meet me in the living room?" Jamie asks. "And bring your computer and your script. Okay?"

"Okay, it's a long walk," I say sleepily, "but I think I can make it."

Jamie CHUCKLES, but I'm not kidding. It is a long walk, down endless corridors, down a couple of flights of stairs, through more corridors. I arrive a little out of breath. We sit on facing couches that frame the huge fireplace.

"I always like to put the pages through the computer one last time before we shoot," Jamie says. "So why don't you just type through tomorrow's work. Then give it to me and I'll do the same. You know, I think my fingers are smarter than my brain. As I'm typing, I often find things I never would have noticed just reading."

"Okay," I say.

"See, making a movie is sort of like putting together a jigsaw puzzle," she says. "Except it's a magic jigsaw because the pieces keep changing shape. No scene is ever quite what you expect it to be. You'll see. Maybe when the actors play it, the scene turns out to be smaller than you imagined. Or maybe it takes on a life of its own and gets bigger. Or maybe just weirder, a different shape. See?"

I nod, but I'm still trying to work it out.

"Anyway, when one piece changes shape, you have to change the shapes of the other pieces, or else they won't all fit together. Right?"

I nod.

"And the only pieces you can change are the ones you haven't filmed yet. So that's why I believe in rewriting. Not just rewriting but rewriting every day. Or usually every night. It's a lot of work, but it's worth it. You up for it?"

"Sure," I say, not sure what I am letting myself in for. "But we haven't shot anything yet. Nothing's changed sizes. Nothing's done anything."

"Don't get smart."

"Right."

To prove I'm game, I open my computer and press power. The machine grumbles softly and starts up. I call up the script file now entitled Untitled Goodnight Picture. Using my computer's search engine, I find the dugout scene right away. Then I flip my script open to the right pages because the printed version isn't always exactly the same as the version in my laptop. Trying to balance my computer on my knees and my script on the arm of the couch, I feel as if I am auditioning for some sort of circus act. Step right up, ladies and gentlemen, boys and girls, and see the writer tie himself in knots. I drop the script twice—amusing Jamie—but manage to hang on to the computer. I start typing, making small cuts as I go:

```
EXT. RED CANYON — AFTERNOON

The Sanborn family make their first entrance into
the canyon escorted by U.S. CAVALRY TROOPS. MR.
SANBORN is evidently important. MRS. SANBORN and
her daughter Revelie arrive riding in a U.S. Army
ambulance.
```

"Good, you keep working on that," Jamie says. "I've got a couple of things I need to get done for tomorrow's shoot. I'll come back and check on you in half an hour or so. Okay?"

"Sure."

She gets up and goes. I go back to typing:

```
                  MRS. SANBORN
              (wearing white gloves and a
              pink ribbon)
          Where's your ranch, Mr. Goodnight?

                  GOODNIGHT
          You're lookin' at it, ma'am.

                  MRS. SANBORN
          Where's the ranch house? Where's
          the bunkhouse? Don't ranches have
          bunkhouses? I've heard so much about
          this kind of house. But what is it?
          Some sort of a cowboy hotel?

The COWBOYS are trying to hide their smirks.
Goodnight glances over at Revelie with an
expression that begs for help.
```

GOODNIGHT

Well, ma'am, I'm afraid we don't have a
regular bunkhouse or anything like that.
We just live in an ol' dugout. Or sleep
under God's own leaky ceilin'. Someday ...

MRS. SANBORN

A dugout? I thought a dugout was a
canoe. You don't live in a canoe, do
you, Mr. Goodnight?

GOODNIGHT

No, ma'am.

MRS. SANBORN

Then could you explain to me what
you're talking about? I'm afraid I
don't speak cowboy.

I stop typing and reread what I have done so far. I've made a few
trims here and there as I've typed, but the dialogue still seems wordy.
I look for more cuts but can't bear to part with anything. Not only
do I not know what to do, but my hands start to tremble badly. I
need help.

I tell myself: I'm all alone. It's late at night. Jamie won't be back
for twenty minutes or more. Why not?

I hurry upstairs and fetch my batons. Twirling them, I descend the
staircase once again. I could do my twirls in the privacy of my own
room, but it has a low ceiling. The living room's two-story ceiling is
high enough for me to throw and catch my batons.

I twirl, I whirl, I hurl spinning propellers into the air. And of
course I catch them like a gold-glove shortstop. I'm good and I'm
beginning to relax.

"Hey, you're good." Jamie's voice comes from behind my back. "I never could get the hang of it myself."

Startled, I drop a baton.

"Didn't mean to scare you," she says. "Forgot my notebook. Sorry."

I want to die. I want to melt and sink into the floor like the Wicked Witch. I want to run and hide and stay hidden for the rest of my life. I don't want to turn around but I do. Jamie gives me a big, dazzling smile.

"By the way," she adds, "what the fuck is going on here?"

"It's my parents' fault," I stammer.

"Sure, blame it on Mom and Dad. Especially Mom, right?"

"No, both of them. They both gave me batons for Christmas way back when. Really, they did."

"You've got strange parents."

"I suppose so, but they meant well. See, when I was growing up, if Mom and Dad gave me a present, they also gave my sister a present, too. And not just any present but exactly the same present they had given me. And it also worked the other way 'round. If they gave her something, they always gave the same thing to me, too. That was so we kids would know they loved us the same, exactly the same, and so we wouldn't grow up believing in sexual stereotypes."

"No kidding?"

"No kidding. When I got a gun, my sister got a gun. When she got a doll, I got a doll. And we both got batons. My sister turned out to be a pretty good shot, and I turned out to be a hell of a twirler."

"I can see that."

"I can also shoot in case you're wondering. But when I'm worried about something, twirling is a lot more calming than shooting. Anyway it is for me."

"Good," she says, shaking her head. "You're a man of many parts, Chick Goodnight. I'll let you get back to work now."

"Don't tell anybody, okay?"

"Okay."

Jamie picks up her notebook and hurries out of the room. I am so
shaken by what has just happened—by her discovery of my secret—
that I have to keep twirling for another ten minutes to calm down.
Then I collapse on the big couch. But the longer I sit there idly, the
more I remember my sharpshooter sister who died in a car crash
when she was just sixteen years old. I try never to think about her, for
my sins, but this memory has flown in under the radar.

Eventually, in an effort to banish her memory, I go back to work,
back to typing, now making deeper cuts:

                         GOODNIGHT
     Well, ma'am, mebbe I better just show
     ya. It's right over here. Just follow
     me, ma'am.

The dugout is located in a small grove of cedars. It
is just a shack, half in the ground and half out of
it. No windows.

                       MRS. SANBORN
     Do I understand that you live in this
     so-called dugout, Mr. Goodnight?

                         GOODNIGHT
     Yes, ma'am. I mean I sleep here
     sometimes. I mostly live outdoors.

                       MRS. SANBORN
     What about your cowboys? Do they have
     their own dugout things?

                         GOODNIGHT
     No, ma'am. They's just one dugout and
     we all sleep in it.

MRS. SANBORN

Really? May I look inside, Mr. Goodnight?

GOODNIGHT

Okay, if you want to.

She has to stoop to get through the small doorway,
and she isn't a tall woman. Goodnight stays outside
because there isn't much room inside and he has no
desire to be trapped in close quarters with this lady.

MRS. SANBORN

(poking her head outside, she

holds her nose)

Mr. Goodnight, your home smells. You
and your poor men, you live like
prairie dogs.

When Jamie returns, I can feel my face heat up as I blush.

"Don't worry," she says. "I didn't tell a soul. Your secret's safe with me."

"Good," I say, "but I didn't want you to know either."

"Too bad. Let's see what you've done."

Since we don't have a printer here in front of the fireplace, I hand my laptop to her. She starts reading and crossing out. My cuts were mere nibbles compared to the big bites she is taking. My fingers tremble faster and I keep twisting in my seat as I watch her. When she finishes, she hands the computer back to me. I start reading:

EXT. RED CANYON — AFTERNOON

The Sanborn family make their first entrance into the
canyon escorted by U.S. Cavalry troops. MR. SANBORN
is evidently important. MRS. SANBORN and her daughter
Revelie arrive riding in a U.S. Army ambulance.

MRS. SANBORN
(wearing white gloves and a
pink ribbon)
Where's your ranch, Mr. Goodnight?

GOODNIGHT
You're lookin' at it, ma'am.

MRS. SANBORN
Where's the ranch house? ~~Where's the~~
~~bunkhouse? Don't ranches have~~
~~bunkhouses? I've heard so much about~~
~~this kind of house. But what is it?~~
~~Some sort of cowboy hotel?~~

The COWBOYS are trying to hide their smirks.
Goodnight glances over at Revelie with an
expression that begs for help.

GOODNIGHT
Well, ma'am, I'm afraid we ~~don't have a~~
~~regular bunkhouse or anything like that.~~
~~We~~ just live in an ol' dugout. ~~Or sleep~~
~~under God's own leaky ceilin'. Someday . . .~~

~~MRS. SANBORN~~
~~A dugout? I thought a dugout was a~~
~~canoe. You don't live in a canoe, do~~
~~you, Mr. Goodnight?~~

~~GOODNIGHT~~
~~No, ma'am.~~

~~MRS. SANBORN~~
~~Then could you explain to me what~~
~~you're talking about? I'm afraid I~~
~~don't speak cowboy.~~

                    GOODNIGHT
~~Well, ma'am, mebbe~~ I better ~~just~~ show
ya. It's right over here. Just follow
me, ma'am.

The dugout is located in a small grove of cedars. It
is just a shack, half in the ground and half out of
it. No windows.

                    MRS. SANBORN
Do I understand that you live in this
so-called dugout, Mr. Goodnight?

                    GOODNIGHT
Yes, ma'am. ~~I mean I sleep here~~
~~sometimes. I mostly live outdoors.~~

                    MRS. SANBORN
What about your cowboys? Do they have
their own dugout things?

                    GOODNIGHT
No, ma'am. There's just one dugout and
we all sleep in it.

                    MRS. SANBORN
Really? May I look inside, Mr.
Goodnight?

                    GOODNIGHT
Okay, if you want to.

She has to stoop to get through the small doorway,
and she isn't a tall woman. ~~Goodnight stays outside~~
~~because there isn't much room inside and he has no~~
~~desire to be trapped in close quarters with this~~
~~lady.~~

```
              MRS. SANBORN
         (poking her head outside, she
         holds her nose)
      Mr. Goodnight, your home smells. You
      and your poor men, you live like
      prairie dogs.
```

"Did I cut anything you can't live without?" Jamie asks.

"Well, uh, you did cut some lines I like," I reply. "Some lines I think are funny."

"Tell you what," she says. "We'll type those up and mail them home to your mother. She'll be proud of you." She pauses. "In America, movie scenes are usually short. The short scenes and quick cuts give American movies their energy. As I was reading through this, it seemed to me that it belonged in a French movie where scenes go on longer than a seven-course dinner."

"Right," I say sheepishly.

29

THE NEXT MORNING I'M EXCITED BUT TRY NOT TO show it. The movie begins for real today. My first movie. The movie my whole life has been pointing toward. The sky is a beautiful clear blue. No rain will fall today, bad for farmers, bad for ranchers, good for filmmakers. The wind is blowing.

I join Jamie for an addictive breakfast burrito at the caterer's wagon. Eating on the move, we make our way to a Mack Trucks–driven SUV. We tuck ourselves into the backseat and kick up dust on our way to Goodnight's dugout. We pull up and park next to a long, black motor home. I have no idea what it is doing here, but I don't ask. There are a dozen eighteen-wheel trucks scattered across the landscape. I don't know why they are here either.

We get out. Jamie KNOCKS on the black motor-home door. A POTBELLIED GUY who looks like a teamster opens up partway. Seeing Jamie, he opens all the way. I follow her inside and down a short corridor to a mobile living room. Sitting there are Tom Bondini and the actress who will play my great-great-great-great-ever-so-great-grandmother, Dolly.

Her name is BROOKE BROOKLYN, which probably wasn't her original name. She is an old friend of Jamie's, which is why she has this role. Not that we gave it to her because of old ties, but old ties got her the audition. And she really was the best. Anyway I thought so. Or maybe Jamie persuaded me to think so. I'm not sure. But I'm happy with Brooke Brooklyn or whatever her real name is. It's like the Old West where and when Robert Leroy Parker could change his name to Butch Cassidy and go down in Western history.

"Here are some new pages," Jamie says, handing the actors last night's revision of today's scene. "We just made it a little shorter."

Jamie and I sit down next to each other on a short sofa. On a facing couch, the actors hurriedly read through the newly revised scene. Brooke reads considerably faster than Tom does. Finally he finishes and looks up.

"Sorry," he says.

"Good," Jamie says. "I'd like to run through the scene very informally before we do it for real. I hope that's okay?"

"Sure."

"Fine."

"Very good. Just see how the scene feels in your mouths. Whenever you're ready . . ."

We all stare at Brooke, who is wearing white gloves and a pink ribbon on the back of her head, like a schoolgirl.

"Where's your ranch, Mr. Goodnight?" Brooke asks. She is sixty, thin, and has condescension down to a fine art.

"You're lookin' at it, ma'am," Tom says.

"Where's the ranch house?"

"Well, ma'am, I'm afraid we just live in an ol' dugout. I better show ya. It's right over here. Just follow me, ma'am."

Tom makes a *T* with his hands as though he's calling time out in a football game.

"What's the problem, Tom?" Jamie asks.

"That's kind of a mouthful," says our leading man. "Could I just say 'Well, ma'am, I'm afraid we live in a dugout. Follow me, I'll show you'?"

"Fine with me," says Jamie. "Any objections, Chick?"

"No," I say, even though I think the change will make our hero seem more confident than I imagined him. "Fine."

"Good, less is almost always more," Jamie says. "Let's take it from the top again."

Jamie takes up her favorite position just to the right of the camera. I stand behind and a little to the right of her.

"Action," Jamie almost whispers.

I feel a surge of energy that has nowhere to go. I'm a filmmaker now. My definition of myself has changed. I am reminded of that night when I happily bid good-bye to my virginity. My celluloid maidenhead is now broken. I woke up this morning as one thing, but I will go to bed tonight as something else.

Then I suddenly, unexpectedly, find myself wondering if they will let me dedicate this movie to my cousin. Tears well in my eyes and I quickly wipe them away. Too happy, too sad, too bad. One side of the coin can never escape from the other side.

As the camera rolls, an ambulance—a glorified surrey like the one with the fringe on top—rolls into the frame and comes to a halt. Sarah, Brooke, and an actor named AMBROSE SMYTHE descend. He plays Sarah's father, Brooke's husband, and my great-great-great-great-ever-so-great maternal grandfather H. B. Sanborn. A banker by trade, rich, and an anglophile. So far none of the actors has said a word.

"Cut," Jamie almost whispers. "Very good, everybody. Let's do it again. Back to first positions."

Everybody LAUGHS.

"Nice work," I say.

"Thanks," Jamie says, turning to face me. "I love easing into a movie with a scene like this. No lines. No real acting. Nothing to frighten the horses."

I am feeling good until a voice behind me says: "You don't want to spend a lot of time hanging out on the set." I hadn't noticed Buddy Dale's arrival. "It's too boring. You should be back in your room writing your next movie. Trust me."

"I'm surprised you're not back in your room auditioning farmers' daughters," I say as my fingers play sixty-fourth notes and my heart turns into a kettledrum.

"I'm headed there right now," Buddy says. "Want to come along and join in the fun? It'll be you, me, and Chris the stud stuntman. Plus all the ranchers' daughters. Of course, you might be afraid you won't measure up."

"No thank you."

"I'm not going to have a problem with you, am I?"

Unable to write a great comeback in my head, I walk away. Jamie falls in beside me and walks with me.

"I can't believe you said that to Buddy," Jamie says. "You're normally so shy and reticent."

"I can't believe it either," I say. "I thought I was going to have a heart attack mid-sentence." I pause for a deep breath, my heart still booming. "I'm just so angry at him—all the time."

She thinks a moment. "But you're not used to expressing your anger, are you? Generally, you just hold it in, right?"

"I suppose so."

"You're this quiet volcano, aren't you? Your anger builds up and build ups, and finally one day you erupt and it all comes spewing out. Right?"

"I don't think I really erupted. I just spewed a little steam."

"Right, but the mountain is rumbling. The warning signs are there. Just try not to get burned, okay?"

After lunch, we finally tackle Dolly's visit to the dugout. Lighting takes longer than it used to take to drive a herd up the trail to Dodge. Lights are carried in, then carried out again.

"Watch your backs!"

New lights are carried in.

"Flying in."

I have no idea what is going on, but I am nonetheless fascinated. Well, fascinated may be too strong a word, but I am interested. I am sitting on an apple box and surveying the scene when I notice a new arrival. She is a top-heavy Barbie in pale blue spandex. I get up and walk over to Jamie, who is seated in her canvas-backed director's chair with her name on it.

"Who's the hooker?" I ask.

"Aren't you a sports fan?" Jamie asks. "I took you for a sports fan."

"I love sports," I say defensively. "My father was a football coach."

"Then why don't you recognize the cover girl of *Sports Illustrated*'s swimsuit issue?"

"Swimsuit isn't a sport."

"I hear she has some great athletic moves. Buddy flew her in last night from L.A. I imagine she thinks she's going to be in this movie. Doesn't she look frontier to you?"

"Hollywood doesn't really work this way?"

"Most of Hollywood doesn't. Like most politicians aren't all that crooked. What money is to a pol, sex is to Buddy Dale. It's Hollywood's special twist on corruption."

I look up to SEE (POV) MISS SWIMSUIT bearing down on us. Long legs, heavy breasts, a face as immobile as Barbie's own.

"Hi, I'm Billie Jo Houston," says Miss *SI* Swimsuit. She reaches out and shakes Jamie's hand. "I don't mean to interrupt, but Buddy Dale said I'd have a line in this movie. Only nobody seems to know what my line is."

"We really haven't decided yet," Jamie says. "It's the first day."

"But I'm supposed to fly back to L.A. tomorrow. Maybe I could just say 'Hi, there.' How about that?"

"The thing about the frontier," Jamie explains patiently, "is there weren't very many women. The only extras in this scene are cowboys, and I don't think you could pass."

Everybody LAUGHS.

"But I'm not supposed to be an extra. I've got a line. Maybe I could be the cook. 'Dinner is served.' Something like that."

"Sorry."

"But Buddy said—"

"Then I'm really very sorry."

I'm thinking: Some of Buddy's victims deserve what they get, but not my cousin! Then I reconsider: Actually the dumb ones don't deserve it either. They're helpless.

Billie Jo turns and stalks away.

"Wait," I say.

Miss Swimsuit turns.

"If you value your life," I warn her, "don't give Buddy too hard a time. He's a killer."

"Then I hope he kills the two of you," Billie Jo hisses, turns again, and marches away on long legs.

I watch her telling Buddy what assholes we are. He scowls in our direction, but that's all. He has evidently already gotten what he wanted. As the two of them march away, Chris joins them. Vultures of a feather.

"We're getting close," says diminutive cameraman Victor Hammer.

Half an hour later, we are ready to shoot. Rolling. Speed. Action, spoken softly.

"Mr. Goodnight, your home smells," says Brooke, poking her head out of the dugout. "You and your poor men, you live like prairie dogs."

I love hearing the words. They seem the sweetest words I've ever heard in my life.

"Hi, handsome," says a familiar voice.

I look around and SEE (POV) Sarah flashing me. Somehow she has managed to unbutton her complicated Victorian bodice and has thrown the shutters wide open. I gulp. Her nipples are brown and erect. I can't help wishing it were Jamie flashing her tits at me.

As if taking a cue from my thought, Jamie steps into the frame of my vision. "Hey, Sarah, nice rack," she says.

Everybody LAUGHS.

———

"How'd you like your first day of shooting?" asks Jamie as we drive "home" together. "You were bored, weren't you? I mean bored except when Sarah was showing you her tits."

"No, not really," I say unconvincingly.

"You aren't a good enough actor to lie," Jamie says.

"Okay, I was excited at first, then a little bored, but the longer I watched, the more interesting it became."

"Because you understood more?"

"Well, I finally figured out there was a rhythm to it. At first, I thought everybody was just sitting around doing nothing. Then I realized it was sort of like a relay race. Only races are usually faster. But one group works and then they hand off the baton to another group and then another. And at the end, here come the actors."

"Very good."

I can't believe how pleased I am by this offhand comment. "And you did great," I say.

"Shut up," Jamies says. "I'm going to close my eyes, no offense. Wake me when it's over."

We ride in silence through the gorgeous desolation that is West Texas. Being an English major—well, let's face it, I got my Ph.D.—I have long thought that this bleak landscape is to traditional beauty as the modern poets are to traditional poetry. You have to find the beauty in the ugliness. Easy beauty is excluded. Like all those beautiful actresses who were too beautiful for our show. And the wind is blowing hard.

"Trucks," I say, keeping my voice down so as not to wake Jamie, "I was wondering if you ever drove Buddy Dale back in California."

"Sure, sometimes," Mack Trucks says.

"I guess I'm kind of a voyeur, but I was wondering if you ever drove actresses to his house."

"Yeah, sure, and there was some beautiful ladies. Real beautiful. The most beautiful ladies I ever seen."

The flatness rolls by. The wind makes the SUV swerve, then correct its course, then swerve again.

"Do you remember any of their names?" I ask.

"Not usually," Trucks says. "Not unless they was real famous."

"What about a girl with the same last name as mine? That would be my cousin, Sharon Goodnight."

"No, sorry."

"Or it might have been Sharon Loving. That's her stage name."

Mack Trucks thinks for a long time. I look over at Jamie to see if she is still asleep. Her eyes are closed and she is breathing regularly.

"Sorry," Trucks says at last. "I don't remember her." He pauses. "I'm not sure, but I don't think so."

"Well, thanks anyway," I say. "If you wouldn't mind, maybe you could ask some of the other drivers."

"Be my pleasure."

"Just ask quietly."

Mack Trucks stops the SUV in front of the great rock cowboy castle where we are staying. The moment we come to rest, Jamie's eyes open. We get out and climb the front-porch steps.

"So you've still got blood in your eye, huh?" Jamie says.

The wind blows.

30

I AM SURPRISINGLY TIRED FROM STANDING AROUND all day. I'm more tired than if I had been baling hay or mucking out the barn. My feet hurt. My back hurts. I'm in bed by 10 P.M. and asleep a minute or two later. I sleep dreamlessly until a pounding sound awakens me at three in the morning. It takes me a few moments to realize somebody is KNOCKING at my door. With my head still full of cotton, I stumble out of bed and lurch toward the sound. Wearing underwear and a T-shirt, I struggle with the door until it finally opens.

"Hi, handsome," says Sarah. "My night's been a disaster. What about yours?"

"Uummm," I yawn.

"Well, I've got to tell somebody, so I thought I might as well tell lucky you."

"I can't wake up."

"Go back to bed."

I don't need convincing. Turning my back on my guest, I stumble back toward my bed.

"You've got good legs," Sarah says.

"Uuummmhhh," I yawn.

I collapse on the bed, and she lies down beside me. We are both on top of the covers.

"I have to tell somebody or I'll explode," she says.

"I'm against exploding leading ladies," I say.

So she proceeds to tell her tale with energy and detail and venom. She tells it so well I feel as if I am there. It's the way I feel about the scenes in the script. Writing those scenes about Revelie and Goodnight, I felt I was right there even though I obviously couldn't have been. Imagination, or trance, or empathy, or self-hypnosis, or whatever the hell writers rely on, is a wonderful thing. As Sarah talks, I see her story as if it were scenes in a movie:

INT. TOM BONDINI'S ROOM IN COWBOY CASTLE — NIGHT

Tom HEARS a KNOCK at his door. He goes and opens up.
Sarah enters carrying a book.

SARAH

I thought maybe we could do some
research. I hope you're game. This is
how I love to work.

TOM

What's the book?

SARAH

It's *Lady Chatterly's Lover*. See, it's
about this great lady who falls in love
with her gardener or gamekeeper or
whatever he was. And that's like our
story.

TOM

No it isn't. I play a cowboy.

SARAH

But that's the American equivalent.

TOM

You think a cowboy is the equivalent of
an English gardener?

SARAH

You're missing the point. Our story is
about the daughter of an aristocratic
family who marries beneath herself.

CLOSER ON TOM — who isn't pleased.

TOM

You think your marrying me is beneath
you? Who's got top billing? Who's
getting paid what?

CLOSER ON SARAH — who looks both irritated and
defensive. Why doesn't he get it? Why won't he play?

> SARAH
>
> You're right. In reality, in the here
> and now, in Hollywood, you're the lord
> and I'm the servant girl. But in this
> movie I'm your social superior.

BIG CLOSE-UP OF TOM — who is tired of this
conversation.

> TOM
>
> So let's wait until they turn the
> camera on to play that game.

BIG CLOSE-UP OF SARAH — who tries to be seductive.
She will seduce him into playing her game.

> SARAH
>
> It's a very sexy book. You might like
> it. I thought we might read it together.

WIDER ANGLE

> TOM
>
> Let me see it.

Sarah hands over the book. Tom hefts it. Then he
looks at the last page.

> TOM (CONT)
> It's too heavy and too long.

> SARAH
> We don't have to read it all. We could
> just read the dirty parts.

                    TOM

I'm tired. I'm sleepy. And I never read
anything but scripts.

                    SARAH

Like that's something to be proud of.

                    TOM

You need your beauty sleep. Good night,
see you in the morning.

                    SARAH

Good night, Mr. Goodnight.

                    TOM

I'm not Mr. Goodnight. I'm me and
you're you. For better or worse.

                    SARAH

For richer, for poorer.

                    TOM

For Christ's sake, Sarah, leave me
alone.

Lying stiffly on her back, Sarah stares up at the ceiling.

"Tom makes me so mad," she hisses. "What's wrong with him?
What's wrong with me? I just wanted to get something going between
the two of us. I need a relationship. We need a relationship. We're
married, for Christ's sake. Only it feels like we're already divorced.
What am I gonna do?"

31

THE NEXT MORNING, THE ALARM IN MY CELL PHONE BURPS, but I don't spring out of bed. Well, I never actually spring, but I usually do get up. Instead I lie in bed making excuses for my lack of motion. I tell myself that Sarah kept me up half the night. Even after she finally left, I couldn't go back to sleep for what seemed hours. So I deserve sleeping in. Besides, I now know how long it takes to set up a scene. I'm pretty sure I can sleep another hour—maybe two—and they still won't be ready when I get to the set. Persuading myself of the justice of my cause, I drift back into delicious stolen slumber.

My cell phone is BURPING again. I thought I turned it off, but I must have hit the snooze button instead. Before throwing the phone across the room in a fit of early-morning temper, I glance at the face. The alarm isn't going off. I have an incoming call. I stop breathing: from Jamie.

"Hello," I say, trying to sound more awake than I feel.

"I woke you up," she accuses.

"No," I lie.

"Well, it sure sounds like it. Get your ass over here right now. I need you. Hurry. We can't wait for you all day."

My hands are shaking so badly I can hardly get my pants on. I'm lucky I don't hurt myself. Skipping showering and brushing my teeth, I race down the hall, down the stairs, and out the big front door. I'm surprised to SEE (POV) Mack Trucks parked in front of the house.

"Git in," says the Truck. "Jamie sent me to git you. She says you're late."

"I didn't know I was on the clock."

Mack Trucks drives like a posse chasing bank robbers. Bouncing up and down, I try to comb my hair with my fingers. The rough road makes me bite my tongue. The wind is blowing so hard it pushes the big SUV around.

The huge SUV makes a hockey stop spraying gravel. I jump out and run toward the crowd around the camera. I'm out of breath when I reach Jamie, sitting in her tall, canvas-backed chair with her name on the back.

"Well, hello, sleeping beauty," she says. "Nice of you to favor us with your presence."

"I'm sorry I'm late," I say. Then, coming to the point: "What do you need me for?"

"I've got something to show you."

"What?" I'm still trying to catch my breath.

"Not so fast. Before I show you, I have to ask you a few questions. For instance, did you know that Buddy Dale flew back to California last night?"

"No, I'm afraid Buddy doesn't ask my permission to leave the state. But if he had, I'd've said go by all means."

"He said he had to go to a meeting, but I suspect he'd just run out of coke. Anyway he left. We'll have to get along the best we can without him."

"That'll be hard."

People are starting to crowd around us: grips, gripes, gaffers, best boys, makeup, hair, little Victor Hammer the cameraman. What is going on? I feel I'm the new kid in class and they are all playing a trick on me.

"Now, Chick, knowing Buddy as you do," Jamie says, "would you suspect that he is a tidy person? Do you think he cleans up well after himself?"

"I don't know where this is going, but I wouldn't think so. That's what servants—the help—are for in his world."

"Exactly. You're exactly right. And that's exactly what he did. He left his mess for the help to clean up. But the help here in Texas aren't exactly like the help back home in Beverly Hills. The help here found a few things that Buddy left behind, and they were good enough to share them with us. Want to see?"

"Of course. What?"

The crowd around us contracts.

"Polaroids. Most of them aren't that interesting. Just shots of Miss *Sports Illustrated* in bondage. You don't want to see those, do you?"

"Of course not," I lie.

"But here's the masterpiece. The one Michelangelo among all the pretenders. It might just be the best Polaroid ever taken in the history of—what?—the whole world."

"Can I see it?"

"Of course."

The crowd contracts even tighter. Soon I won't be able to breathe.

"Here."

Jamie hands me a Polaroid. The man in the photo is dressed like Michelangelo's Adam, meaning nude, but he does have a scrap of clothing that Adam had to do without since it hadn't been invented yet. Buddy Dale has a green tie—tied with a perfect Windsor knot—wrapped around his balls.

"Not bad," I say, "but I'd prefer a noose."

"How soon can we get it on the Internet?" asks Victor Hammer.

"Not yet," Jamie says. "We may need it later."

In the photo, Buddy Dale has a very self-satisfied smile on his face, which I hope to wipe off someday.

"Go on, show him the other one," says munchkin Victor Hammer.

Jamie hands me a second Polaroid. This is Chris, whose balls are tied not with the school tie, but with a red bandana.

"Okay, so two masterpieces," she says.

32

BY THE END OF THE DAY, WE ARE FINALLY FINISHED shooting all the footage for our dugout scene. Master shots. Group reaction shots. Two shots. And singles. While we are doing the close work, Jamie confides to me that some actors deliberately mess up the masters so you have to use their close-ups instead. She suspects Sarah may well be capable of such tactics and is watching her closely. We get one last shot of sunset over the dugout and then shut down.

"That's a wrap," says KIM KURUMADA, a tall son of Chinese immigrants, who is our first AD, the first assistant director.

"Let's go," says Jamie. "Tonight you'll see your first dailies. I hope you like the way they look. I hope I like how they look."

"I can't wait," I admit.

Mack Trucks drives us. On the way, we spot four deer, two wild turkeys, and accidentally kill a dove that suddenly swoops in front of the SUV. There is a sudden explosion of feathers.

"That's not good," Jamie says.

"No," I agree, a little shaken.

"I'm real sorry," says Trucks.

"Not your fault," says Jamie. "Good thing I'm not superstitious."

"You sound superstitious," I say.

"Shut up, she explained," she says.

"Ring Lardner in *The Young Immigrunts*, right?"

"If you say so, Professor."

"That's *immigrunts*, with a *U*."

"You don't say."

Seeming irritated with me, Jamie takes out a notebook and starts making notes. I can't help wondering what she is feeling as well as what she is writing. Is she jotting down new dialogue? Scribbling notes for fresh cuts? Writing home to mother? Compiling an encyclopedia of my faults? What? I warn myself not to ask because she is already in a bad mood.

"What are you writing?" I ask.

"A list," she says cryptically.

I wait. I tell myself once again not to be too inquisitive.

"What kind of list?" I ask.

"I don't have to tell you about my list," she snaps. Her tone says: Leave me alone.

I lean back in my seat and watch her work on her list. She turns her notebook so I can't see what she is writing.

One dove feather still clings to the windshield as we turn down the drive that leads to 6666 HQ.

"Drop us at the barn, please, Trucks," Jamie says, putting away her notebook.

Mack Trucks pulls up in front of the great red barn with the distinctive 6666 emblazoned in white paint on its forehead. After thanking MT, we enter the barn, which has been transformed into a screening room. A huge white screen has been installed at the far end. Instead of chairs, bales of hay have been arranged in rows. The projector stands tall like a prize bull.

Jamie and I are among the first to arrive, but others begin showing up shortly. Sarah, anxious to see herself on-screen, is the first actor to appear in the barn. Soon the other players begin straggling in. Sarah's movie mother and father enter together. The cowboys saunter in. The actors are all still in costume.

"Some directors don't want their actors to see dailies," Jamie tells me. "The theory is it makes them too self-conscious. Which may well be. But it also pisses them off if they can't see themselves. So you have to take your pick: pissed off or self-conscious. Maybe I'm just taking the path of least resistance."

"Where's Tom?" I ask. "Doesn't he want to see himself?"

"Of course he does," she says. "But he told me he wanted to change first."

"None of the others changed."

"Exactly."

The barn quickly fills up with not only actors but also representatives of all the other movie arts: hair, makeup, wardrobe, sound, set design, camera. Plus every level of assistant director from the first AD to the last. They collectively begin to grow restless. I see them all asking the same question: Where is Tom? They all seem to wonder, as I wonder, if Tom is grandstanding, preparing a big entrance, wasting everybody's time.

The barn door cracks open and Tom Bondini finally slips inside. Everybody naturally looks in his direction. He is transformed: His cowboy boots have given way to his bright puce running shoes, which make his feet look like giant plums. He wears sweatpants and a sweatshirt. He is the anti-cowboy.

"Thanks for condescending to join us," calls Sarah. "We didn't have anything to do except sit around and wait for you. And of course play with ourselves."

"Shut up," Jamie explains again. "Let's see what we've got here. Lights."

Somebody clicks off the lights in the barn. The big screen now dimly illuminates the room. I like what I see. And one thing I see is that Sarah, whom I hardly noticed when we were shooting the scene, is something else entirely on-screen: I can't stop looking at her even when the action and dialogue are elsewhere. And I don't know why. It seems she does it just by being there. Just by breathing. Just by being embarrassed "mit out sound," MOS, by her mother's antics. Just by . . . what? I wish I knew.

As the dailies wind down, I'm actually thrilled. It's not just my words that are coming to life on the screen, it's my past, my heritage. It is time travel. I like what I see so much that I reach for Jamie's hand and give it a tight squeeze. She pulls her hand away. Sarah wouldn't have.

33

WE SHOOT SIX DAYS A WEEK AND THEN, LIKE GOD, REST on the seventh day. For our one day off, I have surprised myself by arranging an outing. I'm not good at arrangements, but for the good of the movie, I have organized a lunch with the cowboys at the Pitchfork Ranch. I want our cast to meet real ranch cowboys who do real ranch work. I could have set up a similar lunch at the 6666, but I thought our actors should see other ranches. Besides, I know the folks at the Pitchfork much better. They are old family friends. We eat Christmas dinner together every year.

I am a nervous wreck before the lunch. I desperately want Hollywood to like these cowboys, whom I think of as my cowboys. And I fervently want the cowboys to like Hollywood. Which side will let me down? Which "family" will embarrass me more? Why did I ever think this would be a good idea? Why did I ever suppose I could wrangle such an event? I am standing on the spacious front porch of the castle losing my mind.

"Hi," says Jamie.

I jump as if I have just been bucked off something lethal.

"Don't have a heart attack," she says. "What's the matter? Nervous about playing 'hostess'?" Her fingers do the quotation marks.

"Yeah, how'd you know?"

"Because you're you."

Soon we're en route to the Pitchfork. This trip rates a big van. Mack Trucks is at the wheel with Jamie, Sarah, Tom, and me in the back. I'm all the way in the back, the third row. It's a beautiful ride past wheat fields. I wonder if I should tell the others that the wheat is raised to feed the cattle, not to make bread, but I decide not to press my luck.

The wind is blowing. The windmills are spinning like airplane propellers straining to take off but forever nailed to the ground.

We pull up in front of an elaborate wooden mansion. I would have suggested this ranch as our headquarters, but Goodnight's castle was definitely made of rock.

As we emerge from the van, BOB MOORHOUSE, the Pitchfork Ranch manager, comes up to welcome us. He has closely cropped dark blond hair and an uncropped bushy mustache that looks like 1880. He wears jeans with a crease tucked into ostrich-hide boots that come up to his knees. To me, knowing him so well, liking him so much, he looks like the spirit of the West. The old spirit.

As I make the introductions, I am afraid I will forget Tom Bondini's name or Sarah's or worst of all Jamie's. I pass this test. Barely. I actually stumble on Bondini, the biggest star in the world, but more or less recover. Nobody laughs.

"This way to the cookshack," says Bob Moorhouse, the Pitchfork boss.

Following him, we walk over uneven ground to the cookshack, which is just that. A small thrown-together building. Inside, the shack is divided between a spacious kitchen and a somewhat cramped eating area with a long white table and white benches.

The COWBOYS are already there looking just the way cowboys are supposed to because Bob Moorhouse takes ranch and cowboy traditions seriously, almost reverently. He enforces a cowboy dress code at the Pitchfork Ranch from the crown of the ten-gallon hats his "boys" wear down to the jingling rowels of their spurs. Cowpokes at other ranches may sometimes wear Nike running shoes and baseball caps, but not at the Pitchfork. Moorhouse believes being a cowboy is a sacred trust. Treating it otherwise would let down Old Goodnight, Billy, Wild Bill, Jesse and Frank, Butch and Sundance, the Wild Bunch, the whole Hole in the Wall Gang, and all the other ghosts of the West. His cowboys also wear leather chaps of various designs. One puncher even sports leather cuffs, chaps for the wrists, and a leather collar. Their jeans are all tucked into boots that come up to their knees.

Moorhouse introduces his cowboy gang to my Hollywood gang. The cowpokes are too shy to say anything. Our actors—like many in their trade—are shy, too. So it is a quiet cookshack.

We all stand instinctively in a double line on both sides of the long table. Tom, evidently believing they are all politely waiting for him, the biggest star in the world, to sit down first, takes a step forward. But as he lifts his leg over the bench to sit, there is an unmistakable sense of disapproval, MURMURS, LAUGHS.

"I'm sorry," says Bob Moorhouse. "I should've warned you. There's a custom that you cain't sit down till the dinner bell rings one last time. Going beforehand is sorta like bein' an Oklahoma Sooner, you know. But, Tom, you didn't know. Really, I'm sorry I didn't warn you."

The dinner bell CLANGS again. There is a rush as if this were Oklahoma Sooner musical chairs. The cowboys start grabbing for food. Chicken-fried steak. Gravy. Green beans. Red beans. Black beans. And most of all biscuits.

"Mr. Moorhouse—" Jamie begins.

"Call me Bob, please."

"Okay, Bob, I'm Jamie. Tell me, Bob, how many cattle do you have here on the ranch?"

"We've got about five thousand mother cows," Moorhouse says. "There's also lots of steers destined for McDonald's and the Four Seasons and Arby's. I'd have to check on—"

"How many windmills? I noticed quite a few."

"Well, ma'am, we've got a hundred and thirteen. We've even got a cowboy, his full-time job's just ridin' herd on all them windmills. Keepin' 'em turnin' and pumpin'."

"And how many cowboys do you have?"

"Usually about a dozen."

"We liked to have had one less today," says ranch foreman JAMES BURNETT.

"What happened?" asks Jamie.

"Well, this mornin', I looked over at Charlie here, and he was doin' this dance. I thought it was St. Vitus's dance. Or maybe he was on fire. Figured he musta been burnin' down—goin' right up in actual flames—to jump around like that. Turned out, what happened was, a tarantula run up his leg."

"I'd rather have a rattlesnake up my leg," says poor CHARLIE DUNBAR.

"Now that tarantula never hurt you none," says the foreman, "but you like to hurt yourself havin' a fit like that."

"Give me a rattler any day."

I'm congratulating myself: This lunch idea is working out. The actors are getting to hear how real cowboys really talk. How they interact. How they kid each other and overstate everything. A cowboy bunkhouse is like a locker room. I award myself a silent "nice going."

Then a cell phone BURPS. Everybody looks at everybody else. Sarah finally answers it.

"No, you can't talk to me now . . . I'm in the middle of . . . no!!!" She listens some more with a look of absolute horror on her face. "No! No! I can't stand it! What? What? Can you hear me? I think I've lost the connection."

She hangs up.

"What?" asks the cowboy with the wrist chaps.

"My dog Pete," Sarah whimpers. "He's been taken to the vet. I hated to leave him. Studio rules and all that. They said I couldn't bring him. He's in guarded condition."

Now the whole lunch becomes about Sarah. Never mind that Tom Bondini is the biggest star in the world. Sarah is the biggest star in this scene. And the chance for real cowboys to inform our actors is wasted. Now it's all about poor Pete. And poor Sarah in the bargain.

"I might need to fly home to be with him."

"You can't," Jamie says coldly. "Your contract and all."

"You would deny me the opportunity for a last word—"

"Yeah. Tell him your last word on the phone."

Sarah's phone BURPS again. She answers.

"Hello." Pause. "Oh really."

Sarah bursts into tears. "He's dead." Sobbing. "I have to go home for the funeral."

"Sorry," Jamie says.

"But I have to bury him."

"Put him in a deep freeze and bury him later."

Riding "home," leaning close so nobody can hear, I ask Jamie: "Why did you give Sarah such a hard time?"

"Why are you suddenly on her side?" Jamie whispers. "Did she let you squeeze her tits again?"

"No, I was just wondering."

"Okay, it's because she doesn't have a dog," Jamie whispers even more softly. "Pete's the name of her boyfriend. Pete Axelman. He's an actor, too. And I'll bet he's still alive and kicking. That was probably him on the phone. Or else she set her phone alarm."

"Oh."

The wind blows dust as thick as fog across the road.

"This is how I try to look at it," Jamie says.

"What?" I ask. "How?"

"See, actors are artists and they need to practice. I mean, if Sarah were a pianist, what would she practice on?"

"The, uh, piano," I say, still a little confused.

"Very good. And if she were an oboist, she'd practice by playing the oboe. And if she were a bassoonist, she'd practice by playing the bassoon. You do another one. I want to make sure you're keeping up."

"Okay," I say, "if she played the tuba, she'd practice by oom-pahing on a tuba."

"Excellent. But she isn't a pianist or an oboist or a bassoonist or an oompah player, is she?"

"Not as far as I know."

"No, she isn't. She's an actor. And what is an actor's instrument? Himself or herself. Sarah practices on herself. She plays herself. And what are her notes? Her emotions. She plays her emotions over and over, and if that pushes the buttons of the people around her, well, that's just too bad. As far as she's concerned, she's just practicing her scales."

"Do you like Sarah?"

"Not much. But that doesn't mean she can't act. Maybe just the reverse."

34

I AM SOUND ASLEEP–DEEP IN MY SUNDAY AFTERNOON siesta—when I'm awakened by a KNOCK at my door. Still deep among the lotuses, I ignore it. The KNOCKING gets louder. I can no longer pretend it is part of a dream. Reluctantly, very reluctantly, I get out of bed and slouch toward the door. Slouching toward I don't know what . . . Opening the door, I should have known what. Even known better.

"Hi, did I wake you?" says Sarah.

"No," I lie sleepily.

"Liar," she says. "Why can men never admit they were asleep? Is it because they're always supposed to be awake to ward off danger and protect the village and their womenfolk? Men are so atavistic."

"Real men don't even know what 'atavistic' means," I say and then yawn. "What about women? They never want to be caught napping either."

"Wrong. Real women like to whine about somebody waking them up. I almost said 'bitch about' but 'whine' is more womanly."

"Okay"—another yawn—"what's up?"

"I want to go shopping in Spur."

"That's because you've never been shopping in Spur."

"I don't want to go shopping as myself. I want to shop as Revelie. Shopping as a character is one way I build a character. Won't you help me? Surely you know all the best places."

"There aren't any best places. There aren't even any good places. I love Spur, but it's dying. Just a few skeletons left."

"I want to see it. I need to see. This is research. I can't believe you won't help me."

Mack Trucks takes us on a tour of Spur, which does not take very long. We drive slowly down Main Street. There is the Piggly Wiggly grocery store, followed by the Campbell Funeral Home (the oldest establishment in town), then Duckwall's Variety Store, then the office of the *Texas Spur* newspaper, then the hardware and video stores. Full stop, that's all. The tone of the town is somehow set by the boarded-up movie theater. The name is spelled out in long-faded letters:

"This used to be a big-deal town," I say. "A market town. A where-to-go-on-Saturday town. But then the railroad passed us by."

"Really?" Sarah asks as if she is interested.

"Well, actually," I say as if she is interested, "Spur did once have something of a broken-down train connection, but everybody called it the Wooden Railroad."

"So why'd we come here?" asks Sarah.

"Because you wanted to. You insisted. I tried to tell you."

We stop at the one traffic light in the whole town. We are the only car at the intersection.

"Why do they have this stoplight?" asks Sarah.

"To handle all the traffic jams."

"Yeah, right. Does anybody really believe they need this red light?"

"No, everybody knows you could plant your cotton crop on Main Street and not have to worry about anybody running over it."

"So why don't they get rid of the light? You know, pull the damn plug?"

"That's just it. Because it would be like pulling the plug in a hospital. It would be admitting the town's finally dead."

"Let's get out of here."

"Okay, where do you want to go?"

"Where's the nearest town where Revelie really could go shopping?"

"Lubbock."

"How far away is that?"

"Seventy miles."

"Let's go."

We take Highway 70 north eleven miles to Dickens, the county seat.

"We can't shop here?" Sarah asks.

"It's smaller and a lot sadder than Spur," I say.

We turn onto Highway 82, pointing west.

The next town is Crosbyton.

"What about here?"

"No."

Then Ralls, home of the Fighting Jackrabbits.

"No?" she asks.

"No," I say.

Lorenzo.

"No?"

"No."

As we are driving out of Lorenzo, I can already see the next town rising out of the oceanlike plain up ahead. Like the mast of a ship, the top of the water tower appears first. Then come the tall grain elevators. Finally the buildings of the town itself.

"Is this beginning to look familiar?" I ask.

"No, I mean it looks like all the others, but no," she says.

"This is Idalou."

"So?"

"You lived in Idalou. You must have gone to school here."

"What've you been smokin'? I've lived all my life in L.A."

"You said you'd lived in Idalou. You know, at the audition."

"Did I? I don't have a very good memory. But if you say so, I guess I did. You've probably never done anything to mess up your head. Yeah, right, your memory's gotta be better'n mine."

"You mean you lied?"

"I acted. There's a slim but important difference. See, one of the secrets to auditioning is pretending that you are in real life the character they want to cast. If you walk in the door playing the real thing, and convince them you're the real thing, then you have a chance. But it's all acting."

"You conned us."

"That's what acting is. If the movie were set in New York, I'd be from Brooklyn. You seem upset."

"I am."

"So fire me. Of course, you'd have to burn all the film we've already shot. Studios don't much like that, but be my guest."

"We're going back to the ranch."

"What about shopping?"

"I'm no longer in the mood."

"Fine! Fergit it! Forget all about Lubbock. But I thought that's what you wanted, an actress. And if I was good enough to fool you, maybe I'm not too bad. An audition happens from the moment you walk into the room until the moment you walk out the door. Everything is acting. The getting-to-know-you. The chitchat. All of it. Take that personally if you want to."

"Is anything real for you?"

"Acting is real! Roles are real! They're as real as the lines in your script. Is every line historically accurate?"

I turn up the radio. Too loud. I don't want to talk or think.

"Fi-i-ne!!"

Her accent is almost perfect, lingering on the "eye," making it a two-syllable diphthong, maybe even a three, as if she really were born in Idalou.

35

I SLOUCH BEHIND THE WHEEL OF AN OLD, FADED-RED pickup. Beside me sits Jamie. I owe the truck to my dad, who swears he can live without it for a few weeks. Until I bring it back, he'll just share my mom's car, an ancient, faded-red Cadillac. I love this pickup the way I love old boots.

"Nice wheels," Jamie says.

"You say the sweetest things," I say.

"Nice of your dad to lend it to you," she says.

"Yeah, he's a nice guy," I say and then startle myself by adding: "I love you."

"Would it offend your masculinity if I asked you to slow down? And I don't just mean your driving."

"You were right about Sarah," I say as I glance at the menu. "She wasn't born anywhere near Texas."

"Duh," says Jamie.

We are seated at a table opposite the counter in the Dickens Café. The stools at the counter are occupied by cowboys and farmers and one wide-frame man with a gun on his hip. I hope he is connected to law enforcement.

"What should we do about her?" I ask.

"Nothing," Jamie says. "Acting is her job and her acting fooled us. Could be a good thing. She's persuasive."

"But she's dishonest."

"The dishonest actor. Really. It's the reverse of an oxymoron. It's inevitable. Actors act. Liars lie. I don't like it, but I expect it. With actors, you're always dealing with an alternate universe."

"Oh."

The waitress, a fat girl named AMANDA, plops Diet Cokes down in front of us. None of the eat joints this side of Lubbock have a liquor license.

"Chick, what'll you have?" asks Amanda, with whom I went to high school. Then I went on to college; she didn't. "Chicken-fried steak?"

"How'd you know?" I say.

"You're easy," she says. "Her, she's harder. I'd say fried chicken, but I'm not sure."

"Do you have anything that isn't fried?" Jamie asks.

"Pie," Amanda says.

"I'll have the fried chicken."

"I knew it."

As Amanda retreats, Jamie says: "Tell me about your cousin. I mean if you don't mind."

I hesitate.

"I'm sorry. I thought it might help to talk about it. Were you close?"

"Yeah, I guess so. We grew up together in Spur. We were both part of the Goodnight cousins club. There were quite a few of us. Sharon and I got closer living together in L.A. She was okay until I came to town. Then I show up and she gets killed."

"That's crazy. You can't afford to think that way."

"I keep remembering one Saturday when I took Sharon out sailing on White River Lake. I'd borrowed a friend's Sunfish, basically a flat plank with a sail attached. And I was showing off. Pushing the tiller as far as it would go—hard alee—so the boat did tight circles. One after the other. Until she got dizzy. I was laughing at her until she fell overboard. I dove in after her because I knew she couldn't swim."

"Wasn't Sharon wearing a life jacket?" Jamie asks.

"She was, but I jumped in anyway. And I hugged her to me. And somehow she squirted out of my arms and the life jacket and sank like an anchor. I'd never felt so guilty about anything in my whole life. There I was hugging an empty life vest. Hugging it to death. I dove down, but the visibility in the lake was about six inches. I kept flailing around, and then miraculously I felt her long hair. I grabbed a strand and hauled her up to the surface screaming. She didn't like getting her hair pulled."

"You saved her, so now you feel responsible for her life."

"No, I almost got her killed. Her life slipped through my hands, my arms. I was just lucky to grab a hair."

"But you saved her."

"Not this time. Somehow she slipped through my arms again. And this time I wasn't lucky."

The tears come just as the food arrives.

"What've you got to cry about?" asks Amanda.

After our fried dinner, I am driving Jamie back to the Four Sixes when I have an inspiration. Without warning, I turn left at a sign that says DICKENS SPRINGS. Jamie doesn't protest. So far, so good. We wind down a dirt road to a circular turnaround dominated by a metal covered wagon that disguises a picnic table. I park beside it where there should be a magnificent view of the breaks country, but the moon is dark tonight. Not good.

"You used to make out here?" asks Jamie.

"Sometimes," I say, embarrassed. "The view is better when the moon cooperates."

"I'm sorry if that was your plan tonight. See, if we fuck, it could end up hurting the movie. It could alter power relationships. I'm supposed to be the one in charge, but what if I'm sleeping with you? Who knows what evil that way lies? Unquote."

"I just brought you here to enjoy the view."

"Some view."

"You don't like black? What would movies be without the occasional fade to black? Can I at least kiss you?"

"I think that would be all right."

The kiss tastes like delicious darkness itself.

36

AT SIX IN THE MORNING, MY PHONE *RINGS*.

"Hello."

"It's Trucks. I'm sorry to call you so early, but if I waited somebody might overhear. Anyhow there's a driver who remembers driving your cousin to Buddy Dale's home. He isn't sure of the time or date. But it was after dark and it wasn't too long ago."

I'm fighting mental mist. "What's his name?"

"I promised I wouldn't tell you. He's scared to talk to you."

"Unpromise!"

"No, sorry."

"Trucks, you have to tell me."

"I wish I could."

"But this is about my cousin."

"I know. I'm sorry."

"Okay, thanks."

Lying in bed, flat on my back, looking up at the ceiling, I tell myself: Everybody is afraid of Buddy Dale, and so he is going to get away with murdering my cousin Sharon. I can't let that happen.

I click into what has become my recurrent fantasy about killing Buddy Dale but this time with more detail. What weapon should I use? Perhaps a gun. This is certainly gun country. But guns are traceable. What about a knife? But then I would get his blood all over me, which might well lead to my arrest. Besides O.J. used a knife and I don't want to follow in his bloody footsteps. How about an ax? That would be appropriate. Maybe too appropriate. Besides, it would be too *Crime and Punishment.* I am looking for crime without punishment. Which leaves what? A blunt instrument? There have to be lots of bludgeons lying around the 6666. The blacksmith's hammer. A random piece of pipe. A rock, God knows there are plenty of rocks and they don't have serial numbers. But I keep coming back to the ax. I imagine the feel of the ax in my hands as I bring the blunt end down to crush his skull. It feels good. Very good. I have the sense that I sometimes have when I am writing: that what I am imagining is really happening. Yes.

Now I need an alibi. I like this game, but is it a game? Am I playing or plotting? I have to admit: I don't know. Anyway if an alibi is so important, I could hire a hit man, an assassin. But hit men for hire often turn out to be undercover cops. Then Buddy would live forever and I would go to jail for the rest of my life. Not a happy Hollywood ending. Think some more.

What about torturing Buddy to death? I imagine his agony. I see his contorted face. I enjoy the sweat and the blood.

I remember my recurrent dream. It isn't about showing up for school naked. (Oh, I've dreamed that one but not often.) It doesn't involve walking out onstage and not knowing my lines. (Dreamed that one, too.) But my real repeating dream that I dream all the time is: I have murdered somebody. I used to believe that everybody had this dream, but I have eventually realized—to my embarrassment—that I was wrong. But now I am daydreaming as well as night dreaming about turning killer. I wish I could go back to sleep and really dream, but it is time to get up and make a movie. Back to work in the dream salt mine.

But maybe, one of these windblown days, my dream will come true. I remember what somebody once told me: "Dreams come true, not free." What would be the cost of this dream?

I meet Jamie downstairs in the big living room. Seeing her, I feel some of the hate and tenseness begin to dissolve. She is wearing jeans and a cowboy shirt. She looks good.

"Good morning," she says with a smile. "Are you ready to go hang Sarah by her thumbs?"

"I'm ready." I smile back. "This could be fun."

"Ya think?"

37

I VISIT A PLACE I HAVE SO LONG TRIED TO IMAGINE: the town of Tascosa that disappeared from the face of the earth about a century ago. I love this sham shell of a town. The original was born on the bank of a river back when rivers were America's superhighways. When the new steel river—the railroad—passed it by, the town failed and died. But now it is born again—not where it originally stood, on a riverbank a hundred miles north of here—but in a field not far from the 6666 Ranch airport. Jamie and I stride down "Main Street" like a couple of gunfighters. There is Henry Kimball's blacksmith shop, yes. There is the office of W. S. Mabry, Surveyor, yes. There is the Wright & Farnsworth General Store. The North Star Restaurant. And the Jenkins & Dunn Saloon, yes, yes, yes.

"How do you like it?" asks Jamie.

"I love it," I say. "I'm in a time machine. Eat your heart out, H. G. Wells."

Jamie LAUGHS.

This isn't my first visit to this town. Over the past few weeks, I've dropped by from time to time to watch the Paramount carpenters at work building it. But this is the first time I have seen the finished Tascosa, the town where my legendary forefather met my foremother. To re-create this place, our art department used old black-and-white pictures of the town that I had collected over the years. Now here it is in living color. I'm surprised at how thrilled I feel. For some reason, I try not to show it.

"When we finish shooting the movie," I say, "maybe we can take this set back to Paramount."

"Don't count on it," Jamie warns. Raising her voice, she says: "Trucks, you can drop us right here."

We pause in front of the saloon.

"Let me buy you a drink," Jamie says.

She leads the way with me right behind. We step up on the wooden sidewalk and push through the swinging doors and come face-to-face with nothing but a black curtain behind which there is more nothing. The Paramount carpenters have only built the front of the saloon, not the tables, not the bar, not the gamblers and dance-hall girls. Of course, I had known there would be nothing inside, so

I'm not really disappointed. Besides, I can see the dance hall girls and gamblers anyway.

"What'll you have, cowboy?" asks Jamie.

"A double shot of you," I say.

"Don't talk like that. Now let's stop playing and get to fucking work."

"It's 'Git to work,'" I say, "and you split an infinitive."

"Git out of here, and split this," she says as she affectionately gives me the finger.

Emerging from the saloon, I enjoy the sight of Tascosa's Main Street once again. We are walking down the uneven wooden sidewalk toward White's Hotel when Sarah intercepts us.

"Ready to get hung up by your thumbs?" asks Jamie.

"That's what I wanted to talk to you about," Sarah says. "I want to do all my own stunts. Not just the close shots, the long shots, too."

"Okay," says the director.

"Really?"

"Sure."

Looking a little disappointed, Sarah slinks away.

"She was expecting a fight, wasn't she?" I ask.

"Of course, that's why I didn't fight with her," Jamie says. A silence descends upon us and then expands. "Besides, I'd love to hang her by her thumbs and leave her there all day."

In the movie scene—as in my family history—outlaws hang my great-great-great-ever-so-great-grandmother Revelie by her thumbs. They are torturing her to try to force her banker father to open up the bank's safe. Into this painful crisis rides Goodnight and his cowboys. And that is how my forefather meets my foremother. Of course, our Revelie has already shot several scenes with our Goodnight, but nonetheless they still haven't met yet, because we haven't filmed their meeting yet. I wonder how hard it is for the actors to shoot scenes out of sequence, to move back and forth in time, the way we have been doing, the way all movies do.

"But what if Sarah dislocates her thumbs?" I ask.

"You're on her side now?" asks Jamie. "What've you two been up to?"

"Nothing," I say too quickly.

"You're so naïve."

"No, I'm not."

"Yes, you are, but it's one of your more attractive qualities. Anyway you're naïve to think we would hang anybody up by their thumbs. Not our leading lady. Not even a stuntwoman. There's a harness that goes around the wrist so it only looks like she's being hung by her thumbs."

"Good," I say, relieved. "But a little disappointing."

"Still, being hung by your wrists is no sunny day in a Texas paradise as Sarah would soon learn if I actually let her do her own stunts."

"You're not going to let her?" I ask. "But you said—"

"Of course not. I was just playing with her mind. After all, she's always playing with everybody else's."

"But she thinks—"

"That's where you come in. You have to talk to her. Tell her you're worried about her. Say you're afraid she'll dislocate her shoulders."

"Could that really happen?" I ask.

"Absolutely. So go play her shining knight and rescue your princess from pain and suffering."

"She's not my princess."

"But you care about her?"

I feel I am being forced to choose between my two leading ladies.

"No," I say at last.

"I don't believe you. Go talk to her. Talk her out of being silly."

"No."

"As the director of this movie, I'm your commanding officer," Jamie says sternly. "And I'm ordering you."

"No."

"Do you want to be banished from the set?"

"You wouldn't do that."

"Okay, no, I wouldn't. But I'd be very disappointed in you." Jamie gives me a look of utter disappointment. "And be convincing. Because if she gets hurt bad, we could be shut down for weeks."

I KNOCK on the door of Sarah's tiny dressing room. Hers is one of three identical rooms packed into a single motor home. Our leading lady has neighbors: the cowboy named Suckerrod is to the left of her, the cook named Coffee to her right. Meanwhile, big star Tom Bondini has his own motor home all to himself, and it is even longer than this threesome. Sarah is forced to be content—or discontent—with much, much less. I know she has noticed this disparity because she has complained to me many times over. I KNOCK again. The door opens.

"Hi," Sarah says.

"I'm worried about you doing the stunts," I say.

"Yeah, sure, great. But what about the wicked witch of the Wild West?"

"She's worried, too."

"Yeah, right, she's worried about her shooting schedule, not about me."

I take too long to say: "That's not true."

"I knew it." She looks down at her boots, then lifts her eyes. "She's backing down on her promise and she sent you to tell me."

"No," I lie.

"Liar. It's just very important to me to live the role. That's how I work. I need to experience the pain and everything else."

I think it over. "What if you were supposed to get shot? What if you were supposed to get stabbed?"

She doesn't need to think at all. "I haven't decided yet. Never had to. I'll bear that cross when I get to it. Or not. Okay?"

"You're crazy."

"For me it always has to be real. You can tell the wicked witch of the Wild West that I'm doing my own stunts. She said I could and I'm holding her to it."

"She didn't mean it. She just didn't want to fight with you."

"Well, I do mean it!"

She slams the door in my face.

I find Jamie pacing back and forth in front of White's Hotel. As I approach, she looks up and then frowns.

"She whipped your ass, right?" Jamie asks.

"Sort of," I say.

"Sort of? Admit it. She whipped your rear end. She paddled you."

"Okay, right, she still wants to do her stunts."

"We'll see about that. It's one thing to whip a candy-ass writer. It's another thing to go up against Chris. He's anything but a candy-ass. She'll listen to him." Jamie turns and looks around. "Sally Benn, come talk to me."

SALLY BENNET, a lowly assistant director, an AD, with a walkie-talkie strapped to her belt like a gunfighter's six-gun, comes running.

"What can I do for you?" she asks.

"Find Chris Crosby," Jamie says. "You know who he is?"

"Of course," Sally says with feeling.

"Round him up. I've got a job for him."

Sally hurries away on her errand. Since I would rather avoid another chance to shake hands with Chris, I retreat across Main Street and sit on a hitching rail in front of the surveyor's office.

Ducking my head so my cowboy hat hides part of my face, I watch as Sally Benn, acting like an AD in heat, or so it seems to me, escorts Chris Crosby down Main Street. He is good-looking if a girl is shallow enough to like a straight nose, squinty blue eyes, broad shoulders, and hard muscles.

Jamie gives him a dazzling smile. I loathe him. They talk for a few minutes. Then Chris goes off, presumably to bend Sarah's iron will, a bending at which I had failed. He will probably tie her will in knots like a lasso.

A little ashamed of myself, I follow some fifty yards behind him to see how he goes about succeeding where I got knocked on my candy-ass. Reaching the movie's impromptu parking lot, I detour into Jamie's motor home and peek out through one of her windows: I have a clear view of Sarah's one third of a trailer.

Feeling part spy and part Peeping Tom, I watch Chris knock on her door. It opens. She smiles at him. He says something. She frowns and starts YELLING. He tries again. She slams the door in his face. I like her better. I tell myself I'm not the only candy-ass on this movie.

The next three hours are spent lighting, measuring, tweaking, and who the hell knows what else. Moviemaking is the slowest business on earth except for the manufacture of fossils. Shortly before noon, we are finally almost ready. I edge up closer to my director.

"Go get the stuntwoman," Jamie tells Sally Benn, AD, who hurries away.

Sally returns shortly with stuntwoman STACY REEVES in tow, closely followed by our leading lady. I see Chris Crosby lurking in the background.

"Sarah, you can't do your own stunts," Jamie says sternly.

"Then I'm not doing this scene at all," says an angry version of my foremother. "I mean it. Let Stacy do my lines."

"Nice try, but no."

"Okay, I'm done."

To underline her point, Sarah starts taking off her costume right there in the middle of Main Street. It seems to take her forever to undo all the buttons down the front of her Victorian dress. At last, it falls around her ankles and she steps out of it. Then Sarah reaches behind her back and begins untying and unlacing her corset. Dropping its whiteness in the red dirt, she attacks the layers of nineteenth-century underclothing beneath. She takes off old-fashioned articles of clothing—things I don't even know the names for—until she is naked except for her high-top, button-up boots. Then she stalks off down the street toward her cubbyhole of a dressing room.

"That girl knows how to make an exit," Jamie says. "Of course with most women, when they say no, they keep their clothes on instead of taking them off." She turns to the stuntwoman: "Stacy, you're up."

"What if she means it?" I ask, still watching Sarah's bare-ass retreat down Main Street. "What if she doesn't come back?"

"She'll come back."

"But what if she won't? Will you fire her?"

"These days, you want to fire everybody, don't you? But no, I can't. We've already shot too much film. Spent too much money. We can't afford to start over now."

"That's what I thought."

"That's what you thought, and that's what she's thinking. But I hope she also remembers that I could make sure she never gets another job." Jamie flashes a brilliant smile. "Not that I'd ever do anything like that." She savors the idea. "Give her an hour to stew and then go talk to her again."

"You want me to do it because I did such a good job the first time?"

"Right."

"No."

"Yes. You'd better tell her that she can do some of her own stunts, just not all. She can't do the long shots, but she can do the medium stuff, which is what I wanted all along anyway. But make it sound like you finally convinced me. Wrestled me into submission. Tell your girlfriend she's won and you'll be her hero. She'll be in your bed tonight if not sooner."

"She's not the one I want in my bed."

"Don't talk nonsense. Go seduce our leading lady into returning to her movie. Okay?"

"You sure you don't want Chris to do it?"

"If you fail, I'll send Chris to beat her into submission."

"Very funny."

"Not really."

38

GOODNIGHT AND HIS COWBOYS RIDE INTO TASCOSA to discover Sarah hanging by her thumbs, her feet some six feet off the ground. She dangles, like a caught fish, from a fence post sticking out of one of White's Hotel's second-floor windows. We have already shot the long views of the scene starring stuntwoman Stacy. Now we are ready to come in closer, medium close.

Sarah is hanging there, but Jamie does not seem to be in a hurry. There are last-minute fiddles with the lighting. There are more rehearsals for camera. You can't hurry art.

"What the fuck are you waiting for!" YELLS the suspended Sarah.

"You asked for it," Jamie says a little too smugly.

"My shoulders are killing me."

"We can always use Stacy."

"Go to hell!"

"Well put." Jamie turns to the first assistant director, Kim Kurumada, and mentions: "I think she's a little too low in the frame. Raise her six inches."

"Lower the camera!" SCREAMS Sarah. "That's faster."

"That would destroy the composition of the shot," says Jamie.

"We really appreciate your hanging in there." Another dazzling smile.

Five minutes later, Jamie whispers, "Action," and Tom-as-Goodnight lurches into the frame, pretending to be drunk, acting as if he has no idea what is happening.

"Wasss goin' on?" Tom/Goodnight slurs.

Our big star hiccups as a tall, good-looking outlaw steps forward.

"Just havin' a little fun," says an actor named JOE PLATE, who is playing the dashing badman Jack Gudanuf. "Who wants to know?"

Tom sways in his saddle, loses his balance, and falls to the ground at the feet of the outlaw leader. Then he starts drunkenly climbing up Gudanuf's leg as if it were a tree.

"No," Joe Plate protests, "stoppit."

I look up at Sarah, whose face says stoppit, too. Which is how her face is supposed to look in the scene. But is she acting or is she suffering? Or both? Does she want to kill me? Or is she luxuriating, orgasming in the pain?

Stumbling to his feet, Goodnight bear-hugs the outlaw as if hanging on to keep from falling down.

"Git off me," Joe/Gudanuf orders.

Tom/Goodnight tightens his grip with his left hand but stops hugging with his right hand, which draws his pistol. Still moving drunkenly, staggering, almost knocking the outlaw over, Tom jabs the muzzle of his gun under Joe's chin. Joe grunts as if it really hurts, which it probably does.

"Drop your gun!" Tom orders in a sober voice. "Drop it or I'll shoot your head off. Right now!"

Tom presses the gun even harder.

"Ouch!" says Joe, a line not in the script.

"Drop it!" Tom says again. "And tell your men to drop their guns, too."

Joe opens his hand and lets his pistol fall to the ground. Then one of his men drops his gun. Then another and another. Tom stops hugging the chief of the outlaws and steps back.

"Yeooowwwooww!!!"

That scream isn't in the script either, but perhaps it should have been. A woman hanging by her thumbs would scream, wouldn't she?

As soon as the outlaw guns hit the ground, the townspeople pour onto Main Street, most of them carrying weapons. There are buffalo guns and carbines and brooms and clubs and even a couple of muskets. An old man with white hair actually carries a sword. I can't help noticing an especially beautiful extra wielding a pair of scissors and "acting her ass off." She is so lovely that she looks out of place here on the western frontier. I am puzzled for a moment but then realize: She must be one of Buddy Dale's girls. So unfortunately he must be back.

"Cut," Jamie says softly. Then she raises her voice: "Very good, everybody. Let's do it again. Back to number-one positions."

"Get me down!" SCREAMS Sarah.

"But we're going to shoot another take," the director says pleasantly.

"Get me down! Get me down right now! My shoulders are dislocating. Hurry!"

"Okay"—dazzling smile—"somebody find Stacy."

"You're in a good mood," I say.

"Yes, I am," Jamie says. "You will be, too, later on tonight."

"That sounds promising," I say, imagining the best.

"I've got something to show you."

"Good. Very good."

Then Stacy—whose hair is dyed the same shade of brunette as Sarah's—appears with Chris in tow in his capacity as stunt coordinator. Thanks to me. But I can't stand him being there. Being among us. Like a disease.

"Chris," I say. "This is the perfect scene for you, right?"

"What're you talkin' about?" he asks.

"I mean you like hurting little girls"—there goes that pesky volcano again—"don't you?"

"No, I like hurting guys who think they are big men."

Chris sucker punches me on the point of my chin. I land on my candy-ass.

39

AFTER DAILIES IN THE BARN, JAMIE LEADS ME, STILL rubbing my jaw, back to the rock castle. With every step, I am growing more excited. But we don't climb the stairs as I have been hoping, imagining. I follow her down the hall to a door I have often passed but never opened.

"It's in here," Jamie says.

She opens the door and leads me inside. I SEE (POV) tall shelves lined with film cans. Trolleys with reels of film. Bins filled with writhing celluloid snakes. The individual frames look like the diamonds on a diamondback rattler. And there are all sorts of strange machines.

"Where am I?" I ask.

"The cutting room," Jamie says. "It used to be the formal dining room, but they agreed to let us take it over for a while."

That is when I notice the chandelier made of cow horns. I also recognize DAVE RALSTON, our film editor, sitting at a table, cutting film with a contraption that looks like a miniature guillotine. His thumb depresses the blade, chop.

"Be with you in a minute," Dave says.

"I'm an old-fashioned director," Jamie says. "He's an old-fashioned cutter."

"How so?" I ask.

"He likes to actually get his hands on the film," Jamie says. "Feel it between his fingers. Cut it with a real blade and hear the little film strips scream."

"Today most everybody else uses an Avid," Dave says. "You know, computer editing. But I don't do that. Either because I like the old ways better or because I don't know how to use an Avid. It's one or the other. I don't know which. So I just stick to my old flatbed."

Studying the flatbed, I SEE (POV) three reels of film lying flat like records on turntables. In the middle of the table is what looks like a television screen. And on the other side are three flat take-up reels. The contraption resembles a six-burner stove.

"It looks pretty high-tech to me," I say.

"Then you haven't been keeping up." Dave is dressed all in black topped with a black cowboy hat. His hair is long, black, and stringy. "This is Stone Age moviemaking. Welcome to my cave."

"You've got something to show Chick, right?" Jamie prompts. "I mean as a favor."

"Yeah, sure."

"See, there are all kinds of union rules. Dave doesn't have to show a lowly writer anything if he doesn't want to. But he's going to because he's a nice guy."

"I'm only a nice guy if he likes it," Dave says.

"He'll like it. I did. And we're in sync."

"I'm a little confused," I say. "What is it that I'm going to like?"

"Dave's cut together a scene," Jamie says. "I thought you might like to take a look at it. See your first assembled footage. Find out what the movie's really going to look like in about a hundred years."

"Great," I say. I try not to sound too thrilled, but thrilled I am. "Thanks."

"Step right up," says the cutter in the black cowboy hat, "and sit right down."

Jamie and I pull up red-plush dining room chairs and sit on either side of Dave as he does some last-minute fiddling.

"Why three reels?" I ask.

"This one's picture," Dave says. "That one's dialogue. And the third one's music. I just stuck in some music I had handy. The real stuff comes later, so don't panic."

"Okay."

"You know, that's where George Lucas got the name R2D2. He was in the cutting room, and somebody asked for R2D2—you know, reel two, dialogue two—and he liked the sound of it. Anyway, here goes."

As Dave reaches for a switch, I HEAR a KNOCK at the door of the dining room. His hand freezes on the controls. (As if the governor is on the other side of the door and has come at midnight to stop the execution.) We all look at each other with expressions that ask: Who the hell could that be? I naturally suspect that Buddy has come to cause trouble. The KNOCK, KNOCKING repeats, louder this time.

"Chick, would you mind seeing who it is?" Jamie asks.

I get up stiffly and make my way to the door. Suspecting Buddy, I am reluctant to open it. I had been in such a good mood and now . . .

KNOCK, KNOCK, KNOCK.

I open the door and SEE (POV) Sarah smiling at me.

"I heard you were looking at assembled footage," Sarah says. "Can I watch, too?"

"Who'd you hear that from?" Jamie asks sternly.

"Not me," Dave says unconvincingly.

"Well?" asks Sarah.

"I'm sorry," Jamie says, getting up and approaching the door. "It's not fair to Dave—"

"Dave doesn't mind," our leading lady says confidently.

"Really, I didn't tell her," says the cutter.

"Then it's not fair to your fellow actors," Jamie says, taking up a position beside me in the doorway, as if to block it. "If I show cut film to you, I'd have to show it to everybody. And everybody would have an opinion. We'd end up with a movie edited by committee. No, I'm sorry."

"I'll bet you'd show it to Tom," Sarah says, her eyes narrowing. "Maybe you already have."

"No, I haven't. And Tom hasn't asked. He wouldn't. He knows what's proper and what isn't. He would never ask for special favors."

"I just wanna see the damn scene!" Sarah explodes.

"Unless you leave right now, nobody is going to see it. We'll all just go to bed. Chick, I'll show you the footage later."

"Fuck you!" Sarah says and slams the door in our faces.

"Always a pleasure," Jamie says to the still-quivering door. "Now where were we?"

Dave shows me the scene and it is thrilling. Seen from Goodnight's POV, the ambulance bearing Revelie, her father, and her mother snakes down the steep wall of the red canyon as guitars gently strum. CLOSE-UP of Tom looking anxious. Back to POV. Reaching the canyon floor, the ambulance comes to a stop. WIDE SHOT as Goodnight rushes forward to meet his unexpected guests. As Revelie's mother emerges from this vehicle, a bass fiddle goes THUMP THUMP THUMP, which reminds me of an understated reprise of the shark theme in *Jaws*.

CLOSER ON MRS. SANBORN, who asks: "Where's your ranch, Mr. Goodnight?"

CUT TO GOODNIGHT CLOSE-UP, who says: "You're lookin' at it, ma'am."

The scene unfolds like a dream. Literally a dream. I have so often imagined this scene that I have also dreamed it. The cuts from take to take remind me of the fast cutting in dreams. My dreams. My dreams of this moment, which are history and myth and I hope someday movie myth. Mrs. Sanborn enters Goodnight's dugout, where the lighting is almost opaque.

"The Prince of Darkness could have shot this," Dave says.

"Who?" I ask. "What?"

"You know, Gordon Willis. The cinematographer. He thinks dark equates with serious."

"Sometimes it does," says Jamie.

Revelie's mother emerges from the underworld and tells Goodnight that he and his cowboys live like prairie dogs. I have heard the line hundreds of times—what with auditions and rehearsals—but I still LAUGH.

40

I AM TAKING OFF MY PANTS TO GO TO BED WHEN I change my mind. I decide to pay a visit to a girl down in tent town. I get out my contact sheet with numbers and addresses for everybody, cast and crew. Moving my hand down the list, I finally find a Reeves, Stacy: She currently resides in tent number 106. God, I didn't realize we had that many. Our payroll must be impressive. No wonder making movies is an expensive hobby.

I head out.

Soon I am moving through the mowed wheat field looking at numbers stenciled on tents. Number 106 turns out to be in the last row at the back of the field. My hands tremble faster as I try to decide how to knock on the front door of a tent. Why don't they have doorbells? Eventually I decide to SCRATCH.

"Come in," Stacy calls.

Pushing aside the tent flap, I enter a surprisingly spacious and even luxurious bedroom. The bed, on which Stacy is sitting, is a real bed, not a cot. There is a night table, a chest of drawers, a desk, a sofa, even a television set.

"Oh, it's you," Stacy says with a gulp.

She looks like a version of Sarah—which is how she got the job—but prettier. Really much prettier. I remember one of Sarah's many on-set rants: There oughta be a Screen Actors Guild rule, the stunt double can't be prettier than the leading lady! Stacy is wearing jeans and a tank top.

"Yeah, it is," I say brilliantly. "I'm sorry to disturb you at this hour, but I was hoping you could help me out with something."

"Okay," she says, looking and sounding apprehensive, as if she is auditioning for a part in *The Rape of the Sabine Women.*

"I wanted to talk to you here because it's kind of private," I try to explain.

"Okay." Now Stacy looks like she is trying out for the lead in *The Rape of the Sabine Women.*

"Private because it concerns Chris. I was wondering if he ever mentioned somebody named Sharon Loving."

"Oh, yeah, he was crazy about her," Stacy says, relaxing a quarter of an inch. "That was so sad. He was really broken up. Why do you ask?"

"Uh, well, she was my cousin."

"I'm so sorry. I really am."

"Thank you. Did he ever say anything about any trouble in their relationship?"

"No. Why are you asking?"

"Well, he used to beat her up. Really. So I was just wondering."

"He always said that was because he loved her. 'You always hurt the one you love' sort of thing. If he hadn't loved her so much, he wouldn't have hurt her so bad."

Oh, my God! I shiver but decide now is not the time to debate how to treat the woman you love. Now I'm after information. "You wouldn't happen to know where he was on the night she died?" I ask.

"Sure," she says defiantly, "in me."

"Was he in you all night?" I ask, embarrassed.

"Let me see." She thinks. "Well, no, I don't think it was all night."

"When did he leave?"

"I think it must've been around ten. He was pissed."

"Pissed drunk, or pissed mad?"

"Pissed mad."

"What was he pissed about?"

Stacy looks around the interior of the tent as if she is thinking of doing a little remodeling. She takes her time. Maybe a different color canvas would help.

"Well, if you must know," she says at last, "he was pissed at your cousin because she was seeing Buddy that night. You know, for an 'audition.'" She makes quote marks with her fingers.

"Really?" I say, making an effort to keep my voice flat. "Are you sure the audition was at night, not in the afternoon?"

"Yeah, I'm sure. She'd seen Buddy in the afternoon. The night thing was supposed to be a 'callback.' Yeah, of course. Anyway, Chris figured it was more than an audition. I guess he was jealous."

I spend some time mentally redecorating the tent. The bed is too narrow.

"But now Chris and Buddy are thick as bandits," I say at last. "You'd think, if he was jealous, Chris might not like Buddy very much."

"Oh, that's just Chris being Chris," Stacy explains. "He always sucks up to power—or tries to—on every show he's ever been on."

"Oh," I say definitively. "Can you remember anything else about that night that might be helpful?"

"Yeah, maybe. Chris said he had to leave that night because he was supposed to meet Big C at the Polo Lounge, and he was already late."

"Who's Big C?" I ask.

"Oh, that's right, you above-the-line folks don't condescend to know us below-the-line types. Big C is part of Chris's regular stunt crew. He's in tent one-fifteen. Back here in the stunt ghetto."

After leaving Stacy's tent, I have an argument with myself: Have I done enough for one night, or should I seek out the provocatively named Big C? My boots seem to make the decision for me—110, 111, 112, 113, 114. I stop in front of 115 and am about to scratch with a trembling hand when I hear something unmistakable. Unnnhh, unnnhh, unnnhh, unnnhh. Inside the tent, somebody is either chopping wood, lifting weights, or making love. Deciding this interview can wait, I demurely turn away and head back toward the castle.

But I can't sleep. Eventually I decide to make another trip to tent town. Maybe Big C's guest will be gone by now. I get dressed and head for our below-the-line ghetto, where all the people drawing union-scale wages live. I know the way now, so this trip goes faster. Reaching tent 115, I SCRATCH on the flap.

"Git on in here," says a voice from within.

Hesitantly, I pull back the tent flap and look inside. I SEE (POV) a big, sandy-haired, good-looking man in his twenties seated on a narrow bed. I don't see a woman. Good, he didn't ask her to sleep over.

"Come on, if'n you're comin'."

I duck and enter.

"Hi, I'm Chick Goodnight—"

"I know," he interrupts. "I'm Big C, and don't ask me how I got that there nickname."

He stands up and sticks out his hand. I shake it. He doesn't try to prove how strong he is at my expense.

"Sorry to come by so late," I apologize.

"Oh, thass okay," he says. "Don't need much sleep. What can I do for you, Writer Man?"

"Well, as you may know, my cousin Sharon Loving was killed recently in Los Angeles."

"Sure, and I'm sure sorry."

"Thank you. Anyway, I've been trying to reconstruct her last day."

My voice catches on *last*. "Where she went. What she did. But also where her friends and enemies were. And what they did."

"Yeah, okay."

"Which brings me to Chris Crosby. The two of them were dating, Chris and Sharon."

"Yeah, I know."

"So I've been wondering if she might've been with Chris that night." I pause and moisten my lips. "But somebody just told me that Chris was with you, so I guess he couldn't've been with my cousin."

Big C rocks on his boots for a moment. "Well, thass a funny thing," he says at last. "It truly is."

"Funny how?"

"Well, I was s'posed to meet him at some bar, but he never turned up. I was kinda peed off at the time. But the next mornin' I heard about Sharon, and I knew how much he musta been hurtin', so I decided to fergit all about him standin' me up."

"Didn't you ever ask him why—?"

"No," he interrupts. "Why pile on to his burdens?"

41

THE NEXT MORNING, WE RETURN ONCE MORE TO TAS-cosa. We are scheduled to shoot coverage of the scene where my great-great-great-ever-so-great-grandmother, who has been hanging by her thumbs, is finally cut down. I can't believe this is our second day on the scene, and this is as far as we have gotten, but that's moviemaking. Only fossils are manufactured more slowly. Fossils and sedimentary rock. As Jamie paces, we are off to our usual slow start this morning.

"How's Sarah?" Jamie asks.

"I don't know," I say.

"Good."

Then my cowboy radar senses approaching danger, so I look to my left. Nothing scary there. But when I look to my right, I find Chris Crosby bearing down on me. As he comes nearer and nearer, I expect him to stop or at least slow down. But he doesn't. He seems to be planning to walk right through me. He bumps me and I retreat two steps.

"I hear you've been asking questions 'bout me?" he sputters.

"Sure," I say. "I wanted to know where you were the night my cousin got killed. Since you used to like beating her up"—my kettledrum heart is pounding again—"I thought you might like murdering her, too. Especially if you suspected her of getting it on with Buddy."

"Yeah, I figured she was fuckin' him. That's why I went off by myself that night and got shit-faced. Didn't see her then or ever ag'in, I'm sorry to say."

"So how come you're so thick with Buddy? He poached your girl, didn't he?"

"That's just business." Chris comes and stands a half inch from me. "Now you stay out of my business. You give me any more trouble, I'll make you wish *you* had a stunt double."

Involuntarily I take another step backward. Which encourages him to move forward. With his right hand pressed to my chest, he pushes me back some five or six feet. I stumble but catch myself before I fall. He gives me a look of contempt, turns his back, and stalks away.

"You know, you really have a gift for working and playing well with others," Jamie says. "How do you do it?"

Fortunately, Sally Benn, the AD, approaches with a troubled look on her face. I'm sorry she has a problem, but I'm glad for the change of subject.

"What's wrong now?" Jamie asks.

"We can't find Miss Texas," says Sally.

"Who?"

"You know, that girl who was Miss Texas a couple of years ago. Debbie Whitt."

"Oh, you mean Buddy Dale's one-night squeeze."

"Yeah, her. She didn't get on the bus this morning. We've been calling her room, but there's no answer. And she's been established over and over in this scene. What should we do? Look for a substitute?"

"Nobody's going to look like her." Jamie thinks for a long minute. "Call Buddy Dale."

"Buddy Dale?" There is fear in the AD's eyes.

"Yeah, Buddy Dale. Maybe she's curled up nice and warm right next to him. Or maybe they're making the 'beast with two backs.'" Jamie turns to me: "See, I went to school, too." She turns back to the AD: "Tell him to get her ass to the set ASAP, I mean AssAP."

"Really?"

"Really!"

"Okay."

Assistant Director Sally Benn races away.

"Do we really need her?" I ask. "I mean she always looked—to me anyway—out of place in the scene."

"Yeah, sure, but she's already established in the scene. Now, as we do coverage—you really should've gone to film school, you know—anyway, if there are people in yesterday's takes who aren't in today's takes, then we can't cut yesterday's work together with today's work."

I look puzzled.

"It's like, say, a character is wearing a tie in one take, then you cut to another take and he isn't wearing a tie anymore. It's all the same scene. Where did the tie go?"

"Oh."

"Only in this case the tie is Miss Texas. Now you see her. Now you don't. Where did she go? It's the same scene, should be the same characters. Not good. A careful filmmaker doesn't let that happen."

"Oh." I feel dumb. I should get used to the feeling, just accept it.

"Damn Buddy," she says.

"Amen."

Jamie is still pacing. Sally Benn returns looking like a death in the family.

"What did he say?" asks the director.

"He, uh, has a 'do not disturb' on his phone."

"Tell them it's an emergency."

"I did. They still wouldn't ring his phone."

"Call his cell phone."

"I did. It's turned off."

"I'm going over there," Jamie announces angrily.

"I'm going with you," I say.

"No."

Jamie and I climb the front porch steps. We burst through the big front door into the vast living room that now sports fighting deer heads. I have to hurry to keep up with Jamie as she takes the stairs two at a time. Then we race down the hall to Buddy Dale's door. Jamie starts POUNDING on it. BANG BANG BANG BANG BANG. She pauses. I take over the BANGING. I BANG even harder than she did. I stop. She starts again. BANG BANG BANG BANG.

Jamie tries the door. It is unlocked.

"We're coming in," she announces loudly.

She opens the door slowly. It is a slow REVEAL. We SEE (POV) an empty room.

"Buddy!" Jamie calls.

Nothing.

"Buddy!"

No one.

We enter the room, look around. The bed is a mess. Jamie walks over and opens the closet. Empty. I open drawers. Nothing. We bump into each other trying to get into the bathroom. No toothpaste. No deodorant. No shampoo or comb or razor. Not even any Polaroids.

"He was supposed to be here all week," Jamie says.

"I wonder what happened to change his plans," I say.

"Yeah," she says. "Let's go check on Miss Texas."

I KNOCK. No response. Jamie KNOCKS. Nothing. Then she tries the door. It is locked.

"I'll go get a key," I volunteer.

"No, bust it open," Jamie says.

"But I know these people. We can't break up their home."

"You bust it or I will, which'll take longer."

Taking a deep breath, I hurl myself against the locked door. It gives about an eighth of an inch. Busting down doors is evidently harder in real life than in the movies. I smash into the door again. It moves another eighth of an inch.

"Should I call in the grips?" Jamie asks.

I throw my everything at the door. It moves yet another eighth of an inch.

"I'm calling the grips. Or maybe Chris. How about him?"

I hit the door as if I am a lineman on one of my father's football teams. The door CRASHES open. We burst in like a SWAT team. MISS TEXAS lies in her bed, flat on her back, with the covers pulled up to her pretty nose, which seems strange in midsummer.

"Good morning!" Jamie says in a loud voice.

Miss Texas does not stir.

"Time to wake up!" Jamie SHOUTS.

Miss Texas ignores the order.

I begin edging closer to the bed. I feel Jamie right behind me. I bend down and gently shake Miss Texas's shoulder. She is a beauty all right, especially slightly disheveled, with raven-black hair and Snow White skin. Her lipstick is mussed but not removed, which seems strange. She still wears her mascara and she still won't wake up.

"Is she?" Jamie asks.

"She's still warm," I say. "I was afraid she'd be cold."

"Shake her harder."

I shake her like a dog with a rag doll. She doesn't wake up.

"Check her pulse," Jamie says.

"I'm not sure I know how," I protest.

"Do like on TV. Feel her neck."

I gently press my fingers into the neck of Miss Texas, where I think an artery might be. She doesn't complain. At the same time, I press my own neck, to make sure I am looking for a pulse in the right place. I feel my own blood pumping—but not hers.

"I don't feel anything," I say, "but I'm probably doing it wrong. Do you want to try?"

"Put your hand on her heart," Jamie says. "See if you can feel a beat."

I start pulling back the covers—which are still warm—but I stop when I realize Miss Texas isn't wearing any nightclothes.

"Don't be shy," Jamie says.

Feeling as if I am violating a beautiful woman—which might be okay in fantasy but isn't in life—I pull the covers down to her waist. Her dark-nippled breasts are beautiful and probably real. I'm a Peeping Tom. Taking a deep breath, I place my hand on the left breast of Miss Texas. Not full center. Off to the side. Now I'm afraid she will suddenly wake up and scream. She doesn't and I don't feel a beating heart.

Looking up, feeling queasy, I shake my head. Jamie is already dialing her cell phone.

"Buddy did it," I say.

"Maybe it was Chris," she says.

"Why would he?"

"I'm kidding."

"Not funny."

"Sorry."

"Buddy did it," I repeat.

"Shut up!" says Jamie. "You're getting boring."

We are seated on a couch in the great living room—now our jail—waiting to be interviewed by deputy sheriffs. Filming has been shut down for the day, which will make the studio grieve.

"But he did."

"You don't take direction very well, do you? This character flaw is going to hurt your acting career."

"Do you mean I'll never play Hamlet?"

"There's the rub," she says, digging her elbow into my ribs.

"Ouch. Don't rub so hard." I take a deep breath. "Buddy did it, and that means he killed my cousin, too."

"So now you're ready to kiss and make up with Chris Crosby, our much maligned stunt coordinator?"

"No."

"Why not?"

"Well, because I'm not sure, I guess."

"On second thought, you could play Hamlet. Maybe this. Maybe that. Maybe he did it. Maybe he didn't. Maybe, maybe, maybe. Hamlet, the Prince of Perhaps. Be a perfect role for you."

"Thanks."

"You're welcome. Now shut up and leave me alone. Let me think."

I silently watch her thinking. I like what I see. I like her intensity. I like her intelligence. I even like her ordering me around, which puzzles me. I am even more puzzled when she produces a notebook out of nowhere and starts writing in it.

"What's that?" I ask.

"You know, it's my list," Jamie says. "Don't ask. Just leave me alone."

I watch her scribbling. She turns the back of the notebook to me.

"Are you making a list of suspects?" I ask.

She ignores me.

"Is Buddy Dale's name on it?"

"His and Chris Crosby's and yours," she says.

42

A DEPUTY SHERIFF ENTERS THE BIG ROOM WITH THE big fireplace. It takes me a moment to recognize JIMMY LEE JOHNSON with whom I went to Spur High School. He played center on the football team. I played right end because I was tall. I could even catch a little.

"Go long," says Jimmy Lee.

"What's he talking about?" asks Jamie.

"It's a 'Y' chromosome thing," I say. "We played high school football together."

I introduce my director to my friend the Texas lawman. He was wide in high school, and he is double-wide now.

"Chick, I'm supposed to talk to you," Jimmy Lee says.

"Sure," I say.

"I need some fresh air. Let's go out on the porch, okay?"

I follow the deputy out onto the vast 6666 veranda. We sit down side by side on the steps. The wind is blowing.

"What do you know?" asks the long-ago center.

I can't help mentally criticizing his interview technique since, as a former reporter, I have conducted so many. I wonder why he isn't leading me chronologically through what I know. Beginning at the beginning.

"I'm not sure if you know that my cousin Sharon was killed recently in L.A."

"Of course," Jimmy Lee says. "I was so sorry to hear what happened to her. Condolences, really, heartfelt. Hit-and-run drivers should get the needle."

Deciding to let the hit-and-run comment go for the moment, I HEAR BARKING and look up. A big dog chases a small cottontail rabbit across the front lawn. They disappear around the corner of the castle.

"And now we have another suspicious death," I say.

"Not all that suspicious," says Jimmy Lee, "not accordin' to what I hear. Looks like just another drug overdose."

"Maybe," says the Prince of Perhaps. "Maybe not."

"Keep talkin'," says the deputy.

"Well, two young women are dead. Both connected to this movie."

"Whoa there. Was your cousin workin' on the movie, too?"

"She auditioned for a part the day she was killed."

"Good for her. How'd that go?"

"I don't know. She died before I could talk to her about it. But the interesting thing is, Sharon auditioned for Buddy Dale. And today's dead girl, well, she was sleeping with Buddy Dale. Coincidence or pattern?"

"I got no earthly idea," says Jimmy Lee. "We got ourselves a hit-and-run in L.A. And we got ourselves a drug overdose in West Texas. And you seriously think the two gotta be connected?"

"I think it's worth looking into."

I decide not to overload my old teammate's mental agility with my suspicions about our stunt coordinator Chris Crosby. Girl beater and Ted Bundy wannabe. Such knowledge would only confuse him. I know because it confuses me.

"Jeez, I dunno," says my friend the lawman.

"I could be wrong," I say, "but I think we owe it to Sharon and Miss Texas to try to find out what really happened."

"Miss Texas?" asks Jimmy Lee. "You mean that there dead girl was Miss Texas?"

"She was last year, or maybe the year before that."

"You mean I touched Miss Texas?" Jimmy Lee stares at his hand. "I even saw her naked."

"I know you're really busy right now, but could I come by and talk to you later?"

The deputy shrugs. "Sure."

"Or how about dinner tonight?"

I meet Jimmy Lee at the Dickens Café at eight o'clock. By this time, the dinner crowd has mostly cleared out. This is hardworking, early-eating country. We sit at a table beside the picture window that gives us a great view of a burned-out gas station. The waitress Amanda takes our orders. Jimmy Lee, the double-wide deputy, wants two chicken-fried steaks. I make do with one.

"Did you make much progress today?" I ask.

"Well, I didn't catch a murderer," Jimmy Lee says, "but I still ain't too sure it's murder. The tox report ain't come back yet—gotta send to Lubbock for that sorta thing—but I'm still bettin' on an accidental overdose. We found a few loose grains of cocaine on her night table. Murder sure seems like a long shot."

"I didn't say Buddy murdered her," I protest. "I said he killed her. Homicide."

"I know you're a writer and all and like to make them vocabulary differntzes, but that don't mean a whole helluva lot to me."

"I just mean I don't think he shot her or stabbed her. When he gave her the coke, he didn't intend to kill her. But when he handed her that stuff, which she probably wasn't used to, it was like giving a loaded gun to somebody who doesn't know how to use one. And encouraging her to point it at her head."

"How do you know she waddn't used to it? You think that just because she was purdy. Lots of purdy girls got ugly habits."

"I know, but beginners are much more likely to overdose than hard-core users. The veterans have built up a tolerance."

Jimmy Lee thinks for a long time. He is still silently pondering when the food arrives. His steaks are stacked one on top of the other. I expect him to separate them, but he doesn't. He cuts into them as if they were a stack of pancakes and takes a bite.

"Mebbe," he says with his mouth full.

"Yeah, right," I say. "Now, did you manage to find out when Buddy bugged out?"

"Yeah, we did." He stops to take in another double-decker mouthful. "But I dunno if I should be tellin' you inside stuff. It don't seem right somehow."

"Jimmy Lee," I say, "we used to be teammates." I pause and glance down at my trembling hands. "Maybe we could be again."

"Whaddaya mean?" he asks, still chewing.

"I mean I'm asking you to work with me on this. I'll tell you what I find out, and you tell me what you find out."

"I dunno. That might be a problem."

"Why? What's the matter? Have you got something against me all of a sudden?"

"Not all of a sudden."

"What's that supposed to mean?"

"I mean it goes back a while. I guess you oughta know I thought you was standoffish in high school. What they call aloof. Superior kind of thing."

"I was just shy," I say, becoming aware of my trembling hands. "It's a family tradition. I had a great-grandmother who used to run out and hide in the fields whenever company came. I'm a long way from figuring out what that's all about. But I'm sorry."

"Hmmm. Your great-grandma, huh?"

"Please. This means a lot to me. Do it for old times' sake. Do it for my cousin."

Jimmy Lee chews. As he is swallowing, he is already cutting another massive bite. He chews it, too. I wonder if his mind is working as well as his jaws. Is he considering helping me, or is he just eating? Maybe eating takes his full concentration.

"Okay, your man left the ranch around six in the mornin'," Jimmy Lee says at last. "One of your drivers done drove him to Lubbock, where he caught the first flight out. Eight in the mornin'. He must've had some nooner in L.A. to get up that early."

"Yeah," I say, mulling. "You know, he was scheduled to stay all week. I wonder what happened to change his plans."

"You don't wonder. You think you know, don't you, Mr. College Man? But I'm afraid I've got some bad news for you. You ain't quite as smart as you think you are, in spite of all your studyin'. See, accordin' to the coroner, Miss Texas didn't die until around eight in the mornin'. So how'd your Buddy kill her then—or manslaughter her, whatever—if he was gittin' on an airplane to Los Angeles at the time?"

"Oh," I say. "I wonder how he fiddled that."

"Thass not all," he says, still chewing. "Would it surprise you to learn that Miss Texas was out partyin' with somebody else the night she died? I mean a non-Buddy person. Git it?"

My mouth full of chicken-fried steak, I chew faster and then swallow in a painful gulp. This is no way to treat the Dickens Café's specialty.

"Who?" I ask, a little breathless.

"So maybe you ain't so sure no more, huh?"

"Just tell me: Who was it?"

"Did you ever hear of a stuntman named Chris somethin' or other?"

"Yeah," I say. "Chris Crosby. Met him once or twice."

"What do you make of him?" Jimmy Lee asks.

I don't tell my old teammate he was my cousin's abusive boyfriend. I'm not sure why not. I suppose I don't want to admit any evidence that might exonerate Buddy Dale.

"He's just some stuntman," I say.

"Just some stuntman, right!" says the deputy. "A stuntman who used to date your cousin. Who beat her up. And he's got priors. A few fights in bars. But mostly beatin' up women. You ain't exactly been lev'lin' with me, Chick."

I look around as if searching for a back door, a way out, an escape route. I don't see one.

"I don't think Chris had anything to do with this," I say lamely, defensively, "but I guess I should've mentioned him. How'd you find out about him anyway?"

"Chick, I do this for a living," says the deputy. "All that teammate palaverin' and you was holdin' out on me. What kinda teamwork is that? You'll tell me if'n I tell you? Yeah, sure! Thanks a lot. You tryin' to insult me or somethin'? I can about half understand all your Hollywood friends treatin' me like I'm a small-town idiot—but not you."

"I'm sorry," I say. "I really am."

"Go to hell. Now what makes you think this here Chris is as pure as uncut cocaine?"

"Just a feeling."

"A feeling? And you used to be so smart. Seems to me like the things you done said about your Buddy, well, they fit ol' Chris, too. He was datin' your cousin out in L.A., and he was datin' Miss Texas back here, and they're both dead. Whut was it you said—coincidence or pattern?"

"So I'm guessing we aren't going to be teammates on this one, huh?"

"Wrong again, college boy. Teammates is teammates. Now and forever. *Semper* what the fuck. Gatorade's thicker'n water, you know.

Just don't treat me like I flunked outta kindergarden, and we got our-selves a deal. Until I catch you lyin' to me ag'in. Then I'm gonna lock you up for obstructin' justice."

I decide this is not the moment to tell him that it is "kinder-garten," not "kindergarden." When Jimmy Lee asks if I am going to eat the rest of my chicken-fried steak, I shake my head and tell him the lie he wants to hear: "No." Jimmy Lee volunteers to eat the rest of it if I really don't want it. Am I bribing a duly sworn law enforcement officer? Yes I am.

"Be my guest, partner," I say tentatively.

"Thanks, uh, pardner," he says.

Amanda appears, startling me.

"How 'bout some dessert?" she asks.

"Pie," says Jimmy Lee. "Ever' kind you've got. He's payin'."

Outside the restaurant, as we are saying our good-byes at the edge of Highway 82, I have an idea.

"Jimmy Lee, maybe you could look into something for me," I say, "now that we're teammates again."

"Like whut?"

"Well, the Los Angeles cops won't tell me anything about the death of my cousin. They just say it was hit-and-run and nothing else. No details. No evidence. Good-bye, get lost."

"Yeah, I'll bet."

"But I was just thinking, maybe they would tell more to one of their own. A brother officer. Member of the blue fraternity. In short, you."

"I wear khaki," says the deputy.

"You know what I mean."

"Yeah, I reckon I do."

"Would you call them for me? See what they'll share with a fellow lawman."

"Whut'd be my excuse for botherin' 'em?"

"Let's see, you could say there's been a murder down here that you think may be connected."

"But I don't think they're connected. You do."

"I didn't say you had to tell the truth."

43

IT IS A DAY TO MAKE FARMERS SMILE AND FILMMAKERS weep. It is raining bobcats and prairie dogs. We cancel our outdoor shooting schedule and move to our emergency covered set. Inside an abandoned building in Spur—unfortunately, there are lots in my dying hometown—our carpenters have built the interior of Revelie's Tascosa home. For the first time in over half a century, Spur's Main Street is a busy thoroughfare. It is crowded with movie trucks and movie motor homes. It is alive with our swarming crew, who resemble locusts in short pants. (Why do crews dress this way? It certainly isn't because the grips and gaffers and best boys have pretty legs.) A small crowd of spectators watches at a respectful distance: Spur isn't big enough to generate a big crowd.

Unfortunately, a Ford pickup suddenly roars out from a cross street, barrels through Spur's lonely red light, and collides with one of our prop pickups. The driver, an eighty-year-old man who works at the bank, quite reasonably never expected that there would be any traffic on Main Street. There never had been. Why would there be now?

Since we didn't know we would be shooting this scene today, we hadn't put it through the computer one last time last night. So I sit at the dining table in Jamie's motor home, computer open, trying to catch up. By accident rather than design, the scene we are about to shoot follows chronologically—also historically—the thumbs scene we just finished shooting.

To thank Goodnight for rescuing her and her poor thumbs, Revelie has invited him to dinner. In this scene, our poor hero will meet for the first time Revelie's memorable mother. Even though, thanks to our shooting schedule, he has already shown her around his dugout ranch house. Typing through it, I don't make many changes. But I do severely cut some stage directions, which will make the scene appear shorter. Jamie always wants everything shorter. When she walks in, I hand her the new pages.

"Good," Jamie says, "you shortened it. Always a good instinct. You're learning."

I smile bashfully outside, broadly inside. I love her praise.

She reads through the scene rapidly. Then she looks up and frowns.

"You just shortened the stage directions. You didn't shorten the scene. Do it again."

Busted. Jamie turns and storms out of the motor home.

I frown externally and cry inside. I never get away with anything. I type through the scene again. This time I make cuts in dialogue. They are painful cuts. I feel I'm cutting heart muscle. As I am printing out, Jamie returns. She grabs the still-warm pages from the printer tray and reads quickly.

"Okay," she says and races out the door again.

Okay? That's all I get? I slump, depressed.

"Action," Jamie almost whispers.

A door opens and Tom walks through it.

"This is the purdiest house I ever seen in my whole entire life," says Tom/Goodnight. "It surely is."

"I'm glad you think so," says Sarah/Revelie.

"It's a shack," says Brooke as Revlie's mother, Dolly. She is wearing a red dress with a dangerously low-cut neckline. "Nothing but a shack. I feel like Robinson Crusoe. I really do."

"Mother, this is Mr. Goodnight," Sarah says.

"Please call me Jimmy," says Tom.

"I don't know you well enough," says Brooke. "Are you a religious man, Mr. Goodnight?"

"No, ma'am," Tom stammers. "I'm a teetotaler but not religious."

"Then you've never read the Bible?"

"Well, frankly, ma'am, it's the only book I own, so I do read it some. So I won't fergit how, you know. And because it's full a good tales. But it's a little too bloodthirsty for my taste, ma'am."

"I see."

Tom looks devastated.

"Cut," Jamie almost whispers. Then she raises her voice: "That was great. Let's do it again. Right away."

"How did you think it played?" I ask, fishing for a compliment.

"Brooke was great."

So I fished for a compliment and caught one for Brooke Brooklyn.

"We've got that one," Jamie says, "and it was great. Now let's go for something a little different. A slightly different color. I don't know what that color should be, but a different shade. Play with it. Everybody except Brooke. You do just the same. That was just about perfect. Poor Goodnight. What a mother-in-law you're gonna make."

"Thank you," says the mother-in-law from the inferno.

When we break for lunch, I take out my cell phone and dial the sheriff's office. I ask for Jimmy Lee, who isn't there. I leave a message asking him to call me on my cell. Then I walk outside because the rain has stopped and the sun is out. I sneeze. I always sneeze in the sun.

"Bless you," says Victor Hammer, the little cameraman with the big name.

"Thank you," I say.

Then I amble over to the catering cart. There is a long line. I know I'm allowed to cut in at the front, but I would feel guilty. I join the end of the line. But soon the others in the line are pushing me forward. I am intensely embarrassed, but—remembering my sometime Taoist philosophy, he who would be last will be first—I allow myself to cheat. Soon my tray is being heaped with ribs and potato salad.

I survey the tables set up on Main Street. Now I face my nightmare: Where to sit? I have flashbacks to school cafeterias where I never knew where to sit because I was always the new kid in town and my dad was the new coach. Every time he had a winning season, we moved to a bigger town and a new school cafeteria full of even more strangers. I seem to SEE (POV) a sea of strangers before me now even though they aren't. How the hell did I end up in a business where lunch mimics lunch in school?

I finally sit down at an empty table, having failed another social test. I have eaten three lonely ribs when I sense an energy behind me. I flinch. I don't want anybody to notice me eating alone.

"Didn't mean to scare you, Doctor," says Sarah.

"Don't call me 'doctor,'" I say.

"But you got your Ph.D., right?"

"That's a secret."

Since I'd decided not to go into teaching, I've always avoided the label that only reminds me of what I perhaps should have done instead. Since I'm not a teacher, the title *doctor* seems to be an affectation. Besides, I suppose both cowboys and actors equate Ph.D. with sissy. I love the values of the West, but its anti-intellectualism isn't my favorite. I don't want anybody calling me "Doctor." Okay?

"Well, Doctor," Sarah says, "if you don't want me to blab the scandal of your Ph.D. all over town, you'll put down that rib and come with me."

I go with her. Not just because of the blackmail. I feel rescued.

"Where are we going?" I ask, hurrying to keep up.

"Tom's trailer," Sarah says.

"He's invited us to lunch?"

"Not hardly. He invited the Pitchfork Ranch cowboys to have lunch with him at the Dickens Café. I'm sure the boys're having a high old time. Makes you wonder about his sexuality, doesn't it?"

"So why are we going to his trailer?"

"Because I want to make him jealous."

"How?"

"We'll have a little surprise for him when he gets back from his lunch with the cowboys. First, we'll talk our way into his motor home. Then we'll curl up in his bed. That's how he'll find us. That'll make him jealous, don't you think?"

I'm not so sure that the biggest star in the world is going to be jealous of a screenwriter under any circumstances. Not in this world.

"Sure," I say.

"Good," says Sarah.

She leads me to Tom's trailer. She KNOCKS. His potbellied driver opens the door and surveys us.

"Hi," Sarah says. "We're going to surprise Tom. Don't tell him we're here. Okay?"

Potbelly shrugs and moves aside. We climb the steps and enter a world, once again, where the trailer park meets the luxury hotel. I follow Sarah down a familiar narrow corridor past cupboards and the bathroom. The hall empties into the bedroom with black walls and black sheets.

"Take off your clothes," orders Sarah.

"What?" I ask.

"You heard me. And hurry. I'll race you." She starts undoing the hundred buttons that stretch down the front of her nineteenth-century dress. "On second thought, the race part is off. Didn't your fucking ancestors ever hear of Velcro? By the time they got undressed, I'm surprised they weren't too tired to do it."

Not sure I want to take off my clothes, I just watch her getting naked. She steps out of her full-skirted dress and attacks her layers of old-fashioned underclothing. She manages to strip faster than I would have thought possible. There she is, dressed only in breasts and pubic hair, and I'm the one who feels embarrassed.

"Not bad," I say with real admiration.

"Shut up and strip," she says in a gruff voice.

"You sound like a guy."

"You're acting like a girl."

She comes right up to me, grabs the front of my cowboy shirt, and rips it open. Luckily it has mother-of-pearl snaps instead of buttons. I take off the shirt and toss it on a chair. Then I look down to see if there is any visible evidence of the spare ribs I have just eaten. Am I fatter? The answer is yes, at least in the eye of the beholder.

"Come on, come," Sarah prompts. "Stop staring at your belly button and take off your pants."

Obeying orders, I push down my jeans and underwear in one motion. They are down to my ankles when I realize I still have my boots on. I feel trapped and ridiculous and tied in knots. Taking pity, Sarah kneels down and helps me finish taking off the boots and the rest of my clothes.

"Don't just stand there admiring yourself," she says. "Lie down."

I lie down on the bed and she plops down beside me. I imagine an OVERHEAD SHOT of our white bodies on the black sheets.

INT. BIGGEST STAR IN THE WORLD'S BEDROOM — NOON

Two naked bodies.

                              SARAH
          Put your arms around me.

                    CHICK
                 (VOICE OVER)
When I do, I love the softness of her
skin. I even catch myself thinking: She
feels like a leading lady, like a star.
When I pull her to me, her breasts
spread against my chest. Giving in to a
stupid impulse . . .

Chick tries to kiss Sarah.

                    SARAH
Don't do that.

                    CHICK
                 (retreating)
Okay. Sorry.

                    SARAH
Wait until he gets here. Then you can
kiss me all you want to. And do
anything else you want.

                    CHICK
Okay.

                    SARAH
He's late.

                    CHICK
No, he isn't, not very.

                    SARAH
Who does he think he is, anyway? Some
big star who can just show up for work
whenever he feels like it? He doesn't

care if the whole cast and crew are
waiting for him.

CHICK

But he's not late. Not very.

SARAH

The arrogance.

CHICK

But—

SARAH

What's that?

We HEAR the door of the motor home opening.

CHICK
(VOICE OVER)

As Hemingway would say, the earth moves.
Somebody enters the black motor home,
causing it to shift on its springs. I've
never felt more naked in my entire life.

SARAH
(whispering)

Now.

CHICK
(whispering)

Now what?

SARAH

Kiss me.

Chick kisses Sarah. The earth moves again as steps
approach. Still kissing her, Chick looks up and SEES
(POV) Tom — and Jamie.

This scene no longer feels like a scene. I am no longer on the outside looking in. I am in the painful now and here. I want to disappear. To cease to exist. To shrivel into nothingness. I stop kissing.

Tom looks at us as if we are a couple of throw pillows. Sarah has gone to all this trouble to make him jealous, and he doesn't even react. He seems to know that the best way to hurt Sarah is to do nothing at all.

Jamie smiles down at us. Amused. My earth moves again, shifts, loses its bearings. Has she lost all respect for me? Will our working relationship, which has been so important to me, change forever? Will our personal relations, for which I've had such hopes, be dashed forever? And for what? Because I couldn't—or didn't—say no to Sarah. Because I was embarrassed about eating alone and wanted to escape from the school cafeteria. Because I'm still the new kid in town even though this town is a movie. How could I ever explain all this to Jamie?

"Hi," says Sarah.

"Hello, fun couple," says Jamie.

Tom doesn't say anything.

I twist out of Sarah's embrace and turn onto my stomach, trying to hide. Then my cell phone starts BURPING in my discarded shirt pocket. I want to answer it—it could be my friend the deputy—but I don't want to expose myself again. I know how foolish I would look scrambling naked to take a call.

I scramble.

"Hello."

"It's Jimmy Lee."

"Thanks for calling back," I say, sitting on the floor, my knees pulled up to hide my nakedness. My voice is unsteady as I ask: "Any news?"

"Sounds like this is a bad time. Like you was in the middle of somethin' interestin'. I'll call back later."

"No, no, this isn't a bad time. Nothing's going on."

"Coulda fooled me," says Jamie.

"Me too," says Sarah, staying in character.

"Please tell me," I say. "What's new?"

"Well, we got the tox stuff back."

"Good. What?"

"It's kinda like what you said. There was cocaine but not a whole helluva lot. Not enough to kill most folks. Not enough to kill a junkie. But, like you said, it was enough to fuck up the beatin' of a virgin's heart. Which looks like the causa death. How'd you know that's what we was gonna find?"

"I was Philip Marlowe in another life."

"Phil who? Is that some kinda cigarette or somethin'?"

"I'll tell you later."

"The problem is—I mean the problem for your theory is—this kinda thing happens real quick. You take a hit or maybe a second hit or a third and then suddenly your heart starts filibusterin'. It ain't no long-delayed action kinda thing if you git my driftin'. I mean your buddy Buddy was long gone—too long gone—by the time she bought the farm. Which brings me back to Mr. Stuntman. He was certainly here in the right time frame. Course he says he was fast asleep in one of your damn tents, but no witnesses."

I don't know what to think: I desperately want Buddy to turn out to be a killer. It would justify all my contempt for him as a producer. At the same time, I hate Chris for abusing my cousin. Was it the devil at the top of the food chain who killed her, or was it the villain at the bottom? But this is not the moment to have that conversation with a cop.

"Well, thanks for keeping in touch. I appreciate it."

"Hold up, I ain't finished yet."

Oh no, I can't stand to talk any longer. With everyone watching. With everybody listening. With my naked ass trembling.

"I'll call you back," I say.

"No, no, just a damn minute," Jimmy Lee says, irritated. "I thought you said there was nothin' goin' on."

"Okay, what?"

"Remember you asked me to call the L.A. cops? Well, turns out your cousin had a coupla smudges of somebody else's blood on her. Differ'nt blood type and all."

"God," I moan. "I gotta call you back. I can't talk about this right now."

"You sure you ain't in the middle a somethin'?"

I punch out the call and curl into a fetal ball on the floor. The stares actually hurt my skin.

"Action," Jamie whispers.

This afternoon, I'm standing too far away actually to hear the soft command, but I imagine I hear it. The actors are seated around a dining room table that belongs in Boston, and Dolly lets everybody know it, radiating the news. She is considerably too good for Tascosa.

"Don't you like your chicken?" Brooke asks.

(My great-great-great-ever-so-great-grandfather hated chicken, but he didn't on this day.)

"It's delicious," Tom lies.

"Then try to show a little more enthusiasm, Mr. Goodnight," Dolly instructs. "My chicken is famous all over Massachusetts."

"I thought I made the chicken," says Revelie.

"Yes, dear, but you made it from my recipe."

After we wrap, I am a zoo animal in my room, pacing, pacing, pacing, back and forth, back and forth, until I'm exhausted. I sit on my bed to rest, but I can't stand being still. I get up and pace some more. Why did I do it? Why didn't I say no? Why had I ruined everything?

The pacing is supposed to numb my mind, but it isn't working. I speed up. It doesn't help. I feel trapped in the cage of my own stupidity.

I keep glancing at the cell phone on my night table hoping it will ring. It doesn't ring. It won't ever ring again. Jamie won't call, as she usually does, inviting me to dinner. The caterers serve dinner every evening in a big dining tent—since this part of the country isn't exactly littered with good restaurants—but my director prefers to eat out. The food in the food tent might be better, but it has its drawbacks. At the ranch, she would be barraged with complaints, questions, pleas between every bite. So she usually calls me and we usually go out and it is almost like a date. A business date. But she should have already called tonight if she is going to call at all. I realize how much I miss Jamie's call, how much I miss her, how much I have lost. Thanks, Sarah. Did she plan this?

At last I do what I have been longing to do all night: I pick up my cell phone. I start to dial Jamie's number but can't. I call Deputy Jimmy Lee instead. He answers on the first RING.

"Hi, it's Chick."

"Come on, Chick, fess up," the deputy says. "You was fuckin' your leadin' lady when I called, right?"

"No, not really," I say.

"Not really?"

"I'll tell you later. What about the blood they found on Sharon?"

"Yeah, they done found a smudge on the left side a her neck. And another one on her left wrist."

"So it *was* murder." I am breathing rapidly and shallowly.

"Not so fast. The cops got a differ'nt theory. They figure the driver that done hit her got hurt in the accident hisself. And so he was bleedin', see? So he stops, sees her lyin' there, and scampers to check her pulse. You know, the jugular, then the wrist, or t'other way 'round. That's how come he got blood on her in them two spots. When he done seen she ain't got no pulse, he got scared and skidaddled."

"Do you believe that?"

"I dunno, but that there's their story."

"So they just stopped investigating?"

"Well, they went through the motions anyhow. Whether their hearts was in it or not. They done sent them blood smudges fer a DNA checkup. Then they run them results ag'inst their bad-guys database. No hits."

"But did they check Buddy Dale's DNA? Or Chris Crosby's for that matter?"

"I dunno fer sure, but I wouldn't count on it."

"Then maybe we could."

"Now how in hell we gonna do that?"

"You get the DNA report from the LAPD, and I get samples of Buddy's and Chris's DNA."

"Come on, Chick. Thass—"

"Go, Spur Bulldogs."

"Okay, okay."

I go back to pacing. I am still walking back and forth at midnight when I finally lie down. Ten minutes later, I'm up again. I pace. I lie down. I pace. I lie down. I get up and get out my batons.

44

IT IS RAINING AGAIN. THE FARMERS AND RANCHERS are counting their profits, the movie company its losses. We move to another commandeered empty building and another time in the lives of our characters. Now Revelie and Goodnight inhabit their great stone castle: The exterior will of course be the 6666's stone ranch house, but the interior is a failed furniture store, where we are now. Today the store will be a battleground. Revelie and Goodnight are going to have an epic fight.

Sarah taps me on the shoulder. Oh no, I don't want Jamie to see me talking to our leading lady. I try to make myself small, which doesn't work for me. I SEE (POV) Jamie notice us and then turn away. I wonder if my director and I have eaten our last dinner together.

"I just did something bad," Sarah tells me. "It felt good, but it was bad."

"What?" I ask, irritated.

"I told Tom that the crew hates him," she says. "That they make fun of him behind his back. That they call him a pussy."

"I've never heard that," I say.

"I didn't say it was true. I said that's what I told him. I already admitted it was bad."

"But why would you do such a thing? I thought you wanted him to like you. That's a strange way to make him fall in love with you."

"I wanted him to like me when we were doing romantic scenes. But today we're doing a fight scene. I want him to hate me now. I want him to want to kill me. I'll make an actor of him yet."

"Jesus," I say.

"Just watch. There are gonna be sparks."

Sarah gives me a big leading-lady smile, turns, and marches away.

"Are we getting close?" asks Jamie.

"Yes," says Victor Hammer.

"Liar," she says. "How close?"

"Half an hour," he says.

"That's not close! Damn!"

Jamie turns away from the cameraman and marches over to me.

She looks mad. Mad at Victor. Mad at how long everything takes. Mad at me, too?

"Do you know what your girlfriend did this morning?" Jamie demands.

"I don't have a girlfriend," I protest.

"I'll tell you what she did," she says. "She told Tom that the whole crew laughs at him behind his back. That they think he can't act and he's an arrogant prick. Can you imagine?"

"No," I lie.

"What's wrong with her?" asks Jamie.

"I don't know. I really don't."

"She's an asshole. She's a cunt."

I almost say: Make up your mind which one. Instead, I say: "Maybe she's priming the pump for the big fight scene."

"You and your down-home clichés. Well, if that's her plan, she's smarter and stupider than I thought."

"I have no idea what that means."

"Good. I remain a woman of mystery."

She turns her back on me and marches away. Moviemaking is much more emotional than I ever supposed it would be. And it takes longer.

"Action," Jamie whispers.

We are in Goodnight's study, his office, his "brood room." The door flies open. In the doorway stands Sarah. She holds a basket in her left hand. Reaching into the basket, she pulls out an egg. She cocks her arm and throws the egg at her husband's head. Except she is actually throwing at an imaginary target. Because the camera sees only the thrower, not the thrown at. The egg explodes against the wall above an empty couch. Sarah reloads and throws a second egg at her imagined husband. Then a third.

"Cut," whispers Jamie. She raises her voice: "Very good. Let's go again. Sarah, let's go for a little different color. Say, red. You see red and you throw."

"The problem is what I don't see," says Sarah. "Where's Tom? Is he a coward or something? Do I scare him?"

"Sometimes you scare me. But, you know, our insurance company wouldn't want you throwing missiles at your costar."

"Thanks for nothing," sniffs Sarah. "Still, I ought to have somebody to throw at. Otherwise it isn't real."

"Okay, I can see that," Jamie says. "But it has to be somebody expendable." She pauses, then smiles. "Chick, how about you? Go sit on the couch."

"But—" I protest.

"Do you want to help or not?"

Jamie gives me a big smile as I slink to the couch. Sitting down, I hunch my shoulders, trying to make myself a smaller target. Doesn't work. I don't feel littler. I do feel scalded. Normally I would love to help out, to justify my presence on the set, but now I think it is retribution. Jamie is spanking me.

"Chick, before we start," Jamie says, "I believe it's your right to consult with the stunt coordinator if you feel you are in any physical danger. Would you like me to call Chris?"

"No, thank you," I say.

"Very well," she says. Then she whispers: "Action."

The door flies open and Sarah opens fire. The first egg hits me on the chin and yellow goo splashes up into my nose. I sneeze and struggle to catch my breath. She throws a second egg. When I duck, it hits me right on top of the head, soaking, matting my hair.

I think: Thank God, she's throwing eggs instead of bullets, because she's a damn good shot. Well, eggs would be a woman's weapon, wouldn't they? I feel deservedly humiliated. I feel like an omelet.

We do the scene fifteen more times. We never do fifteen takes.

Either Jamie is being paid off by the local egg farmers or she is making a point. My face is a map of bruises.

"Turn the camera around," Jamie says at long last.

Now the camera faces the couch. Tom Bondini sits where I sat. Now he is the target.

"I still think this is crazy," Jamie says. "What if she accidentally hits you in the face with an egg?"

"Accidentally on purpose," I say softly.

"Yeah, exactly," says the director.

"I don't think an egg is going to hurt me much," Tom says.

"What if she's hard-boiled them?" Jamie says. "I wouldn't put it past her."

"I'll take that chance. She called me a coward. What's the crew going to think of me if I back down now?"

"Jesus, nobody tell Paramount." Jamie walks to the closed "office" door and opens it a crack. "Sarah, remember, don't hit his face. You can hit him anyplace else but not the head, okay? If you hit him in the face, you'll never have another close-up in this movie. Do you understand?"

Closing the door, Jamie returns to Tom. "Okay, when she starts throwing, close your eyes and duck. She's not supposed to come anywhere near your face, but I don't trust her. So please remember, duck, duck, duck. You tell him, Chris."

"She's right," says Chris Crosby. "Like this." He demonstrates by bowing his head as if he is praying. "You know, like a girl in a rainstorm."

"Like anybody in a rainstorm," Jamie says. "That way"—she ducks her own head—"the worst she can do is mess up your hair instead of breaking your nose. Got that?"

"Yes, ma'am, close my eyes and duck."

"Okay."

Jamie walks back and takes up her favorite position just to the right of the camera. She pulls down a deep breath and lets it out.

"Action." Jamie moves her lips MOS.

The door flies open and the first egg is launched. Tom doesn't duck, but it misses the biggest star in the world by three feet. Good. Sarah rearms, fires, and hits Tom directly on the point of his famous nose. He YELPS involuntarily.

"Cut!" SCREAMS Jamie. "Sarah, why did you throw at his head? I warned you! I told you! Dammit!" The director hurries over to the star. "Tom, are you okay? Are you hurt? Is anything broken? Somebody, get our phony doctor. Hurry." She stands there panting.

"This isn't my fault," says Chris Crosby. "I warned you it was dangerous."

"I'm okay," Tom says.

"You sure?" Jamie asks.

"Yeah."

"I thought I told you to duck."

"I'm no coward."

Jamie shakes her head as the egg thrower approaches her costar.

"Maybe you're not a coward," Sarah says, "but are you an actor? See, I'm pretty sure the real Jimmy Goodnight would've ducked. It's what any real person would do."

"Goddamn you!" Tom YELLS.

"Save it for the scene," says Sarah.

"That's enough," Jamie commands. "Get Tom's stand-in."

"No," says Tom. "I'm not giving in to her."

"Nobody says you are. I'm the one giving in to her." She pauses. "No, I'm not. Tom, stay where you are. Sarah, go to your dressing room."

"What did I do!" Sarah protests. "He was supposed to duck."

"Go to your dressing room!" Pause. "Right now!" Pause. "Move your fucking ass!"

At last, Sarah slouches away.

"Good." Jamie exhales. "Okay, Chick, you're now Sarah. You're Revelie. You throw the eggs."

"But—"

"The camera's not on you. Nobody'll know. By the way, you don't throw like a girl, do you? I mean like a real girl, not like your girlfriend Sarah."

"She's not—"

"Save it. We're in a hurry."

"I'll throw the eggs," announces Chris Crosby from nowhere. "That'll be the safest." Stepping forward, he holds out his hand for the egg basket.

"Sorry," Jamie says. "Go sit down."

"Then I abdicate any responsibility—"

"Get out of the way."

So I take my place in the doorway holding a basket of eggs. I am playing my own great-great-great-ever-so-great-grandmother. I deliver five strikes to Tom's famous chest.

"Good," Jamie says. "Turning the camera around."

I am thrilled at her praise even though it is for egg pitching.

It takes a while to relight the shot.

"The shark is dying," says Kim Kurumada.

A quarter of an hour passes.

"The shark is dying," says Kim.

Another fifteen minutes.

"The shark is dying."

I finally go up to him and ask what he is talking about.

"Well, you see, sharks can only breathe if they are moving forward. Why? Because they are primitive monsters who have no other way of forcing water to flow through their gills. If the shark stops moving forward, the shark suffocates. Like us. When we bog down, we're dying."

"Oh," I say.

"The shark is almost dead," Kim says in a big voice.

"We're ready," says cameraman Victor Hammer.

"Good," says Jamie. "Where's Chris? Jesus, fuck, what happened to Chris?"

"He's on the lam," I say, "running for the border before they arrest him for murder."

"I'm right here, asshole," Chris says from behind me.

I turn and he takes a swing at me. He is kidding. The punch misses my chin by an inch. Just like he was taught in stuntman school. But, expecting the worst, I fall down anyway. What is weaker than a glass jaw? At least I don't hurt myself, anyway not too badly. Everybody LAUGHS. I wish I could say their laughter makes me feel like a director, but actually it makes me feel like an idiot and a coward.

"Good, you're here," Jamie says as if nothing has happened. As if I am not lying in the dust. "Walk through this with the actors, okay?"

I get awkwardly to my feet, brush the dust off my clothes as subtly as possible, and watch the stunt rehearsal.

"Chris," I say, "make sure she doesn't get hurt. Really. I know how much you like to see girls in pain."

He swings again, but I dodge this time. I am a slow learner, but I do eventually learn. I can hear the crew murmuring behind me.

"Chris, get back to work," orders Jamie. "We're waiting on you."

Giving me the finger, our stunt coordinator turns his back on me and walks away.

"Okay, heroes, let's do this in slow motion," says Chris. "Now, Sarah, don't forget to roll when he tackles you. And Tom, remember to come in low. Put your shoulder into her belly."

"Sure," Tom says.

"Let's do it by the numbers. There should be one and only one movement per number. Tom, number one is your first step, number two is your second, and so on. Here goes—one—two—three—four—five—six . . ."

While Chris slowly counts, Tom slow-motion "charges" Sarah, who pretends to slow-motion "throw" eggs. The camera faces her, which she loves. The biggest star in the world comes "running" from behind the camera, "charging" into frame, and stops just before he tackles her. She falls down anyway. Is she mocking me or trying to make it real?

"Roll when you land," Chris coaches. "Roll, roll."

Rolling over, Sarah LAUGHS and LAUGHS.

"The shark is dying," says Kim.

Sarah keeps on LAUGHING.

"Are we getting close?" asks Jamie.

"We're ready," says Tom.

He may be the biggest star in the world, but wardrobe, makeup, and hair nonetheless proceed to waste fifteen more minutes. The makeup part is kind of fun: They reapply raw eggs to the face and body of Mr. Box Office.

"The shark is dying."

"Remember, roll, roll."

"Are we close?"

"That's enough," says Tom. "We're there."

"Good," Jamie says and exhales. It is as if she has been holding her breath through all the lighting, all the rehearsals, all the tweaking of how the actors look. "Let's go."

"Settle down, everybody," says Kim. "Picture is next."

The crew stops walking and talking.

"Action," Jamie mumbles.

Tom rises from the couch and charges full-speed, head-down at Sarah, who is throwing full-speed eggs. One explodes like a yellow hand grenade on his back. As he nears her, Tom rises up from a semi-crouch. Then he smashes into her hard. The top of his head slams into her face.

"Owwwoww!" Sarah SCREAMS through broken teeth.

When they hit the floor, nobody rolls.

"Cut," says Jamie.

I SEE (POV) Sarah spit out a bloody tooth.

We all rush forward, tripping over each other. Tom, his scalp bleeding from its collision with Sarah's teeth, is still lying on top of her. Blood runs down his face and drips on her. Blood spews from her mouth.

"Print that one," says Sarah, her words garbled by a mouth full of blood. "That was real."

45

NOW SARAH HAS A CHOICE OF WHICH ROLE TO PLAY: "poor me" or her normal "tough guy." She opts for the more flamboyantly dramatic victim's pose. She dissolves in tears. She is inconsolable.

"My teeth," she mumbles through broken ivory. "Old people lose teeth, not young ones. I'm old before my time. I'm mortal."

Still flat on her back, she starts crying. Tom has a bloody gash on the top of his head, but her pain easily upstages his, even if he is the biggest star in the world.

"Hello, insurance company," says Jamie.

"The shark just died," says Kim Kurumada. He shakes his head. "Where's the nearest hospital?"

"Crosbyton," I say.

"How far away is that?"

"Thirty miles. The nearest good hospital's in Lubbock. That's seventy give or take."

"What's the life expectancy around here," asks Jamie, "with medical help so far away?"

"Most folks only live to be ninety-something," I say, "probably because hospitals are so far away."

"Yeah, probably," she says.

"I'll call the local ambulance folk," I volunteer.

Soon we HEAR the SIREN.

The medics put Sarah on a stretcher, start an IV, and hoist her into the back of the ambulance.

"Chick, come with me," Sarah calls.

I look around and SEE (POV) Jamie, who is frowning. I have to make a choice, my leading lady or my director? Well, the choice isn't really hard.

"No, I'd better not," I say. "I've got work to do."

"Please." Poor me.

"Go with her," Jamie says. "Your girlfriend needs help, and you know the local customs."

"She's not—"

"Go with her!"

With a sagging heart, I climb into the back of the ambulance. Tom crawls into the passenger seat in the cab. He needs medical help, too, but is again upstaged. With siren shrieking, we scream up Highway 70 north to Dickens, where we turn west onto Highway 82.

"Hold my hand," says Poor Me. "I'm scared."

I hold her hand. I wanted her in the movie. Now I've got her, but what am I going to do with her? Yes, beware answered prayers. Her scheming—her provocation—has just shut down production.

"Did you know that there Miss Texas?" asks the medic who is riding in the back with us. His name is ABBO BARTHOLOMEW and I have known him all my life.

"Not really," I say. "But I found her body."

"That's what I heard," says Abbo. "You know, there's been lots of talk. Gossip. I figured you was probably sleeping with her."

"No, we had somebody else assigned to that duty. Our producer."

"Never mind 'bout that. What I wanted to ask you is, well: Did you notice anything unusual when you done found her?"

"No, but I did have a strange feeling. I thought something was wrong, but I wasn't sure what. Do you know something?"

"Not really, but I 'companied the body in the ambulance. And so I felt I had an interest. So I asked questions. And I heard there was something kind of unexpected when they cut open her stomach. You know they always do that."

"What was it?" I ask, wanting to retch.

"Well, she s'posedly had undigested steak and lobster in her tummy. Nice last meal. Anyhow that's what I heard by the watermelon wine. I'd like to know fer sure. I was hoping you might could tell me one way or t'other. True or false, you know?"

"I don't know what she ate," I say, puzzled.

"Well, you know, if they's any truth to it, that'd raise some questions."

"Right?" I prompt, still puzzled.

"Because if she ate at a normal time, or even kinda late, say before midnight, her stomach contents shoulda been digested long before she died off early in the mornin'."

"Right."

"Of course, maybe Hollywood people eat surf and turf at four in the morning. You'd know about that."

"No, I wouldn't. But I don't think so. Thank you."

I am left wondering who fed Miss Texas her last supper: Was it Buddy, her last boss, or Chris, supposedly her last date? And why so late? And where had that lobster come from? Steak is easy to get out here, but lobster is harder. I promise myself I will try to find out even if it means talking to strangers.

Both Sarah and Tom survive their contact with Crosbyton Hospital. His scalp is stitched up and he is released. It turns out she has two broken teeth and a broken rib. Two other ribs are cracked. So she is forwarded to Lubbock, where she is told she is lucky her broken rib didn't puncture a lung. Her injuries once again trump Tom's.

We shut down for a week. Millions are involved.

46

WHILE WE'RE SHUT DOWN, I DRIVE UP TO CROSBYTON to pay a call on the coroner. Not a stranger. I've phoned ahead, so he is expecting me. I'd been afraid I might have to interview him in the morgue, but he receives me in a normal-looking doctor's office. He does have a plastic—I hope it's plastic—skeleton standing in a corner, but nothing else screams death.

DR. CHANDLER is a short, square, heavyset man with reddish hair and a red mustache. I don't know him well, but I've met him in passing several times before. As often happens in small towns, he combines working on the dead with treating the living. There is a joke that the good doctor kills enough of his patients to keep himself in business as coroner. We shake hands. He grips mine firmly.

"Thanks for making the time to see me," I say.

"Of course," says Dr. Chandler. "We're all excited about your movie. Tell me, what can I do for you? Where does it hurt?"

"Oh, I'm sorry," I say. "I'm not sick. I wanted to talk to you about the death of, uh, Miss Texas. I can never remember her name. That's terrible, isn't it?"

He makes a sound in his throat that isn't really yes or no. It is a kind of grunt that serves the same function in conversation that zero serves in math.

"I assume you did the autopsy, didn't you, Dr. Chandler?"

"Yes, as a matter of fact, I did. What a sad business. What a beautiful girl."

"I wonder if I could ask you: Was there anything unusual about her stomach contents? I've heard gossip that there was."

"First, let me ask a question: Why are you so interested?"

"Well, it's my movie, so I feel partially responsible." I was afraid he might ask me such a question, and so spent the ride here trying to come up with a plausible answer. "I guess a guilty conscience makes me want to find out as much as I can about what went wrong."

"I don't think you need to feel that way," says Dr. Chandler, "unless you gave her the coke." He LAUGHS to prove he knows that's impossible.

"I didn't," I hurriedly refute the joke anyway. "But what about the gossip about what was in her stomach?"

"Well, that was somewhat curious as a matter of fact." Then he stops talking.

"In what way?" I ask a little breathlessly.

"She still had a big dinner in her stomach. Of course, everybody digests their food at a different rate. But if she ate her dinner at dinnertime, her stomach should have been almost empty by the time she died at between seven and eight in the morning."

"And how do you know when she died?"

"Liver temperature."

"So how do you account for the stomach contents?"

"Well, there are often anomalies in cases. Maybe she had some sort of digestive problem. Or perhaps she was taking some new diet drug that kept her from processing her food."

"You did a tox screen. Did you find any diet drug?"

"No, unless you consider cocaine a diet drug. Some do, you know. Speeds up your metabolism and all."

"But that would make her digest her food faster, wouldn't it?"

"You've been watching *CSI*, haven't you? Or is it the Discovery Channel?"

"Both actually, from time to time."

"Anyway, you're right. There does seem to be a contradiction between liver temperature and stomach contents. But since cause of death was obvious, I didn't worry too much about contradictions. There are always things we can't explain."

"What about lividity?" I ask.

"You really have been watching television."

"What about it?"

"Am I on trial here?"

"Of course not. I'm sorry. But I understood that once the heart stops, the blood begins to settle according to the laws of gravity. The longer a body has been dead, the more discoloration, right?"

"Right. As a matter of fact, that's a good question. The lividity was more advanced than I would have expected. Another contradiction. But liver temperature is usually the best measure of time of death. That's what I relied on. As would *CSI* and the Discovery Channel and Dr. Kay Scarpetta."

"Right," I say, but I don't mean it.

Trying to fall asleep that night in my third-floor bedroom, I keep reliving the discovery of the body of Miss Texas. What had I missed? What does her liver temperature mean? Temperature, temperature? What? I see myself leaning over her, turning back the covers—which are warm. Were they warmed by the body heat of Miss Texas? Or possibly something else? What? The only possibility I can imagine is an electric blanket. Especially since I remember how warm her covers were. I just figured it was because she was literally and figuratively a hot girl. But maybe she had some help staying that hot that long.

Vaulting out of bed, I dress hurriedly and race to the room where Miss Texas died. I am about to try the doorknob when I realize somebody may be asleep inside. Maybe Buddy's latest is in there. Hell, I don't care. I grab the knob and try to turn it. It turns. Maybe Miss Michigan or Miss Guam—like my cousin—is just a trusting soul who doesn't lock her door. I ease it open slowly.

The room is empty. Closing the door behind me, I hurry to the bed. Bending down, I touch the covers and feel the embedded wires. It is an electric blanket! I've got him now! That's how he kept the body warm while he raced to the airport. I pull the blanket off the bed with one violent jerk.

Then I sink to my knees. There is no electrical cord! This was once an electric blanket, but it is no longer. The cord appears to have been jerked loose, probably when the blanket stopped working years ago. From my knees, I lie down on the floor and try to reenter the womb. Good luck.

47

BACK IN MY ROOM, I FEEL DISAPPOINTED, LONELY, AND abandoned. The movie has abandoned me because we aren't shooting. Jamie has abandoned me because I played that dumb stunt with Sarah. I haven't even heard from our leading lady lately. Maybe I should pay a visit to my mother and father. But it's late.

So perhaps I should pick up a book. Books never sleep. I look at my night table, where a dozen are stacked. T. H. White's *The Once and Future King*. Malory's *Le Morte d'Arthur*. Raymond Chandler's tattered *The Big Sleep*. Anthony Trollope's *The Way We Live Now*. Trollope is actually my favorite author although I generally keep this to myself. His chapters are short and about one thing only. With my new knowledge of screenwriting, I see his writing as cinematic. By now, I have read all his sixty-plus novels, so I'm rereading them. I believe Trollope came up with two of the best titles in all of literature: *The Way We Live Now* and *He Knew He Was Right*. (Closely followed by *Debbie Does Dallas*.) I pick up *The Way* and begin to enjoy the familiar Trollopian cadences—punctuated with lots of dashes—that I have come to love.

Reading the story of the original stock market cheat in literature, I begin to feel better, but nonetheless my mind keeps darting away to thoughts of Jamie. Where is she? What is she doing? Why hasn't she called?

I think: The way I live now is unhappy. Which is crazy. I'm telling the story—making the movie—I've always wanted to tell. The story that has fascinated me all my life. So why am I so unhappy? Then I realize I know why. But why can't I fix it?

I pick up the phone and dial Jamie's number. My parents would be asleep by now, but maybe she won't be. I've been waiting for her to call me since she is the director and I'm only the writer. But enough of that. I HEAR her phone BUZZING. Good—I am cowardly enough to think—she isn't there. I exhale.

"Hello," Jamie answers.

"Hi," I say.

"Do you want to have dinner tonight?" she asks.

"More than I want eternal life," I say, playing it cool.

We have dinner at the Lake Restaurant, which is perched on the bank of the White River Lake ten miles west of Spur. This tiny box of an eatery has huge windows overlooking the water. The moon shimmers on the waves.

"This is where I learned to sail," I say.

"Really?" Jamie says. "So far from the ocean? I never think of sailing cowboys."

"Well, as I believe I've already mentioned a time or two, the wind always blows here. It never stops. It would be the perfect place for the America's Cup."

A waitress stops at our Formica table. She is either a junior or senior in high school, and she is absolutely beautiful. Blond hair that is more or less real. Eyes as blue as my cousin's. Well developed. I say a little prayer that neither Buddy Dale nor Chris Crosby will ever stumble into this restaurant and "discover" her.

"Hi, Molly," I say.

"Hi, Chick," says MOLLY KANTREL.

"Molly, this is Jamie."

They nod at each other.

"What'll it be?" Molly asks.

"What's good?" asks Jamie.

"The fried catfish is my favorite," I say.

"Why am I not surprised that it's fried?" asks the director. "Do you have anything that isn't fried?"

"Pie," Molly says.

"I'll have the fried catfish," Jamie says.

"Good choice," I say. "Me too."

The beautiful Molly turns and marches away with active hips.

"What was it like growing up here?" Jamie asks. "I mean West Texas is sort of like a combination of *Our Town* and life on the moon."

"There's no wind on the moon," I say. "Let me see. It was sort of like growing up in slow motion. But intense slow motion. Everything meant so much." I watch the light on the lake. "How about you? What was it like growing up back East? What was the name of that town again?"

"Swampscott, Massachusetts. It's north of Boston. Small town near a big city."

"Like Spur and Lubbock?"

"Not nearly."

"Did you live in a mansion on the cliffs overlooking the ocean?"

"As a matter of fact, I did. For a while anyway. The most beautiful place in the whole world. Then when I was in fourth grade, my father lost all his money. He was in the real estate business. One day he owned skyscrapers. The next day we didn't even own our own home. Bottom fell out of the real estate market and took us down with it. Right to the bottom of the bottom."

"Really?" I say stiffly. "I, uh, I don't know, I guess I thought everything had always been easy for you." My fingers tremble worse. "That you'd never been roughed up by life. I'm babbling."

"It's okay to babble in real life," she says. "Just don't let your characters babble. Babbling takes too much screen time." She reaches across the table and takes my hand. Her touch is a live electrical wire. I try not to jump but am not completely successful. "I knew things were bad when we started selling our pictures. My family had this great art collection. Matisse, Modigliani, even a Picasso vagina."

I LAUGH. Which makes me self-conscious because I know everybody always laughs at everything a director says. But I can't help myself. Besides, maybe it wasn't supposed to be funny because she isn't smiling.

"We even had a Van Gogh from his potato-eaters period, in other words, back before he figured out how to paint. And a Monet and a Manet. That reminds me, Billy Wilder used to say he didn't mind people confusing him with Willie Wyler. Or as he put it, 'Wilder, Wyler, Monet, Manet, what's the difference?'"

I LAUGH.

"Anyway, the parents of my friends started dropping by our house on the cliff to shop for paintings. It was deeply embarrassing. Later, I would see our pictures in other people's homes. I started out being angry at my dad, but ended up loving him all the more. He was the wounded bird who couldn't fly anymore. Anyway, all the pictures went, then the house, too." She looks out at the lake, which is a poor substitute for her lost ocean.

"I'm sorry," I mumble feebly, not knowing what else to say to her sad story.

"Worse things happen," she says, "but that was tough."

Jamie's eyes brim with tears, but she doesn't cry. I remember her telling our actors that fighting back tears is more effective than crying. I start fighting back my own mirror tears.

"The thing about Van Gogh," Jamie says to move us beyond the emotion, "is that he started out as a terrible artist. Any critic seeing those potato paintings would've told him to give it up. No hope. And they did. But a crucial part of his talent—the defining part— was keeping going. Just keeping going. His first paintings weren't any good. He kept going. They didn't sell. He kept going. Eventually he started getting better. They still didn't sell." She pauses. "So my dad bought one of his worst paintings, so what? So much the better. Because it tells us that talent is not just genius but also never giving up. Maybe mainly not giving up." She shrugs. "My dad gave up."

"Now I know why you're a director."

"It's never that simple. Anyway, bankruptcy and selling the paintings and losing the house killed my father." A tear starts to roll down her face, but it only gets a couple of inches before she quickly brushes it away. "I hate weepy women," she says.

"How do you feel about weepy men?" I ask, brushing my own cheek.

Beautiful Molly brings our food. The fried catfish seem to be writhing in pain. They remind me of the snakes in the snake pit in *Raiders of the Lost Ark.*

"They look like those snakes in *Raiders,*" Jamie says. "I'm glad I know they're dead."

"Yeah," I say, trying to control a shudder. "That was just what I was thinking."

"Of course," she says.

I wait while she takes a bite.

"This is actually very good," she says at last.

"Long live frying," I say.

After dinner, we climb down the rocks and walk along the beach. I take her hand. She doesn't resist. I notice that the hand holding hers isn't shaking, even though my other one is.

"I know you're used to better," I say. "The Atlantic Ocean and all. But the White River Lake is all I have to offer."

"It's beautiful," Jamie says. "Besides, as some producer or other used to say, 'A rock's a rock, a tree's a tree, and water's water. Shoot it in Griffith Park.' I mean we could shoot *Mutiny on the Bounty* here, if we wanted to. It's lovely. Don't apologize for anything, but especially not for where you come from."

"Okay, I really do love it here. When I was growing up, this lake was my favorite place on earth. Of course, back then I hadn't seen much of the earth."

"That sounds like another apology."

"Sorry."

"Growing up, did you ever go skinny-dipping here?"

"Well, ma'am, yes, I did."

"Coed skinny-dipping?"

"That's the best kind."

"Is it? Is it really? Hmmm. Would you mind proving that?"

"What?" I ask, surprised.

"Would you mind taking off your clothes and jumping in the water?"

"Is this a test or a joke?"

"How Jewish, answering a question with a question. I thought I was supposed to be the Jew, not you. Anyway, it's not a joke or a test. It's a proposition."

"What?"

"You're unusually slow tonight. I thought you could read my mind."

"Not always."

"Would you go skinny-dipping with me?"

"Uh . . ."

"I'll take that as a yes." Jamie starts taking off her clothes. "Last one in is a rotten egghead."

We race. I strip faster and shyly plunge into the dark water seeking cover. She is not far behind me. Surfacing, I HEAR her SPLASH. I realize that now I have seen my director naked, but only as a kind of dimly lit blur. She comes up shivering next to me.

"Is this what it was like in high school?" she asks.

"No, the girls weren't as smart," I say.

"I don't feel that smart tonight."

I put my arms around her and we kiss underwater. One hand strays to her breast. She pushes me away. Gently.

"I don't feel *that* dumb either," she says when we pop up. "We still have to work together."

When we emerge on shore shivering, we dry off with our clothes. So now the clothes are wet and cold. I start to get into my jeans anyway.

"Ick," Jamie says in the language of women. "Don't do that."

"Huh?" I say in the confused male language.

"I hate wet clothes. Let's ride back naked. But don't speed. I'd rather not get pulled over."

Back on the two-lane blacktop, stark-raving, birthday-suit naked, I keep the faded pickup below fifty. Not only because Jamie asked me to cool it. Not only because the police might uncharacteristically show up and find nudists unusual. I'm not sure what law we would be breaking, but I don't want to find out. Anyway, I am driving slower than usual because I never want this ride to end.

"You're beautiful," I say.

"Do you mean I'm only beautiful with my clothes off?" Jamie asks.

"No."

"Yes, you do."

I try to concentrate on the road, on my driving, although it is hard.

"I didn't realize, uh, I mean—" I begin uncertainly.

"You never noticed I've got tits?"

"On the contrary—"

"'On the contrary'? You think that's dialogue?"

I pull to the side of the road into an unexpectedly steep ditch. My father's pickup leans at a precarious forty-five-degree angle. I reach for her breast. She doesn't stop me this time. Soon I am worried about whether our acrobatics will tip over my father's pickup. How would I explain that to dear old Dad? But she stops me before the earth moves and the pickup falls over.

"I've got a code, too," Jamie says. "No fucking the fucking people you fucking work with."

Pain and suffering.

48

WHEN WE FINALLY GET BACK TO FILMING, WE WRAP up the Revelie-Goodnight fight scene in four hours.

Then Kim Kurumada, the first assistant director, YELLS: "Wrong set!"

Meaning we are moving on. And the new set—the right set—is miles away in Palo Duro Canyon. Which will waste a lot of time, but what are you going to do? Soon we hit the road in a convoy: vans, motor homes, trucks, tractor-trailers, and honey wagons. Jamie and I ride in her middle-sized motor home.

An hour later, we pull up in front of a strange-looking pioneer home. It consists of two log cabins built about ten feet apart with a single peaked roof connecting them. The space between the cabins—a breezeway—is called a "dog's run."

"Nice work," Jamie tells our set designer, MICHAEL MAL-ROOD. "Nice aging."

"Thanks," he says.

Leaving him behind, we amble up to the dog's run, where there is some shade.

"People don't always laugh," I say. "He didn't."

"That's because he didn't know I was making a joke," she says.

"Were you?"

"Only partially."

"What's wrong?"

"Mike's aged the cabin, but I think it should be right out of the box. This is Goodnight's present to his bride. It hasn't been sitting around aging for years. His instincts were right, but he didn't read the script closely enough. Like all those people who illustrate book covers. Anyway, there's nothing we can do now unless we want to rebuild the whole thing."

"We can't un-age it?" I ask.

"As I'm sure you'll eventually discover in life, it's a hell of a lot easier to age than roll back the clock. Even in the movies."

The scene we are about to shoot is called "the wedding ball" in the script, but it isn't going to be a ball as usually understood. Our ballroom will be the dog's run between the north room and the south room. The dance floor is packed earth. As in real historical life, there unfortunately won't be enough women to go around. Revelie is, after all, the only Eve in an Eden full of Adams, so measures will have to be taken if the ball is to be a success. Our first shot will show the cowboys drawing straws to see which ones will be girls and which ones boys. Those who get the short straws will be the females, the long straws, the males. The short straws will tie white handkerchiefs around their left arm to indicate that they are the weaker and fairer sex.

I am smiling in anticipation of what is to come until I look up and SEE (POV): Buddy Dale, dressed in black, approaching with a girl who looks like his granddaughter on his arm.

"What's wrong?" asks Jamie.

"Darth Vader is back in black," I say.

"Oh," she says but doesn't look.

But I do, and I see Chris Crosby following Buddy like a faithful dog. They all three have runny noses. Good. This could be my chance to get a sample of Buddy's DNA. Chris's, too. All I have to do is follow along behind and pick up discarded tissues filled with DNA, among other things.

"Hey, Jamie," Buddy Dale calls.

Now she has to look, but she doesn't have to smile, and doesn't. Ignoring me, Buddy, his "granddaughter," and Chris stop in front of Jamie.

"Jamie, I'd like you to meet Heather," says the producer.

HEATHER looks like a beautiful and promising fourteen-year-old. She has blond hair, clashing brown eyes, an unlined and perfectly symmetrical baby face with an upturned nose. She LAUGHS. Buddy doesn't introduce me, which pisses me off even though I know it shouldn't. What do I care about being slighted by a lint ball like Buddy? Hmmm.

Jamie and Heather shake hands.

"She's here for the wedding ball scene," Buddy says. "Won't she look fabulous in a ball gown?"

"I'm sure she would—" I begin.

"She *will*," Buddy tells me.

"Not unless she's willing to have a sex-change operation," I say, talking back to Buddy once again.

"What are you raving about?" asks Buddy.

"If you'd read the script, you'd know that the only woman at this wedding ball is Revelie. Period. That's the point," Jamie says. "The very feminine Revelie is the only female—marooned really—in an all-male world. Kind of like me."

"But the script says it's a wedding ball," Buddy says.

"Can you spell irony?" asks Jamie.

"Maybe Heather would be willing to read the script to you," I say. Meanwhile, the two chambers of my heart are trying to beat the shit out of each other. "Prevent future casting malfunctions."

"Someday . . ." Buddy threatens.

Jamie gives me a look that says: Be careful, Vesuvius, you're about to blow. A little rumbling is okay, but that's enough.

So I keep my mouth shut.

"Does this mean I'm not getting a ball gown?" demands Heather.

"I'm sorry," Jamie says, "but it means you're not getting a part. Not in this scene."

"Buddy, you promised me," Heather complains. "What are you going to do? I passed up a fashion show for this gig. You owe me for that and lots more. I thought you were the boss around here."

"I am," Buddy assures her. "We'll work something out. You'll be in the scene. I promise."

"I'm not so sure about that," says Jamie.

"You have to use her in the scene," Buddy demands.

"Fire me," Jamie says.

"Heather, would you mind waiting for me in my trailer? Chris, would you escort her? I'll straighten this out and see you in a few minutes."

Watching Heather and Chris retreat, I think: So Buddy's got a trailer now. Must be handy for casting. Maybe that's why he went back to Los Angeles: to line up more perks. I follow Chris with my eyes to see if he will blow his runny nose and discard a tissue. He doesn't, but I will keep watching.

"Okay," Buddy tells Jamie in hushed tones, "you don't really have to use her. Let her prance around in a couple of expendable takes. So she'll be on the cutting-room floor. So what? Editing happens."

"So you really do have her best interests at heart," Jamie says. "I was afraid you were just using her."

"Do you want this movie made or not?"

Buddy turns and walks away, presumably on his way to his new motor home and his new actress. I watch him go hoping he will shed a Kleenex. He doesn't.

"I think he's bluffing," Jamie tells me, "but I don't think I'm willing to call his bluff. Do you think less of me?"

I think too long. Then I say: "It seems to me that I never fully appreciated Faust."

"Damn you! I'm trying to make your movie. I'm trying to realize your dream. And you give me this kind of shit! You accuse me of making a deal with the devil. Damn you!"

She storms off toward her trailer. I just stand there because I don't have a trailer. I feel irritable and homeless.

"We're getting close," Kim Kurumada, the first AD, calls a couple of hours later.

Our actors are milling about in the dog's run, looking comparatively washed and shaved. After all, they are going to a ball. Jamie and I are circling each other warily. My Buddy radar warns me that he is approaching. I look around and spot him bearing down on Jamie. Walking a half-step behind him is a short, baby-faced cowboy who doesn't need to shave. I recognize her right away, and I head toward the confrontation.

"How about this for a compromise?" Buddy asks Jamie. "Now she's a cowboy. She'll fit right in."

"No," I say. "She doesn't look like a boy, much less a cowboy."

Jamie gives me the cool-down look.

"That's the reason people hate having screenwriters on the set," Buddy explodes. "I've had it with you. You're off the set. You're banned from the set. Get out of here."

"No!" says Jamie.

"No?" Buddy asks. "No, he's not banned? Or no, Heather can't play a man in the scene?"

We all stare at our director. She won't meet my eyes, but she does meet Buddy's, not a good omen. We all wait.

"No to both," Jamie says at last. "Chick can stay and Heather can't be in the scene. Sorry. It would compromise the whole sequence."

"We'll see about that," Buddy says. "Chick, you're fired. Get off this set or I'm calling security. You're trespassing. If you resist, you'll suffer the consequences."

I just stand there hating him with my eyes. Chris materializes from somewhere and stands beside Buddy. Is our stunt coordinator supposed to represent the consequences?

"Go on," Buddy orders. "I'm serious."

"I'm not going anywhere."

"Yes, you are! Security!" Buddy is looking all around. "Get me a guard!"

Glancing around, I SEE (POV) teamsters, a rent-a-cop, and Chris Crosby all converging on me. I flinch in spite of myself.

"Buddy, I've got a little something to show you," Jamie says.

She opens her script in the middle and plucks from between its pages—where she always keeps it—the Polaroid of Buddy with a green tie tied around his genitals. In the West Texas sunshine, the colors are strikingly vivid.

"Just a suggestion," says Jamie, "lighten up."

Buddy lunges for the photo. She pulls it out of his way like a matador pulling away a cape. The producer stumbles and falls on the red earth. Chris rushes in to lift him up.

"Are you okay?" asks the stuntman.

"Yes, of course." He struggles against helping hands. "Get your hands off me. Stoppit! Stoppit!"

"Just tell us who you want us to beat up," says a huge truck-driving teamster.

"Me," says Jamie, stepping forward. "He wants you to beat me up and steal this picture." She holds up the Polaroid for the teamsters to see. The behemoths freeze. "Nice likeness, don't you think?" She looks around. "Heather, come here. Have you seen this?"

Heather approaches.

"Damn you!" Buddy actually snarls. "Give me that thing right now. That's my property. Hand it over or I'll have you arrested for stealing."

Heather keeps coming, squinting at the photo. She must be near-sighted.

"Sorry, Buddy," Jamie says. "I'm afraid pictures don't belong to the subject, namely you, but to the photographer, namely some bimbo. If she asked me, I'd have to give it to her. But you? No, sorry."

Buddy seethes but can't think of a rejoinder.

"I wanna see," says Heather, running now.

"No, you don't!" Buddy SHOUTS. "Heather, get back to the trailer right now!"

The model dressed as a cowboy keeps coming, but she slows down.

"Heather, you'll love it," Jamie says.

"I said go back to the trailer!" Buddy YELLS.

"No," says Heather. "I'm through listening to you. You told me I could be in the movie. You told me I'd have a ball gown. You told me I'd have words to say. And none of that's true. I wanna see the fuck-ing picture."

"Be my guest," Jamie says.

As she attempts to hand the Polaroid to Heather, Buddy charges, trying to grab it, but once again he misses, loses his balance, and careens into a teamster. Who by this point isn't sure whether he wants to touch the great producer or not. He might catch something.

"Oh, my God!!" Heather SCREAMS. Then she starts LAUGH-ING. And *LAUGHING*. And <u>*LAUGHING*</u>. The clay cliffs ring with her LAUGHTER.

Buddy storms off in the direction of his new trailer.

"Behave," Jamie calls after him, "or I'll put it on the Internet."

"Good going," I tell her.

"Get away from me," she hisses. "You accused me of selling my soul to the devil, damn you."

"I was confused. Right play, wrong character. Now I realize you're not Faust, you're Helen."

"Nice compliment, but—but—uh, nice compliment."

"You're welcome."

"The shark is dying!" YELLS Kim Kurumada.

"We should give it mouth to mouth," SHOUTS Sarah, the blushing bride. "I volunteer."

I find myself wondering whose teeth would be sharper.

49

WE SPEND THE REST OF THE LATE AFTERNOON AND evening shooting the wedding ball and worrying about what Buddy Dale will do to exact his revenge. We know he cannot stand being thwarted and hates being embarrassed even more. Laughed at even by his bimbo.

"Action," Jamie says self-consciously.

EXT. DOG'S RUN — EVENING

Half the cowboys—the short straws—wear white
handkerchiefs on their arms. The bride in her
elegant wedding dress and the groom in his cowboy
duds are poised to lead off the ball. The fiddler is
COFFEE, the cook.

> COFFEE
>
> Whaddle I play?

> TOO SHORT
>
> It's gotta be a waltz.

> COFFEE
>
> Whichun?

> TOO SHORT
>
> The one about Froggie the Frog.

> COFFEE
> (to bride and groom)
>
> That okay by you, folks?

> REVELIE
>
> Of course, the Blue Danube Waltz would
> be lovely.

> GOODNIGHT
>
> Shore, play Ole Froggie.

The fiddler starts fiddling and the groom takes the
bride in his arms and they dance. To help him keep
time to the music, Goodnight SINGS softly in
Revelie's ear:

GOODNIGHT
Froggy the frog, hop hop, hop hop,
jumped over a log, hop hop, hop hop . . .

MONTAGE: BLACK DUB dances with Too Short. LOVING
whirls TIN SOLDIER around the dance floor. And
Goodnight dances with the bride in her wedding
dress. They kick up a lot of red dust. The bottom of
the bride's gown is almost blood red.

ANGLE ON COFFEE: He plays "After the Ball Was Over."

VARIOUS ANGLES, MOVING HANDHELD CLOSE-UPS: Goodnight
dances with Tin Soldier. And Loving dances with the
bride in her flowing white and red gown. POV:
Goodnight is always watching his new wife and his
best friend. Loving guides Revelie around the dance
floor with skill and assurance. He dances the way he
rides, the way he does everything, with an economy
of motion that has a special charm. And Revelie in
his arms mirrors his economy and matches his charm.
They seem made to dance together.

"Cut," breathes Jamie self-consciously. "That was perfect. Let's do
it again. Back to number-one positions."
"If it was perfect, why would you—?" I begin.
"Shut up!" she orders.
"She explained," I say.
"Ring Lardner," Jamie says. "Right?"

"Moving on," Jamie announces ten takes later. "Somebody go get the
Steadicam." She turns to me. "Are you pleased?"
"Pleased as prickly pear punch," I assure her.

"How quaint."

"I just made that up. There's no such thing as prickly pear punch, but it alliterates."

"Find a place to put it in the script."

"But it's made up."

"So are movies, professor."

Wanting to change the subject, I say: "I can't wait to see the Steadicam in action."

"Yeah, but speaking of 'in action,' take a look at your friend Sarah."

I turn and SEE (POV): Sarah is still in the arms of Loving as played by Kelly Hightower, the actor who almost lost a job because he put on the wrong hat. Sarah's head is still tucked in just below Kelly's chin. It is as if she thinks the music is still playing, the waltzers still waltzing. Sarah and Kelly look like a freeze frame. Motionless. Beyond time. Then Sarah destroys the effect by rising on tiptoes and whispering something in Kelly's ear. It is a peculiarly intimate gesture. I feel a pang of jealousy for God knows why.

"She's a piece of work," Jamie says, "with the emphasis on piece."

"Yeah," I agree.

"You know what she's doing, don't you?" she says.

"Trying to get laid," I say.

"That too. But she's still trying to make Tom jealous. Not just 'acting' jealous—not just there's-a-writer-in-my-bed jealous—but real jealousy."

I look around for Tom Bondini to see if he is even aware of his costar's performance. He is. He is glaring at Sarah. Tom is Arthur watching Guinevere whispering to Lancelot. Noticing Tom's interest, Sarah bites Kelly's earlobe. Revelie bites Loving. Guinevere bites Lancelot. The snake in the Garden of Eden bites man.

"Watch," Jamie whispers to me. "Tom will either play into her hands or he won't. Let's see what he's made of."

Tom strides toward Kelly. It is high noon. The studs are in the street. Duel in the sun is coming down. Sarah smiles. Perfect. She is getting just what she wants. She happily awaits the explosion as if she were a psychological suicide bomber.

"Watch," Jamie whispers. "Watch, watch." As if anybody is watching anything else. "My money's on Tom."

Seeing the jealous "husband" bearing down on them, Sarah and Kelly unclench. Still close, they turn to face the threat.

"No, don't," Sarah says, still playing her role, telling her rival lovers not to fight over her. "Please don't."

Tom Bondini—a.k.a. Goodnight—brushes past Sarah as if she were not there at all. He rushes up to Kelly Hightower—a.k.a. Loving—and envelops him in a Hollywood hug. Which goes on. And on. And on. Tom's hands are moving on Kelly's back, caressing, massaging. The biggest star in the world is making happy sounds and nuzzling the cowboy's neck. Then Tom nibbles Kelly's still-wet earlobe. Sarah just stares, shocked, horrified, angry, and jealous.

I feel Jamie's hands tightening around my arm. Her fingernails hurt as they press into my skin.

"I wish we could use this in the movie," my director whispers.

Then Tom Bondini turns Kelly Hightower's face to him and kisses him full on the mouth. Goodnight kisses Loving. Arthur plants a big wet one on Lancelot, and Guinevere doesn't like it. It was supposed to be her party, but she is left out.

"Ouch," I say.

"Sorry," whispers Jamie.

The kiss is still going on. Tom is kissing Kelly so hard that his cheeks crater. He looks like a famine victim. Sarah abruptly gets tired of waiting and waiting for Arthur and Lancelot to unclench. Guinevere hikes up the skirts of her wedding dress and marches away, beaten, bested, furious, ignored, and still jealous. A nervous LAUGHTER ripples through the cast and crew.

As soon as Sarah is gone, Tom immediately releases Kelly. It is as though somebody has just said "cut." The performance is over.

50

SITTING AT MY COMPUTER IN MY ROOM, I KEEP TRYING to rewrite tomorrow's pages, but I'm having a hard time concentrating. I blame my lack of concentration on Buddy Dale because I am sure he is plotting retribution. Will he plant drugs in my room—or Jamie's—and then call the cops? Will he spread rumors about my having sex with cattle? Or worse, especially in this country, sheep?

I am still trying to read his twisted mind when my cell phone BURPS. Picking it up, I expect to find Jamie's number on the tiny screen, but instead I see a number I don't recognize. Could it be Buddy?

"Hello," I say suspiciously.

"Hi, it's Stacy," says Sarah's stunt double. "Chris just told me something I thought you might find interesting."

"What?" I ask, not exactly sounding like a trained interviewer.

"Chris said he has Buddy by the balls. He owns Buddy's balls. He's leading him around by the balls."

"Why? How?"

"He's got evidence Buddy did something bad."

"What did Buddy do?"

"I don't know, but it must be pretty awful because Chris says he is going to be the new stunt coordinator for all of Paramount, the whole studio."

"What about the evidence? Did Chris give you any hints?"

"No, and I even fucked him to try to find out, but he wouldn't tell me."

"Oh," I begin but don't know quite what to say. *Nice going* doesn't seem appropriate. "Are you sure he didn't let anything slip?"

"Sorry. Like I said, I tried."

"Thank you. Anything else at all?"

"No, nothing."

"I really appreciate this. Please let me know if you hear anything more."

"Okay, I better go."

I am hanging up the phone when I change my mind.

"Wait," I say. "Are you there?"

"I'm here."

"Good. I just thought of something." But can I bring myself to put that thought into words? "You, see, uh . . ."

"What?"

"Well, see, uh, you said you kind of did it with Chris, right?"

"Yeah, I fucked him."

"Right, and, well, I need a sample of Chris's DNA. And I thought, well, you might have one. You know . . ."

"You mean between my legs?"

"I'm sorry. I mean you probably used protection. Forget I asked."

"Protection? In Texas? The bareback state? Don't worry. You'll have your DNA. Be my pleasure." She pauses and sniffles. "Chris hit me tonight."

Returning to my keyboard, my concentration is worse than it was before. I stand up and head for the door. Maybe a drive will help clear my overcrowded head.

Leaving the 6666 castle, I head west on Highway 82 with no destination in mind. I pass the entrance to the Pitchfork Ranch on my left. A few miles farther on, I speed past the rodeo grounds on my right. I can feel the wind hitting my pickup broadside trying to blow it off course. And all the while I keep replaying tomorrow's lines, but there is interference, static. Buddy is still crying havoc in my head. And I keep replaying Stacy's phone call. What evidence of which crime? My Sharon? His Miss Texas? What?

Then I SEE (POV) the sign for the turnoff to Dickens Springs. Having always loved this place, I hope it might be a soothing setting to regroup and really think. I turn right onto the dirt road and climb the steep bank. Then the road levels out. Passing the picnic table disguised as a covered wagon, I remember indelible nights of discovery here when I was in high school and dating a cheerleader. And of course, I also recall my less rewarding visit with Jamie. Another dark night.

I drive to the very brink of the cliff that marks the beginning of the breaks country. I sit there staring into the darkness, barely able to make out the canyons within canyons, the interlocking arroyos, the infinite succession of dark humps in the night. I hope this familiar black and gray panorama will fine-tune my head, but the static keeps on crackling between my ears.

I get out of the car and walk to the edge of the cliff. The wind hits me in the face smelling of dry earth and something pungent. I scare myself by inching even closer to the drop-off. I dare myself to jump.

My mind does seem to be clearing at last when I SEE (POV) a pickup coming down the road toward me. Its lights are off. Puzzled and a little apprehensive, I start back toward my own truck. A dark figure gets out of the pickup. Like an outlaw in the movies, he is wearing a bandana over his face and he is carrying a large stick. I start running toward my truck. He runs to meet me. We are like long-lost lovers racing to embrace.

As the masked man swings his stick, I think incongruously, stupidly: I'm about to find out how it feels to be a baseball. I half turn and the blow catches me on the right shoulder. Now I recognize the outlaw's weapon. It isn't a bat, it's an ax handle. How odd. Or how premeditated. How carefully chosen. How perfect and how horrible. To be beaten with the handle of an ax, my forefather's scepter, his Excalibur.

"Why!" I SCREAM.

But I know why. Only someone close to our movie would know to choose this uniquely apt weapon. So I not only know why but who. Don't I?

The next blow hits me just below my knee. He was probably aiming to shatter my kneecap, but he missed, not much of a low-ball hitter. Crying out in pain, I jump on one leg. Then he just misses the other kneecap. I fall in a heap on the ground. He hits me on the back trying to crack my ribs. Instinctively, I curl up like an armadillo and cover my balls with my hands. I don't know why I pick my balls instead of my head, but I do. Instinctive priorities.

Now I am not only in pain but frightened. The fear is as palpable as the pain. The fear actually hurts. It throbs. It paralyzes. Is this masked axman going to kill me? Is he going to take away my one and only life? Is he going to put me in the same ground as my poor cousin?

I discover that I hate Buddy Dale more than I have ever hated anyone in my whole life. I hate him for what he did to my cousin, and I hate him for what he is doing to me. I tell myself I have to survive in order to extract, extort, compel vengeance. Now I cover my head with my hands because I want to live even more than I want to procreate. I have to live. I can't let Buddy win. The ax handle breaks my left hand. Strangely, I think: This is going to cramp my twirling.

The next blow misses my hands and seems to shatter my skull. I feel hot pain, hotter hate, and I drop over the cliff of consciousness into the darkest badlands.

51

"ANYBODY HOME? ANYBODY HOME? THE LIGHTS ARE out, but is anybody home?"

My eyes flicker open and I SEE (POV) Jamie leaning over me. She is out of focus.

"I love you," I say, out of my mind, babbling.

"You only say that because you are out of your mind," she says.

"No." I try to reach out to her with my right hand but discover it is taped to a board with an IV bag draining into it. I attempt to reach out with my left and find it in a cast. "Damn," I say, frustrated, "am I going to live?"

"I'm afraid so."

"Afraid? I can tell you about afraid. I was afraid shitless. Do you think less of me?"

"Absolutely," she says.

"Where am I?"

"Methodist Hospital in Lubbock. I hope you're not against Methodists."

"No, I used to be one," I say. "How did I get here?"

"You were lucky."

"If this is good luck, I think I'll try bad luck next time." My light-headedness makes me say: "Everything hurts. Even my pubic hair."

"Yeah, well, anyway, you're lucky because a couple of high school kids drove out to the springs looking for passion and found you instead. They thought you were a dead body and called the cops."

"I thought I was dead, too, until I just woke up hurting."

"I guess it was a close thing. You've been out cold for a couple of days now. Nobody was real sure you were going to wake up."

"Really?"

"Really."

"How's the movie going without me?"

"Okay. Luckily movies only shut down when actors get hurt—not writers."

"Did I mention I love you?"

"You love working with me. You love our movie. You don't love me."

"It's a good thing you're pretty because you can be awfully dumb sometimes."

"I was dying for you to wake up. Now I'm dying for you to go back to sleep again."

"Maybe I, uh, maybe, I mmmm . . ."

I am just drifting off when I HEAR a KNOCK at my door. Before I can say "Come in," it opens, and in walk my mother and father.

"So you're finally awake," Dad says. "Son, if you ain't careful, you're gonna sleep your life away."

"How are you?" Mom asks anxiously. "How do you feel?"

"Everything hurts," I say. "Even the pupils of my eyes."

"You really scared us," she says.

"Mom, Dad," I say, remembering my manners, "I'd like to introduce you to—"

"We're already old friends," interrupts my father. "While you been loafin' there sleepin', we been gittin' to know each other. Who done this to you, do you know?"

"The producer," I say. "I mean not him personally. He must've hired somebody to do it. And, I don't know, maybe he even had help finding that somebody. Maybe a certain stuntman auditioned leg-breakers for him. I haven't got it all worked out yet." I yawn. "I'm sorry, I'm getting sleepy again. I don't know if I can stay awake much long—"

When I wake up, I am all alone. It doesn't seem fair. Wondering what time it is, I try to look at my watch, but there is a cast where my time-piece should be. I scan the room for a clock. There is a big one on the wall right in front of me. It reads twenty past eight, but is that morning or night? I am lost in time. The window admits gray light, but is it dimming or brightening?

"Hi," says Jamie.

I hurt myself swiveling my head from the window to a chair in the far corner of my hospital room.

"Ouch," I say. "Is it morning or night?"

"Evening. How are you feeling?"

"Lost. I guess. Lost and sore and pissed off."

"Of course."

"I thought I was all alone."

"You're not alone. Even when I'm not here, you're not alone. Can you understand that?"

"I'm trying. But it's easier to understand when you're here."

"I know."

"Have you been here all the time?"

"Whenever I could get away."

I notice that she is paying more attention to what she is writing on a legal pad than she is to me, and I'm instantly jealous.

"You're making a list," I accuse.

"What else have I had to do all these hours?"

"I'm sorry you've been bored, but I'm awake now."

"Good, do you happen to know a crime category that begins with *Y*? I've come up with several but they aren't very satisfying. Well, do you?"

"Yelling," I say.

"That's not a crime," she says.

"It is in my family."

"Okay, *Y* is for yelling."

"Look, I've helped you. I'm part of the list game now. You have to tell me the rules. Please."

"No! Now I need the name of a movie that features yelling."

"Let's see, what about *Who's Afraid of Virginia Woolf?*"

"Very good. Any others?"

"Anything with Liza Minnelli."

"I need titles."

"Uh . . . uh . . . *A Streetcar Named Desire.* Remember, 'Stella!!'"

"I remember. What else?"

"I know, *Scream* and *Scream 2.*"

"Screaming isn't yelling."

"Yes it is."

"It's my list and I say it isn't. Let's move on to *Z*. Do you know any crimes that begin with *Z*?"

"Oh, I get it," I say. "Alphabetical crimes followed by the appropriate movie titles, huh? *A* is for ax murder. So you need a chop-'em-up movie, say *Crime and Punishment,* right? How'm I doing?"

Jamie doesn't say anything. She just glares.

"Let's see, *B* is for burglary," I guess. "Say *To Catch a Thief. C* is for, uh, I don't know what. But *D* is for decapitate as in *A Tale of Two Cities.* Like that. Right, right?"

"You think you're so smart," Jamie scolds. "Well, if you're so smart, why can't you come up with *Z?*"

"I can," I say confidently, but then I can't think of any *Z* crimes. Zebra murder? No. Zoo graffiti? No. "Would you accept zealotry?"

"Hmmmm. I don't know."

"What about *Elmer Gantry?*"

"I'm liking zealotry better."

Unfortunately, all this thinking is making me sleepy again.

I wake up—who knows how much later?—when I feel Jamie touching my shoulder. It is an affectionate gesture, but it still hurts. I wince just as I HEAR a KNOCK on the door.

"Are you decent?" my father's voice booms through the wood.

"Moderately," I call back.

The door opens and Mom and Dad enter once again.

"Are you feeling any better?" asks my mother.

"Everything still hurts," I say, "even my—toenails."

"You should clip those," she says, staring at a foot protruding from the covers, and unable to keep from being momlike. "But I'm sorry they hurt."

"How're you doin'?" my father asks my director. "Did you get any rest?"

"A little," Jamie says. "How about you, Mr. Goodnight?"

"There you go again with that 'mister.' Please, call me Clyde. Say, when you finish this here movie, I got another picture show you can make. Did Chick here ever tell you 'bout that there great goat drive?"

"No, sir"—catching herself—"no, Clyde, he didn't."

"Well, see, I had this crazy old uncle named Hool and he owned a coupla thousand goats. Back about eighty years or so, when this here part of the country got rained on even less'n usual. So crazy Uncle Hool makes up his mind he's gonna drive all them goats to New Mexico, where he hears they's better grass. He up and hires some old cowboys and drives that there big old herd of goats about five hundred miles acrosst badlands and over mountains and through the damn White Sands. Hell of a story. You could even call it *The Great Goat Drive*. Be like one of them cattle drive movies only different. Whaddaya say?"

I am of course embarrassed. What is my father doing trying to pitch a movie to my director?

"I love it!" exclaims Jamie with what seems genuine enthusiasm. "Kind of a cross between *Red River* and 'Billy Goat Gruff.'"

My father LAUGHS. Jamie LAUGHS with him. They are getting along famously. Why was I worried? Why embarrassed? Somehow I had momentarily forgotten how charming my father is. I overlooked the effect he always has on women of all ages.

"Clyde, have you ever thought of acting?" Jamie asks.

"No, ma'am, I ain't never thought no such thing."

"Well, maybe you ought to. We might even have a part for you. I mean you've got the accent, right?"

"Are you pullin' my leg, purdy lady?"

"I wouldn't do that, Clyde. I'm serious. Of course, you'd have to read a scene for me. Or read a scene with me. Kind of an audition."

"Well, that would be my pure pleasure, ma'am."

"Great. I'll set it up. Okay?"

"Okay, but it better not be too big a part. I'd sure hate to have it interfere with my sol time."

"Sol time?"

"The time he devotes to playing solitaire every day," my mother explains.

"Clyde, I see you haven't spent much time on movie sets. When you're making a movie, you have all the time in the world to play sol. In fact, you'll have more time than when you're doing nothing."

"Well, that's sure a load off my mind, purdy director lady."

"Clyde, come on," says my mother with a slight edge in her voice, "buy me a cup of coffee. Let's leave the young people alone for a little while."

My dad politely opens the door for my mom and escorts her out the door.

"I love you," I say.

"No, you don't," Jamie says. "But I love your dad. He'd be perfect as one of the other ranchers. Or maybe the judge or even the prosecutor. We'll see."

"What about my mom?"

"Oh, I forgot about her, didn't I? Well, she can be an extra. How about that?"

"My dad's a charmer, isn't he?" I say jealously.

"He certainly is."

I lift my broken hand and stare at it.

"This is what I was afraid of. Looks like I'm going to have to cut back on my baton twirling."

52

HALF WAKING FROM A NAP, I HAZILY BEGIN TO PLAN my revenge. Dreamily I wonder: How shall I do it? What about a baseball bat? Then Buddy would have the pleasure of knowing how a baseball feels. I imagine it is the bottom of the ninth inning in the World Series. Here comes the pitch. It's a big, fat curveball. I swing, I connect, there goes the producer's head over the left-field wall. I like it, but it seems hard to arrange.

Okay, well, how about this: I put poison in his coke? Or how about poison in his black hair dye? Vanity kills. Or poison in his botox? But that's already poison, isn't it? Well, then make it stronger. Make it strong enough. He'll die with no wrinkles and leave a good-looking corpse. Better yet, feed him a poisoned bimbo. I LAUGH and it hurts my bruised face. Ouch.

But what if Chris turns out to be the one who deserves to die? I could Super Glue him to a mechanical bull and buck him to death. I could put arsenic in his Skoal. Or I could poison his steroids.

What about something more practical? Let's see, blunt instruments seem to be the least traceable and don't require background checks. I could arm myself with a rock, or a pipe, or a hammer. What about a crowbar, and then the crows could pick out guilty eyes? Premeditating Chris's—or Buddy's—pain takes my mind off my own bruised and broken body. Okay, how do you get an anonymous gun? And how do you know you're not buying it from an undercover cop?

When a deputy sheriff walks into my hospital room, I jump because I feel I have been caught in the act. The law has walked into the middle of my murder plans.

"Didn't mean to scare you," says Deputy Jimmy Lee Johnson, my friend from Spur High football. "Do you feel up to answering a few questions?"

"Sure," I lie.

"Could you kind of start at the beginning and tell me what happened?" he asks, his interviewing technique improving.

But I don't play along, don't begin at the beginning: "I'll tell you just what happened," I say. "Buddy Dale hired a thug to beat me up."

"But what about that other guy? That stuntman? You know, the one who's always beatin' you up on the set?"

"He isn't always beating me up," I say indignantly. "He just hit me once."

"Not what I heard." He shakes his head as if he is disappointed in me. "I heard you was done down for the count at least three times."

"Those other two"—the fake punch and the chest push—"I just sorta fell down on my own."

"Good, I'd hate to hear that a fake Hollywood cowboy could beat up on a real Spur Bulldog. I mean more'n oncet or twicet."

"It was just once. Who've you been talkin' to anyway?"

"Ever'body. And now I'm talkin' to you. Tell me what happened that night?"

"Okay, you wanna read me my rights?"

"Naw, victims don't have no rights, just vicious criminals."

53

THREE DAYS LATER, I LIMP TOWARD THE BIG, RED 6666 barn that we have transformed into a movie theater. Dailies will be starting soon. I'm glad to be out of the hospital, happy to be reuniting with my movie, but I'm uneasy, too. It always makes me nervous to be the center of attention, which I am sure to be this evening. How could I not be with two black eyes and my arm in a sling? My hands are trembling. Both the good hand and the broken one. Not even the plaster of paris cast controls my shakes. Reaching the big barn door, I take a deep breath and push it open with my better hand. Time to make my big entrance.

Inside, I find that most of the cast and crew have already gathered. They all turn and look at me the way I knew they would. Their stares seem to form a force field propelling me back out the door. It takes an act of will to stand my ground. Needing reassurance, I look for Jamie but don't see her. I do SEE (POV) Sarah sitting with Kelly: Her hand rests on his shoulder like a brand. He's mine!

Most faces are happy to see me, some look pleased but concerned, but one face has a big shit-sandwich smile: Buddy Dale's. Sitting next to him is a smirking Chris. Now the shaking has spread contagiously from my hands to my whole body. Embarrassed, I turn to go, and I find myself face-to-face with Jamie.

"Oh, good, you're here," she says.

As always, her mere presence calms me. I begin to relax, to settle into quiet, to be less self-conscious.

"Yes, I am," I say, "and glad to be here."

"Sit with me," she says.

She leads me to her regular hay bale close to the screen. I sit on her left. Becky, her assistant, sits to her right. But we still wait. Then Tom Bondini walks in wearing his T-shirt and bright puce running shoes.

"Let's get started," Jamie says. She squeezes my good hand, then releases it.

The lights go down and movie footage jumps onto the screen. I realize that it is coincidentally, weirdly, the scene in which Goodnight wakes up from a coma.

INT. PRIMITIVE HOTEL ROOM — DAY

Loving sits beside Goodnight's bed. Goodnight's eyes blink open. He SEES (POV) his best friend looming above him.

                    GOODNIGHT
          It's you.

                    LOVING
          Ain't nobody else. Who was you
          expectin'? Some kinda archangel? Or
          mebbe the devil hisself?

                    GOODNIGHT
          If I ain't in heaven or hell, where the
          hell am I?

                    LOVING
          At the Grand Hotel in Hot Springs. Only
          it ain't all that grand if'n you ask my
          opinion. Closer to hell than heaven.

                    GOODNIGHT
          How'd you find me?

LOVING

```
Wisht I could claim credit, but just
ain't so. You was lucky. Old prospector
name a Jensen come acrosst you. He
figured you was dead till he tried to
steal yore money. You surprised him by
bein' able to cock yore gun.
```

The master, the wide shot, plays over and over on the screen. We see not every take filmed but just the takes the director wanted printed. While we watch take one, followed by take five, followed by take eight, Jamie keeps whispering in the ear of Becky, who scribbles nonstop notes. She records which takes the director likes. Which mannerisms might be curbed in the future. General advice to actors on what is working and what isn't.

Seated beside Jamie, I am no longer trembling. I am enjoying myself. I even manage to forget that I am looking out of two black eyes.

After the master, we look at the close-ups. Kelly Hightower's face fills the screen.

LOVING

```
Ain't nobody else. Who was you
expectin'? Some kinda archangel? Or
mebbe the devil hisself?
```

At the end of the scene, Jamie says: "Nice work, Kelly."

"Thanks," he says.

"See, I told you, you're great," Sarah tells the new man in her life, her Loving. "You're gonna surprise ever'body." Then she adds in a stage whisper: "You're much better'n he is."

Thankfully, I am no longer the center of attention: He, Tom Bondini, is. Everybody turns and stares at him. He just CHUCKLES and shakes his head as if to say: What do you do with a problem child?

We see the scene again, a different take, the same words but a slightly altered coloring. Kelly has more fun with the lines this time. Then another take. This time Kelly comes down harder on the word "devil." And on and on, again and again.

Then come Tom Bondini's close-ups. Take after take, repetition and more repetition, but I am far from bored or anxious to move on. Not only because I like watching dailies—and trying to decide which takes are the best ones—but I am actually beginning to dread the moment when they will end. Because then I will have to talk to people.

Be careful what you dread because it is likely to happen. Soon people are coming up to me, asking me how I'm doing, patting me on my sore back and worse shoulder. I keep mumbling that I am fine even though I know I don't look fine. Luckily I don't have to do a close-up because I would scare the audience out of the theater.

As he is leaving the barn, Buddy pauses to shake my hand. He is still grinning. I start to turn away, then change my mind. I take his hand with my good hand and squeeze as hard as I am capable of squeezing. I try to break his hand bones but fail. I have to work out more. But his grin fades.

When he is gone, I go back inside the big barn and search around the bale of hay where he was sitting. I know it is his bale because grains of cocaine lie atop it like tiny snowflakes. I find four used tissues scattered carelessly on the floor.

54

THE BUFFALO KEEP ARRIVING ALL DAY. THEY COME IN horse trailers and cattle trucks. They arrive from all over Texas, New Mexico, and Oklahoma. One load even rolls in from Yellowstone. We are assembling the greatest buffalo herd to roam these plains in well over a hundred years. For a few days, it will be 1868 in old Texas once again. I keep expecting a hunting party of Comanches to appear on the horizon.

"This is moviemaking on a grand scale," says Jamie.

"Amazing," I say.

"It really is."

Jamie and I are walking slowly along a barbed-wire fence that surrounds our burgeoning buffalo herd. I am still having trouble believing the great lengths to which Hollywood will go to make a movie.

"How do you feel?" Jamie asks. "All healed up?"

"Pretty much," I answer. It has been three weeks since my beating. "Everything except my hand." I hold up my cast.

"Do you feel well enough to ride?"

"Ride? Why do you ask?"

"Well, you can ride, can't you?" Jamie asks. "You can't come from a town named Spur and not be able to ride."

"Sure, I can sit a horse," I say, "but I'm no rodeo rider like some of my cousins."

"You have cousins who are rodeo riders?"

"Of course, doesn't everybody? Some of them even went to college on rodeo scholarships."

"You're kidding."

"Really I'm not. Anyhow I can ride well enough not to fall off too often. Why?"

"Do you ride well enough to herd cattle?"

"I've herded cattle, but I'm not much of a roper."

"You don't have to rope. Are you good enough to herd buffalo?"

"That's a good question because they're supposed to be real hard to herd. Got minds of their own. Hard to make them do anything they don't want to. You know, like cats and quail."

"No, like actors," Jamie says. "But I'll try to herd the actors if you'll try to herd the buffalo."

"What are you talking about?" I ask.

"I thought you might like to be an extra in the buffalo sequence. I like putting people I know—people I like—in my movies. Just as extras, you know."

"Sure," I say, flattered. But I keep remembering how ornery buffalo are supposed to be and what the scene is going to be about: a buffalo stampede.

"Good, your call is five A.M."

What I don't say is: I've never been a morning person.

I am sleepwalking as I make my way—before dawn—to the ramuda. Inside the corral, the horses are milling about. They are probably nervous because they suspect I have designs on riding one of them. I was a little less than frank when I told Jamie I could punch cattle (much less buffalo). When I was growing up, I had my own horse named Judy and spent a lot of time in the saddle. But that was years ago and I haven't kept up my skills. I am as apprehensive as the horses. More so.

"So you're actually up this early," Jamie says, having crept up behind me.

"Of course," I say.

"Sure," she says dismissively.

The movie's WRANGLER approaches us.

"Good mornin'," he says. He looks like a slightly taller Billy the Kid. I expect no mercy.

"Morning, Billy," Jamie says. (Oh no, that's really his name.) "Billy, I'd like you to meet Chick. He wrote the movie—"

"She helped," I interrupt. "More than helped."

"Anyway, he wrote it, including the buffalo scene. So it's only fair he should help us herd our unherdable beasts. That means he needs a good horse. One with some spirit."

"I really think spirit in horses is overrated," I say, surprising myself. But then there is such a thing as self-preservation.

"He's being modest," she tells the wrangler. "Billy, what horse would you pick for yourself if you were going to be herding buffalo today?"

"But I *am* gonna be herdin' buffalo today, ain't I?" Billy says, confused, defensive. "Has things changed?"

"No, it was just a figure of speech," she says.

"I wouldn't want to take his horse," I say.

"I'm sorry, Billy," she says. "I should have asked what horse would be your second choice."

"Well, I dunno. Less see." He ponders as he studies the horses. "Mebbe Twister. He's got some energy. Course his mouth is kinda hard, but that goes with the spirit thing there."

"Is that Twister as in tornado?" I ask.

"Yeah, thass right, but it's also kinda the way he bucks. Kinda like a bull, you know, twists and spins. But he won't do none of that unless you get on his bad side."

"How do I stay on his good side?"

"It's kinda a matter of attitude. If he knows you know what you're doin', he won't give you no trouble."

"Otherwise he's a cyclone?"

"Not always but could be."

"Could be?"

"Yeah, I reckon."

"Okay, why not?" I say because Jamie is there. "I'll take my new friend Twister. He couldn't beat me up worse than the guy with the ax handle, could he?"

"We'll see," says Billy. "I'll saddle him up for you and bring him around."

Sitting on the steps of the sweeping front porch, Jamie and I watch the frenzied activity as our movie company prepares for a buffalo drive. Stuntmen are running here and there as if they are late for their next injury. Real 6666 cowboys, whom we have recruited for the sequence, saunter about slowly with the air of men who never hurry. Trucks are kicking up dust. Buffalo bulls are roaring, which is their way of propositioning the females. And Jamie is making a list.

"What letter are you up to?" I ask.

"*N* if you must know," Jamie says coolly.

"Hmmm, *N* is tough." I consider for a long moment. "What about 'nuke'?"

"I'm not sure 'nuke' is a crime."

"Well, it isn't very nice. Then you could use *Fail-Safe* and *Dr. Strangelove*. Or if you prefer, *N* could be for 'napalm.' That's not nice either, but it smells lovely in the morning, as Bobby Duvall pointed out in *Apocalypse Now*. Are you writing these down?"

Then Sarah walks into our frame.

"I have to be in this scene," our leading lady says.

"Good morning to you, too," says Jamie. "What are you talking about?"

"My character would be a member of the posse."

This sequence is about a Goodnight posse that goes in search of a young woman who has been kidnapped by outlaws. While they are looking for her, they come across a herd of buffalo.

"You? A member of the posse? I don't think so," Jamie says. "Revelie is a Boston lady who by misadventure finds herself in the Wild West. But she's still a lady. She isn't Calamity Jane."

"I disagree," Sarah says. "I think Revelie embraces the Wild West. It's her new home. She's out to prove that she's up to it. That she's tough. Tough as the guys. Maybe even tougher than Goodnight himself."

"That may be your story," says the director, "but it's not Revelie's. Let's stick to the script."

"But it *is* Revelie. Anyway my Revelie." Sarah turns to me with blazing determination: "Chick, what do you think?"

"Well," I say, flustered, flapping my fingers like a butterfly that has had too many cups of coffee.

"Well, what?" Sarah demands.

"Well, the fact is, the real Revelie didn't join the posse," I say at last. I pause to pick my words. "There's no such person as Your Revelie, but there was an actual woman named Revelie Goodnight. I think we should try to be true to her."

"You're so fucking weak," Sarah says. She turns and marches away mumbling loudly: "Pussy-whipped, pussy-whipped . . ."

"I think your girlfriend is having second thoughts about you as a he-man," Jamie says. "Sorry about that. I really am."

"No, you're not," I say. "Anyway I hope you're not."

Ninety minutes later, stuntmen are still running, real cowboys still sauntering, the trucks are still churning dust, but the buffalo are gone. They have been herded away—herded with considerable difficulty—to our set, where they await collective stardom. Jamie and I are still on the veranda, but we have moved to a porch swing, still watching. She is still working on her list. Buddy Dale walks into our frame, blowing his nose.

"Good morning, Jamie," Buddy greets our director, ignoring me.

"Morning," she says, evidently not sure whether it is good or not.

"You know, I was thinking," he says. "I'm a pretty good rider. I'd like to be in this scene. You can always use another extra, right?"

"What wannabe starlet are you trying to impress now?" I inquire, but my delivery is a little too hot and hesitant at the same time. Unused to venting my rage, I'm not very good at it. But I vow to keep practicing.

Ignoring my question, he asks: "How about it?"

"It's okay with me if it's okay with Billy," she says. "But he doesn't usually like too many civilians riding in big, complicated scenes. I wouldn't get my hopes up."

"Billy the Kid, I already checked with him. He said it's okay with him if it's okay with you. So I guess it's okay. Thanks."

Buddy Dale turns and goes.

"Damn," Jamie says.

"Look on the bright side," I say. "Maybe he'll get killed in the buffalo stampede."

"Just make sure that honor doesn't go to you."

55

I REPORT TO THE COSTUME DEPARTMENT TO GET gussied up for my acting debut. They let me keep my Levi's, but they add batwing leather chaps. They give me a beat-up, working cowboy's sweat-stained cowboy hat, and spurs. I am surprised when they hand me a gun belt complete with six-shooter. I decide to wear it low-slung and tied to my leg, gunfighter fashion. One can dream, right?

Then I report to the set. It is a vast field some five miles from 6666 headquarters. This land looks much as it did a hundred fifty years ago thanks to a government program. For arcane reasons having to do with a surplus of cotton, the United States pays cotton farmers to turn their fields back into range land. Good for the farmers, good for us, not so good for the taxpayers. This range is beautiful, with grass tall enough to tickle a horse's belly. The wind is blowing, making the tall grass ripple, making it wave.

Spying Jamie, I swagger in her direction, thinking I look pretty good. Chaps and a gun give a fellow sexual self-confidence.

"Don't we look deadly?" Jamie says.

"I'll take that as a compliment," I say.

"You would," she says.

My hands almost stop shaking when she tells me the first shot doesn't involve me having to get on a horse. It is essentially a TWO SHOT featuring the biggest star in the world and the biggest buffalo bull I have ever seen. Tom is supposed to talk to the big woolly because my ancestor Jimmy Goodnight used to do just that. A Comanche chief taught him this trick, explaining that animals may not understand your language, but they will understand your tone of voice.

We've been assured that the giant buffalo is usually quite tame but can sometimes be erratic. While we all stand off at a respectful—and we hope safe—distance, Tom Bondini and the buffalo face off. Tom "forks"—as the cowboys say—a red horse named Red. Like the rest of us, the camera is way back, not only for safety reasons. By backing off, we can shoot the scene with a telescopic lens that will shrink the distance between Tom and the huge bull. They will look as if they are almost face-to-face even though they aren't. I keep studying Tom to see if he looks frightened. He doesn't, but then he is a good actor.

"Action," Jamie says softly.

Nothing happens.

"They couldn't hear you," I whisper.

"Action!" she YELLS.

"Where did that come from?" I whisper.

So prompted, Tom Bondini, who is wearing a radio mike,

launches into his dialogue. The buffalo chief really should be wearing one, too, but nobody has had the nerve to mention it to him. Jamie wears earphones as she often does. Today I am wearing them, too. Otherwise, at this distance, we wouldn't hear anything but the wind. Tom sounds as if he is standing next to me:

> GOODNIGHT
>
> O Great Chief of the Buffalo, I have a
> big favor to ask.
>
>   (pause to let this sink in)
> It's a real big favor. See, there's
> some outlaws stole this here girl. And
> I gotta git her back. Them outlaws'
> hideout is just right over yonder in a
> damn rock house. Excuse the "damn." So
> what I figured was this here: If'n you
> and your herd was to run past in
> fronta that there house, well, them
> outlaws just couldn't resist. They'd
> grab their guns and come runnin' out
> to kill theirselves some buffalo.
> White folks is like that. Well, you
> know that.

The big bull just tosses his head as if mildly annoyed. Is he telling Goodnight to get the hell out of there? Or is he just chasing flies away?

> GOODNIGHT (CONT)
> Good, you didn't say no right off. See,
> the idea is that when they come runnin'
> out wavin' their guns, well, we're
> gonna be waitin' for 'em. They'll be

```
huntin' buffalo, but we'll be huntin'
them hunters.
```

Goodnight lets the woolly chief think the matter over.

```
                GOODNIGHT (CONT)
    I shore hope my plan's okay with you,
    see, 'cause I cain't think a no other
    way to git them there rapin' outlaws
    outta their rock hideout. That there
    place is some kinda fortress. So we
    really do need your help. Might even be
    a chance for you to git some revenge
    if'n you ever think a that sorta thing.
    Well, now, how about it? Whaddaya say?
```

The old bull nods or maybe just shoos a pesky fly.

```
                GOODNIGHT (CONT)
Thanks.
```

I love the way the scene looks and sounds. Tom's tone is just right. It is almost exactly as I imagined it, and surely much the way it really happened. I believe it is some of the best work we have done so far. I even admire the writing.

"Don't worry," Jamie says. "There's no time to rewrite it now, but we'll save it in editing."

"What do you mean?" I ask.

"It's much too long, but we can cut it in editing. I've already got some ideas for deep cuts."

"But I loved it."

"You would."

I feel as if somebody else is beating me up. And not just any somebody. The somebody I care the most about. Hollywood is bruising.

Now I have to get on a horse. Will Twister bruise me, too? Very possibly. It's not that I don't ride, it's just that I've never ridden with iron-banded confidence. To me, horses are like people: They all make me nervous. Especially ones I don't know very well.

Billy the wrangler leads up two horses: Twister for me and a palomino mare for Buddy, who suddenly appears.

"Which one's mine?" asks the producer.

"This one," says Billy, nodding toward the palomino. "Her name's Babe."

Which isn't exactly the truth. Babe's real name is Black Widow. I had persuaded my new friend Billy the wrangler to give Buddy the meanest horse in our ramuda. According to local cowboy lore, she leaves you dead or on your head.

"Thanks," says Buddy, taking the reins.

Babe stretches forward and bites him on the cheek, drawing blood. Fighting her off, Buddy swears as if the horse would understand: "Fuck you, fuck, fuck, fuck. Fuck you forever right up the ass."

"You sure you can handle her?" I ask, goading. And I LAUGH, which is completely inappropriate and absolutely involuntary.

"Of course I can handle her!" Buddy snaps as he uses his sleeve to wipe blood from his damaged face. Like me, he is wearing wardrobe chaps (now spattered with blood) and a six-gun.

"Neither of you *have* to ride," Jamie says. "I mean you're both acting like Miss National Velvet on a hot tin roof. So you can beg off if you're really that worried."

"No." My voice shakes along with my hands.

"Never," declares Buddy, sounding like a cartoon Churchill. "Never, never, never."

"Tallyho," I say.

"Cowboys don't say that," Jamie says. "You should know better."

"Oops."

"Get on your horse!"

"I was afraid you'd say that."

Meanwhile, standing in front of Black Widow, Buddy looks the horse in the eye and gives her bridle a sudden jerk to show her who is in charge here. In response, she rears and comes down on top of him, knocking him down.

"Buddy, are you all right?" Jamie cries, crouching down. "Buddy, Buddy, talk to me."

"I'm fine," Buddy says, crawling from beneath the mare. "I ducked. Don't worry about me."

He stands up, brushing the red dust off his wardrobe clothes.

"We're getting you a different horse," Jamie announces.

"No, you aren't," Buddy says shrilly, his manhood and horsemanship challenged. "I can ride this horse. I'll show her who's boss."

My shaking fingers on the reins do not impress Twister. Neither does the cast on my wrist. He keeps stopping and lowering his head to munch on the impressive prairie grass. I grab the reins with both hands and pull up hard. If Twister and I were all alone, I wouldn't really mind if he stopped to nibble, but I know the other riders will think less of me if I am a permissive horseman. None of the real riders are putting up with this kind of behavior. It takes a while to convince the horse that I am serious, but he eventually lifts his head and starts moving again. I'm not sure whether he stopped eating because I was pulling on the reins or because he was no longer hungry. I hope he's good and full. Now we can get on with our business.

No, Twister stops again, lowers his head again, and begins another meal. I pull up on the reins, but he ignores me. He realizes he is stronger than I am and knows my hands are shaking. I am a quivering fly on his back. Looking up, I SEE (POV) the other riders getting farther and farther ahead of me.

"Hey, Chick," Buddy Dale YELLS back at me, "put another nickel in. Let's go. Try to keep up."

All the other riders LAUGH. The crew LAUGHS. Somewhere in the general laughter, I think I discern Jamie's LAUGHTER. Feeling as if the laughs are lashes, I pull at the reins harder than ever and nudge Twister with my costume-department spurs. The hungry horse lifts his head and trots forward. I grew up in Spur, Texas, but I have never before used spurs on a horse. I have discovered a new tool. If only I could use spurs on producers . . . or even myself . . . I spur again and Twister breaks into a gallop.

I catch up.

"If you need another nickel, let me know," calls Buddy, who has a large Band-Aid on his face. "I've got plenty." He LAUGHS. "I'd even pony up to buy you some riding lessons, cowboy."

"Action!" Jamie says over a bullhorn so we can all hear.

Now we unleash our quail drive. With multiple cameras rolling, we advance at a trot upon our manufactured buffalo herd. Ranged in a concave crescent, we latter-day buffalo drivers bear down on the bison. Eat your heart out, Buffalo Bill, what did you kill? The buffalo are still here, and where are you? I am on the far north side of the crescent, where my messing up won't be center stage. Buddy Dale, at his insistence, is in the middle.

Tom Bondini raises his cowboy hat and waves it over his head. Seeing this prearranged signal, we all kick our horses into a gallop. I'm glad for the change of gait because it is easier to ride a galloping horse than a trotter, less wear and tear on the balls. "Goodnight" beats his hat against his chaps to make noise. A cowboy named TIN SOLDIER bangs his tin hat on the pommel of his saddle to make even more noise, CLANG, CLANG, CLANG. Another cowboy named BLACK DUB SHOUTS and whirls his lariat over his head.

The buffalo take off and head right for our art department's conception of an outlaw cabin. It is made of papier-mâché rocks but looks like a real fortress. And we are right behind the woollies, nipping at their hocks. This is great. Not only have I not fallen off, not only is this dashing ride lots of fun, but the buffalo are doing exactly what they are supposed to, charging the outlaw hideout as if they have read the script. So much for them being like cats, quail, or actors. I am having a great time until my six-shooter bounces out of my holster.

Then things get even worse. The buffalo herd suddenly veers to the left, perhaps spooked by the "rock" cabin, maybe moved by their own zeitgeist. Or are they just ornery? They miss the outlaw's hideout by half a mile and just keep going. So much for them not being like cats, quail, or actors.

"Riders, hold up!" Jamie SCREAMS over the bullhorn.

I pull back gently on the reins and Twister slows to a stop. I glance to my left in time to SEE (POV) Black Widow screech to a stop, almost sitting down on her haunches. But Buddy Dale doesn't stop. He is launched headfirst between the horse's ears. He makes a one-point landing on the top of his head and just lies there. I feel a little guilty for having set him up on a killer horse, but that feeling quickly passes. I'm just glad I turned my head quickly enough to see it.

The producer of the movie is soon surrounded by actors, 6666 cowboys, and then our medical team, consisting of one male nurse with what looks like a fisherman's tackle box. I hang back. The crowd bursts into applause as Buddy gets unsteadily to his feet. I move closer. He looks more or less all right. Now instead of guilty, I feel disappointed.

"I'm gonna show her," Buddy mutters under his breath. "Teach her some manners."

Having seen and heard enough, I go back and start searching for my lost gun. Which I never find. To my infinite embarrassment, props has to issue me another one. They tell me they are going to dock my pay.

Take two.

It has taken over two hours to round up the buffalo and reassemble the herd. This work was done by the professionals, the 6666 cowboys. Now we are ready to shoot the scene again, but this time we will be taking precautions. A fence consisting of a single strand of barbed wire has been erected on both sides of the path we want the buffalo to take. The posts are cedar branches with the leaves still attached. We hope the fence won't look like a fence on the screen. Especially as everything will be moving so fast.

We drivers once again are lined up in our semicircle. I am again on the far right flank. Buddy is again in the middle and still on Black Widow. He was once again offered another mount, but he wouldn't admit he couldn't ride a spirited horse.

"Action!" Jamie's voice comes over the bullhorn.

We advance at a trot. Ouch, ouch. Then Tom swings his hat over his head, and we charge at a gallop. Better. And this time I have tied my new gun into my holster with a strand of thread. The buffalo break into a run that turns into a stampede. They respect the single string of barbed wire and bear down on the outlaw fortress where the kidnapped girl is being held and abused. Since I haven't fallen off, this dash is so much fun that I forget to keep my eye on Buddy. At the rock house, the herd divides like a river going around an island, which is just what it is supposed to do. Good. Perfect.

Alerted by some unnumbered sense, I glance to my left and SEE (POV) Black Widow bucking. Although I keep hoping Buddy will lose his seat, he doesn't. I must admit he holds on well. But he does lose his grip on the reins as he clings to his saddlehorn with both hands. Evidently realizing her rider can no longer steer, Black Widow stops bucking and goes back to running but in a zigzag pattern.

I am surprised to SEE (POV) Buddy Dale draw his six-shooter from his holster and aim it at Black Widow's head. Right between her ears. I can't believe it. What is wrong with him? Is he panicking? Doesn't he know the gun is unloaded? Does he plan to pistol-whip the horse? Or is he just stoned out of his mind? I am stunned to HEAR an EXPLO-SION. Black Widow somersaults and winds up lying on Buddy's right leg. He is trapped, pinned down, motionless. Could he be dead?

Nobody stops. Nobody yells "cut." Nobody does anything. Nobody seems to care.

I ask myself the obvious question: Did we get that on film?

"Did we get that on film?" I whisper to Jamie when I find her.

"Yes," she whispers back. "Anyway, I think so."

We are both staring down at Buddy Dale, who is unconscious but breathing. One leg is still trapped under the dead mare. I feel guilty, not about our producer's problems, but because I seem to have set in motion events that have caused the death of a horse. We HEAR a SIREN a long way off but getting closer.

The tow truck actually arrives before the ambulance. It was Jamie's idea to call the wrecker to lift Black Widow off the producer. The truck backs up until I am sure it is going to run over the poor dead animal. The mechanics get out and attach the lift cable to the horse's hind legs as if this is a regular occurrence. Could it be? Then they hit the winch switch. The legs come up. Then the hindquarters. Then little by little the torso.

Just then the ambulance SCREAMS up. Medics pile out and descend upon Buddy Dale. For no apparent reason, they get an IV drip going in his arm. Working gingerly, they encase his injured leg in an inflatable cast. Then they lift him almost lovingly into the ambulance and it SCREAMS away.

"Did you see that!" I ask ten minutes later.

"See what?" Jamie asks.

"The dead horse just swished her tail."

"Did you fall on your head, too?"

"There it goes again."

"Is this a joke?"

"No."

"Our movie is in jeopardy and you're wisecracking."

"But I'm not."

"Cut it out!"

Black Widow whinnies long and loud.

We call a veterinarian named J. R. KEYS. There are no human doctors within a ninety-mile radius, but there are plenty of animal doctors. And they all make house calls. Doc Keys arrives half an hour later. By now, Black Widow is back on her feet. The horse doctor talks to her soothingly, strokes her forehead, and feeds her a carrot.

"How is she, Doc?" I ask.

"I think she's gonna be fine," he says. "Looks like the bullet just grazed the top of her head. Knocked her out, probably gave her a concussion, but that should pass. Still, I'd like to take her back to my barn and watch her for a coupla days."

So we call the horse ambulance. The cowboys help Doc Keys load Black Widow into it. Then the horse doctor and the horse drive away.

"Buddy couldn't even shoot straight," I say.

"Hush your mouth," says Jamie. Then she adds: "Let's go see what we really got on film."

I follow her to the camera "truck," which looks like a high-tech street peddler's hot-dog stand. It even has a big umbrella. This rolling cabinet is crowded with technology, including video of what we have just filmed. Jamie may be an old-fashioned director who shuns new gadgets, but Victor is an up-to-date cameraman. He records all takes on videotape.

"Rack up camera three," Jamie says.

We watch on a small black-and-white television screen as the buffalo drive begins. Trotting. Now galloping. And Buddy Dale is in the center of the telescoped shot.

"You've got a camera trained on him?" I ask incredulously.

"He's the producer," Jamie says. "He asked me to. Ordered me to. What the fuck? Anyway, I did. Let's see what we've got."

On the small black-and-white screen, Buddy Dale looks surprisingly good chasing the buffalo. He has a good seat. Black Widow is behaving and responding. Horse and rider cover the ground smoothly. Then for no apparent reason, Buddy digs his spurs into his horse. Black Widow responds by bucking. Buddy spurs again. Black Widow bucks harder and almost dislodges her rider. Desperately grasping the pommel, he drops the reins. As Black Widow stops bucking and starts zigzagging, Buddy pulls the prop gun from his holster. Only as it turns out, it isn't like the other prop guns. It's loaded. Did he load the gun after that first fall? Was he just waiting for a chance to kill his enemy, Black Widow, to settle the score for embarrassing him? Or is he simply scared to death and trying to save himself? In his drug-addled state, does he believe shooting the horse is his only way out? We see the six-shooter exhale smoke and the horse somersault.

A production assistant comes up. "He's got two compound fractures."

"That's all?" I ask.

56

"THAT'S RIGHT, BUDDY DALE SHOT HIS HORSE IN THE head while it was galloping with him in the saddle. Don't say where you got this. Deep Throat rules. Deep stomach. Deep duodenum. Deep sphincter. Okay?"

I'm on the phone to a friend of mine, TERRY DINNERSTON, at the *Los Angeles Times*. Reporters will agree to anything as long as they are convinced something is true. I've known him for a long time.

"Okay," he says. "But did he actually kill the horse?"

"No, but he tried hard enough. Case of attempted horse murder."

"Does he say why?"

"Oh yeah, the other side of the story. Why not? Well, he says he didn't know the gun was loaded. Ever heard that one before?"

"Please, go on."

"And according to him: He pulled his pistol because he thought it would add drama to the buffalo chase. He was going to pretend to shoot in the air, but the gun ejaculated prematurely. A very Buddy thing to do, or so I'm told."

This story—picked up by every paper in the known world—provokes an international outcry because people will stand for murder but not cruelty to animals.

"You leaked the story!" Buddy Dale SCREAMS in the big 6666 living room.

"You shot a horse," I say, sounding like somebody else.

"Then you admit you leaked it?"

"No, I admit you shot a horse," I say, my voice thickening. "I saw you. We all saw you. We've got it on film. The papers got it right. It's not your fault you didn't kill the horse."

"You've jeopardized the movie."

"No, you have"—not only my hands but my whole being is shaking—"by trying to kill a horse. It's one thing to murder my cousin, but now you've gone too far."

"You're fired!"

"Maybe."

"You'll see!"

"We'll see. Not too many people like people who hurt horses."

I think—perhaps it's just my melodramatic imagination—that he wants to lunge across the living room at me, but he is stopped by the heavy cast on his twice-broken leg.

The studio works out a compromise: I am not to be fired but neither
is he.

"I can't believe it," I say. "It'll hurt the film."

"Wise up," Jamie says. "Nobody gives a shit who produces a movie.
Except in Hollywood." She waits for me to say something. I don't. "I
agree with you. He should be gone for all kinds of reasons, but he isn't."

"You mean I've got to kill him?"

"Don't even joke about that kind of thing."

"Who says I'm joking?"

In my 6666 room, I return to what has become my mantra: How
should I kill Buddy? How do I kill Chris? Maybe I should go back
and look at all the movies where the killer got away with it. I pick up
a pad of paper and a hotel pen. I'm now going to make my *own* list,
which might even contain some lessons to be learned. Deciding to
list the movies in alphabetical order, I write down: *Anatomy of Murder?* No, nothing usable there. What about *Arsenic and Old Lace?* They
got away with it for quite a while. But Buddy doesn't really go for old
ladies. Too bad. *Dial M for Murder* should have worked, but it didn't.
Not a good model. *Murder on the Orient Express?* No, too many con-
spirators. *Psycho?* He got away with it, didn't he? But do I want to kill
Buddy in the shower? Not really. *Sunset Boulevard?* I would love to
leave his body floating in a swimming pool, but there's not one
within miles. Maybe a stock tank would do. I begin to realize the
paucity of got-away-with-murder movies. It seems there should be
more.

Then I have not the big idea but a little one. I call Victor Hammer
and ask him if he can lift a still photograph from our footage—now
developed—of Buddy shooting Black Widow. He says no problem. I
call my friend at the *Los Angeles Times.*

The picture—as published in the *L.A. Times* in eye-catching color—reveals a man shooting a running horse in the back of the head. The caption reads: THEY SHOOT HORSES, DON'T THEY?

I show the picture to my friend Deputy Sheriff Jimmy Lee Johnson. I want him to arrest Buddy, but he informs me it isn't actually against the laws of Texas to shoot a horse. Steal a horse, go to jail. Shoot a horse, go to dinner.

"You leaked that picture!" Buddy SCREAMS in the 6666 living room.

"No," I lie shakily, "but you posed for it."

Meanwhile protesters are marching in front of our great rock castle. They are carrying signs that say: SHOOT THE HORSE SHOOTER . . . HORSEWHIP HOLLYWOOD . . . TAR AND FEATHER BUDDY DALE, and many more helpful suggestions. Television cameras record the event. I hope all publicity is, as they say, good publicity because we are getting a lot of it. Maybe I should be a press agent. Don't even kid about something like that.

57

TODAY WE WILL BE SHOOTING IN THE 6666 CASTLE itself. When I come downstairs, a little late, I feel a special energy in the big living room. I look around, not sure why. It is as though there is a secret I'm not in on. I find Jamie and make my way to her.

"What's going on?" I ask.

"I'm not sure," she says. "Sarah told me to expect something different this morning."

"It would be Sarah."

"Yes, it would. She said we needed a change of pace after the horse shooting. Something to pick up our spirits."

"Get ready to duck."

I don't have to worry about any dialogue today because we are just filming dancing. A dance party at the castle. The Goodnights have invited families from many miles around.

"We need the cast on the set," Kim Kurumada says into his walkie-talkie. "Rehearsal coming up."

The cast begins drifting in—stark raving naked. The extras are naked. Of course, Sarah is naked.

"What's going on?" Jamie demands.

"Naked dance call," Sarah explains. "When things get tough, the tough get naked. Pretty much guaranteed to cheer everybody up."

"Oh," agrees Jamie.

Naked bodies keep arriving. Kelly is naked. Even Tom, the biggest star in the world, is naked. What is more, the assistant directors are naked except for their walkie-talkies. We have a surprisingly good-looking band of naked moviemakers. I don't know why I am surprised by their comeliness, but I am. My God, look at that . . . and that . . . and those! Thank God the grips, gaffers, and best boys don't strip off their clothes, too.

"Maybe I can write this into the movie," I say.

"Pervert," Jamie says.

"That's a good thing, right?"

Our imported choreographer, MELINDA ROY, who is also nude, places bodies artfully around the big living room, which has been cleared of all furniture. It is as if she is arranging a bouquet of naked flowers.

"Five, six, seven, eight," Lindy calls at last.

Naked bodies press against naked bodies. I almost feel the frissons. I expect giggling, but there isn't any. The nude dancers are businesslike. They are all so comfortable with their bodies, even proud of them, they don't care who sees.

"Maybe you should take your clothes off too?" I suggest. "Could be a bonding experience with your cast and crew."

"Fuck you," Jamie suggests.

"Good idea."

A naked Tom watches a naked Kelly dance with a naked Sarah. A naked Arthur watches a naked Guinevere and a naked Lancelot waltzing circles around a great living room beneath the locked horns of two doomed deer. This is a fulcrum in the story, where the king's wife begins falling in love with the king's best friend. And here we have it in the flesh. As she dances with Kelly, Sarah's nipples are at full West Point attention.

"We should try this more often," I say.

"In your wet dreams," Jamie says.

"You don't feel overdressed?"

"No!"

The playback on our sound system changes to a polka. Soon breasts are bouncing like pigs in sacks.

I find myself staring at Buddy's latest fly-in date—MISS ALABAMA—who is stunning in every way. She is the most beautiful yet. Or maybe I am just swayed by her not having any clothes on. Her breasts come to sharp points like pink-tipped footballs. Her legs are as long as buffalo rifles and perhaps as deadly. I hate Buddy Dale more than ever. He doesn't deserve such beauty. And he isn't even up yet. Blaming his twice-broken leg, he has taken to not showing up until noon or later. But today the lay-a-bed is missing the Birthday Suit Ball. There is some justice. With one of his members in a cast, I wonder how Buddy and Miss Alabama do it. Unfortunately, I can't seem to take my eyes off the Southern belle.

"Your tongue is hanging out," Jamie says. "Be careful you don't step on it."

"Ouch!" Sarah YELLS.

She has—or pretends to have—a splinter in her bare foot. She hops up and down, tits bouncing like some juggling routine. All eyes move from Miss Alabama to Sarah. Nude pain trumps simple nude perfection. The rehearsal comes to a momentary halt. Naked bodies converge on our leading lady.

"I'm all right," Sarah says bravely. "Let's go on. I'll wash the blood off the floor when we're done."

I am in awe of her gift of self-dramatization. In a sea of nude bodies, many of them more compelling than hers, she has nonetheless made the scene about her. Soon she is bravely and nakedly dancing on. I don't see any blood on the cedar floorboards.

58

LATE AT NIGHT, I START CLIMBING THE WINDMILL. THE rungs are cool against the palms of my hands. I climb and climb and climb. I feel the windmill but can barely see it. It is as if the windmill has melted away and I am simply climbing the night. Hand over hand, one handful of darkness after another. The closer I get to the top, the louder grows the roar of the whirling wheel. Its sharp-edged blades remind me of spinning swords. Knights of old are up there fighting it out. When I reach the platform just below the killer wheel, I pause to study the threat posed by all those flashing knives. I remember that a windmill blade once cut off my favorite uncle's finger. I know to respect this screaming banshee of a machine. Don Quixote fought slow-moving Dutch windmills, which were pussies. I'd like to see him joust against a West Texas windmill when the wind is blowing, and the wind is always blowing. I carefully ease myself up onto the square platform beneath some insane cheerleader twirling swords.

Lying flat on my stomach on the platform, I study the dark landscape below. The great stone house. The trees. The 6666 barn. The memories. I recall my mother telling me many times how she always climbed up the windmill when she had heard bad news or needed to make a difficult decision. This tower was the quiet place spiritually—although incredibly noisy actually—where she could think and reflect. Maybe it even helped that the roar of the blades drowned out minor thoughts. Only the most important ideas fight their way through what sounds like the cockpit of a WWII bomber. Suspended in time and space and the West Texas wind, I recall Mom telling me that she climbed the windmill when her father died. This memory leads to mourning my cousin. Without warning, I am crying. My tears fall away into the void, seemingly dropping forever and ever.

Little by little, profound sorrow spirals down to current problems. I am worried about the scene we are supposed to shoot in the morning. That's why I couldn't sleep, why I came up here. I hate the scene. Well, "hate" might be too strong a word. After all, I wrote it. But it somehow seems wrong. I just don't believe these people—Revelie and Goodnight—would talk to each other in that way.

The scene is about their childlessness. They both desperately want children. In my pages, Revelie and Goodnight accuse each other of being at fault. It's your feeble juice. No, it's your uppity womb. But would they really express those thoughts out loud, much less shout them louder and louder at each other? I feel the Revelie and Goodnight in this scene are not the same heroine and hero we have come to know so far. My dialogue is—as they love to say in Hollywood—too on the nose. There must be some way to say it without saying it. But I can't stop tomorrow's work from going forward. All the plans have been made. All the calls have been given. Money has been spent. I see myself standing in front of an onrushing train saying: "No, I don't think so."

Hanging up here in the night, fretting, worrying, I feel peculiarly self-destructive. I want to jump. It would be so easy. It would be so quick. I realize I'm not really suicidal, just experiencing an age-old urge brought on by looking over the edge of the abyss. So I turn my head and look up. I wonder what it would feel like to touch the spinning wheel. I imagine losing a hand and watching it fall darkly to earth. Time to climb down.

Going down is faster. The rungs are still cool to the touch. The black earth creeps up to receive me. Dodging trees in the night, I weave my way back to the castle. I climb the stairs toward my room, but then I surprise myself by taking a detour. I find myself standing outside Jamie's door. What am I doing here? Reaching for the doorknob, I half hope the door will be locked, but it isn't. I turn the knob slowly, quietly, and ease open the door.

"Oh, hi," Jamie says. "I was just thinking of calling you. Good, you're here. I don't have to worry about waking you."

"Why were you going to call?" I ask in an unsteady voice.

"There's something wrong with that scene tomorrow," she says. "A few minutes ago, I just woke up and thought: No! There's a problem. The words don't sound like them."

"I know," I say. "That's what I came to tell you."

"We'll fix it."

"Now?"

"No, I'm miles too tired. We'll fix it on the set tomorrow."

"Thank you."

"You mean you didn't invade my bedroom in the middle of the night to ravish me?"

"That too."

"I'm miles and miles, donkey miles, too tired for ravishing unless you've got a gun. I mean a real gun."

"I've been thinking of getting one." I look down at my boots. The left one has a skinned toe. When did that happen? "Uh, well, I should probably go now, but you could talk me into staying." She doesn't say anything. "Could I—stay?"

"Only if you promise to keep your clothes on," she says.

"I promise," I agree immediately. "But can I at least take my boots off?"

"Just one of them."

I take off the one with the skinned toe. Then I slip under the covers fully dressed except for one boot and my cowboy hat. I am thrilled to discover that she isn't wearing anything at all. I run my hand down her naked back, but she is already sound asleep and snoring softly, which gives rise to some self-doubts on my part. I consider waking her. No, probably not a good idea. I ponder pulling back the covers to see her naked body. I decide I'm either too much of a gentleman or too much of a chicken.

When we wake in the morning, Jamie starts plucking feathers out of my hair.

"Did these come from your pillow?" she asks.

"Maybe I grew them," I say, "living up to my name."

She plucks another feather. "He loves me." She plucks one more. "He loves me not." She studies my head. "I don't see any others. I guess that's it."

I retrieve one of the discarded feathers and stick it back on top of my head.

59

IT IS AN UNUSUAL BLOCKING SESSION. WE HAVE GATHered in the Goodnights' bedroom—built in an abandoned variety store in Spur—to rehearse the scene. The married couple is seated on their marriage bed.

"I hope you didn't spend too much time memorizing your lines," Jamie says, "because we've had second thoughts."

"Why?" asks Sarah.

"Good," says Tom.

"The dialogue just doesn't seem right," Jamie says. "TOTN."

"What's that supposed to mean?" Sarah asks.

Jamie just touches her nose.

"But I love confronting him," Sarah says.

"But not in these words," Jamie says. "It's our fault. I'm sorry. But meanwhile I hope we can block the scene."

"You must be kidding," says our leading lady. "There's no scene."

"There will be."

We proceed to block the scene.

"Sarah, you get up off the bed and walk to here," Jamie says. "Okay, go."

Our leading lady stands up and walks to a position near a window. Then she turns to face her husband.

"Mark it," says Jamie.

A camera assistant rushes in to place two pieces of tape on the floor so that they form a *T*. With a Magic Marker, he writes "B second position" on the tape.

"Okay, let's try that," says Jamie.

Sarah stands up, walks to the mark, and turns.

"But what do I say?" she asks.

"We're not sure yet," Jamie says. "But that's where you stop and turn. If you don't, you'll be out of focus." A dire threat to any leading lady, much less ours. "Sarah, do you remember all those Spencer Tracy scenes that begin with his head bowed? Most people think that's because he was humble or contemplative, but that was never it at all. He was just looking for his mark because he didn't want to be fuzzy, and neither do you."

Point taken.

Sarah gets up off the bed, marches to the tape, turns, and opens her mouth wide but doesn't say anything. She holds the pose. She is making fun of us, but we deserve it. We have no idea what she is supposed to say, not yet.

"Good," Jamie says. "Now, Tom, you lie down on the bed. Motion for her to join you."

"Do I say anything?" asks the biggest star in the world.

"Of course, not sure what. But that's where you'll lie when you say it. Mark it."

His position is marked with chalk on the covers.

"Thanks, everybody. Go to makeup. Victor, do your lighting magic. We'll have pages soon."

We retire to Jamie's motor home, which isn't as big as Tom's but is much grander than Sarah's tiny dressing room. I am in such a hurry to get started—we are in a race now—that I bump my head entering the directorial coach.

"Ouch!" I yelp.

"Women are smarter to be shorter," Jamie says.

We sit down at her mobile dining room table and I hurriedly open my computer. Then I pause. I have been in a rush to get started, but now I don't know what to type.

"What?" I ask.

"What?" Jamie answers.

Then Sarah sticks her head in the door.

"I've got an idea," she announces.

"What?" Jamie asks.

"What?" I ask at the same time, even more hungrily.

"What if I ask my husband: Do you suppose my not getting pregnant has anything to do with your fucking the cowboys instead of me?"

I look at Jamie. She looks at me.

"Great idea," Jamie says at last. "We'll write that right in. Why don't you go start rehearsing it?"

Sarah withdraws.

"Well, that was helpful," Jamie says.

"Extremely," I say. "Kind of makes me think nobody should say anything."

Jamie thinks. "You may be right." She thinks again. "Tom motions for Sarah to join him on the bed. She walks out of the room instead. That says it. I mean that says it without saying it. Without saying anything at all."

That is the scene we shoot. Sarah gets up off the bed and walks to the window. She hits her mark. She is in focus. Of course. Tom motions her to join him on the bed. She walks away.

"Cut, print. Moving on."

"Wrong set," says Kim Kurumada.

I happen to be close enough to overhear Sarah tell Tom (not softly): "I told them to let me say the reason I never get pregnant is because you're gay. But I guess they thought it might hurt the movie."

"Go fuck yourself," Tom says.

"I guess I'll have to if you're too gay to do it for me."

"Too bad you had to say that. I was about to offer to switch dressing rooms with you. I hate to think of you in that actors' ghetto trailer. But I guess you're just going to have to stay there. Sorry."

I think: He's good.

Sarah storms off with no place to go except her tiny dressing room.

60

I CAN'T SLEEP. TONIGHT THE PROBLEM ISN'T A SCENE that isn't working, but rather my imagination working overtime. I keep reliving my limited exposure to Jamie's very naked body. She is probably naked tonight, too, lying there like an undiscovered vein of gold. Almost undiscovered. I know the treasure waiting there. Tossing and turning, I keep running my mental movie of Jamie naked in bed over and over. My head feels empty. There is nothing in there but a little movie theater. Jamie is projected on the white bone of my inner skull.

Turning over once again, I wonder if my father—who will be coming in for his audition tomorrow—is having any trouble sleeping tonight, too. I would like to think that we are both lying awake and looking at the same darkness, but I doubt it. I have almost come to the conclusion that my father never worries. Something else I haven't inherited from him. He told me that he worried back in college when the doctors told him he had an enlarged heart and shouldn't do anything too taxing mentally or especially physically. He almost worried himself to death. Then he made a conscious decision to stop worrying. The next day he went out for football and made the team. He didn't die and he quit worrying for good. Besides, according to him, worry gives you wrinkles. He has surprisingly few.

Who else could be awake? Sarah because she is plotting. Buddy because he is trying to prove that, even crippled, he is good in bed. Miss Alabama because Buddy won't let her alone. These are my unchosen companions in the long night.

I get up out of bed, pull on my jeans, and walk down the corridor to Jamie's room. I just stand there staring at her door. What am I doing here? She's tireder than tired. She needs her rest if she is going to direct this movie. My movie.

Turning away, I head for the stairs. I cross the vast living room—which reminds me of the Great Plains indoors—and pass on out of the house. Shirtless, I head for the windmill. I start climbing. The cool rungs feel good against my hands and bare feet. I pull myself to the top and lie down on the wooden platform beneath the giant metal wheel. For once, the wind isn't blowing and the great fan is still. Fortunately, all the chickens are bedded down for the night, so they don't fall over. It is absolutely quiet up here in black space. I begin to feel drowsy and drift off to sleep in my high-rise bedroom.

61

"I COULDN'T SLEEP," JAMIE SAYS THE NEXT MORNING.

Seated in the breakfast booth in her small motor home, we are drinking much-needed coffee. The motor home is parked on a side street in Spur. Studying Jamie, I don't see any dark circles under her eyes, but she is wearing makeup.

"Really?" I say, as if she might be lying to me about not being able to sleep.

"Yeah, I don't know what was wrong," she says. "I thought about coming down and knocking on your door, but I didn't want to wake you."

"I was awake," I tell her.

"Really?"

"Yeah, and I got up and went down the hall to knock on your door. But I lost my nerve. I didn't want to wake you or scare you."

"You should have."

"I know."

"Did you ever get any sleep?" she asks.

"Not until I went out and climbed the windmill. I fell asleep on that little platform way up at the top."

"Now you're scaring me."

"I didn't intend to fall asleep. I just did. It was so peaceful up there. The wind wasn't blowing and the wheel was quiet."

"I don't believe it. There was really no wind?"

"Not a whisper."

"How were the chickens?"

"Asleep."

"Lucky them."

There is a KNOCK on the motor home's door. Then a production assistant named ANDREW pokes his head inside.

"There you are," he says. "Chick, you've got a visitor."

"Is this visitor tall and charming?" asks Jamie.

"Uh, well, as a matter of fact, I think he is," says the baby-faced boy.

"We've been expecting him," she says. "Show him in."

Andrew opens the door wider, and my giant of a father squeezes himself through the narrow portal. He isn't fat, just big. He doesn't so much enter the trailer as put it on like a sweater. He is wearing black boots, khaki pants, a pale blue cowboy shirt, and a dove-gray cowboy hat with a narrow brim. He takes off the hat.

"Clyde, welcome to the movie!" Jamie says enthusiastically. "It's great to have you here at last. Would you like coffee?"

"I surely would, purdy director cowgirl."

"Clyde, sit down right here by me. Chick, would you mind pouring your dad a cup of coffee. And use the good Styrofoam, please. He's a special guest."

While my father squeezes in next to my director, I get up and pour him a cup of coffee. My dad takes a sip of the coffee, doesn't grimace, takes a deck of cards out of his shirt pocket, and lays the cards out on the table beside the Styrofoam coffee cup.

"Now I'm ready to go to work," my father says.

"Good," says Jamie.

"Did you sleep all right?" I ask.

"Like a baby calf," Dad says. "So here I am, what can I do for you, purdy one?"

"I thought we'd just read through a scene," Jamie says, "and see how you take to it." Her briefcase is on the table. She opens it and takes out two pages stapled together. "Why don't you take a look at these? You don't have to memorize the lines, just get familiar with them."

"Are there many hard words?" my father asks with a twinkle.

"Lots," Jamie says. "That's why we need you, Clyde."

I've been wondering which scene she plans to read with my father. I've wanted to ask but don't want to interfere. I've recused myself from this particular audition. So I squint at the pages in Jamie's hand trying to read the words, but she keeps moving them, waving them around.

"Now this is a scene between Revelie and Goodnight," Jamie tells my father. "You'll play Goodnight and I'll be Revelie. Not that we're offering you the part of Goodnight. The biggest star in the world has already got that role. You may turn out to be a better actor, for all I know, but he's better known. This is just a test. So pretend you're a young man again and we'll play a kind of love scene together. All right?"

"Sounds awful good to me. I gotta say you make a mighty purdy Old Lady Goodnight, as we always called her." He gives her a big smile. "In her latter days, she dipped snuff. You ain't gonna dip snuff, are you? I don't know if I could kiss a girl who had a mouth full of snuff."

"It's not that kind of love scene, and, no, I won't be gobbling snuff."

"Good. Stay away from it. Nasty stuff."

Jamie hands my father the pages, and he starts reading silently. It takes him about half a minute to digest the scene. My dad even reads faster than I do.

"Okay," he says, looking up. "It's purdy good." He takes a deep breath. "Less go."

"Would you like to read it again?" asks Jamie.

"No, I think I got it," he says.

"Well, okay," she says doubtfully. Then she looks around the trailer. "Clyde, let's you and me go sit on those chairs over there. You take the one on the right, I'll take the left."

"Is that what directors do?" he asks. "Tell people where to sit?"

"That's right," she says, LAUGHING.

Goodnight and Revelie cross the motor home and sit down facing each other. I stay put in the breakfast nook. My hands and heart boost their rpms. I want him to do well for several reasons. I love him. I don't want him to be disappointed. But most important, I don't want my father to embarrass me.

"Ready?" asks Jamie.

"Rarin' to go," my dad says.

I cringe.

"Chick, you say 'Action.'"

Surprised, I say in a choked voice: "Action."

Opening her script, Jamie reads: "You have a hard time talking to women, don't you?"

Of course, my father doesn't at all, but Goodnight did, so that's what the line says.

Clyde reads: "Sometimes." A man of few words.

Jamie: "But Too Short told me you can talk to animals."

Clyde: "I used to could."

"How'd you learn?"

"I just learnt."

"Nobody taught you?"

"Uh?"

"Please tell me. I'm really interested."

"I, uh, I, uh—"

"Tell me!" Jamie snaps.

"Well, I used to live with the Comanches," my father says reluctantly in a tone that suggests every word hurts. "And they done taught me how. That's about all I can tell you." He pauses and squints at the distant horizon of the motor home. "If I told you more'n that, I'd go crazy."

"We wouldn't want that," Jamie says. "I'm sorry. I didn't know it was so private. Please disregard the whole thing. I'm sorry I asked."

"No, no, I can—I mean sometimes—I can talk to stuff. Animals, plants, other stuff. I just talk to them like they was people. That's all. Nothin' much to it. Them things understand your tone if'n not your words."

My father folds the script pages and puts them in his shirt pocket.

"Don't you want to go on?" Jamie asks, surprised. "You're doing so well."

"Course I wanna go on. This here's fun, purdy director. It's yore turn."

Jamie takes a moment to collect herself.

"Well, then," she says at last, "maybe you could turn that around. Maybe you could talk to a person as if she were an animal. Think of me as a buffalo or something."

"I swear you don't look much like a buffalo, Miss Revelie," my dad says from memory.

"Well, then some other creature," Jamie reads, a curious expression on her face. "What else do you talk to? Trees? Do you talk to trees?"

"Sometimes."

"Well, make believe I'm a tree. Talk tree-talk to me. What about that? Do I remind you of a tree? I mean any particular tree?"

My father studies Jamie, trying to see her as a tree.

"You're not one tree," he says softly, his eyes down. "You're lotsa trees." He looks up at her. "You're a whole forest of them trees."

"What do you mean?" Jamie asks, still reading every word, and sounding like it. Slightly stilted.

My father looks down again, like Spencer Tracy searching for his mark, but there isn't any mark. He is shy. He is pensive.

"Well, the Comanches figure," he says, still looking down, "that we're all a part a nature." He looks up. "Right? Thass on the one hand. But we're a reflection a nature, too. Thass on the other hand. See?"

"No, not really," she says, expressing the confusion of both Revelie, the character, and Jamie, the director. What is going on here? Who is this?

"The Comanches figure we've all got forests inside us. And rivers inside us. And springs inside us. And canyons inside us. And thunder and lightnin'. That sort a stuff. See?"

Yes, I see, I'm seeing something I don't believe.

"I think so," Jamie says. "Tell me what you see in me."

My father studies her again. He seems glad to have the license to stare at her.

"Well, I reckon I see a dark forest in you," says the slightly tongue-tied poet. "It's full of big ol' trees. Not mesquites or cedars or chinaberries like we got out here. But oaks. Live oaks. Like they got down in East Texas, where I used to live before this here. So there's lotsa shade in your forest. It feels cool. And it's kinda mysterious-like."

"That's what you see?"

My father nods and smiles. "The forest in you is quiet and calm. It seems safe. But they's wild animals in it."

"What kind of animals?"

"Deer." He looks and sounds fifty years younger. "Lots of deer."

"I like deer."

"But they's also coyotes and wolves."

"I don't like wolves."

My father shrugs. "Too bad, you got 'em, right there in your insides."

Jamie drops her script and claps. I clap, too. The two of us give my father, Clyde, a standing ovation in the cramped motor home.

"Clyde, I love you," Jamie says.

"That was kinda the point a the scene," my father says, "waddnit?"

"It was indeed," she beams. "Now, Clyde, if you'll just bear with me for a moment, I'd like to confer with my partner here. Chick, would you follow me into the bedroom?"

"He's done been waiting all his life to hear you ask that," my father says.

Jamie LAUGHS.

"That's true," I mumble.

I follow my director into the tiny bedroom in her motor home. She sits down on the double bed and motions for me to sit beside her. I obey.

"Your father's amazing," Jamie says. "Why didn't you tell me about him?"

"He surprised me, too," I say. "I mean I knew he was a great storyteller. And charming. But I had no idea he could act."

"I couldn't believe it," she says. "He read that scene once and he had it by heart."

"I knew he had a good memory, but I didn't know it was that good."

"How old is he?"

"Seventy-one."

"Just amazing." She pauses and looks at the motor home horizon. "I've been wracking my brain to find what part we should give him."

"What about one of the other ranchers?" I suggest.

"That's what I was thinking before, but I'm thinking bigger now. What's left of any consequence?"

"Well, there's the judge in the trial scene."

"I was thinking more along the lines of the prosecutor."

"That's an important part," I say, surprised.

"That's the point," she says. "I'll offer it to him if it's all right with you."

"Of course," I say with some trepidation, hoping he is up to it, still a little afraid of being embarrassed by my amazing dad.

"Let's go tell him."

I follow her out of the bedroom, down a claustrophobic passageway past the john, and into the living room. We find my father sitting in the breakfast nook, hunched over a game of solitaire. Jamie takes a seat opposite him on the other side of the table.

"Clyde, sorry to interrupt, but we would like to offer you a fairly important part in our movie," Jamie says. "As you may or may not know, our story involves a murder trial."

"I know about that there trial," Dad says, "from old family tales."

"Good," she says. "We would like you to play the part of the prosecutor."

My father thinks a moment and then smiles. "You mean today I was makin' love to Revelie, and tomorrow or when-some-ever I'll be tryin' my best to hang her?"

"That's about it. Are you game?"

"You bet, purdy director lady."

"I don't suppose you have an agent?"

"Sure I do. What do you take me for? A greenhorn?"

Jamie looks at me, surprised. I look back at her, even more surprised.

"Good, who is it?"

"Him," my father says, pointing at me.

"Fine." Jamie smiles. "I'll put in a call to your agent and see if we can't work something out." She actually winks at me. "Now there's one more thing I'd like to discuss with you, Clyde."

"Discuss away," he says while moving cards on the tabletop.

"I was wondering if you would consider becoming our dialogue coach. It would be a significant time commitment, but I assure you there would still be more than enough time for solitaire. You'll see."

"What exactly would I be doin'?"

"You'd be teaching your accent to our actors. I just love the way you sound. Before we shoot a scene, you'd read it to the actors so they could hear how it should sound. Then they'll rehearse the scene while you listen. Then you tell them which words don't sound right and help them improve. Something like that. It wouldn't really take too much time, but it would mean you'd have to be here every day."

I flinch inside. What would it be like to work with my father every day? Would I be more inhibited? What would it do to my relationship with Jamie? And would I ever get over being afraid he would somehow embarrass me? Or, more likely, upstage me?

"You just cain't git enough of me, can you, purdy director? Well, that's okay because I cain't git enough of you neither. It's mighty fine with me, but you're gonna hafta check with my agent ag'in."

"You do catch on fast."

"No, I waddn't tryin' to be funny. I mean you really gotta check with him. Fathers and sons can be a touchy thing. We've always got along real good, but I ain't sure he'd want me underfoot ever'day. And I'd understand. 'Cause I wouldn't of never wanted to work with my own daddy. Course, he was a mean son of a bitch that carried a gun ever'day of his life. Once pulled it on me."

Listening, I can't believe it. My father has turned out to be not only a great reader of scenes but an even better reader of my emotions.

"Do it," I say.

"No, you think it over," he says. "Call me tonight."

"But I was hoping you could start today," Jamie says.

"Dad, do it. Do it, really. Do it today."

"You gotta listen to your agent, right?" says Dad.

62

WE ARE INSIDE THE OUTLAWS' ROCK CABIN HIDEOUT, but this interior of the cabin is miles away from its exterior. The outer shell of the hideout is still out there in that grassy field where the buffalo so recently roamed. But we are finished with it, which is a good thing because the buffalo did some damage to it as they stampeded by. When a buffalo hits papier-mâché, the paper rocks really don't have much of a chance. The hideout's interior sits inside yet another abandoned appliance store in downtown Spur. I say "downtown" as if there were suburbs. There aren't.

"I swan, them rock walls, they look like the real thing," my dad says.

I find myself idly wondering if these interior rocks match those we used on the exterior. They should correspond since they are two sides of the same wall. I decide not to worry about it. My father RAPS on the wall with his knuckles. It sounds like he is knocking on an empty egg carton.

"Imagine that," he says.

"Clyde, could you join us, please?" Jamie says. "We need you."

My father walks over and lowers himself into a tall, canvas-backed folding chair with his name hastily written on the back with a Magic Marker. He completes a circle—a circle now unbroken—made up of Jamie, several actors, and me, all seated on similar director's chairs. Well, everybody but me. I'm seated on an apple box which has nobody's name on it. Writers get no respect. Jamie hands my father the pages for the scene we are about to shoot.

"Now, Clyde, maybe you would just read the scene out loud," she says, "playing all the parts. I want the actors to hear how you talk. I want them to absorb your accent. Okay?"

"Fine and dandy," my father says, but "fine" has become a two-syllable word in his mouth.

"Good," Jamie says. "Now just to set the scene for you, Goodnight and his cowboys are in the process of rescuing a girl who was carried off by outlaws. They find her chained to the fireplace."

"I see," Dad says. Then he points: "That's the chain right there, ain't it?"

"That's right."

"Is it a real chain or paper like everything else?"

"It's real enough. Whenever you're ready."

My father adjusts his glasses, studies the page for a moment, and then begins as if he were telling a story, his specialty: "Well, Goodnight comes in this here cabin and sees this girl with a chain locked around her neck. He heads on toward her, but that scares her.

"So Goodnight says: 'Don't worry. I won't hurt you. You're safe. I promise.'"

(My father actually says something between "don't" and "don'," something between "won't" and "won'.")

"The poor girl don't say nothin'," my father continues. "She's too ascared and untrustin'.

"So Goodnight says: 'Really, it's aw right. We come to git you back.'"

(*Right* has become a two-syllable word.)

"So the unfortunate girl says: 'Where are they?'"

(My father has raised the pitch of his voice ever so slightly, playing the girl.)

"Then Goodnight says: 'They's all dead or tied up.'"

(What he actually says is somewhere between "dead" and "daid.")

"The outlaws' plaything asks natural 'nough: 'You ain't foolin' me, hunh?'"

(I notice Jamie and all the actors staring at my father raptly as if he were telling a great story around a campfire. They listen as though they don't already know what is going to happen.)

"So Goodnight says: 'No, ma'am, we ain't foolin' atall. Can I come closer? I don't mean you no harm.'"

(His "can" is halfway to "ken" but not all the way.)

"So the chained-up girl just sits there woolgatherin' and tryin' to figure out what in the world to do."

"Goodnight says: 'By the way, my name's Goodnight. These here are my boys. We're from the Home Ranch down in the red canyon. Maybe you heard tell of it?'"

(I had written "heard of it"; he improved the line to "heard tell.")

"She still don't say nothin', so he says: 'I reckon you're Katie Russell, hunh? From the Exchange Hotel?'

"This here's when that there girl in chains nods just a little and says: 'Come on.'

"He'd done won her trust."

Jamie starts the CLAPPING, and the others readily join in.

At that moment, when we are all feeling good, Buddy Dale comes bumping onto the set with his noisy cast and crutches. He points at my father.

"Who's he?" Buddy demands.

"Our new dialogue coach," Jamie says. "He's great. You should hear him."

"I didn't give you permission to hire a dialogue coach," he says angrily. "You can't spend money unless I authorize it."

"We need a dialogue coach," she says.

"No you don't. Clark Gable didn't bother with one in *Gone With the Wind*. Besides, this is just some dodge to slip Chick's down-on-his-luck daddy some money. He is Chick's dad, isn't he?"

"Yes, I am," my father says, getting up slowly. "And proud to be so. What's it to you, if'n I may inquire?"

"I'm the producer! That's what it is to me. And I'm firing you right now."

"If you're the producer," my father says softly, so that you have to lean forward to hear him, "then you are the low-down son of a polecat with bad breath and bad habits who murdered my little niece, ain'tcha? Come see me when you heal up, and I'll show you what I really think a you."

Once again, Jamie leads the CLAPPING, and the others immediately jump in. The clapping goes on and on.

"Old man, you're fired!" Buddy Dale BELLOWS. "I don't want to have to tell you again. If you don't get off my set right now, I'm calling security and I'll have you thrown off."

The clapping stops.

"If he goes, I go," Jamie says. "Clyde and I are a team."

"Okay, both of you, get the hell off my set!"

"If she goes, I go," says the biggest star in the world.

"Oh, go to hell, all of you!"

Buddy Dale turns awkwardly and thumps off the set.

"Shall we go on with the rehearsal?" Jamie suggests.

"Should I leave?" asks my father.

"Nobody's leaving," says Jamie. "Especially not you. Clyde, we couldn't get along without you."

"Thanks," he says. "Not only is that fella a mean cuss, but he's sure got a bad case a dandruff."

"Clyde, that wasn't dandruff," she says. "That was cocaine."

"I always thought it was dandruff, too," I say.

"I guess we're both just a coupla hicks," my father says.

"Right," she says.

Getting back to work, Jamie asks the actors to read the scene this time. My father takes notes all the way through. When they finish their reading, there is no clapping.

"Well, Clyde, what've you got for us?" Jamie asks.

"Okay, I mean I hate to be presumptuous. I mean, what do I know 'bout actin'? But, Tom, you ain't gitting 'right' exactly 'ri-ight.' See, 'ri-ight' oughta be a two-syllable word because the *I* is a two-syllable vowel. Alri-ight? Wanna try-y it?"

"Ri-i-ight," says Tom.

"Thass good. Thass very good. Only you kinda overdid it. You done made it a three-syllable vowel. So just ease up a little, and you'll be perfect."

Sensing somebody approaching, I look around and SEE (POV) Becky bearing down on us. She is carrying a cell phone in her out-stretched hand—carrying it as if it were hot, burning her fingers.

"Jamie," Becky calls from ten feet away, "the studio's on the line. Shelley Bingham."

The whole set tenses. My hands shake faster.

"I'll bet I know what this is about," the director breathes. Plucking the phone from Becky's palm, she says: "This is Jamie." Pause. "Oh, hello, Shelley. What can I do for you this fine morning?"

"Fine morning!" Shelley exclaims in a voice so loud I can hear her end of the conversation. "Buddy tells me everything and everybody is running amok. He says you've lost control of the movie."

"That's just Buddy being Buddy," Jamie says. "You know, an ass-hole."

"But he's the producer. That means he's allowed to act like an ass-hole. That's his job."

"Not this time. He wants to fire Chick's father, Clyde Goodnight, whom I've hired as a dialogue coach."

"I know."

"But if he goes, I go. And if I go, Tom goes, and I'm pretty sure we can shame Sarah into going, too. Who knows, Chick might even quit."

"I don't like this. Are you sure you're not losing control of the show?"

"The film's going great, anyway I think it's great. I hope you're pleased with the dailies you've seen."

I can't make out what Shelley says, but Jamie smiles.

"The only trouble on this movie is Buddy Dale. So far, he's already killed one of our extras and tried to kill a horse."

"He killed somebody?"

"Not that we'd ever be able to prove it, but I'm sure she died of an overdose he gave her."

Again I can't hear Shelley's response.

"And today, when he appeared on the set to fire Mr. Goodnight, he had cocaine sprinkled down the front of his black sweater. You know, Chick's good friends with a deputy sheriff down here. Played football together or something. Anyway, if Buddy gives Clyde Goodnight any more trouble, I'm going to have Chick ask his friend to bust Buddy on coke possession charges. Let him try to run this movie from a cell in the Dickens County jail. And that's the worst jail I've ever seen in my life. It's medieval."

"Jamie, you sound different."

"I am different. I'm in Texas. Here it's be tough or the buffalo will run right over you."

"I'd better watch out or you'll be running this studio one day."

"And the first thing I'll do will be fire Buddy Dale."

63

THE NEXT DAY, WE ALL FILE INTO THE BIG 6666 BARN for dailies. Jamie sits on her bale of hay at the front.

"Clyde," she calls, "come here and sit by me." Then she notices that her new dialogue coach is accompanied by his wife. "You, too, Annie," she adds.

My father sits on Jamie's left. Her assistant, Becky, sits on her right as usual, so her boss can whisper comments to her that she dutifully writes down. My mother sits down beside my dad. I take up a position on a bale of hay directly behind Jamie and her party.

"Now, Clyde, as you know, we're going to see several takes of the same scene," she explains. "I want you next to me so you can tell me which takes are the best in terms of accent. Don't worry about the acting. That's my job. Just concentrate on whether or not they sound like Texans. Okay?"

"Fine and dandy," says my father.

My mother doesn't say anything, but I notice her gently elbowing my dad in the ribs.

"Where's Buddy?" Jamie asks the barn at large.

Nobody knows.

"Well, let's go. He can see them later if he wants to. Let's see what we've got."

Somebody turns the lights out and the screen lights up with a scene depicting Goodnight's first encounter with the kidnapped girl. The walls look like rock instead of papier-mâché. The girl—played by actress BETH HEMMING—looks scared to death.

"Good, Beth," Jamie calls out.

On the screen, Tom Bondini says: "Really, it's all ri-ight. We come to git you back."

In the next take, Tom says: "Really, it's all ri-ight. We come to get you back."

In the third, he says: "Really, it's all ri-i-i-ight. We come to git you back."

"What do you think?" Jamie asks my father in a low voice.

"The first one's the best," my dad whispers. "In the second one, he said 'get' insteada 'git.' In the last one, he said 'ri-i-i-i-ight,' or some such. He turned that there *I* into some kinda roller-coaster ride. Don't tell him I said that."

"Thanks," Jamie says. Then she turns to Becky and tells her what my father said, plus some observations of her own, which I can't quite make out.

"Thanks for waiting for me." Buddy Dale's voice cuts through the darkness.

"Lights," says Jamie.

Somebody flicks the light switch.

Buddy stands in the middle of the barn, momentarily dazzled by the sudden light. Then he stares at the front row where Jamie, my father, and my mother sit, half turned toward him.

"We didn't think you were coming," Jamie says.

"You should have waited a few minutes anyway," Buddy says.

"We're sorry," she says. "Shall we proceed?"

"Who's that?" he explodes, pointing.

"Who's who?"

"That. That woman." I realize he means my mother and grow even more tense. "I've never seen her before. She isn't press, is she? Or have you hired somebody else without my okay?"

"She's a guest," Jamie says.

"What's her name?" Buddy demands.

"I'm Mrs. Clyde Goodnight," my mother says calmly.

"Who invited you?" he asks harshly.

"My husband," she says.

"Well, he had no right. Our dailies aren't open to the general public, to anybody who just happens to drop in. Wait and buy a ticket, madam, like the rest of the world. Who do you think you are anyway? I'm afraid I'm going to have to ask you to leave."

My mother doesn't move.

"Leave now!"

My mom starts to get up, but my father pulls her back down. Then he gets up and advances on Buddy.

"That ain't no way to speak to a lady," my father says. "Yore just lucky we got a code in these parts. And that there code says it ain't right to insult a lady or to bust up a cripple. Otherwise I'd take them crutches away from you and beat you to death with 'em." He says all this without raising his voice.

"We'll see about that!" Buddy SCREECHES.

And he swings his right crutch at my father's head. Moving gracefully, my dad reaches out and grabs the crutch. He jerks it away from Buddy, who almost topples over.

"Give it back," Buddy whimpers.

"Sure thing," my father says.

He crushes that crutch with his bare hands. He doesn't break it over his knee. He doesn't slam it against the ground. He doesn't need to. He simply squeezes and bends and the crutch explodes, sounding like gunshots in the quiet barn. Splinters fly. People duck as if trying to get out of the way of bullets.

Dropping the ruined fragments, Clyde reaches out, grabs the other crutch, and jerks. This time Buddy does go down in a heap. My father destroys the second crutch, again with his bare hands. Then he drops the ravaged pieces, turns his back, and walks away.

"How'm I gonna get back to my room?" Buddy complains.

My dad stops, turns, and says: "Crawl." But he makes it a two-syllable word.

The barn resounds with CLAPPING. Everybody is on his or her feet.

Then Chris Crosby doubles his fists and bears down on my father, walking fast from halfway across the barn. Oh no, I think, looking around for a weapon. But I don't need one, because Tom Bondini, the biggest star in the world, steps in front of Chris and stops him.

It all gives me a warm feeling like a Disney movie. One of their good ones made way back in my childhood.

"That wasn't very nice," my mother tells my father.

"Waddn't tryin' to be nice," says my dad.

"Good," says my mom. "Then you succeeded admirably."

They hold hands.

After dailies, I sit with Jamie on a cowhide couch in front of the giant fireplace. She is making one of her lists and I am twirling an imaginary baton.

"Did you see what your dad did to those crutches?" she asks.

"I saw," I say.

"I had no idea he was that strong."

"When he was younger, he used to pick up cars."

"You're kidding."

"Well, he only picked up one end at a time."

"What are you talking about?"

"When his car would slide off the road and get stuck in a ditch, my dad would get out, lift up the rear end of the car, and set it back on the road. Then he'd pick up the front end and put it back on the road, too. I never quite measured up to my dad."

"Chick, don't sell yourself short. You have your own quiet strength. I see it all the time. Besides you're as good-looking as your father ever was."

"There is no way," I say with feeling.

"The difference is he knows he's good-looking and you don't."

64

I AM ALMOST ASLEEP. THE SCENE OF MY FATHER CRUSH-ing Buddy's crutches keeps playing over and over in my mind, half memory, half dream. It is a good dream-memory to go to sleep on. I feel very comfortable, very snug, very . . .

Then a light KNOCK at my door rouses me. If my sleep were

deeper—as it would have been in a few moments—I wouldn't have heard it. I open my eyes and shake my head in a vain attempt to clear it. I consider calling out, "Come in," because the door is unlocked. But what if it is Buddy Dale or one of his minions? It takes me longer to disentangle myself from the bedclothes than it should. I'm still half asleep. Finally free, I pull on my jeans and head for the door.

When I open the door, there is nobody there. Did I dream the knocking? Probably. I close the door and start back to my bed, but then change my mind. I open the door again and stick my head out into the hall. I look to my right. Nothing. I look to my left and SEE (POV) Jamie retreating down the corridor. She is fully dressed, cowboy shirt, jeans, boots.

"Wait," I call softly.

She stops but doesn't turn around. I hurry toward her and touch her on the shoulder.

"I couldn't sleep," she says softly. Then she turns around. "How about you?"

"No, me neither," I lie.

"Liar. Why did it take you so long to answer the door?"

"I decided to take a shower first."

"Liar, liar."

"What's wrong? Why couldn't you sleep? I thought you were exhausted."

"I am, but I can't relax. Everything has gotten to be too much. You know, Buddy's call to Shelley, then hers to me. It's hard."

"But you handled all that so well."

"Only on the outside."

"I'm sorry. Especially since a lot of it's my fault."

"I just want to get away from it all. For a little while anyway. Chick, would you take me away?"

"Sure. Where do you want to go?"

"To the top of the windmill."

"I'll get my shirt."

Returning to my room, I put on not only a shirt but my boots. Then I rejoin Jamie in the hall. We walk as quietly as we can in cowboy footgear. Descending the stairs, we cross the great living room, glance up at the fighting deer on the wall, and walk out into the night air. We both take deep breaths. I smell cedar and pecans and cow manure as I lead the way through the trees to the base of the windmill.

Staring up at it, Jamie says: "It looks taller at night."

A billion stars are out, but there is only a sliver of a moon. It is dark.

"You can always change your mind," I say.

"Are you calling me a coward?"

"No, ma'am. Okay, you go first. I'll be right behind you just in case. When you get to the top, lie flat. If you try to sit up, you could get your head cut off. And it's so dark, I might have a hell of a time finding it."

"Are you trying to scare me?"

"Just trying to save your life, ma'am."

Jamie starts up the windmill, and I follow her. We climb the metal rungs bolted to one leg of the tower. As always, they are pleasantly cool to the touch. Slowly, the earth falls away beneath us. We mount into the heavens. As we crawl higher and higher, the fan wheel roars louder and louder. Jamie stops.

"Are you all right?" I ask.

"Just give me a moment," she says. "The air's too thin up here. I'm a sea-level girl."

After a brief rest, she starts up again with me right behind her. It is so dark that I can barely see the ground. The vivid stars seem somehow closer than the earth. I feel like the Little Prince going home again to tend his single rose on his small planet. I loved that book growing up, long before I even began to understand it. Long before I even knew there was something that needed understanding. Our small planet is the wooden platform just below the wheel.

When we reach it, the fan roars like a twister, a blow-your-house-away tornado. Jamie says something that I can't hear because of all the noise. Then she pulls herself up onto the tiny platform that resembles a collar around the neck of the windmill just below its spinning head. As instructed, she lies flat on her stomach. I pull myself up and lie beside her. The wheel races above our heads like a hundred swords of Damocles. We stare down into the black void.

"Welcome to my small planet," I say, "and you're my rose."

Jamie shakes her head and points to her ear. Maybe I only said it because I knew she wouldn't be able to hear. She leans over and kisses me lightly on the lips. Kissing is a good way to communicate in a tornado. Carefully, because there isn't much room, she turns over onto her back. Following her lead, I also turn carefully. Now we are staring up at the stars, which are brighter and friendlier than the earth. I half turn, lean over, and kiss her. This kiss lasts a long time. The wheel roars. My mind whirls. We seem suspended in time and space, and I never want this kiss to end. Finally she ends it, pulling away. But then she turns toward me. Now we both lie on our sides, face-to-face, our arms around each other. We kiss again, even longer this time. I wonder what it would be like to make love up here on this now sacred platform, but I conclude that we would probably fall off or be slashed to pieces. We keep kissing and hugging, lost in space, swallowed up by a thundering cyclone. We are from the tempestuous earth but no longer of it.

The wind blows harder up here, harder and colder. Jamie eventually starts to shiver. I lead the way back to earth.

"That was great," Jamie says, with her feet once again on dirt. "By the way, did you ever read *The Little Prince*?"

I LAUGH.

"What's so funny?" she asks a little indignantly.

"I was thinking of *The Little Prince*, too," I explain, "when we were up there."

"Oh, of course you were. Well, what I was thinking was: This platform was like his tiny planet."

"I know," I say. "And you were the single rose. The one he waters and takes care of."

"I did feel you were taking care of me up there."

"And you remember what the fox tells the Little Prince? You know, the secret of life? The most beautiful rose in the world is the one you take care of."

"I do remember. You took care of me up there, but I take care of you on this movie. So, mister, who's the rose, you or me?"

She kisses me lightly on the lips and we start back to the castle.

65

TODAY MY FATHER WILL STILL BE OUR DIALOGUE coach, but he will also have to act. We are finally ready to begin shooting our big trial sequence. My dad doesn't seem to mind that he will be trying to convict his own great-great-great-grandmother of murdering a man. She didn't mean to kill him, not at all. She meant to kill my dad's great-great-great-grandfather, the hero of our movie, Jimmy Goodnight. Her bullet went through Goodnight's side and hit a Jewish cowboy named Simon Shapiro in the stomach. Goodnight was hurt. Simon was killed. And now Sarah/Revelie is about to be tried for her crime.

We are back in Spur where our courtroom has been built inside an abandoned restaurant. Cameraman Victor Hammer is still lighting it when my father enters wearing a nineteenth-century black frock coat. Father and son shake hands. His hand is twice as big as mine.

"Are you nervous?" I ask.

"I ain't nervous," my dad says, his voice steady. "Thass the sorta thing gives you wrinkles."

"Good," I say.

Then I SEE (POV) tiny Victor Hammer approaching. He comes up almost to my father's belt.

"Mr. Goodnight, I've been looking forward to meeting you," Victor says, sticking out his hand. "I'm the cinematographer."

"The sin-a-matographer?" asks my dad. "Does that there mean you photograph sin?"

"Well, I must admit, I've filmed considerable sin in my time."

"Then I figure you're my kinda sin-a-matographer."

"Today it's my job to make you look good. Very good. Practically beautiful."

"Then you got a hard day's work stretchin' out in fronta you. Sorry 'bout that."

"Don't worry about me. I have a feeling you're very photogenic, and I'm seldom wrong about these things."

"Well, good luck, Victor-the-sin-a-matographer."

Then a hush falls over the courtroom and everybody seems to be looking toward the door. I look, too. Sarah is marching down the aisle looking as if she has swallowed a four-year-old child. Her feet are splayed as she attempts to keep her balance. She waddles. I sense the director at my elbow.

"What's she up to now?" Jamie asks.

"I have no idea," I admit.

"Follow me."

I follow Jamie up the aisle, where we almost collide with Sarah.

"That's an interesting choice," says the director in a controlled voice, "but it's rather a surprise. Would you mind explaining your thinking?"

"I'm pregnant!" Sarah says dramatically. "It says so right in the script. Anyway, it implies it."

"Right, but you've only been pregnant for a few weeks, not thirteen months. If you show at all, you barely show."

"I knew it!" Sarah says dramatically, as usual.

The defendant turns and walks out of the courtroom.

"Go see what's the matter," Jamie tells me.

"Why me?" I ask.

"Because she's the other woman in your life."

"No, she isn't."

"Go see what's the matter."

"On my way, okay?"

Walking outside, I am temporarily blinded by a sneeze in the overwhelming sunlight. When my sneezing eyes finally adjust, I SEE (POV) Sarah's three-dressing-room trailer. With trepidation, I walk in that direction. I climb the steps. I KNOCK. No answer. I KNOCK again. I open the door and walk in. The room is about the size of a filling-station john. Sarah is curled up in a fetal position on the floor. But that position is somewhat distorted by the four-year-old hidden under her dress.

"What's wrong?" I ask.

"She doesn't want me to be pregnant," Sarah says.

"She just doesn't want you to be so pregnant."

"No, she wants to deny me my pregnancy."

"What are you talking about?"

"This pregnancy is really important to me."

"Why?"

Pulling herself together, Sarah stands up, but doesn't answer my question.

"Thanks for coming to check on me." She tries to hug me, but the dirigible on her stomach divides us.

"Let's sit down," she says.

We perch on a short bench in her tiny dressing room.

"I'm going to tell you something that I haven't told anybody since grade school. Then I used to tell everybody. I didn't realize there was anything unusual about it. Later on, people told me to shut up about it. So I did."

"Shut up about what?" I ask, just to try to calm her.

"About how I was born," she says.

"How was that?" I ask, confused. Immaculate conception? What?

She takes a long time trying to decide whether to tell me the truth. Or maybe she is taking her time weaving a fascinating lie.

"I was born with a birth defect," Sarah says at last.

"Really?" I ask for lack of a good response. "I don't see any."

"Of course not," she says. "I was born without a vagina."

"Really?" I say with a different tone.

"Stop saying that. Really, I really was born without a vagina. They took a skin graft off my thigh and constructed a vagina. Are you happy now?"

"But can you—?"

"Get pregnant, no. Can I get aroused, yes."

I just stare at her.

"Why are you looking at me like that?"

"I don't know whether to believe you or not. You're always trying to dramatize your life. Is this just a role you're playing?"

"Why would I lie about something like this? It's not exactly something I'm proud of. It was very hard to tell you, and now you don't even believe me. I just wanted you to know why I wanted to be visibly pregnant in this scene. It may be my only chance to be preggers in my whole life. I want to see how it feels."

"Oh," I say.

"Do you believe me now?" she asks.

"I'm not sure," I say uncertainly.

"Well, take a look."

Sarah hitches up her dress. Of course she isn't wearing any underwear. Then she points to a scar on her inner thigh. A piece of skin was obviously cut away. A piece needed elsewhere.

"I believe you," I say. "I'm sorry I didn't before."

"Don't tell anybody," she says. "Promise."

"Okay."

I am already recalculating everything I have ever thought about—

everything I have ever felt about—Sarah Marks. Her feistiness. Her neediness. Her combativeness. Her whole personality. I try to take her in my arms to comfort her. She pushes me away, but she doesn't let her dress fall.

66

FIRST WE WILL SHOOT THE MASTER: THE WIDE SHOT that will anchor all the close-ups that come later. The camera is set up behind JUDGE SAM RAWLINS for an over-the-shoulder shot of his courtroom.

"Victor, can I look through your camera?" I ask.

I know he will say yes, but if I don't ask, I'm pretty sure he would be irritated. On a movie set, the camera is a god—or idol—that shouldn't be approached without permission from the high priest.

"Of course," says the cinematographer.

Pressing my eye to the viewfinder, I see a piece of the judge's shoulder and beyond it: the defense table, the prosecution table, and the spectators. A wounded Jimmy Goodnight, sitting in an improvised wheelchair made with buggy and wheelbarrow wheels, is a dim figure at the back of the courtroom. The jury box is just out of frame on the left. Sarah—looking ever so slightly pregnant if you look closely—sits at the defense table with her lawyer, the only one in town, HANK WALLACE. His suit is shiny but his shoes aren't. Sitting all alone at the prosecution table is my father, who is playing the role of JOHN KING, full-time druggist, part-time prosecutor. As usual, Dad looks extremely confident. Is the defense intimidated?

"Thanks," I say, stepping back from the camera.

Victor continues tweaking his lighting. When it all looks perfect to him, he nods at Jamie, who nods at Kim Kurumada.

"Quiet everybody," says the first AD. "We are rolling."

"Speed," says somebody on the sound truck.

An assistant cameraman named JOHNNY clicks the slate.

"Action," Jamie almost whispers.

And my father begins his motion picture career.

"You about ready?" asks Judge Rawlins, pointing at the prosecutor.

"Yes, sir," my father answers confidently.

Standing beside the camera, I'm nervous for my dad, but he isn't, not at all, or else he really is a great actor.

Then the judge points at Hank Wallace: "You ready?"

"Yes, Your Honor," the defense attorney says, his voice trembling, which might be characterization but is probably stage fright.

"Then we better git started. Time's a-wastin'. You"—the judge points at my father—"call your first witness."

"I call Tin Soldier," says the prosecutor, "otherwise known as Mortimer Jones."

The spectators LAUGH because they never knew his odd first name. Tin Soldier, the Home Ranch blacksmith, reluctantly gets up and heads for the witness stand. He is wearing the metal hat he made for himself to improve his chances of survival in the Wild West. When he sits down in the witness chair, he takes off his steel hat and holds it in his lap.

"Do you promise not to do no lyin'?" Judge Rawlins asks.

"Yeah," says Tin Soldier.

"Good, you're sworn in."

My father, the prosecuting druggist, stands up and approaches the witness chair. Feeling threatened, Tin Soldier puts his steel hat back on. Characterization or fear?

"Where were you on the ni-ight of June twenty-fourth?" asks my dad.

He doesn't seem to be acting. He is simply behaving. And there is a twinkle in his eye that says he knows a secret that nobody else knows. Possessing this secret amuses him and makes him interesting.

"I was in the bunkhouse," the witness says, his voice shaking.

"Well, whut happened?"

Tin Soldier clears his throat. He looks around the courtroom as if searching for an escape route.

"I'm waitin'," prompts the prosecutor.

It occurs to me that I'm glad I'm not in the witness chair facing my father. Growing up, I always found him the gentlest of men, and yet I always knew it was his house and he was bigger than I was. And better-looking and more charming. Was I jealous? Envious? Only my whole life.

"Well, we heard a woman scream and come a-runnin'," says Tin Soldier. "And then we heard Mr. Goodnight tellin' Loving to draw, but he wouldn't fight him. And then the boss pulled out his ol' Peacemaker, and so Miz Revelie grabbed the gun outta Loving's holster. And she shot Mr. Goodnight and my friend Simon Shapiro with the same bullet. And Simon, he fell down dead." He says it all without taking a breath.

"Cut," Jamie almost whispers. "Clyde, that was really very good. Let's do it again."

"But if it was good—" my father begins.

"Let's do it again. And, Clyde, this time give me a slightly different color."

"What?"

"She means—" I begin.

"I mean," Jamie cuts me off, "just do it a little differently."

"Different how?"

"I don't care. Just different. Maybe meaner. Maybe nicer. Whatever you decide. So when we cut the film together we'll have choices. Okay?"

"Fine and dandy."

We shoot the scene again and my father is nicer, and yes, more charming. Then we do a third take in which he is even more charming than before.

"Less go, call your next witness," Judge Rawlins scolds.

"I call Jack Loving," my father says.

Kelly Hightower walks to the witness chair. Loving seems to sit as easily in the witness chair as he does in the saddle.

"Well, whut happened?" asks my prosecuting father.

"Mr. Goodnight and I quarreled," Loving says easily. "He threw down on me. I was faster'n he was. My bullet went clean through him and killt Simon Shapiro, who didn't have no part in our fight. I'm real sorry for that, and I'm ready to take my medicine."

"Hold on," says my dad, surprised, and suddenly seeming vulnerable. An appealing quality. "You mean you did the shootin'?"

"Yes, sir," says Loving calmly.

"Remember," says the prosecutor, "you're under oath."

"That's how come I'm tellin' the truth," lies Loving.

"No!" SCREAMS the only slightly pregnant Sarah. "I did it. I killed that poor man." She points at Loving. "He didn't do anything. He's lying."

"Cut," whispers Jamie. "I think we've got it. Check the gate."

Before moving on, she wants to make sure there isn't a hair or a piece of lint in the gate through which light enters the camera. It is very discouraging to be sitting in dailies when a giant hair fills the screen or lint blocks out a great performance.

"Gate's clear," says Victor.

"Moving on," says Jamie. "Next up is a close-up on Clyde."

With the camera staring him right in the face, almost nose to nose, my father gets calmer rather than more nervous. I tell myself he doesn't know enough to be nervous.

"Action," Jamie whispers.

Now my dad gives the same performance he gave before, but smaller. How does he know that when he gets bigger, his gestures, tics, whatever, need to get littler? I suppose he just knows instinctively. Or has Jamie been coaching him on the side without telling me?

At the end of the day, Tom Bondini, the biggest star in the world, comes over and congratulates my father. They shake hands. Then Tom hugs my dad, who doesn't know what to do at first, but then he catches on and hugs back.

"Terrific," Jamie tells him.

"What, no hug from you?" Clyde asks.

She disappears into his all-enveloping bear hug. As usual, I feel a twinge of jealousy.

A parade of others comes up to congratulate my father. Kelly Hightower. Kim Kurumada. Me. Production assistants. Camera assistants. The cook from the catering truck. When Victor Hammer hugs my dad, he looks like Beanstalk Jack hugging the Giant. Victor's feet come off the ground. Three feet off the ground. I think: Maybe *he* is the Little Prince.

The only one who doesn't congratulate my dad is Sarah, and I think I know why: She is jealous. Jealous of the praise. Jealous of the attention. Jealous of the hugs. I suppose it is the sincerest compliment she is capable of. Then I remember the secret she told me and think I should make allowances. But I don't really feel like it. Blood is thicker than sympathy.

"I hope you're proud of your dad," Jamie says.

"I'm popping my vest buttons," I say.

"That's a line from a Thin Man movie," she says.

"The Thin Man Goes Home," I say. "Doesn't mean it isn't sincerely felt."

"You know, your father made your scene a lot better than you wrote it. That very rarely happens. I've always been a little worried about this trial."

"Me too."

"I'm not worried anymore. Your dad gave you a gift today."

"Yeah," I say with feeling.

I realize that Jamie and I both have something in common: a fascination with my dad. But my emotions are conflicted: I'm jealous of him and proud of him at the same time. And I was afraid he might embarrass me. What was I thinking? I just have to make sure I don't embarrass him. I am surprised when my vision blurs. I hope Jamie doesn't notice my watery eyes.

"You're such a softie," she says.

67

AT JUST AFTER MIDNIGHT, I PUT DOWN MY BOOK—AN amazing biography of Sam Houston entitled *The Raven*—switch off the light, and turn on my side. I wish I knew how to count sheep, but I don't. Maybe I should try counting buffalo. I do try. It doesn't work. Then I just lie there hoping for the best, sooner rather than later.

Sooner seems to be working when I HEAR a faint KNOCK. It is a knock I recognize. I bolt out of bed in my drawers and rush to the door before she can get away. Seeing her distorted face, I'm worried. But not too worried to notice that she is wearing an extra-large man's shirt as a kind of robe with not much if anything visible underneath.

"What's wrong?" I ask.

"They're pulling us back to the studio," Jamie says.

"What?" I must be still sort of dozing.

"Paramount just called," she says. "Thanks to Buddy, the studio thinks we're out of control, and that's a studio's worst nightmare, you know. We're going to have to finish the movie on the lot or locations nearby. Maybe we can make it work, but I don't want to. I love this country. I love this landscape. I even love the Dickens Café and the lake. I don't want to go. Why is this happening?"

"Did Shelley call you?"

"No, it was Rick Livingston, you know, head of production. Shelley doesn't make this kind of call."

Imitating Spencer Tracy, I look down at the floor. I don't see any answers there.

"When?" I ask.

"Tomorrow morning," Jamie says.

"Fuck," I say under my breath.

"You didn't say that like you meant it," she says.

"I never really learned to swear. My mother told me not to, you know. So it's a language I don't speak very well. But I'm going to work on it and try to improve. Let me try it again."

"Okay."

"Fuck."

"No, no, no, it's *fuck!* You're a pussy when it comes to swearing."

"Nice talk. My mother would wash your mouth out."

We both LAUGH even though we are both upset.

"But we can't go back *now*," I say. "We're in the middle of the trial scene. They have to let us finish that at least."

"That's what I said, but they said they'd build us a courtroom on a soundstage."

"What about my father?"

"We'll take him with us."

Then we just stand there not knowing what to say.

"Let's climb the windmill again," Jamie says at last. "I feel like leaving this planet for a little while."

"Just a minute," I say. "I'll get my pants."

"Don't bother," she says.

We hold hands and make a break for it. As we run down the hall, I keep expecting doors to open and disturbed sleepers to laugh at the sight of me in my underwear. In flight, I have flashbacks of dreams about turning up in school wearing nothing at all. Down the stairs. Could anybody still be up in the giant living room? No, just the dead deer. My legs are cold as we sprint through the dark.

We stand at the base of the dark tower staring up at its buzz saw going around and around.

"Isn't there any way to shut that wheel down?" Jamie asks. "I could sure use some peace and quiet tonight."

"I think so," I say a little uncertainly.

Walking to the north leg of the tower, I locate a yard-long lever and pull down hard. High overhead, there is a screech of brakes, and the wheel stops spinning. It is as if the constant wind has suddenly given up blowing. Like a chicken, I stagger. But the wind hasn't stopped. Only the windmill has stopped.

Jamie climbs fast, running up into the night, as if she can't wait. I race after her. Looking up her shirttail, I SEE (POV) that she is wearing underwear. Sarah wouldn't, but Jamie does. Who would I rather be with? No debate, no question. When she reaches the platform—our small planet—she pulls herself up. Lagging a couple of lengths behind, I finally gain the platform myself.

Lying beneath the quiet wheel, I regret the loss of drama but embrace the gain in romance. We are at the still point in the raging universe. We seem more alone than any couple has ever been. I turn to her and she turns to me. We hug and kiss and kiss and kiss.

She squeezes my balls, not to cause pain, the other kind of

squeeze. I unbutton her big shirt. She isn't wearing underwear, after all. The great beheader above us trembles in the wind but cannot punish us, being tied down. I remember Jamie's vow not to make love with an underling. I touch her breasts and she doesn't push me away. I think of the Little Prince, and in my imagination her nipples become rosebuds. I want to take care of them for the rest of my life.

My hands wander down her body. I find the cave of all caves. You can have your Carlsbad Caverns and Mammoth Cave and Cave of Lascaux with its stone-age paintings. I like this one best. She is pulling off my undershorts. I roll on top of her. Our feet hang over the edge of the high wooden platform and the known world.

"Make sure we don't fall off," Jamie whispers.

"I'll try," I whisper back.

As we begin to move together, I am very conscious of the need not to go completely crazy. This isn't a king-sized bed. I tell myself over and over that I must govern my passion. But sometimes limits make sex even more exciting. Yes, it does.

Yes! Yes! *Yes!*

A rooster crows, coyotes howl, a screech owl screeches, earthworms and moles stop digging. Moths clap their wings. And I know my heart has lost its virginity. At long last.

Then I realize we are perilously close to the edge of the abyss.

"Did our small planet move for you?" Jamie asks.

"You know it did," I say.

"Me too," she says. "And I think I got splinters in my ass."

"I'm sorry."

"It's okay. Now let's very carefully move away from the edge or we'll never finish this movie."

BOOK THREE

68

ON A MORE-OR-LESS LAZY SUNDAY AFTERNOON, JAMIE
and I lie side by side in my bungalow at the hotel that sounds like a
bottle of wine. I keep reading and rereading the pages we still need to
film. She is sketching shots on typing paper. Close-ups. Two-shots.
Masters. She is making her version of storyboards, trying to visualize
everything we have left to shoot. She is a pretty good artist, but she
isn't really trying very hard. These are just notes to herself. The only
figure drawn with any kind of detail is Clyde Goodnight, my father,
who at the moment is taking a nap in the bungalow next door.

"That's a good likeness," I say.

"Thanks," Jamie says. "It relaxes me to draw him. I don't know
why."

"Because he's charming."

"Maybe that's it." She adds a few more details to one of his miniature likenesses. "Yeah, that could be."

I go back to reading. She goes on drawing.

"The studio's crazy," I say. "Isn't this move costing them a for-
tune? The new sets. Everything."

"Absolutely."

"But I thought they were bean counters."

"Only up to a point. Their greatest fear is a runaway production.
And Buddy has, well, you know."

"So they should really send the bill to him."

"Yeah, that'll happen, sure. But, you know, I'm trying to work
here. This move means I have to redo everything. Today I've only got
time for two things: drawing and fucking. Nothing else."

"Let's fuck."

"Good idea, but don't mess up my papers."

Which litter the bed. Another limit. Limits can be exciting.

"You messed up my papers."

Jamie is prickly about few things, but her papers are at the top of that short list. Disarranging her papers is considered sabotage.

"I'm sorry," I say. "But it was in a good cause, right?"

"Well, they aren't too bad. Nothing was actually destroyed. And I don't see any stains."

"Good."

"But I still don't like my pages getting messed up."

The next time we make love, I am afraid to move at all. I let her do the moving. It is an experiment to be recommended. And her papers don't get messed up.

We have a room service dinner in bed, and stay in bed until the next morning.

After a quick shared shower, we drive to Paramount in her faded blue, fifty-year-old Mercedes ragtop. The guard at the fancy wrought-iron gate welcomes us back. We don't say it's good to be back.

"Shall we go watch the painters paint each other?" Jamie asks.

"Sure."

Jamie parks in the great car corral and we head for Stage 8, which stands next door to Stage 7, where we filmed our screen tests so seemingly long ago. This great airplane hangar of a soundstage is a short walk down a narrow alley from the parking lot. Passing from light into darkness, from the world of the sun to the black side of the moon, we both stop to let our eyes adjust. We are in the belly of the whale once again and my stomach hurts.

We head toward lights in the distance. Soon we enter a bright room with four walls and no ceiling. And sure enough, there are the painters painting each other. Since finishing our courtroom set is a high priority, some twenty-five painters have been hired and are hard at work. There are so many of them squeezed into a confined space that they can't help but paint each other. The job is already well over half done. Jamie and I sit down on apple boxes in the middle of the room and watch. The painters are painting fast but well. They are craftsmen. I know from summer jobs around Spur, it would take me two weeks to paint this room.

"When will they be finished?" I ask.

"Soon," Jamie says. "We're shooting in here this morning. I hope nobody passes out from the fumes."

"Sarah will," I predict, "just for the fun of it."

"I have a headache," Sarah announces. "I need to go to my so-called dressing room and lie down."

"That's okay," says Jamie. "We're starting with Clyde anyway."

Which is probably why Sarah has a headache. She walks out of the set, her feet splayed, as if she were much more pregnant than she looks.

"Clyde, how do you feel this morning?" Jamie asks. "Are the fumes bothering you?"

"Heck, no, purdy director lady," my father says. "My barn smells worse'n this. I mean I got relatives—who I ain't gonna name—who's got breath worse'n this here."

"Good," says the pretty director, "we're going to move in even closer for this take."

"Closer'n you did back yonder? That was purdy close. I mean it could see the whites of my eyes and then some."

"What I have in mind is something sometimes called the God shot. You'll be the whole screen. Okay?"

"Well, I guess I can stand it if God can," answers my father.

"We only use the God shot on actors we really like."

So motivated, my father hangs out on the set while they tinker with the lighting. He sits in his canvas chair with his name on the back. I sit in Sarah's chair since she has a headache. Jamie comes over and takes a seat in her chair, which is between my dad and me.

"I'm sorry Sarah ain't feelin' well," my dad says.

"Sarah's an actress," Jamie says.

"You mean she's just puttin' on?"

"Probably."

"No kiddin'," my dad says. "Reminds me of when I was coachin' that game ag'inst Post way back when." Of course, I know the story, but I always like hearing it. "We was way behind, and so I called over this here substitute—I misremember his name—and I give him special instructions. I told him: 'I want you to go in and whisper a secret message to Billy-Wayne.' He was our quarterback, see. I said, 'Tell him that Coach wants you to just keel over after the next play. Put on like you're out cold.' And Billy-Wayne done it. He done it good. I went out on the field and picked up that quarterback like a baby and carried him to the sidelines. And I cried—God fergive me—ever' step of the way. And that riled up our players good'n proper. Because they thought the Post players had hurt our leader, see? And we won that game."

"You could be a director," Jamie says. "That's what I do all day, tell people to put on like this and put on like that. You aren't angling for my job, are you?"

"No, ma'am, I ain't purdy enough to be a director."

"Clyde, you're prettier than ninety-nine point nine percent of the directors in the world."

Framing the shot, Victor Hammer looks through the viewfinder at my father. The DP is so short, he has to stand on an apple box.

"Do I look God-like?" my dad asks.

"You certainly do," says the cameraman.

"Victor, I'll just bet you say that to all the gods, don't you? By the way, is my nose gonna be as big as them there noses on Mount Rushmore?"

"Bigger on some screens."

"Well, whaddaya know. If I'da known that, I sure woulda trimmed my nose hairs."

"That's why God made Hair & Makeup. They'll fix you right up."

"Victor, you're a good man, even if you are a sin-a-matographer. Mebbe we oughta break bread together sometime. How 'bout tonight? You ever been to Dr. Hogly Wogly's?"

"No, I haven't. See, being a sin-a-matographer, I'm a very visual person. I only eat at restaurants that have pictures of the dishes. Like Denny's. Denny's is my favorite."

"Victor, I ain't too crazy 'bout Denny's, but if'n you'll have dinner with me at Dr. H's, I'll be proud to draw you pictures. And I do draw mean ribs, if'n I do say it myself."

Still CHUCKLING, I hear the thump of crutches. Turning, I SEE (POV) Buddy Dale entering our set. When he sees my father, Buddy stops suddenly, thinks a moment, then turns awkwardly on his crutches and thumps away with—as my dad would say—his tail between his legs.

69

WITH A MAP ON THE SEAT BESIDE ME, I DRIVE MY
rented any-car east on the Hollywood Freeway. Rush-hour traffic is
hardly rushing. Jamie had offered me a ride to the location but with a
catch: I would have to get up at five-thirty in the morning. I said I
preferred to sleep a little later. She said I was smarter than I looked.
So here I am driving myself, armed not only with a map but directions from the teamsters. The directions come with a warning: Don't
get lost because this is gang country.

I get off the freeway in Silver Lake and begin weaving my way
through a labyrinth of surface streets. All the store signs are in Span-
ish. I feel as if I am in Mexico City or Miami. I pull over every couple
of blocks to consult my directions and my map. I begin to feel better
when I spot a cardboard sign put up by our location scouts: It says
GOODNIGHT ———>. I make a right turn. Soon I discover another
sign: <——— GOODNIGHT. I turn left. Similar signs lead me like
helpful friends to the location where I see trucks and honey wagons
and motor homes and limos and all sorts of cars. The place is throb-
bing with energy. I take a moment to be proud of myself for not getting lost—this time.

After parking, I go looking for the camera. I know by now that the
best way to find it is to locate an electric cable and follow it. All roads
lead to Rome and all cables lead to the camera and the lights. Unless
you are following the cables in the wrong direction, in which case they
lead to the generator. Discovering at last what is essentially a glorified
extension cord, I go where it leads me. Winding my way through vehicles, I emerge from behind the prop truck and SEE (POV) a city of

tents and a few rickety lean-tos. I stop to admire what Hollywood has managed to put up almost overnight. Well, several nights. Less than a week. It is Strike Town not only as I had imagined it, but better. It is called Strike Town, not only in our script but in history, because it is where all the cowboys moved during the first ever cowboy strike. They wanted a raise to $50 a month, but the ranchers refused and most of the cowboys left their spreads and moved to Strike Town.

Here I am, still in the city limits, still in gang country, and yet it looks and feels like wilderness. Los Angeles, especially on the east side, has these lacunae that have never been developed.

The electric cable I am following is soon joined by other cables, like river tributaries, only this river carries not water but electrons. This little Mississippi leads to the camera, Jamie, and the man she is talking to, my father. He rode out with her in her motor home early this morning to check the actors' accents.

"Hello, sleepyhead," says my dad.

I yawn.

"How do you like Strike Town?" Jamie asks.

"I love it," I say.

"Good," she says, "I told them we couldn't shoot until you approved the set. We've been waiting hours for your permission to go ahead. And each hour only costs about ten thousand dollars."

"You're lying," I say.

"Yeah, you're right," she says. "Nobody gives a shit what writers think."

We are almost ready to shoot the death of Jimmy Goodnight. What we are about to stage reminds me a little of the Atlanta-is-burning scene in *Gone With the Wind*. To film that sequence, David O. Selznick burned down some old sets on his back lot. It was a great night in movie history. We intend to burn a city, too. Not Atlanta, but the tents and shacks of Strike Town.

"Are we getting close?" asks Jamie.

"Very close," lies Victor Hammer.

Before my arrival, our crew picked positions for three cameras that will all be shooting at the same time, and the cast rehearsed the scene several times, without the fire, of course. Now we are almost ready to do it for real. Our special effects team is soaking the ground with a clear liquid that smells like barbecue starter. Jamie keeps looking at her watch.

"A watched watch never ticks," I say helpfully.

"Are you saying I've got a face that stops clocks?" she asks.

I let it go.

"Ready," Victor says at long last.

I follow Jamie. As usual, she takes up a position just to the right of one of the cameras. I stand behind her looking over her shoulder at the panorama we are about to film. I SEE (POV) Tom Bondini in the foreground holding his scepter of an ax. Like King Arthur, the king of the ranchers is about to be murdered by his bastard son, a teenager called Justin. Played by a good-looking actor named MATT CAVA-NAUGH, he kneels in the dust in front of the biggest star in the world. In the background, tents and lean-tos stretch to the horizon. It looks and feels like the badlands of West Texas. Of course, if I were to turn around, I would see the sprawling megalopolis, Los Angeles.

"Light it up," Jamie whispers.

I HEAR a great WHOOSH as Strike Town bursts into flames. The cameras roll, three slates clap, and fire dances behind the actors.

"Action," Jamie whispers at last.

I SEE (POV) Justin, the bastard, clutching his stomach, which is covered in blood. He has been bloodied by his own father wielding that magical ax. Goodnight bends to comfort his dying son.

"I ain't quite done yet," says Justin.

He pulls from his sleeve a tiny Derringer pistol, the size of a baby's hand, and aims it at his father point-blank.

"Die, Daddy, die," Justin says. "Go to hell."

BANG. Then a pause. BANG, BANG, BANG, BANG.

Something is wrong! A Derringer can shoot at most two bullets. Didn't the special effects people read the script? One shot! Just one shot! Tom Bondini sinks to his knees, but he clutches not his midsection, as he is supposed to, but his left leg. Didn't he read the script either? Why did I write it if nobody is going to read it?

Then Jamie does the unforgivable: She rushes into the shot. What has come over her? Didn't *she* read the script either? Because if she had, she would realize she isn't in this scene. Or any of the scenes. Nonetheless she throws her arms around the biggest star in the world. I'm jealous. What does she think she is doing?

"Call an ambulance!" Jamie SHOUTS.

BANG, BANG, BANG, BANG.

"Get down!" the director directs. "Everybody, get down! Take cover!"

I look around: Everybody is diving for cover.

Jamie tries to help Tom to his feet, but he is too heavy. Then I see my father walk out calmly, pick up the biggest star in the world as if he were a baby, and carry him to his motor home. He carries the star the way he carried his quarterback so many years ago. Only this time he is crying for real.

I am the only one not moving. I still don't understand. I don't get it. What has gotten into everybody?

BANG. Something invisible kicks up dust six feet in front of me. BANG. A dustup three feet in front of me. BANG. This one kicks dirt on my boots.

Feeling like an idiot, I dive behind the nearest cover I can find: a camera. I am relying on a movie camera to save my life. Many have made that mistake and paid for it. Marilyn Monroe, Montgomery Clift . . . A bullet smashes into the camera, which stuns me. Evidently I have begun to regard the Panovision movie camera as something sacred that no one would dare attack. I was wrong. There are other points of view. It occurs to me: By returning to Los Angeles, against our wills, we have found the real Wild West.

Cringing behind the smashed camera, I HEAR SIRENS but no more gunshots. I wait. I count to a hundred. Then I decide to add another hundred. When I reach two hundred, I open my eyes and stick my head out. I SEE (POV) people running and flames still dancing. Tents and shacks are burning. Smoke billows. Feeling a coward, I still crouch. I am paralyzed. Somebody touches my shoulder. I push the hand away.

"Come on, let's go," Jamie says. "Let's get out of here."

"What?" I ask.

She grabs my hand and pulls hard. I get to my feet, still crouching, and we run like hell. I am disappointed to discover that Jamie is just as fast as I am. If she is even faster, she chooses not to humiliate me, even though her life might be in the balance. We dive under the nearest motor home, Tom's, and roll into each other's arms.

"What's going on?" I babble.

"It appears that somebody dislikes us enough to shoot at us," Jamie says. "This is the kind of thing I thought might happen to us in your hometown, not mine."

"I hear this is gang country," I say.

"Like the Sharks and the Jets?" she asks.

"Except without the singing and dancing."

"Too bad."

Police cars begin roaring onto our set, churning up dust, as if we were making a cops-and-robbers movie. Men in uniform get out and crouch behind their vehicles, weapons drawn.

"What do we do now?" I ask.

"I'm not directing this scene," Jamie says.

We continue to huddle. The cops crouch. The great fire burns. But there are no more gunshots. Eventually the cops stand up and walk around. We roll out from beneath the star's motor home. We try to brush the desert off our clothes and out of our hair.

"How's Tom?" I finally ask.

"Bullet through his leg," Jamie says. "It didn't look life-threatening to me, but all I know about gunshot wounds I learned from the movies."

Then a convoy of armored Humvees snakes onto the set and skids to a halt in the dust. The doors fly open and the shouting begins.

"Get in! Hurry! Get in and lie down on the floor! Hurry! Hurry!"

Jamie and I—among many others, cast and crew—retreat from our set and ignominiously huddle on the floor of the Hummers. I look for my father but don't see him. I'm not too worried. I figure he can take care of himself.

70

JAMIE AND I DRIVE IN HER VINTAGE MERCEDES TO Cedars Hospital, where the biggest star in the world is recuperating. He is registered under the name Clyde Goodnight to throw the press and fans off his scent. A hospital security guard walks us to his room. As we are about to enter, the door opens. TERI MICHELLE BEN-DELE, in tears, brushes past us. She is an actress who has made several movies with Tom over the years, but she does not appear to be acting now. She is hurting.

"Excuse me," she says in a thick voice. And she is gone.

Jamie and I enter somewhat timidly. Tom's room is probably the best in the building, with lots of space and light, but it still smells like medicine. He looks somber but smiles as we near the bed. IV tubes sprout from his arms.

"Maybe this isn't a good time," Jamie says. "We can come back later."

"No, stay," says Tom. "Please. I'm glad to see you. Why wouldn't this be a good time?"

"Uh, well, we just saw Teri," she says. "She was crying."

"She was?" Tom's eyelids quiver and his eyes moisten.

"Yeah. If you'd like us to come back—"

"No. What happened is, she asked me a tough question." He pauses. We don't fill the silence. "Seems this guy's asked her to marry him." Another pause. I sense he wants to be interrupted, but we don't. "She likes him and is leaning toward saying yes, but she wanted to make sure where I stood on the whole marriage thing." Another pause. "Well, not just the marriage thing, because I'd love to marry her, but the boy thing. She asked if I could give up forever and ever boys." We don't say anything. "I told her I'd try, try real hard, but I wasn't sure. That was the honorable thing to do, wasn't it?"

A doctor enters Tom's hospital room, and we make our exit.

"You must never tell anyone!" Jamie says as we are leaving the hospital. "I know you have friends in the press. I didn't mind what you did to Buddy, but I would be hugely, vastly, cut-your-balls-off mad if this turned up in the media. Got it?"

"Got it," I say. "I swear."

"Swear on something. I know, swear on your balls."

"Okay."

"No, you have to say the words. Come on. I know you can do it."

"Fine, I swear on my balls."

"Good, I believe you, only because I know how hard it is for you to adopt colorful language."

"Good."

We walk across the lot toward the blue Mercedes ragtop, zigzagging between parked cars.

"Tom's the only true bisexual I know," Jamie says. "Usually when people claim they are bisexual, it's just a cover. But he's different. You know he's got a 'straw' on this show?"

"What?"

"Poor baby, you are so innocent. A straw is somebody a star gets to put on a movie. Give a job, get a blow job or whatever. You know."

"No, I don't. Do you have a straw?"

She slaps me. It is a good slap delivered from the shoulder. My ears ring and my head wobbles, but I am smiling because I recognize the slap as a signal that she cares for me.

"Point taken," I say. "Do you know who Tom's straw is?"

"Sure, it's Stan the Man Broder."

"Who?"

"One of our stuntmen. Are you shocked?"

"Yes."

"Open your eyes about so-called masculinity."

"I resent that."

"Good. You're feisty. That's very good. That's more-or-less real masculinity."

As we are heading toward the parking lot exit, we notice Sarah pull in. She parks in a space reserved for the handicapped and heads for the hospital's imposing front door.

"Poor Tom," Jamie says with feeling.

71

WHEN I ARRIVE AT STAGE 8 THE NEXT MORNING, I GET two surprises. Jamie tells me that Tom Bondini will be back with us later today. He is a fast healer. But Jamie also has less happy news.

"Paramount is shutting us down in exactly one week," she says in the semidarkness of the soundstage. "We won't get one more hour—not one more dollar—after that deadline."

"But what if we aren't finished?" I ask.

"They'll shut us down anyway," Jamie says.

"They wouldn't."

"They would, so we'd better hurry, huh?"

From now on, the time spent lighting scenes will be cut by one third. Which drives Victor Hammer to the brink of dark mutiny.

"Why don't you just make the actors talk faster?" Victor complains.

"I'll try, but you still have to light faster," Jamie says.

"Do you want it fast or do you want it good?"

"I want it good 'n' fast."

"Very funny."

Feeling the pressure, we rush through the day. On the one hand, I hate this speed because it forces so many compromises. On the other hand, I love this haste because it makes moviemaking more fun. More like working for a newspaper, where you always face a deadline. There are fewer boring waits. There are fewer takes from fewer angles. There is more hustle, more energy, more movement. I think something blasphemous: This is the way movies ought to be made. I tell nobody.

"Action!" Jamie is SHOUTING it now . . .

"Wrong set . . ."

"Action!" . . .

"Wrong set . . ."

"Saving the shark . . ."

"Can we do one more take?"

"No!"

Yes, we are galloping now. We are coming down the backstretch, and our spurs are jingling.

Tom's Goodnight dies with a bullet in his gut while footage from the fire in Silver Lake is projected onto a screen behind him. We have only one more scene to shoot. And one more day to shoot it in.

———————

The real Jimmy Goodnight was buried on the Home Ranch in the center of a hackberry thicket where he and Revelie used to make love. Since our movie company has left Texas far behind us, we are forced to compromise. Our location scouts find us a thicket of mesquite trees in the badlands about a hundred miles east of Los Angeles. We are finished flirting with gangs and other dangers closer to "home."

I drive myself to the location, getting lost along the way, turning a two-hour trip into three hours. I arrive just at lunchtime.

"Nice timing," Jamie says.

"I took a wrong turn," I explain.

"I figured. Where's your dad?"

"When I told him we weren't doing any dialogue today, he decided to stay home and catch up on his sol'. What did I miss?"

"Nothing yet. Except of course you did miss Sarah's fight with special effects."

Jamie leads the way into the mesquite thicket at the heart of which is a small and crowded clearing. The camera somehow looks even more God-like in this setting, which recalls places where Druids might once have met and worshipped.

"Can I look?" I ask.

"Please, look all you want," says Victor Hammer.

"My dad really enjoyed his dinner with you."

"Me too," he says in a bad Texas accent. "That's how come I'm lettin' you squint through my camera."

Squinting through the viewfinder, I see framed in the middle of the shot a granite marker with this simple inscription:

JIMMY GOODNIGHT

1849–1883

RANCHER

And embedded in this stone is the blade of an ax. The sight gives me a chill.

"Thanks," I say.

"Any time," says Victor.

I walk over to the tombstone and give it a thump with my finger. It looks like rock but it sounds like cardboard. Jimmy Goodnight, rancher, has been buried beneath papier-mâché. My chill goes away.

After a lunch that feels like a picnic in the great out-of-doors, the argument between Sarah and the special effects team reignites.

"I won't shoot the shot unless I can do it my way," Sarah says, standing beside the grave.

"Are you refusing to work?" Jamie interjects herself into the battle.

"Yes, I guess I am."

"There can be serious legal consequences."

"This means a lot to me."

"Not just legal but career consequences."

"I don't care."

Jamie turns her back and marches away. She leaves the mesquite thicket—which should be hackberry—and walks in a large circle. I think about going to her, but she does not seem to be in a welcoming mood. Her fists are clenched. I decide to keep my distance.

Buddy Dale arrives and tries to pretend he is in charge. Ignoring Jamie's unwelcoming signals, he falls into stride beside her. But on crutches he can't keep up.

"Wait!" Buddy YELLS.

Jamie ignores him.

"What's going on here?" he demands. "They tell me we haven't even gotten the first shot yet. What the hell is wrong?"

"Nothing," Jamie says, stopping suddenly and turning on him. "Nothing the hell is wrong."

Turning once again, Jamie heads back into the thorny thicket. I hurry after her. Buddy hobbles in our train.

"This is going to be the last shot in the picture," Jamie says. "Sarah, maybe at long last we can compromise."

"What are you offering?" Sarah asks petulantly.

"Well, against my better judgment," Jamie says, "I'm willing to shoot it your way one time only. In other words, one take will be your take. All the other takes will be mine. Okay?"

Sarah takes her time thinking over the offer and then announces: "On one condition."

"What?" asks Jamie, exasperated.

"My one take has to be a close-up."

"Okay, okay."

"And we shoot it first."

"No, we shoot it *last*! We'll shoot that last shot and then we'll all go home. The movie will be over. Take it or leave it."

It takes us three hours to shoot all of Jamie's takes. Establishing shots. Steadicam shots. Tracking shots. Closer shots. Closer still. Singles.

"When's it gonna be my turn?" Sarah asks impatiently, not for the first time.

"I think we're about ready to do yours now," Jamie says with a sigh.

"Great," Sarah says.

But it takes forty-five minutes to tweak the lighting and the makeup and hair. It's the last shot of the movie. Everybody wants it to be just right.

"Picture is next," Kim Kurumada announces at long last.

"Praise the fucking Lord," says Jamie. "Do it."

"Roll film," says Kim.

"Speed," says the sound truck.

Whack! says the slate.

"Action," Jamie whispers.

Sarah walks to her husband's grave. She kneels down as if praying. Then she leans forward, grasps the shoulders of the tombstone, and kisses the blade of the ax. When she stands up and turns around, she is smiling, but blood, her real blood, flows from a cut on her lip. She had to feel it, she really had to bleed. The look on her face is actually ecstatic. But is it because that is what Revelie would be feeling or because the actress playing Revelie has won? And yet in spite of the blood, her blood, I feel let down by her performance in the scene. She is overplaying it.

"Cut," says Jamie. Then she adds: "I hate to say it, but that was really good."

I silently disagree.

"Thanks," Sarah says through bloody lips. "And thanks for letting me."

Our leading lady rushes up to her director, throws her arms around her, and gives her a bloody kiss on the mouth. Everybody gasps and then claps.

"That's a wrap," says Kim Kurumada. "A wrap with a capital *W*. The wrap of all wraps. Thank you all."

The cast and crew burst into APPLAUSE. They CHEER. Everybody hugs everybody. Cowboy hats are thrown in the air. I throw mine, too.

Jamie turns to me and grips both my arms tight. She leans in and whispers: "Do you think bloody Sarah just gave me AIDS?"

72

MY FACE IS WET AND GETTING WETTER AS I DRIVE MY rented car toward Hollywood. Real Hollywood. Literal Hollywood. For Paramount is the only studio still left in geographic—as opposed to metaphorical—Hollywood. Most of the others are located in the Valley.

When I finally reach Paramount, I turn in at the big iron gate that reminds me of a giant peacock's tail. The guard knows me by now, but I still have to show him my identification. The wooden arm goes up and I drive onto the lot. I park beneath the great painted sky. The giant painting is still bright and sunny, but the morning sun is even brighter.

I walk across the big parking lot toward dailies, which will be shown at 11 A.M. in the studio's big theater. I am halfway there when another car races onto the lot and heads right at me. I jump back out of the way just in time. The car screeches to a stop and a beautiful young woman jumps out. I think she is going to apologize, but that isn't her aim at all.

"Where's Buddy Dale's office?" the beauty YELLS. "I'm auditioning for *Goodnight,* and I'm late."

At dailies, we see Sarah's bloody kiss over and over. In the first half dozen versions of the scene, the blood is real, but it once belonged to a pig. In the last take, the blood streaming from her cut lips is really hers. Everybody groans and teases, and Sarah loves it. Once again, in all the takes, she is better on film than she seemed when she was actually doing the scene right in front of me. Nothing is overplayed.

What had I been worried about? What did I expect? Would I never learn? The last take is by far the best.

After dailies let out, as Jamie and I walk back across the studio toward our office, I feel like crying once again because it's over. Really over. No more dailies. No more rewrites. No more anything. But fortunately I remember my cowboy heritage and manage not to bawl on the shoulder of the woman I love.

"I've got an idea I've been turning over and over for several days," Jamie says. "I think it'd be a big improvement."

"Too late," I say. "All the writing's been writ. All the scenes've been shot. You can stop thinking now."

"It's not that kind of an idea," she says. "I don't want to improve the script. I want to improve you. Give you a polish. Make you better."

"Oh?" I say, cringing inwardly, hoping it doesn't show.

"Want to hear?" she asks.

"Sure," I say, giving a very unconvincing reading of the line.

"Of course you do," she says more convincingly. "I knew you would. See, here's the idea: It's time for you to come out of the baton-twirling closet."

"What?" I stammer.

"I am about to explain," she says, laughing but sounding serious at the same time. "It's not right to hide who you really are from people. It's not fair to them, but most of all it's not good for you." CHUCKLING seriously. "Let's face it, you're a twirler. A very good twirler. You shouldn't be ashamed of it. You should announce it to the world."

"You're joking?" I ask hopefully.

"Yes and no. Yes, I think it's funny, but I mean it." She LAUGHS. "And I've got a plan."

"No."

"Yes. You've got to twirl at the wrap party. Put on a show. Wow everybody."

"No."

"You don't take direction very well, do you?"

"No, no, no, and no, ma'am."

73

THE FOLLOWING EVENING, WE HAVE OUR WRAP PARTY on Stage 8. The soundstage is decorated with relics left over from Hollywood's age of westerns. There is a cell from an old make-believe jail. The bars look like steel but are actually made of wood. There is an old outhouse that looks like it is made of wood but is really papier-mâché. There are real saddles and bridles and spurs. There are branding irons and lariats with cobwebs hanging from them. There are wagon wheels that came off the Great Western Movie Machine decades ago. And there are picnic tables and hundreds of bales of hay.

"I'm hungry," Clyde says. "I could eat a Clydesdale."

"Me too," I say, looking around for Jamie.

We follow the crowd to the barbecue pit, which isn't a prop. We stand in line with the grips and gaffers and best boys . . . with actors with one line and actors with hundreds . . . with teamsters and painters and carpenters . . . with cowboys and outlaws. When it is our turn, my father and I both get ribs, links, red beans, and corn bread.

"Smells even better than a Clydesdale," my dad says.

"Yeah," I agree, still looking for Jamie.

"Are you looking for Jamie?" my father asks.

"No."

"Thass what I thought. She's over there. Follow me."

I finally SEE (POV) Jamie perched on a bale of hay with her dinner balanced on her knees. I quicken my pace.

"What's your hurry?" my dad asks.

"I'm not hurrying," I say.

"Thass what I thought," he says. "'Scuse me if'n I git a heart attack chasin' after you."

As we approach the director of the movie, she looks up and smiles.

"I've been wondering where you were," Jamie says.

"Chick took hours primpin' and gittin' ready," Clyde says. "Dunno why he wanted to be so purdy."

"Have a seat," she says.

My father sits on one side of her, I sit on the other. She puts her right hand on his knee. She doesn't put her left on mine.

"Bon appétit," Jamie says.

"I hope that means 'dig in,'" says my dad.

We both dig. The barbecue is good. It's really good. I am wallowing in sauce when it occurs to me that I forgot to pick up any napkins. Now I feel dark, reddish, sticky goo all over my hands and up to my elbows. I feel it streaked across my face like a big saucy clown's smile.

"I always heard that it's not good barbecue," Jamie says, "unless you get sauce on your underwear." She pauses. "Looks to me like Chick thinks this is great barbecue."

My father LAUGHS.

"I forgot napkins," I explain.

"I got extra," my father says, handing me a half dozen.

"Thanks."

I begin mopping up. Of course, I could do a better job if my dad had also brought along a portable shower.

"Would you look at that?" Clyde says. "I mean you could knock me over with a dang buttercup."

I look up. Jamie does, too.

"Ain't that there Tom and Sarah walkin' in holdin' hands? I thought they was s'posed to be at each other's throats."

"That's what I thought," Jamie says.

"Me too," I say.

At the sight of our stars, the cast and crew APPLAUD. Sarah and Tom do mock bows. Everybody is surprised to see them together. They both wear big smiles, happy at the universal amazement. They say hello left and right.

"It's like a mama wolf datin' Bambi," Dad says. "Whass goin' on here? This here Hollywood's sure a queer place." He pauses. "And just look there at what he's wearin'."

I should have seen it before. For the first time since we started the movie, Tom Bondini is dressed in western clothes, not as a costume but by choice. Gone are the puce sneakers and T-shirts. He now sports fancy two-tone cowboy boots, blue jeans, a big belt buckle, a shirt with mother-of-pearl snaps, and a black cowboy hat with a brim the size of a chuck wagon frying pan. What has come over our leading man? He has western duds on his body and Sarah on his arm.

I go to the restroom and take a bath in the sink. My father calls such ablutions "spit baths." When I return to the party, a western band is playing, and cowboys and cowgirls are two-stepping.

Even Sarah and Tom are dancing. When I see them, I stop to watch. He is a better dancer than she is, but they nonetheless look good circling the floor. He holds her close. They kiss as they dance, which knocks her hat off. Without missing a step, Tom leans down, picks up the fallen hat, and returns it to Sarah's head. She puts both arms around him and hugs him tight. He does the same to her. They are pressed together so tightly that I wonder how they can keep dancing, but they do. They float, they glide like ice skaters, their heads never bobbing up or bobbing down. In his arms, she is actually becoming a better dancer.

Then the band takes a break. Jamie winks at me. I have been

dreading this moment all evening. My hands shake worse than they have ever shaken.

"No," I mouth silently.

"Yes," she mouths back. Then she hurries forward and mounts the bandstand. Taking the microphone, she begins: "Attention, y'all! Listen up!" The talk and laughter begin to die down. "I've got a surprise for you." The soundstage gets quieter still. "Through great personal effort, I have managed to line up a virtuoso entertainer to transport you on this fine evening. Is it Willie Nelson? Close, but he's taller. Is it Dolly Parton? No, sorry, he doesn't bleach his hair. Would you like to know who it is?"

"Yes!"

"Shit, yeah!"

"Tell us!"

On and on as my fingers dance faster and faster.

"Ladies and gentlemen, cowpokes and pokees," Jamie YELLS, "clap your hands and stomp your boots for—Chick Goodnight!"

General LAUGHTER. I am embarrassed, angry, frightened, and want to run right out of hulking Soundstage 8.

"Buck up," whispers my father.

I don't buck.

"Chick, come on up here!" Jamie orders.

I sit there paralyzed.

"Better do what she says," counsels my father. "She's the director."

Reluctantly—obeying both my dad and my director—I get up and head for the stage. I crawl up and stand facing Jamie with my back to our cast and crew.

"Bring 'em out here, George," she says.

GEORGE MOON, a member of our special effects crew, emerges from the shadows carrying two batons. They aren't the ones my parents gave me for Christmas so long ago. These are special batons, and they are Jamie's idea. Her reasoning: Nobody will think you are a sissy if the batons you are twirling are on fire.

"Turn around," my director directs.

My shoulders hunching as if I am about to be horsewhipped, I slowly turn and face the crowd. George, the special effects man, hands me the batons. I HEAR the cast and crew LAUGHING. Then George lights them up. The LAUGHTER begins to FADE. The batons look like huge matchsticks burning at both ends. The soundstage is hushed except for the roar of the four fires. I have twirled flaming batons before, but not for quite a while. I hope I remember how.

Taking a deep breath as if it is my last, I start twirling. I do a few unders, a few overs, some finger twirls with fingers that are no longer shaking. With my right hand I hurl a spinning baton into the air. As it starts down, I keep telling myself: Don't miss it. Don't miss it. I don't miss it! As I catch the first baton, I throw the second. Then I launch them both at the same time. Spinning high above me, the batons look like fiery windmills, like gleaming galaxies, like firework bursts on the Fourth of July. I begin to HEAR something I have never heard before in my life. Anyway, not for me. I HEAR the surprisingly thrilling sound of CLAPPING.

The next morning I drive my father to the airport. He is going home. At Gate 46B, we shake hands.

"We're both in the movie business now," Dad says, "so I figure that means we gotta hug. This here Hollywood's a real huggin' place, ain't it?"

"That's right," I say.

We hug long and hard. He hugs harder than I do. Not because he feels more. Anyway, I don't think so. But because he is still stronger than I am.

74

LEAVING OUR OFFICE, JAMIE AND I WALK ACROSS THE
courtyard to our cutting rooms. There are three of them in a row with
connecting doors. This cutting suite looks like the 6666 dining room
in Texas, but not as fancy. Paramount provides no chandeliers and
the chairs are not the plush variety. But there are the same shelves
lined with film cans, the same trolleys with reels of film, the same
flatbed editing machine.

"Good morning, David," Jamie says cheerily. "How are you on
this fine morning?"

"I've been better," says Dave Ralston. "I cut my finger and got
blood all over the film."

"That's okay," she says. "It's a bloody story."

"I know, but I'd rather it waddn't my blood."

"How'd it happen?"

"You know, trying to cut too fast. My boss is a slave driver. Didn't
get my finger out of the way fast enough. Cut film and finger, too."

"David, maybe you should rethink your opposition to the Avid."

"I'd rather bleed to death."

"Looks like that's a possibility. What have you got to show us this
morning? Something bloody, I hope."

"How about a nice thumb hanging?"

"Perfect."

Dave continues fiddling with the reels, making sure they are all
three cued up to the same starting point. Otherwise, Tom Bondini's
lines might come out of Sarah Marks's mouth.

"Okay, here goes whatever," Dave says.

I HEAR the door opening and turn to look. Buddy Dale enters wearing his usual cocaine-flecked black turtleneck and black slacks. He is smiling as if all is forgiven.

"Stop the film," Jamie says under her breath to our film editor. Then she addresses our producer: "Buddy, to what do we owe the pleasure . . ."

"I'm here because this is my favorite part of moviemaking," Buddy announces. "Editing."

"Funny, I thought it was casting," I say under my breath to Jamie.

Buddy glares at me. "What did you say?" he demands.

"Nothing," I say, suffering a failure of backbone.

"No, tell me!"

What should I do? Lie? Stand mute? Ask to call my lawyer?

"I said I thought your favorite part was casting."

"Would you please shut the fuck up!"

"You asked."

"Shut up," Buddy says. "I like editing the best because everybody says it's my strength. I can't tell you how many movies I've saved in the cutting room."

We all stare at each other.

Jamie clears her throat. "Buddy," she says in a friendly tone, "I'm afraid I don't allow actors in the cutting room. Just ask Sarah. And if I wouldn't allow Sarah and Tom, why would I allow anyone else? I'm not going to turn the editing of this movie over to a committee. No matter how well intentioned that committee might be."

"What about him?" Buddy says, nodding at me.

"We're partners," she says. "I couldn't finish the movie without him. You do want me to finish it, don't you?"

Nobody says anything. The producer stares wordlessly at the director. And she glares silently back.

"I'm taking this to Shelley," Buddy says.

"Good," says Jamie. "She's not one of your bimbos."

"Wait till I tell Shelley about the actress who asked me for directions to your office on the last day of our shoot," I say, my hands and heart quieter than usual. "Why did she want to find you? Because she was auditioning for our wrapped movie."

"How could you?" Jamie says.

"She misunderstood," he says.

"I'll bet," I say.

Buddy's countenance is as purple as an overripe plum as he retreats and SLAMS the door in my face. In Jamie's face, too.

"That went well," she says.

"Yes, I enjoyed it, too," I say.

"I was being ironical."

"Oh."

"Let's look at some film."

Jamie and I return to our seats on either side of Dave Ralston. He restarts the film. On the television-sized monitor, Jimmy Goodnight rides into town to rescue a poor girl who is hanging by her thumbs. A CLOSE-UP reveals her thumbs to be as purple as Buddy's face when last I saw him.

In the afternoon, Jamie is called out of the cutting room to attend some meeting in the Tudor castle where the executives work. With nothing to do, I watch Dave edit. Using his little guillotine, he cuts off a section of film. Then he Scotch-tapes it to another piece of film. He uses special movie Scotch tape that is just the width of 35-millimeter film and has sprocket holes punched in it. The tape looks exactly like clear film but is sticky on one side. People have been gluing movies together like this for a hundred years. Dave's practiced fingers move quickly, but the process still looks awkward and ungainly, using technology that dates back almost to the Age of Cowboys. A twenty-first-century art form is waiting on nineteenth-century craftsmanship.

"Wouldn't an Avid be faster?" I ask at last.

"Faster, yes," Dave says. "Better, I don't think so. Tell me: Would you rather have handmade boots or machine-made?"

"I've never had a pair of handmade," I admit.

"You don't know what you're missing," he says, pulling up a Levi leg to reveal a very handsome black boot.

I retreat to a dilapidated couch and pick up a copy of the *Los Angeles Times*. Realizing it is almost a week old, I put it down again. I look at my watch. I lie down on the couch. I look at my watch. I sit up again. I look at my watch. What is taking Jamie so long? Not only do I not know what to do, I miss her.

The door opens and she walks in. I stand up with what feels like a stupid grin on my face. Then I notice that she isn't smiling. I keep grinning anyway.

"Welcome back," I say.

Jamie doesn't say anything, and her expression doesn't change.

"Is something wrong?" I ask.

She walks to the flatbed and sits down beside Dave. I approach, but I don't sit. Feeling somehow unwelcome, I stand and hover.

"Where were we?" Jamie asks Dave.

At the end of the day, as we are leaving the cutting room, I debate with myself about asking Jamie if she would like to get some dinner. I hesitate, first of all, because I'm me, but also because she has seemed cold for hours. I kept waiting for her to warm, but it never happened. I tell myself to keep my mouth shut and wait for a thaw, but I can't help myself.

"Would you like to get some dinner?" I ask as we are crossing the courtyard. "We could go to Lucy's."

"No," she says without looking at me. She doesn't offer an excuse or an explanation. It is just an unadorned: "No."

"Jamie, what's wrong?" I ask.

She doesn't say anything, just keeps walking, looking straight ahead.

"Please tell me."

She doesn't tell me anything. I surprise myself by reaching over and touching her shoulder. She pulls away from my touch and walks farther away from me.

"Jamie, please."

"I know what you did," she says and runs away from me across the courtyard.

Lying in my bed at the Chateau Marmont, I try to sleep but can't. I love Jamie. Even better, she is my best friend. Better still, she is the only person in the world around whom I feel relaxed. When I'm with her, my hands almost stop trembling. But they are shaking now and so is my mind. I feel sick to my stomach. I am seasick on my tossing bed. What did I do? What does she think I did? I ask the question in every way I can think of, but I never get an answer. I want to call her, but it is too late, and I'm not brave enough.

My telephone RINGS. I know it's her. I wanted to call her, so she is calling me. We are still in sync. Our minds still somehow meet. I grab the phone.

"Hello," I blurt out.

"Hello yourself, handsome," says Sarah. "I'm not calling too late, am I?"

"No," I say, wanting to throw up.

"I just had to tell you," she says. "I had dinner with Tom tonight."

"Was he still dressed as a cowboy?"

"Of course. That's all he wears now. But here's the good part: We made love on the hood of his Rolls-Royce. Right there in the restaurant's parking lot. A crowd gathered. It was great."

"Good for you," I say.

"You don't sound like you mean it."

"I've had a hard day. I don't know what I mean anymore."

"There weren't any paparazzi."

"Is that good or bad?"

"I'm not sure."

75

I LIE AWAKE ALL NIGHT. ACTUALLY I PROBABLY DOZE A little, but I never catch myself at it. At five-thirty in the morning, I am tired generally but even more tired of fighting my bed. I get up, shower, and decide to pay an early-morning call to Jamie. Only I don't know where she lives. I hunt around my bedroom until I find a *Goodnight* contact sheet. It has numbers and addresses for everybody involved in the production. And right there at the top of the page is Jamie Stone: 449 Skyewiay LA 90049. Can't they even spell out here? What is wrong with this city? Not recognizing the street name, I go to my computer and ask Yahoo for driving directions. Of course, Yahoo has heard of Skyewiay. I jot down the directions and hurry out of my hotel room before I have a chance to change my mind.

Leaving the Chateau, I drive my rental west on Sunset Boulevard. I turn on my radio loud enough so I can't think. It is just after 6 A.M. The Sunset Strip is deserted at this hour and reminds me of a hooker sleeping off her night. I pass the Beverly Hills Hotel on my right and a little later UCLA on my left. I cross the San Diego Freeway and keep going, running from the morning sun. Now I am watching street signs carefully. Barrington. Bundy. Following my directions, I make a right turn on Kenter. A few blocks later, I take another right on

Skyewiay—what were they thinking?—and wind around until I SEE (POV) 449 painted on a curb.

Pulling over, I study Jamie's surprising home. Her house resembles a redwood aircraft carrier cresting a wave. The "wave" is actually a steep hill. Like a carrier, the house itself is flat. A carrier's deck is cantilevered high above the ocean like a vast shelf. This house is cantilevered, too, and also hangs in space. It is a shelf extending out of the hill. It has a wraparound deck made of redwood. Can this be the right house?

Not knowing what else to do, I sit and wait. I look at my watch. It is only six-thirty. I keep the radio on to jam any serious thinking. I look at my watch. It is six thirty-six. I try to decide what to do, but the radio drowns out my thoughts. As my father likes to say: It is so loud I can't hear myself think. I look at my watch. It is six thirty-eight.

At seven thirty-one, I SEE (POV) Jamie emerge from her front door wearing a big T-shirt that stretches almost to her knees. Without thinking—unable to think—I throw open the car door, stumble getting out, and race up the steep driveway. There is a low redwood gate at the top of the drive. I vault over it. Jamie is just picking up her morning paper when she looks up and sees me.

"What are you—?" she begins.

"Jamie, you have to tell me what's wrong," I say, breathless from running up the hill, desperate from lack of sleep and a night of, well, despair. "What do you mean you know what I did? What did I do?"

"You look terrible," she says.

"I am terrible. Please tell me what you meant. I've been crazy all night."

"I meant: I know what you were spending your money on in Texas."

"Dinners with you and gas."

"And hookers."

"What hookers?"

"Don't play innocent with me."

"Really, I've never been with a hooker in my life"—I try to breathe more slowly—"and I'm kind of ashamed of it. Never had the nerve. Comes from reading *Catcher in the Rye* at an impressionable age. You know, Holden Caulfield goes with a prostitute and she mugs him. Never could get that scene out of my mind. Nothing like an impending mugging to make you lose your erection."

Jamie LAUGHS.

"That's a good sign," I say.

"Not really," she says. "You're an amusing liar, but you're still a liar. He showed me the receipts."

"Receipts of what?"

"Please."

"Tell me, receipts of what?"

"I saw your expense account. Not only were you whoring, but you expect the studio to pay for it. Come on. Not even Buddy would be that crass."

"I've never even turned in an expense account on this movie. I keep meaning to, but I keep putting it off. The studio owes me for hotels and rental cars—and I hope I've managed to hold on to most of the receipts—but I've just never gotten around to totaling them up. I'm not well enough organized to try to cheat Paramount."

"You've never turned in an expense account, not in all this time?"

"No, I swear."

"Can you prove it?"

"I can show you all the receipts I've been saving. If I'd turned in an expense account, I wouldn't have them anymore, would I?"

Jamie thinks a moment. "It's cold out here." The early-morning November wind is whipping her thin T-shirt. "Let's go inside."

I think but this time don't say: That's a good sign. Following Jamie indoors, I feel as if I'm trailing after Alice as we pass through a looking glass. I am disoriented by the accusations, by the lack of sleep, and by the interior of Jamie's home. I SEE (POV) small redwood chairs that seem to have been made for children. I notice a miniature coffee table. I wish I could munch on something that would make me smaller. Then I hit my head on a redwood beam that helps support the roof.

"Ouch."

"Sorry. I should've told you to duck. Frank Lloyd Wright believed that the proper height for a man was his height. Five seven. And he designed his houses accordingly."

"Frank Lloyd Wright?"

"Yes. I thought you knew."

"No." Looking out the window, in the distance I SEE (POV) the Pacific Ocean.

"Yes, the owner went bankrupt and I got it fairly reasonably. It was a fluke. Would you like coffee?"

"Sure," I say, looking around. "Nice place."

Keeping my head bowed, I follow her into the tiny kitchen.

"This place was made for Munchkins," I say.

"Well, it certainly wasn't made for you."

Jamie puts the coffee on and shows me around. Just off the kitchen is a bedroom done over as her office. Behind the kitchen is the master bedroom, which is smaller than my room at the hotel.

"Did you notice," she asks, "that I have no pictures on the walls?"

"No," I admit, "but now that you mention it."

"Wright didn't believe in pictures. He thought they hid the architecture. I could hang some anyway, but I don't mind honoring his wishes. The coffee's probably ready by now."

We carry our mugs to a dining table squeezed between the fireplace and the kitchen. I take a sip.

"Good coffee," I say.

"Thanks, it's the only thing I know how to cook," she says.

We just sit there, across the table from each other, sipping coffee for what seems a long time.

"The hookers," she says at last, "they aren't all of it."

"There's more?"

She sips her coffee. I watch her throat as she swallows. Then I take a sip. When I swallow, the coffee burns in the pit of my stomach.

"More, I'm afraid so," she says and then pauses to take a deep breath. "You also spent a lot of money on Internet porn sites." She takes a deeper breath. "Including sites peddling kiddie porn."

I feel sick. "That's disgusting," I say. "Check my computer, really, check it. You won't find any porn. Check the history tab. No visits to porn sites of any kind, much less . . ."

"And you wanted the studio to pay for that, too."

"No, I didn't. You said 'he' showed you this evidence. It was Buddy, wasn't it?"

"Chick, you've got a Buddy persecution complex. No, it wasn't Buddy, if you must know. It was Edwin Diamond."

"Who's that?"

"The comptroller on the picture."

"I didn't know we had one."

"Well, we do. He's the guy who signs the checks."

"Buddy told him to tell you those lies. Buddy made him."

"You don't know that. If you're telling the truth—"

"I don't like that 'if,'" I interrupt.

"Finish your coffee, go back to your hotel, pick up those receipts and your computer, and meet me at the office. We'll see what we can figure out."

"But you do believe me, don't you?"

"I half believe you. And that's a half better than when you pulled up uninvited in front of my historic house this morning."

76

FEELING LIGHT-HEADED AND HEAVY-LIMBED, I SLOUCH from my car to our office. Becky greets me with her usual bright, optimistic California smile (which is probably redundant). Today I don't even attempt to return it. Frowning, I envy her cheerfulness.

"She got here about five minutes ago," Becky says, answering a question I haven't asked. "She wasn't smiling either, but at least she combed her hair." Becky smiles even more brightly. "Girls always do."

Running my fingers through my hair, I enter the big office. It is supposedly our office, but today it feels more like it belongs to just her. Jamie looks up, tries to smile, but doesn't do a very good job.

"Let's see what we've got," she says.

I place a shoe box full of receipts on her desk. When I remove the lid, several pieces of paper spring out as if they are breaking jail. A couple jump off the desk to the floor, but I recapture them.

"You file the way I do," Jamie says.

She picks up a handful of receipts and starts sifting through them. I watch her like a mother watching somebody holding her newborn. I can't help it.

"You're making me nervous," she says. "Why don't you go get some breakfast. Come back in a half hour or so."

"Okay," I say.

As I creep out of the office, I keep my head down so I won't have to face Becky's neon teeth. Am I hungry? Not really. But breakfast would pass the time, wouldn't it? I feel like an outlaw even though I know I'm innocent. Slinking over to the commissary, I hope I won't meet anyone I know. I don't. Passing by the fancy sit-down dining room—which isn't open yet and wouldn't suit my mood anyway—I enter the cafeteria. There are a few people scattered over the tables, but nobody I recognize. Pushing my tray along what resembles a food assembly line, I order a breakfast burrito and coffee.

I find a table in a corner as far away from everybody else as possible. The coffee isn't as good as Jamie's. The burrito isn't nearly as good as the ones whipped up by the catering truck in Texas. On the commissary's sound system, the Beatles are singing "Yesterday." Nice touch.

When I finish my burrito, I spend the rest of my banishment *not* looking at my watch. And not looking at my watch. And not looking. And not. When I finally give in and look, I see that twenty minutes have passed. Close enough, I decide. I lumber back across the lot.

Becky's smile discourages me. I hesitate before entering the big office. Then I breathe deeply and go in. Jamie's smile encourages me.

"It's like you said," she says. "If you ever turned in an expense account, you certainly left out a lot." She CHUCKLES. "These receipts go back over three years. When's the last time you went through this box?"

"I guess it must've been three years ago," I say. "I don't really remember. I keep meaning to."

"What about your taxes?" she asks. "Didn't you show these to your accountant?"

"I don't have an accountant."

"Oh, my God."

"Sorry."

"Okay, all this helps."

"Good."

"Now let's look at your computer."

I retrieve it from my backpack, set it up on "our" desk, and plug it in to the Internet.

"Do you want to check my computer for kiddie porn?" I ask.

"No, you could have erased it by now," she says.

"Thanks a lot."

"Let's just look at your credit card accounts."

I start punching up the Internet address for American Express, but I am interrupted by Buddy Dale, who enters our office unannounced.

"Chick, I'm surprised to see you're still here," he says by way of greeting.

"Why is that?" I ask, too angry to be nervous. "Is it because you thought your frame job would've gotten me tossed by now?"

"I don't know what you mean by 'frame job,' but I do know that I received some rather disturbing information about you yesterday. As a matter of fact, I've been fighting ever since to keep the studio from going public because it would definitely hurt the picture."

"Thank you very much, but in that case, why did you frame me?"

"Nonetheless, I think it would be best if you absented yourself from these premises starting now."

"It may come to that," Jamie says, "but at the moment, Chick and I are in the middle of something that's important to the movie. I still need him for a little while."

"That's not acceptable," Buddy says.

"Is my resignation acceptable?" she asks.

Buddy storms out.

"Thanks," I say.

"It's not over yet. It's a long way from over, I'm afraid. Now where were we?"

I punch up my credit card account and begin studying it. I see the expected cars and hotels and dinners, but I'm surprised to find some charges I don't recall or recognize. Strange names. Suspicious names. And one outright embarrassing name. I flinch inwardly. My brain shudders.

"What's wrong?" asks Jamie.

I don't say anything. I just keep staring at the screen.

"Tell me," she says. "I know something's the matter. I know you."

I keep studying the columns on the monitor.

"Please, Chick."

"Uh, well," I say at last, "there are some strange charges here. I've never heard of anything called Billco, but it says here I paid them thousands of dollars."

"Oh no," she says with a sharp intake of breath.

"But I didn't," I protest. "I pay close attention when I pay somebody thousands of dollars. It couldn't have just slipped my mind. This is wrong." Feeling myself sweating, I brush damp hair off my forehead. "The only time I ever spent this much money was to buy a car, and I haven't bought one of those lately. Really."

"Is that all?"

I lose my voice.

"Is that all!"

"No, there's something else called Clearing House."

"Is that all?"

"There's also"—I cough—"No No Nanette."

Jamie LAUGHS.

"That's not funny," I scold.

"Sorry," she says. "I know this isn't funny. Nothing about it is funny. Especially those credit card charges. I might take your word for it—that they're bogus, you know—but Paramount won't."

At that moment two men in uniform enter the office.

"Mr. Goodnight," the fat one says, "would you mind coming with us?"

I think I am under arrest, but then I realize they are studio security police.

"Did Buddy Dale send you?"

"Our orders came from the finance department."

They inform me that I am no longer welcome at Paramount and escort me off the lot. At least I'm not in handcuffs, but they won't let me take my computer. It might contain evidence. I wave good-bye to the "officers" as I drive away.

Then I circle back around and park on Melrose in a no-parking zone opposite the showy Paramount main gate. I am no longer welcome where my movie is gestating. I slouch down in my Everyman rental as if Buddy would notice such a car. I wait . . . and wait . . . and wait . . . and . . . and at long last . . .

Here comes Buddy. He is driving his Jag today. I follow in my anonymous car. I trail after him because I don't know what else to do and I've seen it in the movies. He of course is supposed to lead me to evidence of my innocence. He takes Melrose west. I follow him to Highland, where we take a right. Then I realize the radio isn't on. I turn it up full blast. We next make a left on Sunset. I see where Buddy is going and I realize he has won. From the movies, I suppose, I long ago imbibed the notion that in a contest of good (i.e., me) versus evil (i.e., him), good would win out, or what's a Hollywood for. But I was wrong. Today, the snail isn't on the thorn, and there might not even be a God to notice his/her own nonexistence. Buddy is just going home. I watch him turn in at his gated estate.

In my bungalow by 7:30 P.M., I collapse on my bed. Soon the battle begins again with my sheets, with my pillows, with my desire to call Jamie. I know I should be calling my credit card company, trying to sort out the charges to Billco and Clearing House and No No Nanette, but I can't bring myself actually to do it. I feel paralyzed, which amounts to the same thing as being paralyzed. I only get up to go to the bathroom. I don't even turn on the television or the radio.

At a little after 9 P.M., my doorbell RINGS. I almost run to the front door of my bungalow. I can't wait to see Jamie. I want to see her because I love her. I need to see her to be reassured she hasn't abandoned me. A smile comes naturally to my lips. I rip open the door.

My smile collapses.

"Hi, handsome," says Sarah, barging in. "I understand we're both black sheep now."

"So everybody knows?" I ask.

"Yeah," she says, "but it makes me like you better."

Somehow this news doesn't succeed in lifting my spirits. Making herself at home, Sarah sits down on the short couch in my living room. I pace up and down in front of her.

"Sit down," she says, patting a place on the couch beside her.

I lower myself into a chair opposite her. She doesn't seem to notice.

"Tom took me to a porno movie last night," she announces. "We could have seen it, or something just like it, on video. You know, at home. But he likes the danger of a theater, where he might be recognized at any moment."

"Really?" I say.

"Yeah, really. You don't believe me?"

"I do. I'm just surprised."

"I was, too. One of the girls tied her pussy lips in a knot. Really. That got him excited, so he asked me to give him a hand job."

"Did you?"

"Why not? But this is what I couldn't understand: He thought the whole thing would turn me on, especially the knot in the pussy lips. Let's just say he doesn't understand women very well. Wanna fuck? Might cheer you up."

"No, I'm not really up to it."

"Pun intended?"

"No."

"Then I gotta go. Good luck." On her way to the door, Sarah turns and throws open her blouse. "Cheer up."

I do feel ever so fleetingly better as I wonder if she ever does wear a bra.

77

IT IS AFTER 11 P.M. WHEN MY PHONE *RINGS*. MY FIRST thought is: It's Jamie. My second thought is: I've already been burned once. Maybe I shouldn't answer the phone. On the fourth RING, I lift the receiver but don't say anything and wait.

"Hello, hello," Jamie says.

"Hello," I say, relieved, happy, hopeful, trying not to hope too much.

"How are you?" she asks.

"Not too good," I admit.

"Well, I'm calling to cheer you up. I've been working all day on those bad charges. I stared at amounts and dates until I thought I was going to go crazy. So guess what I did?"

"To save your sanity," I guess, "you made one of your insane lists."

"That's right. Good, we're still on the same wavelength. Anyhow, yeah, I started making a list and I got down to *B*, which I decided would be 'beating' today. Then I wrote down *The Glass Key*. You know, Dashiell Hammett, Veronica Lake, Alan Ladd."

"I know."

"Sure, well, remember that great scene where William Bendix beats the total shit out of Alan Ladd? It's really bestial. One of the best and worst beating scenes I've ever seen."

"Yeah, so?"

"I've always liked that name, you know, Alan Ladd. The *L* repeats. The *A* repeats twice. But it's not corny alliteration."

"Jamie, I thought you were going to cheer me up. Could we get to that part?"

"Killjoy. So I was thinking about Bill Bendix hammering Alan Ladd. And that made me think of that thug beating you up. And I decided to check the dates when you were in the hospital and compare them to those suspicious credit card charges. Turns out there's a date when you supposedly charged thousands of dollars to randy No No Nanette, but you were actually in the hospital in Lubbock."

"Thanks to Buddy Dale who hired a Bendix to beat me up."

"Whatever. Anyway, you weren't in any shape to make the day—or night—of any whore."

"I love you," I blurt.

"I'll bet you say that to all the girls who save your ass."

"I'm going to make a list of all the reasons why I love you, starting, of course, with your saving my ass."

"Now don't go all Mrs. Browning on me."

"Come over," I invite. "Let's celebrate."

"Not yet."

78

MY SPIRITS BUOYED BY JAMIE'S NEWS, I DECIDE TO CALL my old teammate Deputy Sheriff Jimmy Lee Johnson. His office extension RINGS and RINGS, but he doesn't answer. Then I realize: How could he? It is after one in the morning in Texas. I leave a message. Then I sleep fitfully, but at least I sleep.

The BURPING of my cell phone jerks me out of a nightmare. I grab the receiver.

"Hello," I mumble, still more or less asleep.

"Hi," says a vaguely familiar voice. "What's up?"

"Jimmy Lee?" I ask.

"None other."

"What time is it?"

"Well, it's eight in the A.M. here in Dickens County. Sorry to wake you up, but you said it was important."

"Yeah, right," I mumble, trying to clear my head. "I was hoping you might do me a favor."

"Like what?"

"Where are you? Are you at a computer?"

"Yep, I'm sittin' at my desk for a change."

"Have you ever heard of any whorehouses billing themselves as Billco? You know, for credit cards."

"Let me check our list."

"Thank you."

I wait and wait and wait. There is evidently a long list—longer than I would have imagined—of whorehouses in and around my hometown.

"Are you still there?" I ask.

"Course," he says. "Here it is. The Bad Baby Escort Service in Lubbock. Should I sign you up?" He LAUGHS.

I take a moment to get my breathing under control.

"Hello?" he says.

"Jimmy Lee, if I fax you a picture of Buddy Dale, could you show it to the girls at Bad Baby and see if they recognize him?"

"Sure, why not. I always wanted to meet some of those girls anyhow."

"What's your fax number?"

When I hang up, I realize I don't have a picture of Buddy Dale. I could get one from the Paramount publicity department, but I am no longer welcome on the lot. If I had my computer, I could find a picture of him on the Internet, but the Paramount sleuths are currently searching it for sin. It is a small problem, but at this early hour it is driving me crazy.

Then my phone BURPS.

"Hello."

"Hi, it's Jimmy Lee. You don't have to send me a picture of your good friend Buddy. Turns out there's a mug shot of him in the system. Seems he got arrested for drunk and disorderly in Players. That's a strip club in Lubbock. He probably didn't tell you about that little incident."

"Great. Get back to me as soon as you can."

"I will, but the Bad Baby girls ain't gonna be awake for another eight hours."

"Wake them up. I'm desperate."

"Okay, I live to serve and protect."

"Thanks."

When I hang up, I sit on the side of the bed trying to decide what to do next.

An hour later, I am still trying to decide. Dithering, I idly take out my cell phone. Instead of dialing, I start scrolling back through its history of calls received. I don't know what I am looking for, but I stop when I reach Stacy Stunts. She called me in Texas. Now I am calling her in L.A. I am about to give up when she answers.

"Hello," she says sleepily.

"Hello, it's Chick," I say. "I know it's early. I'm sorry. But I'm kind of in trouble and could use some help bad. So I thought I might check with you to see if you had learned anything else. Again sorry to wake you."

"That's all right," she says as she yawns. "You know, I've been thinking about calling you." She yawns again. "Because, I dunno, a coupla nights ago, Chris showed me his quote evidence unquote.

You know, what he's holding over Buddy's head. I mean it didn't look like evidence to me, but—"

"What?" asks the trained interviewer.

"Well, it was some kind of electrical cord with a frayed end."

"Thank you, thank you, thank you."

"Well, you're welcome, welcome, welcome."

"Where was it? Where does he keep it?"

"In his bedroom if you must know. Can I go back to sleep now?"

I sit on the side of the bed trying to come up with a plan. I think and think and think, and then I destroy some hotel property.

At seven-thirty, I call Jamie and ask her to pick me up this morning and smuggle me onto the Paramount lot.

79

SHORTLY BEFORE 9 A.M., JAMIE PICKS ME UP AT THE Chateau Marmont.

"Should I hide in the trunk?" I ask.

"As much as that appeals to me," Jamie says, "I don't think it will be necessary. But be my guest if you want to."

When we reach Paramount, the guards see Jamie and just wave us through. Another perk of being a director.

Becky's smile isn't quite so intimidating this morning. Jamie and I sit on opposite sides of our big desk and drink bad institutional coffee.

"I'd better head on over to the cutting room," Jamie says at last. "I don't know quite what you're up to, but good luck with it."

"I don't quite know either," I admit.

I wait. Luckily I have had lots of practice waiting. Waiting on makeup, waiting on hair, especially waiting on lighting. But waiting never really gets easier. I pace. I sit down. I get up immediately. Sit down, get up, sit, up, sit again, up again. I wait for Jimmy Lee to call. I wait for Buddy Dale to come to work. I have my cell phone in my shirt pocket, where I can get at it quickly. Becky calls over to Buddy's office every half hour to see if he has arrived yet. I wait.

At just after 10 A.M. my phone BURPS at last.

"Hello."

"Thumbs up," says Jimmy Lee. "Several of the girls recognized him. Turns out he was a very popular client. Full of Hollywood stories and known for big tips. He wadd't bad in bed either."

"Damn, I was hoping he was impotent."

"Sorry. You cain't have ever'thing."

"Right. Thank you. You've really saved my life. I mean it. Saved my life."

"By the way, I also showed them your picture. Them whores never saw you or else you made a damn poor impression on 'em. Go Spur Bulldogs."

"He charged his fun to my credit card," I say. "And speaking of charges, I'd like to press some. The sooner, the better, today if possible."

"I'll tell Judge Martin whut ol' Buddy's been up to. Fraud and all. Plus I'll throw in he's a suspect in the Miss Texas thing. That oughta light a fire. I oughta be able to git a warrant easy. I mean that ol' judge don't know no more law than I do. Scary, ain't it?"

I call the cutting room and tell Jamie, who WHOOPS.

At lunchtime, Buddy still hasn't shown up at his office. What is wrong? I certainly hope nothing has happened to him. Jamie sticks her head in the office to say she is going to a lunch off the lot. I blow her a kiss. She fans it away.

Buddy, who must have had a hell of a night last night, doesn't show up for work at Paramount until almost six in the evening. Probably no casting sessions scheduled for today.

80

AT 6 P.M. EXACTLY, AN UNCERTAIN DANIEL ENTERS THE lion's den.

"Hi," I say to a new receptionist. "He's expecting me."

As I head for the door to the big office, she says, "Wait." But I don't. I push through the double doors and catch Buddy in mid-phone call.

"Just a second," Buddy says into the phone, "I have to alert security. Another crazy just invaded my office."

I sit down.

"Security, my office has been invaded by a lunatic."

Out of my pocket, I leisurely take an electrical cord. It has a plug at one end and a frayed end at the other. As if it had been ripped from some appliance. Like an electric blanket, for instance. This particular cord happens to have been ripped from the coffeemaker in my bungalow at the Chateau Marmont, but I don't mention its provenance.

"Wait," Buddy tells security. "I'll call you back." He hangs up and fixes me with a stare that has scared a thousand actresses. "What's that supposed to be?"

"I think you know," I say, trying to speak slowly, to remain in control of myself. "Chris gave it to me. Wanna guess where it came from?"

"You're lying."

"No."

"Yes, you are. Where's the temperature-control gauge? Electric blankets have controls."

I hadn't thought of that. Low, medium, high. Of course. I am turning out to be one hell of a trap-setter. Should I just apologize and go on my way? Then something occurs to me.

"I didn't say it was from an electric blanket," I say. "I wonder what made you think of an electric blanket cord. Are you missing one? One that Chris has now and has been using to whip your ass?" My face feels cold but it is nonetheless sweating.

"Get out of my fucking office!"

"That's what I hear. I mean the fucking part." He doesn't laugh at my joke. "Anyway, you should choose your partners in crime more carefully. Guys who aren't given, for instance, to bragging to their girlfriends."

"What the fuck are you talking about?"

"See," I begin, putting the pieces together, "your friend Chris just loves to tell his ladies that you called him up one morning and desperately asked for his help."

"I did no such thing."

"Wait, it gets better." I wipe the hot sweat off my freezing face. "He says you told him you were cooking a former Miss Texas under an *electric blanket*. Since you were on the way to the airport to catch an alibi, you asked him to please wait several hours and then unplug that *electric blanket* before the body was discovered. Throw the coroner off about the time of death. Get it?"

"No!"

"No, you don't get it? And I thought you were smart. Okay, I'll spell it out."

"No!"

"You wanted to make it look like Miss Texas died after you had already left the ranch and were on your way back to L.A."

"You're making this up."

"So Chris did you this little favor. Unfortunately, he is now black-mailing you. Although he probably doesn't call it that. But he tells his girls he now owns you, he now owns your balls. Lucky him. And he is going to be head stunt coordinator for the whole studio."

"You're crazy."

"You wish. Chris actually uses his cord to impress women, to prove to them his power, and to get them into bed. Nice of you to help him out that way."

As I put the cord from the coffeemaker back in my pocket, my hands aren't shaking.

"What do you want?" asks a purpling Buddy. "Money?"

"A confession," I say.

"It wasn't my fault. She died of a drug overdose. Or drug reaction. She wasn't used to the stuff and had a seizure. I sort of covered it up—"

"Sort of?"

"—to protect the movie."

I hope my pocket tape recorder is picking everything up.

"To protect yourself," I correct him. "Why didn't you call 911? That works in Texas, too, you know. You just let her die."

"That's not fair."

"Don't talk to me about fair. You as good as murdered Miss Texas and my cousin, too."

"I didn't have anything to do with what happened to your cousin."

"Liar. She was at your house that night."

"She was, but she left happy and in good health."

"What do you mean by 'happy'? Anyway, I don't believe you. You're lying—"

Before I can finish the thought, the big double doors open. I hurt my neck turning to see if another wave of security cops have come to march me away. But I don't see rent-a-uniforms. I see the cavalry. Four policemen, two in uniform, two in plainclothes, enter the big office without appointments.

"Are you Buddy Dale?" asks the taller of the plainclothes officers.

"What? Get out of here."

"Buddy Dale, you are under arrest for identity theft and fraud. You have the right to—"

"What're you doing here? You're not allowed on the lot. Margaret, call security!"

"Please turn around, Mr. Dale," the officer interrupts. "We are required to handcuff you. Now you have the right to shut up. And if you give up that right you're a damned fool because I already don't like you. I said turn around."

Buddy doesn't move. The uniformed officers step forward, grab Buddy, spin him around, and handcuff him.

"Ouch," Buddy complains. "They're too tight."

"Ain't that a shame," says the tall cop. "By the way, my girlfriend once auditioned for you."

He reaches down and clicks the cuffs tighter.

"Ouch!"

"Let's go."

The cops march Buddy out of his office, across the lot, and out the main gate. Which is where the press and their cameras, still and video, await. The cops must have tipped them off. Good for the cops.

I call out as a policeman pushes the suspect's head into the back-seat of a police car: "So long, Buddy."

81

THAT EVENING, JAMIE TAKES ME TO A CELEBRATORY
dinner at the Palm since I like steak. The official dish of my native
land. We are seated in a booth against the far wall, which is covered in
caricatures. One of them depicts Buddy Dale with an actress on his
knee.

"Poor Buddy," Jamie says with a dazzling smile. "I certainly hope
his cell mates don't force him to audition for the part of Bitch."

"Don't worry about Buddy," I say. "He's out on bail."

"Already?" she asks.

"Yeah, he'll be home before the late news comes on. I sure hope
he gets a chance to see himself doing his perp walk on TV."

"Be a shame for him to miss it."

The cell phone in my shirt pocket BURPS.

"Excuse me," I say, taking it out and glancing at the readout of the
number calling. "Oh, it's my friend the deputy. I'd better talk to
him."

Jamie nods.

"Hello, Jimmy Lee, thank you so much for all your help. You
really saved—"

"Thass all well and good," says the deputy, "but I ain't callin' fer
your thanks. Welcome as thanks always are. I'm callin' with what you
might call a bulletin."

"What?" asks the trained interviewer.

"We just got back the DNA reports in your cousin's case. I'm
afraid them there blood smudges on her don't match Buddy Dale's
DNA."

"Oh," I say, sagging all over, inside and out.

"But they do match the DNA of Chris Crosby."

"Oh!"

"They'll probably arrest him in the morning."

I thank Jimmy Lee several more times and finally hang up. I just sit there, silent in a noisy restaurant.

"What was that?" Jamie asks at last.

"Chris killed my cousin Sharon," I say.

But the police do not arrest Chris Crosby the next morning because he is found dead in the Paramount parking lot at the foot of the great fake blue sky. His neck is broken and he has extensive bruising. Discovered tangled in rock-climbing ropes, Chris was apparently—for his own obscure reasons—attempting to climb to the top of the Hollywood sky. But his reach exceeded his grasp, and he fell. He was like Hemingway's frozen leopard found at the top of snowcapped Mount Kilimanjaro. What was he doing at that height? Didn't he know he didn't belong up there?

Only I don't buy it.

I call the Los Angeles Police Department and after infinite delays finally reach a gold shield who is assigned to the case. I arrange to meet DETECTIVE JOSE MARTINEZ at the Parker Center Police Headquarters, where I give him my recording of my conversation with Buddy. He agrees there could be a motive for murder here. He says he will look into it.

Buddy is picked up a few days later and returned to a cell. Unfortunately, I am not there to witness his discomfort.

82

MY *BURPING* CELL PHONE AWAKENS ME OUT OF A DEEP sleep. At first I don't know where I am. Then I realize I am in the master bedroom of Jamie's Frank Lloyd Wright house. The walls are raw redwood. Sleeping in the raw, Jamie lies beside me. I will my mind to clear and am only partially successful.

"Hi," I gargle.

"This is Detective Martinez," says a recently familiar voice. "I thought you might want to know: Buddy Dale's in the hospital—"

"I thought he was in jail."

"Yeah, he was, but a couple of dozen inmates raped him. He's in bad shape."

"Is he going to live?"

"Too soon to tell."

After thanking the detective for letting me know, I lower my head to the pillow once again.

"Who was that?" Jamie asks in a sleep-thick voice.

"Nobody," I say.

"Good; make love to me the way Goodnight made love to Revelie."

As we are making love, I whisper in her ear:

CHICK GOODNIGHT
Horses whinny. Cocks crow. Mice squeal.
A donkey hee-haws. A hawk screeches. A
baby squalls. A diamondback hisses and

rattles. Spiders stop their weaving and
look around. Prairie dogs come up out
of their burrows to see what has
disturbed the universe.

Jamie SCREAMS like a horse and rooster and mouse and donkey and prairie dog combined.

"I love you!" I SCREAM.

"Frankly, mister," she says breathlessly, "I do—really, absolutely, eternally do—give a damn." She pauses. "Wait, rewrite, strike eternally. We'll see."

We are just settling down and drifting off to sleep when my cell phone BURPS again.

"Tom just asked me to marry him," says another familiar voice.

"Congratulations," I mumble.

"Save your congrats. I told him no. The movie's over."

About the Author

AARON LATHAM is a novelist, screenwriter, and playwright. He wrote the movie *Urban Cowboy* as well as Broadway's *Urban Cowboy: The Musical*. He is the author, most recently, of *The Cowboy with the Tiffany Gun*. A contributor to *Rolling Stone, Esquire,* and *The New York Times,* he lives in New York with his wife, Lesley Stahl.